Mortal Shells

Tales from the Afterworld

Book 3

V. K. Pasanen

Copyright © 2024 by V.K. Pasanen
IngramSpark Perfect Bound Edition
All rights reserved.
ISBN 979-8-3302859-6-9

Editor
Marie Anne Cope

Cover by
JDandJ.com

This book is a work of fiction. Names, characters, places, and incidents are either figments of the author's imagination or used fictitiously. Any resemblance to actual persons, living or dead, businesses, companies, events, or locations is purely coincidental in the reality of the author's imagination.

Mortal Shells

*Welcome back to
tales from the Afterworld.
My road to absolution continues
as I leave Mary and Ryan for a volume
and turn to other players
on the stage of events to come.*

*This is a ghost story
and a tale of two detectives
drawn into Mary's nightmare.
As in the previous volume,
I play no direct role in events.
I am only the reporter
of what the Allseer revealed to me.*

N Reaper

Prologue

Franz Schicklgruber pressed his rifle to his chest as he ran with the wall of fellow comrades. Smoke choked and explosions deafened as men came apart. Soil and gore rained down. He glanced back. His friend, Sasha, turned to retreat and his head rocked back as a bullet from the blocking unit put an end to his cowardice. Franz shook his head and pushed on. No retreat. No surrender. He knew well what Mother Russia would do to him and his family if he failed to kill them all or catch lead trying. Around him, comrades fell like leaves in fall. That reminded him; it was 13 October, his mother's birthday. He tried to think how old she was. He skipped over an arm, a leg, around a mound of corpses, and scaled another. He dropped to the other side, his focus on the nearing German scum behind the machine gun. His rifle was empty but the bayonet was ready. More comrades fell but the barrage of metal and blast concussions did not find him. Ever closer he came, knowing that there were more Soviet bodies than Nazi bullets, or so the General Sokov had said. Franz's focus wavered. He glanced right and left and found himself alone. He looked forward and saw the face behind the machine gun. He recognized the face. It was his, but it wasn't. The gun spat and red hot hail shredded his flesh and cracked his bones. The pain was unimaginable and short lived…

… Franz looked around but saw only tall, naked people of every size and shape, packed tightly around him as they had been on the train when they still had their coats with King David's star. He remembered when his mother had sewn the yellow patch on his coat and had asked her why the letters J-U-D-E were written in the middle. She had looked sad and never answered. That coat was now in a pile with others in the changing room.

Franz thought about the man in the gray uniform and cap who had directed him to go with his mother when they exited the hot, smelly train car. Franz felt like he knew him. But how? He had never seen him before and he had looked like the other mean men who had stood by while other mean men in helmets pushed her and her mother and her twin brothers into the train car after they left their home. The man had brown hair sticking from under his cap, and brown-green eyes. The man had been smoking a cigarette and whistling a tune. He had looked bored. Like the man, Franz had known the tune but could not remember where from. An opera maybe? But his parents had never taken him to an opera and, though they once had a gramophone, it was not like any of the tunes he had heard on the records his father had played for his family as he had smiled while turning the crank.

Franz felt a nudge and moved forward. He continued thinking about the bored man. The man had directed his thumb one way, and Franz had felt a tug as his tall, blonde mother had been yanked in that direction. He had looked back as the whistling man had flicked his thumb the other way and his twin brothers had been pulled away by other mean men in helmets. His mother had screamed and her tears had followed. Franz had cried, too, as his brothers had vanished into the crowd.

He tried to look around. Again he saw only naked parts. Everyone and everything smelled bad. He didn't want to breathe. So many people. He was hot. So hot and sweaty. Why so many people? And why had everyone been made to undress? Franz felt the mass of naked bodies push forward and soon he and his mother were squeezed through an open door.

Franz looked up at his mother. She tried to smile back as he heard a hiss. He smelled almonds and then… and then he could not breathe. He tried to breathe. He panicked as he gripped his mother's hand. He looked up and saw scared faces and people pushing, crushing him, trying to go back the way they came. He tried to cry as darkness closed around him…

... Franz knew he was dying. He thought of his twin brother, Avram. He sensed he, too, was dying. They had always been able to sense the other's joy, pain, and sorrow. How he wished Avram was here now so they could leave this cruel world together. He wondered what happened to Johanna. He hoped she was safe, but he knew that Mother and little Yente were gone. He hoped otherwise, but there was no hope here. Only death and despair lived within the barb-wired fences. He thought about Father's eyes when the man in the brownshirt shot him in the street. Why had Father not taken them away to someplace safe after they burned the synagogue and broke all the windows? But where would they have gone? No one wanted their kind and Franz feared that if Germany won the war there would be no Jews left anywhere, but none of that would matter soon.

Franz coughed. His skin was on fire and every muscle ached as he bathed in sweat. He thought about the whistling doctor's attendant who gave him the last injection. The man had promised it would make him well. He had looked familiar. What was his name? Franz could not remember. Had he ever said? And... Franz lost his train of thought. Oh, yes, he was thinking about the man who had killed him. His face—it had been like... like looking in the mirror. But how could that be?

Franz opened his eyes. Black tendrils writhed over him as more ripped from his spirit-flesh and bone—if such things existed. He believed there were, or had been created to further his suffering. He gagged as the last tendrils slithered from his throat and mouth and sank below the undulating blackness that covered the cell floor. He struggled to his knees as the devilish darkness drained into the floor.

He sat, naked, and hugged his knees. He tried to sob—to release the pent up anguish of the thousands of deaths he had experienced from his victims' perspectives. But the eyes of the damned were not allowed to cry in the Prison of Homicide. That is what the demon lord who called himself the Curator had called this place when he had arrived. How long had it been? Almost an eternity... or less. Franz had suffered every death he had caused doing what he had been told to do, but knew now that it had been an excuse for the monster that he had been and still was. He thought about his Johanna. She had not been a monster, though she suffered as he did in the next cell. Oh, how he wished he could add her one repetitive torment to the thousands that he was condemned to suffer and would continue to relive, forever.

As he sat shivering, he wondered why he had been given a break. He had not expected one and had not received one since arriving in Hell. He thought about the cruel demon guards who had escorted him to this Black Water cell. He remembered the Curator's laugh after that demon lord gloated that Johanna would be suffering nearby.

Franz heard a metallic click and looked up as the cell door creaked open. Two demons stepped inside. They were not the same pair who had first thrown him in the cell. One was obese with a potbelly and man-boobs, and had spiraling ram-horns that jutted from the sides of his head. *Abomination* was carved onto his chest. His face was pulled back tightly and bloodshot eyes bulged from their sockets. His nose looked like a red ball. The other demon was skinny with a skeletal face partially covered with bits of flesh. He wore biker goggles with sharp spikes jutting from the frames that covered cloudy eyes. The almost lipless mouth was sewn shut with barbwire through bone. Maggots crawled in and out of gaps between missing and blackened teeth. *Cruelty* was carved in what remained of his chest flesh.

"Get up, scum. The Warden wants to see you," said Abomination. He did not give Franz a chance to stand and yanked him to his feet.

Cruelty quickly bound him in heavy chains and Abomination wrenched Franz into the obsidian hall with white floors, threw the chain over his shoulder, and dragged Franz as Cruelty followed behind. Soon other pairs of demon guards joined as Franz rolled back and forth at the end of the chain for some time shorter than it seemed.

Abomination finally stopped and yanked Franz to a standing position. His chains dissolved as he looked up at an impossibly high, vaulted, cathedral-style, obsidian ceiling, and then around at the other naked spirits. He counted forty. He saw Johanna and a glimmer of joy entered his existence. He caught her eye and smiled, but her lips remained a line. Franz's gaze darted away, and he felt searing pain in whatever passed for a spirit heart. He saw another familiar face—Otto Dietrich. They had never met but Dietrich had been a close associate of the Führer who was Franz's distant cousin.

The memory of clothing materialized on each spirit and Franz found himself dressed in what he had been wearing when he had hung himself. All but one spirit was silent, and the one who was not, seemed to be getting on well with his demon guards. He was laughing, and even slapped one on the back. He was an odd-looking American with an accent one might hear in their southern region. He was skinny and unattractive with dark hair combed into a strange curl. He had a chin beard, and wore a bowtie, white shirt, polka-dotted dark vest, and black dress coat with large metal buttons.

"Move it. The Warden awaitsh in hish throne room," said Cruelty.

The skeletal biker demon tapped on the bottom of a gigantic black iron double door. The doors crept open and a discordant symphony of war and cackling demons trumpeted out. Franz's demon guard nudged him forward and he marched in a line with the other spirits flanked by their demon escorts along an obsidian walkway many fields wide. The immense walkway was lined with white columns that touched the ceiling that was as high as the sky. Each column told a spiraling story, but the end of each was lost from sight as the tale continued into the heavens. *Heavens?* Franz wondered if such a word was appropriate in his present surroundings. He continued toward a distant mountainous throne where a titan sat with face turned as if observing some grand performance.

As Franz neared the throne, he noticed that the walkway was narrowing and the columns were shrinking. He soon realized that nothing was getting smaller and that he and other damned and demons were growing. Soon the throne and the titan were merely enormous as the din of war grew louder and the cackling became intelligible demon speech.

Nearer, but still far from the throne, Franz reached the last column. To his right, there was a massive sunken courtyard with a large central square pit. Even from a distance, he could see wargames being played with ant-sized participants and toy-sized vehicles. Demons of all shapes and sizes lined the pit's edge, cheering or jeering for victory or defeat as they spoke of wagering whatever demons wagered.

Six titanic demons stood above the hordes. Each was as gigantic as the demon lord on the throne. The six glanced back with red-orange eyes and regarded the approaching visitors. Each titan was finely dressed like princes of a new age in white suits with black shirts, and adorned with gold necklaces, bracelets, and rings. Only one titan had a mortal appearance. He had blond hair and a shimmering white aura. He was strikingly handsome, but the others were less so, or hideous. Two were obese, horned monstrosities

—one had ribbed, vertically oriented horns, and the other, spiral ram-like horns, similar to Franz's current red-nosed escort. Another titan had spines that jutted back from an angular face like a dragon and had a tail that protruded from his white pants. The next titan had three heads, of which two protruded from the sides of its neck. One head looked like a cow, and another like a ram, while the middle head wore an onion-dome crown, and looked like a portly red-faced devil with tall, pointed ears. The last titan was a skinny red devil with horns extending at a shallow angle from the sides of his head and a silver beard that came to a point on his chest. He sat with his legs dangling over the edge of the war pit.

Franz's attention shifted to the other courtyard where a three-headed dog and a strange creature wrestled like two German Shepperd puppies. The dog looked like sketches Franz had once seen of Cerberus, the hound of Hell, but he had never seen anything like its strange playmate. The creature, or dragon, or whatever it was, had yellow scales, a kinky tail, hindlegs of an eagle, forelegs of a cat, neck like a giraffe, a head with two spiraling horns, and a split tongue like a snake.

The beasts stopped rolling around and Franz saw that two of the dog's heads were fighting over something while the third head was playing tug of war with the strange creature with something else. Suddenly the somethings tore in two with a shrieking scream and Franz realized they were souls. With a slurp and a crunch, the four halves disappeared into four different maws. Franz heard more screaming and noticed mice-size souls scrambling away from the beasts as they pawed for their next play thing.

The demon escorts jabbed Franz in the back. "Enough gawking. Move it," said red-nosed Abomination.

Franz looked toward the golden throne. Its finer details were now distinguishable. It was mesmerizing, decorated with stars, crescent moons, circles, triangles, doubled-crossed ankhs, indescribable symbols, and cuneiform letters. Carved serpents slithered through and around the shapes and symbols as if the seat were alive.

Franz arrived at the base of the throne and glanced around. He and the other damned and demon escorts were now a quarter the size of the seated titan who was dressed as the other six, but this demon's eyes were brown and matched his hair. He had tan skin and looked similar to the shimmering mortal-esque white-skinned titan by the pit, minus the shimmer. The titan suddenly began whistling a familiar tune from Puccini's Madame Butterfly, an opera Franz knew well, as his gaze lazily turned toward the summoned. The full weight of the titan's stare fell upon Franz and his soul felt colder.

The Warden grinned and said, "Hello, Franz."

Memories flooded into Franz's spirit. He had known this demon-lord when he still had a mortal shell. The Warden had been the passenger that sometimes drove the one who would have been his executioner, had Franz not saved him the trouble. He had known him as the Benefactor then, and after that, the Curator when he arrived in Hell.

The Warden snapped his fingers. The three-headed dog and the strange beast stopped wrestling, sauntered toward the throne, and sat obediently on either side. The Warden's head turned toward the din of War and the six titans who were still wagering whatever demons wagered. The Warden gritted his teeth and snapped his fingers again. The dragon-headed titan looked toward the throne, tapped the shoulders of the two titans next to him, and then waved his hand. Screams, cries, and moans followed the last explosion and fired round.

Five of six titans made haste to the throne. The seated red devil sighed and slothfully rose. The others took up positions on either side of the throne. Once the slothful one added his presence, three titans stood on each side of the Warden.

The Warden eyed the latecomer.

"The battle was just getting good," said the slothful red-devil. "I was about to win this round and shut Levi and Lucifer's boastful mouths. Mardu…"

"BELPHEGOR!"

"Sorry, I mean… Curator, sir," Belphegor said grudgingly. "Seriously, why do we have to be here for every passenger orientation?"

"Because I command it. And as you well know—I have dominion over the Prison and those within its walls, including you. You may be a prince of Hell, but I can make an example of you to the others," the Warden said as he glared at Belphegor.

"Yes, curator, sir," he said and stared forward.

The Warden eyed each titan. None gave a hint of challenge. "Alrighty then—let's get started. Little demons, leave us and attend to the temporarily dying in the war pit. Those on the side that was winning can return to their Black Water torments, but stake the rest so I can savor the songs of their suffering."

The demons scattered, skipped to the edge of the pit, and jumped out of sight. Quickly, sobs and moans rose to an operatic crescendo of agonized shrieks. The Warden began whistling again and wagging his finger like a conductor in a symphony. "Lovely. Now back to business," he said as his gaze returned to Franz and the other passengers. "Some of you I've had the pleasure of working with, but for most, this will be your first ride. Welcome back, Dr. Morgan Bell."

The American spirit with the bowtie and polka-dot vest nodded with a smug grin.

"And Franz Schicklgruber…"

His head shot forward and up.

"It is so nice to have you here. I look forward to seeing what you can bring to the game. But we will speak later. As for the rest of you—this is your shot to enter the big time here in the Prison of Homicide. You are currently nothing but the lowly damned, destined for eternity to relive the deaths of those mortal shells whose Underspirits you prematurely sent to the Afterworld. As you have experienced, each death remains a fresh, salted wound—a visceral experience. Your Overspirit is mine now and there is no hope of reprieve from this fate unless I choose to permit it. This is your opportunity—your glimmer of hope—and your performance during the game will determine whether you are worthy of demon-hood or not. Well, with the exception of Dr. Morgan Bell. He has already achieved that distinction and will provide guidance to newcomers to the game that me and my ex have been playing since we created the verminous mortal creature. Currently, the Contract Maker is meeting with each of your prospective mortal shells that you'll be wearing, during your stay in Reality 313. It pains to *have to* say this," he said gritting his teeth, "but it is important that you follow the guidelines set forth by the Council of Thirteen in the Rules of Immortal and Eternal Conduct…"

Franz thought to raise his hand, but no sooner had the thought passed through his spirit did he recall all the legalese regarding demon possession.

"... Not doing so will put me and the greater game being played at risk. Failure of any tasks assigned to you will be seen as failure of all, and will guarantee a return to your former hellish existence with an extra helping of prejudice..."

Franz glanced around. All but the demon Morgan Bell were paying attention to the Warden's words. Bell's head was turned toward the war pit. He was grinning and had the air of a spirit who had not a care in the Afterworld.

"... a mortal General who shares consciousness with the Red Horseman, War, will be your commanding officer. You will know him only as the General and will address him with a *'Yes, sir, General, sir.'* Together, their words will be law unless I say otherwise, or it is in violation of," the Warden said, paused, shook his head, and flared his nostrils, "... in violation of *the Rules of Immortal and Eternal Conduct*. That is all. You're dismissed. Your demon escorts will now transport you to the Contract Maker's portal."

Demon guards materialized around Franz and the other demon prospects.

The Warden stepped from his throne. "Franz, we'll have that word now," he said as he shrank to mortal size. "Walk with me."

They passed the others on the way to the war pit and stopped at the edge. Below, Franz saw masses of writhing carnage—each piece staked to the field with an obsidian spear. Absent was the accompanying crimson that soaked Ukrainian arenas which Franz had helped paint, but the cobalt splatters and scrambled tidbits, that left only specks of underlying white, more than made up for it. Dark blue tendrils extended from arms, legs, torsos, and screaming and shrieking heads. The tendrils stretched and snaked without success to make their Overspirits whole.

"Quite a sight and as ghastly as it appears, and more painful than anything your kind has devised for mortal shells, but better in some ways than the torments of the Black Water. And it'll all be yours, and much more, if you fail me in the simple task I'll ask of you. But if you succeed, I'll see to it that your sweet Johanna no longer suffers for killing the one who tried to rape her. I'll also see to it that she has a comfortable existence in a desirable mortal shell working at my new lab in Reality 313."

Fritz bit his imaginary lip and said in a thick German accent, "I do not care what you do to me, but I… I will do anything for Johanna. Anything to make right the evils that I was party to, and for killing her family."

The Warden grinned and draped an arm over Fritz's shoulders. "I know you will. That's what makes this fun. Oh, and if you're curious how old Josef is doing… well, you know how it goes. I gave him plenty of opportunities, protected him until his shell was old, but still he failed me." The Warden chuckled. "And you've experienced a taste of Josef's suffering since you shared in his homicides. But where he failed another has succeeded, and you will be part of the next stage of that game, which is currently in progress."

Franz closed his eyes, sighed, opened them, and asked, "What is it you want to me do?"

"I want you to corrupt one good soul."

"What? That is all? Why?"

"Because I can. And don't you know—every good soul I corrupt erodes the fabric of the realities that my ex loves and nurtures. I do have other reasons, but that's none of your concern." The Warden grinned. "Well, I enjoyed our chat."

Abomination and Cruelty materialized on either side of Franz.

"Would you be so unkind as to escort Mr. Schicklgruber to the Contract Maker's portal?" asked the Warden.

"Yesh, shir, Curator, shir," said Cruelty. "Um, shir. The eashy way or the hard way?"

"The easy way."

"Yesh, shir, Curator, shir."

The guards laid eternally rotting hands on Franz's shoulders and the throne room dissolved.

Franz looked left and right. His escorts were gone and he was alone in a small, circular domed chamber. It reminded him of the planetarium his parents took him to at the Deutsches Museum in Munich in 1927.

In the center was a bush that burned with dark blue fire but produced no heat and made Franz's spirit shiver. Within the flame was a small window. Franz peered through into one reality of the many.

A young, lean, muscular negro man and a handsome pale man sat in a café. Bold white letters behind them spelled *Starbucks Coffee* against a coffee-colored wall. Below the sign was a white mermaid against a green background. Everyone aside from the two men was frozen in mid-whatever they were doing.

The negro man was dressed in casual clothes unlike anything Franz had seen before he had been ushered into Hell by that unfriendly and very old American-looking cowboy in black. The pale man at the table looked like the cowboy's grandson. This was the Contract Maker.

In front of the negro man was an empty inkwell, a feather quill with a double-crossed ankh etched in the nib, and a stack of parchment flipped to the last page. That page was filled with very fine print and a large X, and a line at the bottom. The Contract Maker handed the man a dagger and the man sliced his palm without flinching as his gaze remained unblinkingly fixed on the cowboy's mesmerizing, dark blue eyes. The man filled the well with red. When it was full, the cowboy grabbed the man's hand and ran a finger over the cut and it sealed without a scar or losing a drop to the table. Without looking down, the man grabbed the quill, dipped the nib, and signed, *Joshua Roderick Stone.*

The crimson signature smoked and sizzled. Blood began to phase to black. Franz felt a massive sucking force. It clamped onto him and his soul was yanked through the window head first. Light winked out.

Franz opened his eyes and found himself face to face with the Contract Maker.

"Who are you?" asked the cowboy.

"I am Franz Schicklgruber," he answered.

"No, you are former Colonel Joshua Roderick Stone, and don't forget it," said the cowboy as a negro woman walked into the café with young twin girls.

"Daddy, Daddy, Daddy, can we go now? You promised to take us to the zoo," said one of the two girls as the other nodded insistently.

Franz felt conflicted. He was still Franz Schicklgruber, but the man who was Joshua Stone had already began to flood into Franz's immortal consciousness and he felt nothing but undying love for these two girls and the beautiful woman standing behind them.

Franz glanced back across the table. The Contract Maker and his contract were gone.

The woman kissed Franz on the cheek. He searched Joshua's memories for a name. *Allison... no, Alli.* He tried to speak but his lips wouldn't move.

"How'd your appointment go?"

Franz grunted a response.

"Are you okay?" she asked with a worried expression.

"I... I... I am fine, Alli," he said with a thick German accent.

"Josh, baby, what's wrong with you?"

Franz tried again, searching for his new shell's natural voice as each little girl wrapped an arm around his to get him to stand.

"Oh, nothing, baby. Just... just tired. Appointment went fine. I got the job," he said in a southern U.S. accent.

"Good. You had me worried. I thought you were stroking out on me or something," said Alli.

Franz stood and the twins took one hand each. He willed Joshua's mortal shell to move forward but it would not budge. He tried again as the tug of the twins became more insistent. He stepped forward and began to drive the mortal shell, one foot in front of the next, and so on. He looked down into the girls' eyes and then into Alli's. She kissed him again and he felt the collective warmth of hands and lips and overwhelming love. He wanted to cry. Now he understood why the Warden sent him to do this job. Like everything else, it was for his sadistic pleasure—another torment for an immortal ant who had experienced the coldness of Hell, the memories of the murdered, and the loss of his eternal love, Johanna, who hated him now.

He glanced at the twins again and smiled. *I can't do this*, thought Franz. *But I must... for Johanna.*

Part I

Demons and Prospects

One

11:06 a.m., Dark Tuesday, October 2, 2007. Earth First Food Market, Packer City, Colorado, Reality 313.

The strange, dreary darkness persisted. It was a bit baffling to KNW reporter Kristin Kettlemeyer but it fit her mood as she waited in the mud-covered news van outside the quaint organic food mart. Thirty minutes earlier her fiancé, fellow reporter, Kenneth Prattle (or Kenny as she liked to call him), had gone inside to use the john. She wondered if he might've fallen in the toilet and drowned.

A chuckle escaped but was cut short as she thought of Kenny's failure to seize the day for an interview with Mender concerning his deceased son—patient zero in this lock down mess. And Kenny's face when he returned—*so, tragic*. And oh, how he'd complained about his wrist after that *big bad meanie* Mender manhandled him. Kristen's lips had curled momentarily, sensing a celebrity-assaults-the-media smear piece and then had turned upside down when she saw the footage.

"My God, Kenny, you are such a pussy," she'd said, shaking her head.

"Hey, I saw the handprint," said their cameraman. "It looked like Ken's arm was burned with a steam iron with fingers."

Her lips had scrunched before she'd blurted, "Then show me the footage. Don't have it? Then we don't have a story. He barely touched you, Kenny. Man up, for God's sake."

No sooner had the burning subsided had Kenny started whining about a *"tummy ache."* That's when he ran inside to use the *little boy's room*. No doubt his *tummy ache* was from his meaty breakfast at the Greasy Spoon Diner across the street.

Serves him right, she thought.

She was a vegan and a proud member of PETA. She had no pity for those who supported the *wanton slaughter* of defenseless animals for culinary gain.

It had been at the diner where Kristen had spied Mender pulling into the market and had graciously given Kenny the scoop. She scoffed. *Last time I let love get in the way of business*, she thought as her cameraman tapped the steering wheel.

She checked her makeup in the visor, rolled her eyes, and practiced her most revolted look for the man to whom she'd said "*yes.*" She glared at the entrance and tapped her door, adding to the cameraman's beat. She questioned her relationship with Kenny. Once a star reporter, his job now hung by a thread, while her star was rising. She wondered if it would be the best move to marry someone who'd blown the last chance to save his job. *No, it wasn't. Enough is enough,* she thought.

She slung the van door open with a huff and stormed inside the market. She was on a mission to tell him that they were through.

She beat the door of the lone restroom, and hollered, "Kenny, hurry up!" She listened, but he didn't respond. She beat again. "Seriously, get off the shitter, and let's go." Still nothing.

She crinkled her nose at the putrid stench seeping from under the door. She checked the doorknob. It was unlocked. *Typical Kenny*, she thought.

She brought her sleeve to her face and slowly opened the door. Her eyes went wide. Kenny was slumped on the floor, ass in the air, pants around his knees as blood leaked from behind and pooled around him.

She screamed, tasted the air, and threw up in her mouth. She turned and ran, left the door open, and didn't stop until she reached the van. She emptied her mouth and the rest of her vegan breakfast on the snow-muddy ground.

She gargled with Scope, regained her composure, and went to the front entrance through which Mender had exited. She paused, pushed out tears, and began her heartbreaking report.

"Oh my God. Oh my God, something killed Kenny—not my Kenny. I loved him… I, I, I loved him so much. How will I live… how will I live without him? I'm… I'm sorry, Rick. I didn't know the camera was rolling." *God, I hope he's dead,* she thought. *I should've checked for a pulse. What am I thinking? Of course, he's dead. Kristen, pull yourself together. Come on—you got this.*

Kristen took a deep breath, patted her newly permed brunette hair, stood straighter, and continued the convincing waterworks that she hoped would be remembered at Emmy time.

Two

11:15 a.m., Dark Tuesday, October 2, 2007. Mears County Sheriff's Office, Packer City, Colorado.

"You Goddamn media vulture," Sheriff Pete Maxwell said into the receiver and scoffed. "You're no better than those folks over at KNW. You should've informed me before you aired the story."

WNN News Director Nate Murphy replied, "I'm sorry you feel that way. But I'm informing you now that your woman of interest was last seen heading south a little over an hour ago. Just so you know, I only learned about it after Julie Florid saw the woman on a wanted poster at a coffee shop in town. That's when she reviewed the video that her cameraman captured and recognized the suspect. Once she determined who she'd seen, she called me and asked me what to do. It was my decision to let her run with the story. I apologize for not calling first, but this woman is a prime suspect in the murder of a man—a war hero—who was very important to a friend of mine. I wanted to get her face out there ASAP so she could be brought to justice, *something* your office and the Grayson and Silver City PDs have been *unable* to do."

"You fucking bastard." Pete slammed the receiver. *I shouldn't have said that. I meant it, but I shouldn't have said it*, he thought. He grabbed and heavy-thumbed the remote to KNW in protest. There, Kristin Kettlemeyer was giving a tearful report from the market a few blocks away. It concerned another strange death. "What the hell?" Pete said and left his mouth open.

He shook his head and tried to think straight. *Focus on one thing at a time*, he thought. He was pissed at Murphy but more embarrassed that his suspect had been hiding under his nose. She couldn't have done it alone, and when he found the son of a bitch who'd harbored her, there'd be Hell to pay. After Florid's report, he had an idea and would be speaking with Mr. Batra whether or not they found the woman wearing his familiar jacket and tan backpack.

Now, there was also the matter of Kenneth Prattle's death following contact with Mender. It was too much of a coincidence to ignore. Like most people, Pete believed the Ebola scare was horseshit and the entire lock down was due to somebody's fuck up. He was positive that Alex Mender's death was connected with Melvin Anderson's murder and Mender's rescue of the soon-to-be-identified suspect. He thought about Mender's bandaged hand on September 1. It was odd that the bandage was gone the next morning, and even odder that there was only an old P-shaped scar on the palm. *A souvenir picked up in Iraq? Really?* He wasn't so sure.

Something was off then, and something was certainly off now. Ryan was lying, and Suzanne must've known. He was hiding something. They both were, but what, and why? Yet, if this *Typhoid Mary* infected Mender with something, Pete refused to think that the war hero was knowingly responsible for his son's death. He only hoped Suzanne was okay.

A reporter's death and the strange scar weren't the only reasons for his hunch. After Anderson's Jeep was dragged from the lake, Undersheriff Joe Turner had found a large backpack filled with everything the suspect would need to survive a hike through the mountains. There was also a waterproof map of the Four Corners states with a route drawn to Arizona and a note written on it: *find manycows.*

He figured that *Manycows* was an English version of a Navajo surname. Both he and Turner suspected the woman was headed to New Mexico or Arizona. Pete had alerted authorities around Durango on September 2 to be on the lookout for the woman if, by chance, she survived the mountains without gear and supplies. He had also called everyone with the last name Manycows in the Four Corners states. That didn't take long since it was an uncommon name. When he did reach those with listed numbers, he didn't know what questions to ask and could only tell those who spoke English or Spanish to be on the lookout for the suspect. He'd asked them to call if the woman contacted them, but he wasn't holding his breath.

Four weeks had passed, giving him time to think about the map and his conversations with Ryan. He'd also re-read *The Menders: A*

First American Story. In the tale of Healing Hands, Miller never named the father of Dibé Yázhí, who was Ryan's Navajo great-great-grandmother. This got him thinking. If Ryan's father and grandfather were Utes, why had they spent so much time in the Navajo Nation with very distant cousins? Sure, warm fuzzy feelings had followed the resurrection legend, but historically Utes and Navajos didn't care much for each other. There had to be something else.

Pete did some checking and learned that Ryan's father and grandfather had made frequent trips to Crownpoint, New Mexico, to see a cousin named Wanda Begaye and her grandson, Tommy Yazzie. A little more digging revealed that Mrs. Begaye was the daughter of a respected medicine man named Curtis Chee who happened the grandson of a Manycows who passed away early in the twentieth century. While a connection was a long shot, Pete felt it was worth checking into and attempted to reach Mrs. Begaye without success.

Pete had mulled everything over each night as his wife, Patsy, slept next to him, and had come to the conclusion that Ryan must've known the suspect before Melvin Anderson's death and that she was coming into town to visit him. Why else would he have been so concerned about his *Uncle Mel's* probable killer? Maybe Anderson had known the suspect as well, and that was why he'd stopped to help her outside Grayson.

Yet, if Ryan was party to whatever the woman was involved in, several things didn't add up. Like, why did the woman run after Ryan had rescued her, unless, of course, she was disoriented from the described head injury? Also, there was no way Ryan could've helped her due to two quarantines that kept him contained. Even if he tried, cell service was terrible around the Watchtower and Ryan didn't have a sat-phone. Also, once he was in the containment facility, there was nothing he could've done to help her. Another possibility was that Ryan wasn't the only one in town working with her. This was why Pete planned to have that chat with the owner of Mount Capitol Suites.

Then there'd been that strange incident on September 18 at the Ebola-Colorado containment facility. The Rutherford Hotchkiss Monument had been vandalized and one of its cannon balls had been used to disable the facility's generator. The crazed assailant wearing a balaclava had dressed in black thermal underwear and wool socks. Whoever it was had moved so fast that the only thing the four sent to Grayson Memorial could be sure of was that the assailant was about the same height as the woman Ryan described on September 1. And wouldn't you know—it had been Ryan's unit the assailant had tried to break into. There were also rumors swirling of BNM's (Brigham Norsworthy's Minutemen) involvement in the incident. Add that to the sweetheart deal the Mender's had gotten on Norsworthy's Watchtower. *Yeah. If coincidences were gold*, he thought.

Pete continued to ponder the discrepancies in his theory as he left the office and sent out an all-points bulletin to Undersheriff Turner and all full-time, part-time, reserve deputies, and even the Alpine Ranger. He ordered them to find and capture Melvin Anderson's murder suspect and not return until she was in custody. As before, he instructed them to take necessary precautions to avoid exposure to whatever might've killed Anderson.

Based on WNN's video footage, the suspect was headed south on Grayson Highway toward Bullion Pass. Yet, if Ryan was the only person she knew in the area, there was a distinct possibility she was headed to the Watchtower. Pete figured he'd head out and have a word with Ryan and check on Suzanne. Regardless, he wanted to talk to Ryan privately before bringing him in for questioning concerning the reporter's death. He still respected him, so he planned to keep his suspicions to himself until his theory was more than a hunch.

When Pete reached Lake Hotchkiss, his imagination dove deeper into darker places which his affection for the ex-Army Ranger had prevented his mind from traveling to before. There was no denying that Ryan's time in the service had left permanent scars. The assault of his commanding officer, the current Chairman of the Joint Chiefs of Staff, General Cornelius Adamson, was well-publicized, and since the end of *Berets*, the world outside Grand Junction and Packer City had heard nothing from Ryan. Had he been turned? Recruited by radicals like those who attacked the U.S. on 9/11?

Pete tapped the call button. "All units, proceed to the Watchtower. Suspect likely headed there. I also need back up to bring in Mender for the suspected murder of KNW reporter Kenneth Prattle."

Three

11:34 a.m., Dark Tuesday, October 2, 2007. Lake Hotchkiss Road.

Pete swerved when he saw yellow-orange flashes light up the southwestern sky. Multiple rumbling reports followed as he hugged the edge and righted himself before he repeated the flight of Melvin Anderson's jeep. As he passed the lake's south end, Pete saw smoke billowing against the glowing backdrop at the base of Greenly

Mountain. He hit the call button. "Joe, there's been an explosion on the east side of Crown Lake."

"Yeah, I know. Just got a call from Grayson dispatch about gunfire in the general vicinity. Caller told Rhonda it sounds like a warzone. Said it was coming from the Watchtower. She asked if we needed back up. I told her to ask Sheriff Griggs to send everyone Grayson can spare, but it'll be an hour before anyone gets here. I also told her to call the Colorado Bureau."

"Good thinking. I'll see you in a few. Have all units meet at the base of Greenly Mountain. I gotta check on the Fitzgeralds to make sure they're okay."

"Got it."

Pete rounded the mountainous bend near Crown Lake and saw black and gray smoke rising from the flaming Watchtower.

"Correction. All units meet at the Crown Lake campground. The Watchtower is burning. Repeat, the Watchtower is burning. Call the fire department and tell anyone you see to evacuate the area immediately and head into town. I'm going to the Fitzgeralds' to see if they need help."

He exited onto the Watchtower Private Drive at the southeast edge of the smaller lake. He turned too fast and lost control until his tires found traction in the slushy snow. He pulled into the Fitzgeralds' driveway and passed a truck and SUV parked on the right side of the two-story home. He skidded to a halt.

He hopped out and turned toward Tower Rock. The aspens obscured all but the top third of the Watchtower against the orange background and the billowing black smoke. He heard squealing tires and gunfire. Seconds later, there were more pulses from a semi-automatic, loud discharges from a pistol or a revolver, and more rifle fire. He heard the crackling above and saw flames licking near the Watchtower's ramparts.

Suddenly, a fissure appeared in the blackened sky beyond the orange. Light poured in from above as if through a slit lamp, illuminating the right side of the towering inferno. There was more gunfire. A short silence followed, and then more fissures of light cracked the sky and widened, dissolving the darkness, as if a massive hand had been removed from in front of the sun.

Pete's jaw dropped as night became day, as if a switch had been flipped. "What the…" he began to say and thought, *Well, if that ain't the damnedest.*

Gunfire resumed, ending his wonderment, and then paused again. Only the crackling flames could be heard until they were drowned by the approaching popping-whir of helicopter blades.

Pete moved to the front door and knocked twice.

No answer.

KNOCK-KNOCK-KNOCK.

No answer.

Ding-dong, ding-dong, ding-dong.

Still nothing.

"Damnit, Jeremiah, it's Pete. Sorry about the language. Just… just answer the door if you're home. Sarah! Are you there? Zeke? Blossom? You all need to leave this area immediately!"

He turned to the Watchtower and saw flames cresting over the parapets. His head whipped back to the door.

Ding-dong, ding-dong, ding-dong.

KNOCK-KNOCK-KNOCK, KNOCK-KNOCK-KNOCK.

Ding-dong, ding-dong, ding-dong.

"Jeremiah! Sarah! If you don't answer, I'm busting this door in. This is an emergency. I need to get you and the kids out of here now!"

KABOOOOOM.

Pete spun and his eyes went wide as a cobalt fireball appeared above the trees with matching spiraling tendrils that shot in all directions from a spreading unearthly flame. An icy gust ripped through the trees, stripping them of leaves and snow. Pete shivered, and his fingertips ached as the cold needled through his gloves. Then like the darkness, the smoke and flames engulfing the Watchtower and mountainside vanished. And… and it began snowing, but the snow was dark blue.

"Okay, Jeremiah, I warned you. I'm not paying for your door."

"Understood," said a barely audible voice.

"What'd you say? Dammit, Jeremiah! Is that you? Open the door!" he bellowed as he peered through the peephole.

TEWT-crack-TEWT-TEWT.

Four

11:44 a.m., Tuesday, October 2, 2007. The Fitzgeralds' Place.

Undersheriff Joe Turner jumped out as Deputy Mike Wicker's black Jeep rolled to a stop behind Pete's vehicle. Joe saw Pete hit the ground. Before blood had pooled in the snow around his head, Joe pulled his pistol, fired through the door, and crouch-ran toward the sheriff.

Joe glanced back as Deputy Don Glickman and Reserve Deputy Fred Strickland pulled into the driveway in a green SUV. They avoided Wicker's Rubicon by inches as Alpine Ranger Ronnie Jones and new Reserve Deputy Juan Guzman followed in a red extended-cab. Reserve Deputy Lawrence Lombardi and Jake Tolliver (the other part-timer) was unable to stop his silver king cab and hit Jones and Guzman hard enough to scoot his vehicle closer to Glickman's.

Joe's attention returned to the house. He scanned for movement. The front room window shattered. The last thing he felt was a sledgehammer smash into his face and then he saw sepia.

Five

Deputy Mike Wicker unloaded a magazine in the direction of the shots as a chorus of pistols opened up from the police line.

He ran toward his best friend. It hadn't registered yet that Joe and his father-in-law, Pete, were dead.

A barrage of gunfire erupted from the house, forcing Mike to retreat behind Pete's SUV. Bullets clanged and ripped through aluminum, shattered auto glass, and flattened tires. He leaned against the rear tire, released the empty mag, and inserted a freshie. He racked the slide and looked left. Glickman, Jones, and Lombardi were crouched behind their vehicles. Strickland rolled out of Glickman's driver's side holding an AR-15. Strickland kept his head down and ran to the end of the vehicular barricade, and disappeared around Lombardi's truck. Mike couldn't see Tolliver or Guzman but heard pistol fire coming from the right side of the house. Glickman, Jones, and Lombardi fired numerous rounds and ducked to refresh their mags.

Automatic fire resumed, followed by more aluminum peppering and zinging bullets that sang past aspens or splintered wood.

Mike looked under the vehicle, and saw what remained of Joe's face. His right cheek was gone. The eye hung over the hole by a nerve string. His left eye stared at nothing above the crimson slush. Pete's body was a few feet from Joe's. His head was hidden behind his cowboy hat as the star glistened in the sunlight.

Mike sat back and banged his head against the vehicle as cold reality hit him. He gritted his teeth, breathed hard through his nose, and clenched his fist. He squinted, and his body shook as his rage grew.

He rose and crouch-ran past Glickman, Jones, and Lombardi. He went around Lombardi's truck, Strickland, Guzman, the Fitzgeralds' truck, and finally Tolliver as he crept along the side of the house. Mike turned the corner to the backyard and saw a black-and-white camo-clad bastard running toward the woods. He fired twice, hit, and dropped the man. Tolliver rushed past as Mike kicked in the back door.

TEWT-TEWT-TEWT.

Mike's left shoulder lurched back. The burn followed, but he ignored the pain, aimed for the kitchen, and dodged left as the shooter pulled the trigger.

Nothing—an empty mag. The shooter ejected the magazine as he dashed for cover behind the kitchen bar.

Mike fired thrice before the mag hit the linoleum, tagging the man off-center in the chest and left shoulder. The impact knocked the man off his feet and sent him slamming into the cabinet doors below the sink. The third bullet missed and sent splinters raining from a high cabinet.

He glanced into the living room. A glaring shooter sat slumped against a recliner. Several bloody holes peppered his fatigues. One was punched through his mustache. Mike stepped around the kitchen bar and found the wounded shooter gasping as he held his rifle in his lap. The man coughed up blood, and breathed easier.

Mike aimed at the man's head as a red flower bloomed on the Black Beret's chest. Mike felt warm wetness trickle down his arm and smelled rancid meat that churned his stomach. His eyes watered and he tried not to breathe.

The shooter labored and coughed up more blood as his wild eyes burned into Mike's. The shooter's lips drew into a toothy grin and he guffawed through another cough.

Mike added a bullet to the grinning man's forehead and then lights went out.

At least that was Mike's last thought before he felt like he'd been crammed into a closet. He felt as if he was floating in nothingness. He could still hear outside the closet door, but sound was muffled and seemed like it was coming from somewhere far away.

Six

"Don't shoot! Don't shoot!" said the cocoa-skinned Black Beret in a thick German accent.

"Stay down!" yelled Reserve Deputy Jake Tolliver.

The man struggled to his knees, but kept his hands high.

Reserve Deputies Fred Strickland and Juan Guzman covered while Jake checked the man for weapons. He was unarmed.

"Face down. Hands out. Now!" Jake snapped as he grabbed the man's neck. He slammed his face into the snow and handcuffed him. "You have the right to remain silent, you motherfucker. Any bullshit you utter can and will be used against you in a court of law. Yeah, and you can talk to an attorney and have him there for questioning if you want, you piece of shit."

Warm mist wafted from Jake's nose in furious swirls as he rolled the prisoner over. He saw two wounds and fought the urge to add a third. He removed his belt and tied off the man's leg, then lifted the man's military blouse. Blood seeped from a love handle as yellow fat hung from the wound. He lowered the shirt and, with Guzman's help, yanked the man to his feet. Together, they marched the prisoner to Lombardi's truck.

Jake opened the back driver's side. The prisoner stepped up, and Jake shoved him inside. The man landed face down on the seat as Jake slammed the door.

"Guzman, get Lombardi's keys. No time to wait for an ambulance. Call Dr. Boyd and take this asshole into town and get him patched up," he said, speaking just under a yell. "And when Doc's done, lock his ass in the old jail. And don't take your eyes off him. I'm sure Glickman and Wicker are gonna wanna have a chat with this piece of shit to find out why he and his friends opened fire and killed Pete and Joe and... and why these motherfuckers are still in our county."

Seven

Deputy Don Glickman grimly verified that Pete and Joe were dead as Alpine Ranger Ronnie Jones stood over him.

Don opened the front door with his SIG Sauer raised, entered, and gagged. "My God! What is that smell?"

The officers covered their faces and kept their pistols raised and were greeted by a dead Black Beret slumped against a recliner. He looked left and saw Wicker standing in the kitchen, his face inscrutable, his pistol dangling in his right hand. At his feet, a dead shooter leaned against the cabinet below the sink. The dead man had a creepy post-mortem grin and a third eye in his forehead crying crimson.

"Did you sweep the house?" asked Don.

Wicker nodded, but his gaze didn't waver from the corpse. His head tilted slowly side to side as if he was admiring something.

Don saw Wicker's shoulder as Lombardi entered the front and Tolliver and Strickland came through the back. A quick succession of retching followed. Strickland almost vomited, and all three covered their faces. Only Wicker seemed unfazed by the aroma.

"Mike, you okay?" asked Don.

He didn't respond.

"Can someone stop Guzman before he leaves? We need to get Mike to Doc Boyd."

Don holstered his weapon and took Wicker's gun. He placed it in its holster and laid Wicker's hand over the bleeding shoulder.

Eight

New Reserve Deputy Juan Guzman had made it as far as Castle Lake when Lombardi's voice came over the radio. "Guzman, you copy?"

"Yeah. What do you need?"

"Come back. We got another for Dr. Boyd. One of those dead assholes shot Wicker. Have Boyd send ambulances and a Flight for Life in case there're survivors at the Watchtower. And call Grayson dispatch—tell them to send help. Call Silver City, too. Have them send everybody they can."

"Roger that, but I think Turner already did... Damn, never mind. I'll call again."

Juan u-turned, glanced in the rearview, and saw the prisoner slide. The Black Beret grunted as he hit the door. Juan smirked, accelerated, and turned recklessly onto the private drive, sending the man sliding the other way.

He pulled into the Fitzgeralds' driveway. Wicker was waiting with Lombardi, Strickland, and Tolliver. Lombardi opened the front passenger side and helped Wicker in. Wicker glanced at the prisoner as Strickland closed the door. Juan looked at the Black Beret, and then Wicker. Wicker was holding his shoulder and staring forward with a blank expression.

Juan reversed and shifted into drive. He wanted to say something—anything—to help, but he didn't know Wicker very well. Juan had just moved to the area before the lockdown to replace former Deputy Bob Roberts who left for Seattle in September. He wondered if he should say anything? After all, what can be said to someone who just witnessed their best friend and father-in-law gunned down?

Nine

Early Afternoon, Dark Tuesday, October 2, 2007. The Fitzgeralds' Place.

Don followed Jones outside where Strickland, Lombardi, and Tolliver were solemnly huddled, hats off with heads down, around Pete and Joe's corpses. Don took off his hat. Jones followed and the five continued the moment of silence a little longer.

Don put his hat on and addressed the group. "Strickland, Jones, head up to the Watchtower with me. Lombardi, call an ambulance and contact the Grayson and Silver City PDs. Ask them to send everybody they can A-S-A-P. I guess I'm... I guess I'm acting interim sheriff... at least for now."

"Guzman's already making the calls," said Lombardi. "I also asked him to get us a Flight for Life in case anyone's still breathing up at the Watchtower... or what's left of it."

"Good thinking, Lombardi. Tolliver, go find some sheets to cover Pete and Joe and the stiffs in the living room and kitchen. And don't move anything. And don't touch anything unless you're wearing gloves. And watch your step. And Lombardi, grab your camera and start taking photos. Make sure to get some before Tolliver covers the bodies. The Colorado Bureau, FBI, Homeland Security, ATF, and who knows who else will be here before nightfall. I want this crime scene handled by the book. And for God's sakes, could someone *pleeease* find out where that hellish smell is coming from."

Don followed Strickland and Jones up the drive. The air grew colder with every step. The morning's snow had been shaken from every limb, and even the leaves had been stripped from the aspens and progressively replaced by dark blue ash as the rocky switchbacks came into view at the base of Tower Rock.

As they neared the first switchback-bend, Tolliver came sprinting up the steep road, yelling, "Don, Don..." He stopped, bent over with hands on knees, and caught his breath. "Don, y-you gotta come back to the house. It's bad. Real fuckin' bad."

"What is it?" Don asked as he descended to Tolliver.

Tolliver shook his head. He appeared rattled to the core. "You have to see this for yourself," he said, choking out words as his eyes welled.

"Strickland, Jones—head up without me. And be careful. Don't take any chances, and wait for me before you go inside."

"We won't, and, uh, we will," said Strickland as Jones nodded.

Don jogged behind Tolliver back to the Fitzgeralds'.

Joe and Pete were covered with bedsheets that blended with the snow except for the red around the heads. Don stepped around his fallen friends, entered the house, and covered his nose and mouth. The Black Beret in the front room was covered. Lombardi was in the kitchen snapping photos of the second body and the surrounding blood splatters. Lombardi didn't look up as Don passed and continued to the basement.

Don descended the steps ahead of Tolliver. Don's sleeve no longer helped as his eyes watered and acid bubbled up. He swallowed.

"Oh, my God," Don said at the bottom of the steps as he pressed fingers into his forehead. To the left was a twisted mass of bodies in the corner that he recognized as Sarah and the two Fitzgerald children, Zeke and Blossom. Jeremiah was also dead with his torso secured with duct tape to a chair and a central support. His forehead was likewise taped to the support and his eyelids were propped open with toothpicks while his blue-black lips were sealed with shoelaces. Sarah and the kids were clothed, but Jeremiah was naked. His arms and legs below the elbows and knees were gone, their stumps sutured with different colored shoestrings. Above the amputations and on his chest, muscles had been filleted and slices were missing. Flies buzzed as their wormy spawn flittered in and out of dark, blotchy, graying tissue.

Don bent over and vomited, dry-heaved a few times, and wiped his mouth. He moved closer. Sarah, Zeke, and Blossom had a single bullet hole in their foreheads. Their cloudy eyes were fixed on Jeremiah and their mottled gray faces looked anything but peaceful.

To Jeremiah's left was a picnic table with an open leather roll with surgical instruments for amputation. He'd seen a similar set in a Civil War museum in Frederick, Maryland, but these instruments were covered with dried blood. Next to the roll was a Coleman stove with a black iron skillet, its bottom filled with yellow congealed grease. By the stove was a fine China plate with slices of desiccated, moldy meat. Around it was an empty bottle of cabernet and a dirty, wide-bottom glass with lip prints and little dried red wine in the bottom.

Don felt dizzy. Black spots filled his vision. He tried not to hyperventilate or pass out. He steadied himself on the table. Tolliver didn't notice—he seemed just as unsettled. Don had never seen anything like this (and he was fairly sure Tolliver hadn't either), but the scene reminded him of everything he knew about the Greenly murders of 1892 which occurred not far from here.

Hold it together. Hold it together, thought Don. *You're the sheriff now.* He shook his head, and the black dots disappeared. "Nothing we can do here," he said in a solemn, husky voice. "I'm gonna head up to the Watchtower. You and Lombardi stay here and, uh, guard the crime scene. We should have some help soon. You mind, uh, bringing Wicker's Rubicon into town later?" he asked, rubbing his lips. "Keys are in the ignition."

"Will do," Tolliver said as he wiped his eyes.

Ten

As Don reached the first cobalt-covered switchback, Alpine Ranger Ronnie Jones's voice cracked over the radio. "There's been a massacre up here. Bodies and parts of bodies everywhere—no telling what's inside. I can't see how anyone survived this. Me and Fred'll check the perimeter 'til you get here. We'll meet'cha above the Watchtower."

"Alright. Should be there in under five."

Don stopped at a burned-out Black Hawk fuselage covered with blue frosting. He wiped away a circle of ash from the cockpit and glanced inside. Two charcoaled corpses in seat belts had their heads slumped forward. He continued on and soon rounded the second bend.

Midway up the third, he saw the raised impression of an intact body under the ash and a disembodied hand poking from the cobalt with sinew and bone visible on a few fingers. The air became chillier with every step toward the fallen Watchtower which now was a mass of burned cedar and red rock. Only the rear half of the tower remained. Don scanned three-sixty. Everything for hundreds of feet was dark blue and glistened. Icy air nipped at his nose and ears. He shivered as he reached into a pocket for gloves and put them on.

He stopped at the third bend and peered down to the base of the rock. A second fuselage lay twisted amongst the once exquisite cedar deck. To the west, a third Black Hawk had crash-landed on a cobalt-dusted field. Only its rear rotor was ruined. The pilots had escaped the crash, but hadn't survived. Don could see their bodies sprawled about fifty feet from the fuselage.

As Don neared the fourth and final bend, the blue substance deepened to his ankles. Frost crawled up his boots. He slogged into the driveway and passed frozen, twisted, nearly hidden logs of human remains. A mass of melted metal from a fourth fuselage rested about seventy-five feet from Mender's front door. Chopper pieces were strewn and mixed with broken and melted rifles and blackened and frosty, blue-dusted gore.

Don went to the closed garage and saw hundreds of holes concentrated on the left side. He walked up the four steps to the copper-covered porchway. The front door was missing and three somewhat intact bodies dressed in black and white camo lay face down, punched full of large holes. The aroma of cooked carnage was slightly better than the air in the Fitzgeralds' basement.

He covered his nose and mouth and stepped inside. The front door was in the foyer next to two bodies. He took a few steps and saw more blackened and blue-dusted corpses in what was left of the octagonal-shaped living room. From the foyer, he saw a helicopter blade that had crashed through the stairs to the second floor. Dark blue ash covered everything and sparkled like diamonds in the ceiling-less living room.

He returned to the driveway and looked toward the bedroom over the garage. He pulled out his radio. "Jones, where are you guys?"

"We're above the Watchtower where I said we'd be. There's plenty to see up here before we head inside," he said, waving from the edge.

"I forgot to ask you—did you bring your Canon?"

"Of course. Got my SIG right here," said Jones, stepping forward and tapping his side holster so Don could see.

"No, your camera. That little red dew-hickey you're always snapping pics with."

"Yeah, I've been taking pictures since you left," he said, holding the camera above his head. He lowered his arm and asked, "So what had Tolliver so upset?"

"Those psychopaths slaughtered the Fitzgeralds. Look, let's focus on what we're doing up here."

"What? The kids, too?"

"Jones, not now. Just do your job and take pictures like I asked you to. We need everything documented. I'm heading up."

"Okay. Be careful on that trail. It's steep and the ground's slick."

"Hey—sorry I snapped at you," said Don.

"It's okay. I understand. This kinda stuff isn't supposed to happen here—not in a place like Packer City."

Don climbed the trail and slipped to his knees a few times before reaching the top where four dusted, mangled bodies greeted him by the fire pit. Numerous casings littered the ground behind the solar panels to his left. More large-caliber casings—hundreds and hundreds of them—were scattered near a depression beyond the panels where the ash was thinner.

Don turned to the steep trail leading into the woods. He investigated up to where the ash was thin enough to make out the white snow-cover. He saw no casings, but noted several similar boot prints heading down. He picked his way to the panels and scanned the ground. A pointed object caught his eye before he stepped on it. He crouched down for a better look. It was a dart with a one-inch needle the size of a .45 caliber cartridge. He picked it up, examined it, and set it back where he found it. There were several more nearby.

Jones clicked away.

Don glanced down as Jones almost stepped on a dart. "Ronnie, watch your step."

Jones looked down and took a photo of the dart.

Don continued to a depression beyond the solar panels where a three-foot metal dome was barely visible.

"What is that?" asked Don.

"Haven't the slightest," Jones said with a shrug.

"Let's ask Strickland," said Don. "He knew Brigham better than either of us."

Strickland was atop the tower stairs, framed by a blackened chimney and red rock ramparts that led nowhere.

"Strickland, what're you doing?" asked Don.

Strickland sighed and said, "Nothing. Just thinking about old times. The Watchtower was such a beautiful place once. So sad it had to end like this." He walked down the steps.

Don knew Strickland's story well. He had known Brigham Norsworthy when he was younger. He'd been a frequent guest at the Watchtower for dinner with Brigham and his wife, Angela, when their kids were young, innocent, and spoiled rotten. That was before Strickland became a police officer, and Norsworthy became too radical for him to stomach. Even Angela had more than she could stand. She'd divorced him, took half of everything, and had been happily married to Strickland for the past twenty years.

"You'll have to reminisce later. Can you look at something?"

"Sure," said Strickland. He followed Don and Jones to the small dome. He shook his head when he saw it. "That's a pill tower, and it's recently been deployed." He knelt and brushed away ash. "Look at the carbon scoring around the edge. Probably from an RPG—that's what took out the choppers. I'm sure this isn't the only one. See those casings—they're from a concealed Browning M249 inside. Brigham talked about building something like this to protect his place from the government if they ever came for his guns. He even showed me a schematic. I told him he was nuts. Then he acted like he was joking around. Yeah… that was when he stopped telling me stuff. After that, I left for the police academy, and when I got out, our friendship went south. When Angela left him and we got married, Brigham became a recluse and only spent time with his nephew, Eugene Lee, Charlotte, and elite members of his Minutemen. Who knows what else he has rigged up in this place. Crazier thing is, before he died two years ago, he'd been on life support since his stroke in '93. Then his kids up and sold the place to the Menders. Hard for me to swallow that Mender didn't know anything about Brigham's little defense system. I'm guessing Mender was approached by Brigham Norsworthy's Minutemen and recruited after the ambush in Almawt Lilkifaar. Stuff like that can change a man. I've seen it myself. I hate to think it—much less say it—but I think Pete was right. Mender and that woman were working together, and Brigham's ghost is directing whatever his group has planned." He paused and glanced around at the devastation. "If that blue dust weapon is any indication of their capabilities, it's no wonder these black ops went to so much trouble to bring them in or take 'em down. But I doubt anyone survived what happened here."

"Ryan Mender, a Minuteman and a terrorist? Wow. That's bullshit, Fred," said Don. "Ryan's a good man, and Norsworthy's band of weekend warriors wasn't known for its inclusiveness. And regardless, whatever happened here doesn't remotely justify what they did to the Fitzgeralds."

"What did they do to the Fitzgeralds?" Strickland asked, looking uneasy.

"They executed Sarah, Zeke, and Blossom and tortured and ate parts of Jeremiah while he was still alive from the looks of it."

"What?"

"Yeah. So don't fool yourself. I don't think any of us have a clue what's going on here. But I do know one thing—these guys are fucking evil. Let's get done here. I want to get back to town as soon as possible and have a talk with that sonuvabitch Dr. Boyd is working on before anyone else gets a chance."

"Um, okay," Strickland said as he looked at the ground.

Don led Jones and Strickland down the steps and found four more bodies: three shot in the head and one decapitated. At the scorched deck, he found the way into the front room blocked by a ten-foot debris pile. A few hands and arms poked from beneath. The three headed back up the way they'd come, down the slippery trail, and entered through the front door.

"Can't go that way—stairs are gone," said Strickland, stating the obvious as Don looked at the helicopter blade.

Don lit up the dining room with a Maglite and tip-toed to avoid scattered remains of several mangled and nail-crusted bodies. He scanned the area and found more casings littering the floor under Norsworthy's eclectic art collection in the dining room, kitchen, and the foot of the stairs. He also saw craters in the floor and large holes near the wall foundations. He panned and found similar holes in the ceiling. His light turned to a soot-covered painting in the dining room. The painting was of a mountain with a tower attacked by four giant blackbirds. At the top was a cocoa-colored wizard in brown leather shooting blue-lightning from his fingers. To the wizard's left was a petite silver-armored white female holding a ridiculous blade above her head, ready to strike.

"I've never seen this one before," Strickland said, cocking his head to examine the surrealism. "You know, Brigham painted all of these, like that one over there that looks like Cthulhu. They're weird, but you can't deny that Brigham was a mad genius with a brush." Strickland tilted his head to the other side. He glanced at Don and pointed at the casing wedged and crushed under the frame's lower right-hand corner.

Don eyed it curiously, and then grabbed a corner of the painting and tried to lift it. It wouldn't budge. "Give me a hand," he said.

Jones slid his camera into his pocket, and the three men pulled until the frame tore off the wall. Underneath was a sliding track for a metal door. They pulled and grunted to open the door until a 0.50 caliber heavy machine gun and a pile of spent casings came into view.

Don and Strickland strained to hold the door open as Jones took photos. He gave a thumbs ups and they let go. The door snapped shut with a *CLANG*.

Don headed into the garage and found the floor covered with ice in front of a ruined water heater to the right. Mender's F350 was embedded in the utility room wall to the left, its front and back windshields shot out.

Don stepped carefully to the tailgate. It was riddled with bullet holes. He shimmied to the cab and looked inside. He saw no bodies or blood. He slipped and his ass hit ice-covered cement. He yelled, "Dammit, ow!"

"You okay?" Jones asked.

"I'm fine, I'm fine. Let's hurry this up," Don quipped as he gripped the truck to stand. He saw an open breaker box by two backpacks hanging on hooks to the left. He slipped and slid on the ice to investigate. A red switch caught his eye. He read the note below: *When ravens descend, flip the red switch.* "What the hell?"

Strickland chuckled.

"What's so damn funny?" asked Don.

"Sorry. You know how paranoid Brigham was about black helicopters."

Don and Jones nodded.

"Well, he used to call them ravens," said Strickland. "Guess his delusion came true two years too late."

"You gonna flip it?" asked Jones.

"Best not," said Don. "We'll leave that to the Feds who…" he said and rubbed his forehead, adding, "… will already be pissed about that painting we tore off the wall."

"Yeah, you're probably right," said Jones as he snapped a few photos of the red switch and the message. Don nodded, turned, and followed Strickland into the house, glancing back once to make sure Jones was following.

They left through the front door. Don headed up the stairs to the bedroom over the garage, avoiding the bloody footprints pressed into the cold ash on each step. He paused to view the driveway apocalypse, then stepped into the doorless bedroom. He covered his nose as a wall of rank hit him that rivaled the Fitzgerald's basement. He saw more bodies littering the hall to the game room before his gaze was drawn to a human lump on the right side of the king-size bed. It was Suzanne Mender and she looked like she'd been dead for a whole lot longer than that morning.

Don pushed past Strickland and Jones, leaned over the railing, and dry-heaved. His head swam. Suzanne was dead, but where was Ryan's body? Had he escaped, or was his body buried in the rubble or in the blue snow, or was he puzzle pieces of bones and flesh? Had the suspect been here? Was she also among the dead? Or, if she gave them the slip, was she closer to Silver City or wherever she was headed? Or were Pete and Fred correct? Had Ryan murdered his wife, or was it an accident? And if Ryan and the soon-to-be-identified woman survived, was he now on the run with a suspected terrorist? Don wasn't sure if it mattered anymore and really didn't care at that moment.

He tried not to think of the carnage and evil he'd just witnessed as macabre images clicked through his mind like an old View-Master. His head pounded. He felt dizzy again, and the black dots returned. He held the rail tightly and took deep breaths to calm himself. It wasn't helping. He wasn't the right man for this job and wanted to be as far from this place as possible. When the feds arrived, they would challenge his jurisdiction since the elected sheriff was dead. *I hope they do,* he thought. *They can have this nightmare. I don't want it. Until then, suck it up, buttercup. This is your mess to deal with.*

Eleven

Early afternoon, Dark Tuesday, October 2, 2007. Grayson Highway North, Packer City, Colorado.

Reserve Deputy Juan Guzman crossed the Howard Creek Bridge. Up ahead to the right, Earth First Food Market's small lot was filled with news vans and other vehicles. The front window announced that the store was CLOSED UNTIL FURTHER NOTICE as locals gathered around a teary eyed reporter as she spoke to a camera.

Juan peeked at Wicker, who was still staring forward, blank-faced. Juan glanced in the rearview. The prisoner was staring out the window.

Juan passed a Land Rover outside the Packer City Area Medical Center, and continued to the back entrance where Dr. Raymond Boyd and a woman stood. He hadn't met the town's only doctor, but from the bags under his eyes, he suspected his assistant would be carrying the weight.

"Dr. Boyd, I'm Reserve Deputy Juan Guzman."

"Good to meet you—just wish the circumstances were better."

"You and me both. I thought this town was supposed to be quiet."

"Trust me, this isn't normal, or I would've found someplace peaceful to practice, like inner-city Chicago, or would've stayed on as a combat medic," Dr. Boyd said with a wry grin and somber eyes.

"Anyway, good to have you in town." He motioned to the woman. "This is Tonya Abernathy. She's amazing like my other PA. You'll meet Lei Tran soon enough, but he's off today. We're both recovering from that quarantine and whatever that lab drugged us with last night. But unlike P.A. Tran, I have to be here. Okay, let's get these patients inside."

Juan helped Wicker from the truck and opened the back door as Abernathy walked the deputy the rest of the way into treatment. Juan grabbed the prisoner's arm, pulled him from the vehicle, and followed Dr. Boyd inside faster than the prisoner could comfortably limp.

Dr. Boyd directed the prisoner to an exam table. "Can you get up on the table?" he asked.

The man nodded and stepped up while the doctor held his arm. Juan removed the cuffs and stood with his pistol pointed at the prisoner's back.

Dr. Boyd helped the prisoner remove his shirt. Juan regarded the tattoo on the man's upper right arm. It was of a large skull with a beret and emblem of the 75th Airborne Regiment.

The doctor left the belt tourniquet on the leg and examined the side wound. "Is it true—are Pete and Joe dead?" he asked.

"Yeah, I'm afraid so," said Juan.

Dr. Boyd shook his head and sighed. "Damn shame. Good men. Such good men. The town won't be the same without them. What happened?"

"I don't know. There was a battle at the Watchtower, and then this guy's buddies opened up on us at the Fitzgeralds' place. Pete and Joe didn't have a chance. I don't know much more, and I couldn't tell you if I did. I just need you to patch up the prisoner as quickly as you can."

"I'll do what I can. Is this one of those Black Berets?"

"Yeah. His two friends are dead at the Fitzgeralds'. This coward dropped his weapons and was running from the scene when Wicker shot him," Juan said and quickly added, "but I doubt he knew the man was unarmed."

"So, you taking him to Grayson after I patch him up?"

"Yeah, eventually, I'm sure, but I was told to take him over to the old jail museum. Don's the acting sheriff now and wants to have a word with him before the Feds get a chance."

"I heard what they did to you guys during the lockdown."

"Yeah—talk about a nice welcome to Packer City, especially with a stomach flu and no toilet," Juan said, tensing his jaw as he glared at the prisoner's head. "Thanks to these murdering pricks, we spent the next week disinfecting the place after the Guard let us out. But it's comfy enough now to hold our friend here until we transfer him to a real lock up."

Dr. Boyd cleaned and bandaged the prisoner's flank wound. The prisoner made no sound or show of discomfort. The doctor removed the man's boots and the tourniquet. The prisoner assisted with the khakis, and then Dr. Boyd examined the entry and exit wound. It didn't immediately ooze. He cleaned, packed, and bandaged the wounds. When he was done, he handed the prisoner green surgical scrubs. "Tonya, how's Michael's shoulder?"

"The round passed through the deltoid and missed the glenohumeral joint, but I'll take some radiographs to make sure," she said as she packed and bandaged the shoulder.

"Sounds good. Well, your prisoner is good to go. He should be fine. Let me grab some antibiotics and something for pain," Dr. Boyd said and left treatment.

The prisoner stood, dressed, stepped into his boots, tied his laces, and then sat back on the table and put his arms behind his back. Juan holstered his pistol, cuffed him, and looked at Wicker as Abernathy continued working.

Dr. Boyd returned minutes later and handed Juan two pill bottles. Juan looked at the label as the doctor went over each. "Have your prisoner take two capsules every eight hours until gone and one tablet every twelve. Make sure he takes these with food and water."

"Will do—don't want this piece of shit dying of an infection or getting a tummy ache, now do we? Or, Heaven forbid, he be uncomfortable before his day in court," Juan said with a smirk. He shoved the bottles in his pocket, grabbed the prisoner's arm, and marched him to the exit. Before he stepped outside, he turned to Wicker. "I'll see you later. And hey, we're gonna find out what this asshole knows, and then we're gonna make him pay for what happened to Pete and Joe."

Wicker didn't react and continued staring at something, or nothing, across the room. Abernathy tapped his arm. Wicker stood and followed the PA out of the room.

Twelve

Mid-afternoon, Dark Tuesday, October 2, 2007. Historic Mears County Courthouse and Jail Museum.

Juan fingerprinted the prisoner and set the card on the office manager's desk. He grabbed a sticky note, wrote *process immediately*, and attached it to the card.

He walked the prisoner down the hall to the spotless jail museum that smelled of Pine-sol. The museum was filled with century-old, refurbished furniture that made Juan feel like he'd stepped back a hundred years.

He grabbed a ring with two iron keys from the golden hook on the wooden coat rack. He opened the first cell, removed the prisoner's cuffs, and pushed him inside. The somewhat rusted hinges squeaked as he slammed the door. He tossed the cuffs on the old desk and sat in the historic chair that once belonged to Sheriff Bo Bridger before his murder in 1892. The tale was lore that anyone who loved the old west or was in law enforcement in Colorado knew. Juan wasn't a big history buff and had never been to Colorado before he decided to escape from California. It was Wicker and Glickman who'd told him the story over several Shiner Bachs on his first night in town right before… Juan scoffed. He didn't want to think about the next two nights.

Juan regarded the prisoner as he sat down on the bed. The man met his gaze, then closed his eyes, and held his head. Juan shook his and went to the break room. He returned with a cup of water and Nutter Butters from a vending machine. "Take these," he said.

The man looked up, came to the bars, and took the water and cookies.

"And these." Juan dumped two capsules and tablet in the same hand with the cookies.

The man opened the package with his teeth, ate a cookie, popped the pills, and washed everything down. He returned to the bed and crunched into a second peanutty sandwich, swallowed, and said, "Danke schön."

Juan rolled his eyes and said, "De nada, asshole."

The office manager entered the museum, sobbing, holding fingerprint cards and an ink pad. She was a big woman with rosy cheeks. Like everyone else in town, he didn't know her very well, but had thought her immune to sadness since she always wore an infectious smile that everyone seemed to catch. She had even maintained a positive outlook when the staff was crammed for two days in the cell where the prisoner now sat with plenty of elbow room.

"You okay?" asked Juan.

"Do I look okay?" she snapped, making him recoil. "No, I'm not. Don jus called…" She sniffled twice. "… He… he told me… he told me Pete and Joe are dead."

"Yeah. I know… I was there."

She frowned and glowered at the prisoner. "Is he the one who killed them?" she asked.

"I don't think so. He was running from the scene before… Ahh, never mind. This guy didn't resist, but the other two…" Juan scoffed. "They weren't about to be taken alive. And one of 'em shot Wicker before he killed the guy. Wicker's down the street at the clinic, but Dr. Boyd says he'll be okay. Did Glickman say what the scene was like at the Watchtower?"

"No… he didn't say. He's pretty shook up. I know Don and I think it's from more than just Pete and Joe's death. He said he's finishing up and will be back in about an hour. Besides being shot, how's Mike doing?"

Juan sighed. "He's in shock, but he's alive."

She sighed and asked, "Could you do me a favor? I need to submit these fingerprints, but these won't do. I need the prisoner to redo them."

"Hey, Sauerkraut, can you help this nice lady out, so we can find out who you are since you don't talk much?"

"Yes, but there is no need," said the prisoner. "I will tell you all that you need to know when your new sheriff returns."

"Well, that's very nice of you. You got a name?"

"Like I said—when your sheriff returns."

"Okay then. But let's go ahead and get those prints, though."

Juan unholstered his pistol and opened the door.

The office manager stepped in, made an acceptable set, and exited.

Juan holstered his pistol and closed the door. The office manager looked at him. She appeared to be the verge of another downpour, so he awkwardly opened his arms. She sank into his embrace and broke down on his shoulder. He held her for a moment, patted her back, and then released.

"Thank you, Juan," she said, then wiped her eyes, and left the museum.

Thirteen

Late afternoon, October 2, 2007. Mears County Courthouse, Packer City, Colorado.

Don was greeted by a throng of reporters outside the courthouse. "No comment. No comment. I need you all to stay outside. Thank you." He entered the courthouse, followed by Jones, locked the doors, and said, "Goddamn media vultures."

Guzman was in the hall outside the museum.

"How many chairs we have in there?" asked Don.

"Just Bo Bridger's."

"Seriously? Have you been sitting in it?"

"Uhh, yes. Um, sorry?"

Don scowled. "Don't be sorry—just don't sit in *that* chair again. That's one of the town's most treasured heirlooms. Now, grab us some chairs from the conference room. I need to talk to this asshole, now!"

Guzman set up the three folding chairs. Don removed his hat and set it on the desk. He swiped his hand to move his tuft over his bald top. Jones pulled out his handheld camcorder, sat, turned it on, and pressed record as Don and Guzman found their seats.

Don started the interview. "My name is Don Glickman, interim Sheriff and acting Undersheriff of Mears County, Colorado, and have been for a few hours on account of your friends killing Peter Maxwell, our Sheriff, and Joe Turner, our Undersheriff. That's not to mention what we found in the basement of that house where you and your buddies butchered one of the most beloved families in our community… and left them to rot. One was even partially eaten. Did Jeremiah taste good?" he asked, nearly screaming with fisted hands.

The prisoner opened his mouth to answer, but Don continued before he could speak. "And that doesn't even scratch the surface concerning the massacre of more of your friends up at the Watchtower. But before we talk more about that, let me introduce everyone. This is Ronnie Jones, Alpine Ranger for Mears and San Marcos Counties. He's here today as a reserve deputy and will be recording your statement or confession. I have to tell you—a confession would be nice. It'll speed things along in court. But I have to ask if you're okay speaking without counsel present."

"I am," said the prisoner.

"Good—glad to get that little formality out of the way. Wouldn't want this thrown out of court on account of a technicality. Oh, and I guess you've already met our newest reserve deputy, Juan Guzman. Yet, none of us know who you are, and it might be a few days before your fingerprints return. So, save us some time, and let's get to know each other."

"I will first tell you who I appear to be," said the prisoner in a heavy German accent, "and then I will tell you who I am and that I am guilty of crimes far greater than anything that happened here today."

Don flicked a hand insistently for the prisoner to proceed.

The prisoner nodded and began his confession. "The mortal shell you see before you is Joshua Roderick Stone. He was born on 26 March 1972. He is a retired and decorated U.S. Army Ranger and was honorably discharged at the rank of Colonel. After that, he worked as a military contractor and had no criminal record before taking this job. You will find this common among the other victims wearing the colors of the Black Berets who died today." The prisoner paused.

Don pursed his lips and flittered a hand again for him to continue.

"Before joining the U.S. Army in July 1990, he had been a Boy Scout and a troop leader and regularly volunteered at the Boys Club in inner-city Atlanta, Georgia. When he left the military, he relocated to Boston, Massachusetts. There, he met the love of his life and married Allison Louise Bryant on 23 May 2005. Soon after, his lovely wife gave birth to beautiful twin girls named Jada and Jayla. You will find that he was reported missing by his wife on the thirty-first of July of this year. His name only surfaced in September when an attorney, named James Mender, cited his name in a lawsuit filed over information access during the Ebola quarantine of your town. But I can tell you that who you are now speaking with, is as much Joshua Stone as your town's quarantine was due to the Ebola virus. Joshua is a good man, unlike me. I will confess that I did *not* kill that family in the basement and had no hand in killing your sheriff or undersheriff." He extended his arms, turned his palms up, and looked into Don's eyes. "And these hands…" he said and closed them into fists, "… were never used to take a life during Joshua's years of service, and I made sure that I did not bloody them since I took possession of his mortal shell. I refuse even to use his voice lest I dishonor it."

Don looked confused but played along. "Well, if you're not this former Colonel Stone, then who are you?"

"My name is Franz Schicklgruber. I only took this job for Johanna. She never deserved the punishment she has endured since her murder, and this was the only way I could save her from further torment."

Don stifled a laugh and resisted the urge to open the cell door and senselessly beat the deranged man who was at least an accessory to multiple homicides. He paused, collected himself, and asked, "Who is Johanna?"

"She was my wife and my angel, but I was a monster. I know you will not take me seriously. How could you? Everything I am about to tell you will sound like the words of a madman since you cannot yet hope to comprehend what is going on here. Whether you believe me or not, please listen to what I have to say."

Don glanced at Jones and Guzman, and scoffed. "We're all ears."

The prisoner nodded and continued, "I was born Franz Heinrich Schicklgruber in Munich, Germany. I am a third cousin of Adolf Hitler but met him only once when I was a young child before the first great war. In the difficult years that followed, I was like many Germans and believed my cousin's words when he promised to make Germany great again. So, I joined the National Socialist Party, and when the war came, I enlisted in the Waffen SS and fought bravely on the eastern front..."

Don shifted in the uncomfortable seat as his gaze met Jones's and Guzman's before his attention returned to the prisoner. He opened and closed his fists as he restrained violent intentions.

"… In 1943, I was transferred to Auschwitz/Birkenau, where I served under Dr. Josef Mengele and assisted with his experiments. Only then did I understand my cousin's madness but could not speak out against the doctor or the others lest I wished to face a firing squad or worse. So, I followed orders and tried to understand the necessity of the Final Solution in the larger plan of the Third Reich. It was not that hard before Auschwitz because I hated the Jews, except for one. However, when I met Johanna, I did not know that she was one, and the SS did not discover the truth during her screening process. And when I did, Johanna already owned my heart. I did everything to protect her and to hide the truth from the Gestapo. And never once did I tell her of the hundreds I murdered during Mengele's experiments or the countless thousands I killed in the gas chambers of Birkenau where I commanded sonderkommandos to kill their own people..."

Don ground his teeth, drummed his fingers on a thigh, and rested the tight fist on the other that screamed to open up, and strangle the psychopath in the cell.

"… One day, Dr. Mengele called me into his office concerning news of my wife. As I walked there, I was terrified that the Gestapo had either learned the truth or that she had been killed in an air raid. Upon entering his office, Mengele looked up and gave me his disarming gap-tooth smile and said, *'I have news about your Johanna. It turns out she was a Jew. Did you know this?'* Caught off guard, I denied any knowledge but asked him if she was okay. Still smiling, he answered, *'As okay as any Jew will be after we have won the war. She is dead. It seems the two Gestapo agents who came to arrest her took a liking to her and attempted to rape her. Disgusting. A Jew. She put up a fight and stabbed one in the temple with an envelope opener. His partner avenged the spilling of pure Aryan blood by strangling your whore.'* Dr. Mengele frowned and continued, *'Needless to say, I do not buy your story that you did not know. There will be an investigation, and when it is determined that you knew, you will join your Johanna after a firing squad wastes bullets on your worthless Jew-loving heart.'*

"When I left his office, I knew I was damned and that all the orders I had followed had been an excuse for my cowardice not to stand and die like a man with Johanna. There was never an investigation since I hung myself before they came for me..."

Don glared and slowly shook his head back and forth, simmering, as he breathed deeply in and out his nose.

"… After my life left me, I found myself in an altered yellowish, black and white version of the water closet. A very old American cowboy in black stood next to my hanging corpse. He was frowning and his face was a mask of revulsion. He did not speak to me as three black doors appeared against the wall in front of me. The left door opened by itself and the cowboy in black motioned for me to step inside. I did not argue and obediently walked through the threshold and eventually arrived in the waiting room for a place called the Prison of Homicide…" The prisoner sighed, adding, "… but you probably know this place better as Hell. I did not have to wait long before two demons bound me in chains and dragged me through the Gate of No Hope and to my Black Water cell. There, I believed I would spend eternity paying for my crimes, but before my punishment began, a demon, unlike the others, visited my cell. He introduced himself as the Curator, but I later learned he was the prison's warden and that we had met before when I was a mortal. I knew him then as Mengele's Benefactor. And like I dwell within Joshua Stone, the Benefactor dwelled within the ruthless doctor. I know now that the Benefactor, the Curator, the Warden—they are all names for Satan himself who goes by many, many, more names." The prisoner paused.

Don glanced again at Guzman and Jones. They looked a little pale and their mouths were ajar.

The prisoner continued, "As I prepared for the torments to come, the Curator—as he liked to be called in that role—informed me that my dearest Johanna would be suffering in the chamber next to mine for killing the Gestapo agent. I pleaded that she did not deserve this—that he add her torments to mine—but he laughed and smiled with Mengele's face and slammed the door as I was dragged into the darkness of my soul…"

Don scoffed and rolled his eyes. He looked at Jones and Guzman. Their eyes were riveted on the prisoner.

"… For sixty years, I experienced the fear, pain, and deaths of countless men, women, and children through their eyes and feelings. Yet, my torment was justified, unlike Johanna's, who was forced to relive her rapist's death over and over. Throughout my suffering, that knowledge was too much to bear. But, bear it I was forced to do. After what seemed like an eternity, the Curator returned with a proposition. He knew I would do anything for Johanna, so he offered to allow her to be a doctor at his laboratory in this reality and allow me to escape my torments in return for corrupting one good soul. While I cared nothing for saving myself, I agreed without hesitation for Johanna's sake. However, shortly after possessing Joshua and meeting his wife and girls, I swore that I would do whatever was required to protect him from becoming one of the Curator's minions. Still, I planned to play my part to keep Johanna free from her torments as long as possible."

Don stared into the prisoner's eyes and began clapping slowly. "Wow, that was an incredible story. How long did it take for you to come up with that one, Joshua? You don't mind if I call you Joshua, do you? I mean, that's your name, right? Of course, we still have to verify your identity." He released a short, wry laugh. "Either you are completely insane, or you are trying to make me believe that you are. But I'm not buying your crazy Nazi bullshit. I must admit you have some balls making up a story like that for a cop who had several relatives murdered in those camps. I saw what you and your two sick-fuck friends did to the Fitzgeralds before gunning down two good cops who were close friends of mine. I'm not about to let you escape the death penalty. So, cut the crap and tell me the truth. What happened to you, Joshua, and what the hell happened at the Fitzgeralds' and the Watchtower?"

"I did not expect for you to believe me, but someone seeing this recording may. And by the way…" The prisoner paused and leaned forward. "I have no fear of death. I am already dead and damned to eternal torment for my crimes. This confession will only make my torments worse when the Curator learns what I have done. My only wish is to save Joshua from sharing in my damnation. I have killed no one with his hands—no one! As I have already told you, I took no part in the atrocities committed in that basement or the killing of your sheriff and undersheriff."

Don looked to the door as Wicker entered wearing a blue-plaid long-sleeve button-up. His left shoulder was bulked up from a bandage.

"What are you doing here?" asked Jones as he pressed pause on the camcorder. "You should be at home. We all saw you after the shoot-out. You're in no condition to be here."

"Jones, I appreciate your concern, but I have to see this through for John, I mean Joe, and Peter, and for that *poor* Fitzgerald family. In fact, why don't you two take a break? Don and I can finish up here."

"Mike, how'd you know about the Fitzgerald family?" asked Don.

"Uh, heard it from Guzman," he said.

"What do you mean?" asked Guzman. "I just now heard about it from Glickman, and I still don't know the details."

"Uhh, then I don't know where I heard it, but I must have heard it from someone, or maybe I imagined hearing it. That house smelled like someone died in it and rotted for weeks. Must've been horrific." Wicker walked up to the cell, cocked his head, and glared at the prisoner. "You must have done a real number on that Fitzgerald family."

"Yeah, he, I mean, they did," said Don. "You sure you're okay, Mike?"

Wicker turned with a slight grin. "Yeah, I'm fine as can be expected under the circumstances. Got lucky with that gunshot." He looked at his left shoulder and pointed at the padding. "The bullet went clean through. Sore as hell, though, but I'm a big boy. Jones, Guzman, I outrank both of you, so get out of here and take the rest of the day, I mean evening, off. That's an order."

"Thanks, Mike," said Jones. "I could use a break after everything that's happened today. I'll leave my camcorder so you can finish the interrogation. Just drop it by the house when you're done, or I'll pick it up tomorrow. Guzman, you want to head over to Dr. Bell's for a drink?"

"Sure. I could use a few, but I was told you don't drink."

"Good a day as any to start," said Jones.

"*Dr. Bell's Cannibal Saloon.* Good choice. Love that place," said Wicker as he plopped into Sheriff Bo Bridger's chair and leaned back.

Guzman's face was painted with surprise.

Don felt similar surprise as he thought about Wicker's near catatonic state at the Fitzgeralds' crime scene. He seethed over his strange behavior and uncharacteristic disrespect, but held his tongue.

Jones went to Wicker and placed a hand on his good shoulder. "If you need anything, let me know. I'm always here for you if you need to talk. In fact, why don't you swing by my house Thursday night? I'm having a Bible study with some folks from my church."

"Thanks, Ronald, I appreciate that," said Wicker. "And I'll *definitely* try to make it Thursday. There's just nothing the good book can't fix, now is there?" he said with a sarcastic bite.

Jones squeezed Wicker's shoulder, pursed his lips, and looked into his eyes. He nodded and left with Guzman. Don heard reporters hounding the pair for comments when the courthouse door opened.

"Well, let's get on with the interrogation. I want to hear what this maggot has to say," said Wicker.

"Could you video while I ask the questions?" Don asked, chewing his words.

"Sure, boss-man."

"Call me Don, Glickman, or Sheriff," he said in a low, measured rumble. "And don't you *ever* overstep my authority again. I'm sorry you lost your best friend and father-in-law, but you know the chain of command. And by the way, I loved Pete and Joe, too. Also, get the fuck out of Sheriff Bridger's chair. Show some Goddamn respect!"

"Sorry," Wicker said, not sounding sorry.

The old chair creaked and cracked as he stood. Wicker went and picked up Jones's camcorder, opened the view screen, and pointed it at the prisoner. He fumbled and dropped it on the hardwood floor, leaving a black scuff. The front lens broke along with the view screen. "Shit. Sorry. Ronnie's gonna be pissed."

"Damnit, Mike," Don yelled as he hopped up and grabbed the camcorder. He removed the SD card, slipped it into his pocket, and laid the broken camera on the desk next to his hat. "Watch the prisoner," Don spat, "I need to go over to the Sheriff's office and see if there's another camera or something I can use to record the rest of this insane asshole's confession."

"Sure. Damn butter fingers," Wicker said with an awkward smirk.

Don rolled his eyes, stormed out of the courthouse, and into the media beehive. "No comment, no comment. I'll be holding a press conference soon."

Fourteen

Wicker listened as Glickman's voice trailed off. He turned and regarded the prisoner. "Think you can take care of yourself for a minute? I need to make a call."

The prisoner didn't acknowledge and kept his eyes fixed on the wall.

"Alrighty then. I'll be right back."

Wicker went to the dark break room, pulled a blood-covered cellphone from his coat pocket, and punched in numbers. "General, this is the Surgeon," Wicker whispered in a sudden slow, dignified southern drawl. "All the mortal shells except Joshua Stone have been executed. The only reason we are speaking is that I jumped into a new one and am currently in possession of a local police deputy named Michael Wicker. I am also calling to inform you that Franz Schicklgruber is singing like a canary. I missed the first part of his interrogation, so I do not know how much he has compromised the operation."

"Why were you not present?" asked the General in a gravel-laced voice.

"My apologies, General, sir. When I shot my new shell, Deputy Wicker exorcised my former one with a bullet to the head. After that, he was taken to a medical center for treatment and it took longer than expected to settle into this new body."

"Enough. I understand. Good work. Now, do whatever is needed to get Schicklgruber to execute the deputy tonight. If he refuses to comply, warn him of the consequences."

"It will be my pleasure," said Dr. Morgan Bell.

"Who are you talking to, Mike?" asked Glickman as he rounded the corner.

Bell jumped as he hung up and shoved the phone into his pocket.

"And why the hell aren't you watching the prisoner?"

Bell sobered and replied with his borrowed shell's voice. "It was Mandy. Seriously, Don, you don't have to be such a prick."

"Uh, sorry. How's she and your mother-in-law taking the news?"

"About like you'd expect, but I need to see this through."

"Okay, then, let's get this done. I found Pete's old voice recorder at the bottom of a desk drawer. I can't remember the last time I saw him use it. It's definitely been a while since the batteries were corroded. But it seems to be working okay after I changed them. Just glad he had an unopened package of micro-tapes in the same drawer. I don't even think they make these anymore. Oh, and I didn't mean to snap at you about Jones's camcorder. Accidents happen. I guess audio-only will have to do for the rest of our conversation with the prisoner. But you're still buying Jones a new camera."

Fifteen

Don followed Wicker back to the museum and sat. From his coat, Don removed a voice recorder and a faded yellow package of 3M micro-tapes. He opened the brittle plastic, removed a single micro-tape, inserted it, and pressed record.

Don watched as Wicker went to the bars and regarded the prisoner. The prisoner matched his stare.

"Testing, 1-2-3, testing," Don said, hit rewind, and pressed play.

"*Testing, 1-2-3, testing,*" the machine repeated back.

"Good to go." Don hit record again. "Present are acting interim Sheriff Donald Glickman and full-time Deputy Michael Wicker. We are continuing our recorded conversation with former Army Colonel Joshua Stone. Please verify your name and that you waived your right to counsel on the first part of your interview and wish to continue doing so now."

"The name of my mortal shell is Joshua Roderick Stone, and yes, I waive all of his rights."

"He's good," said Don, glancing at Wicker as he sat without breaking his stare that was now a glare that the prisoner calmly held.

"Uh, um," Don stammered, momentarily losing his train of thought. "Now that, uh… now that we're done with formalities, why don't we begin the second part of our chat with you telling us why you and your friends were at the Fitzgeralds' in the first place?"

The prisoner looked away from Wicker and focused on Don. "I will do so with a heavy heart. After your National Guard arrived on the thirteenth of September, our commanding officer ordered us to find an empty house near Mender's home to use as an observation post."

Don raised a finger and interrupted. "Who was your commanding officer?"

"We were not allowed to know his name, and I never saw his face, but I know he was a possessed mortal and a general, since we were commanded to address him with respect deserved of his rank."

"Okay," Don said as his gaze shifted to Wicker, and then back to the prisoner, "continue."

The prisoner nodded. "We were ordered to wait at the observation post for Mender's return after being released from the containment facility. The General was convinced that the woman named Mary DeMure would seek him out. We were to inform him the moment that she approached so our forces could be deployed in time to capture them together."

"Who is this Mary DeMure, and why did he want to capture her so badly? And what is Mender's connection to her?"

"I… I do not know. I heard that she was a laboratory experiment gone wrong. The General was emphatic that we capture her alive with Mender. That was the purpose of our search of your town, but I played no part in the search since I was assigned to the roadblock at the northern county line. Our forces were unable to locate her before we ran out of time, so the General ordered us to initiate Plan B."

"That still doesn't explain Mender's connection or why you didn't take him when you had him in the containment facility."

"Again, I do not know why, but one of the guards at the roadblock said he believed the lab was incubating something inside Mender. Then the others warned me to stop asking questions and do my job. All I can say is that the General was very adamant that we take Mender and DeMure together or not at all."

"So, what happened at the Fitzgeralds'?" asked Don.

"As I said, our job was to secure an unoccupied home and wait there until DeMure and Mender arrived. Yet, when we arrived at the chosen location, we learned our intel was wrong. But rather than aborting the mission, the Black Beret, who performed reconnaissance, broke into the home and forced Fraülein Fitzgerald and her two children into the basement at gunpoint. The name of the Contractor's shell was Martin Rice. He was once an honored Navy Captain and SEAL before he signed his contract, but his passenger was a vicious demon named Morgan Bell."

"As in *the* 'Morgan Bell'? The Cannibal Surgeon of Packer City? Or are you referring to a different Morgan Bell?" asked Don as he heard Wicker swallow at the mention of the infamous town doctor whose murderous rampage followed the killing of Sheriff Bo Bridger.

"I am not familiar with the crimes that sent the demon Bell to Hell."

"Well if it is, I gotta say—good job, Mike— you killed the Cannibal Surgeon's poltergeist. This just keeps getting better," Don said, shaking his head.

"Yeah—it does," Wicker said with a nervous chuckle.

Don rubbed his chin as he regarded Wicker. Something seemed way off with him. True, it'd been a hellish day—no lie—but still… "Okay… please… please continue, Franz. I mean Joshua. Damnit. Now you got me doing it."

The prisoner glanced at Wicker, and then proceeded. "Bell tied their hands behind their backs and herded them into a corner, and then he placed his muzzle against the young girl's head. The young girl cried, and her mother and brother joined her and frantically promised that they would not tell a soul that we had been there. I pleaded with Bell not to kill them, but he only grinned and said, '*The General gave me orders, no witnesses.*' He fired a round into the girl's head and quickly fired another into the boy's skull. Fraülein Fitzgerald screamed and Bell laughed as he untied her and let her run to her children. As she sobbed and held them, the demon shot her in the forehead.

"A few hours passed before Herr Fitzgerald arrived. We did not hear his vehicle drive up or when entered the home. He must have sensed something was wrong since he came in the back door. At that time, I was upstairs with two mortal shells named Jim Stevens and Hunter Harrison. I had just met Harrison's shell and never learned the name of who possessed him. However, Stevens, who was sitting next to me, was possessed by Hitler's press secretary, Otto Dietrich. But, as I was saying, we were caught off guard by Herr Fitzgerald's arrival, and when he appeared at the top of the steps, he blasted a hole through Harrison's back and showered Dietrich and I with his blood and more before we could react. Dietrich fired a shot and hit Fitzgerald in the arm and he dropped his shotgun. But before the gun hit the ground, the demon Bell appeared and smashed the butt of his rifle into Fitzgerald's skull and knocked him out, and dragged him into the cellar. I assumed he was going to kill Herr Fitzgerald while Dietrich and I were burying Harrison's shell in the backyard."

Don shook his head, and glanced at Wicker again. His eyes were locked once more in a staring contest with the prisoner. Wicker licked his lips as the prisoner continued his confession, noticed Don's gaze, and looked away and down like he was nervous—not angry or any other emotion Don expected—just nervous. Don nodded and felt his brow crinkle as he ruminated further over Wicker's strange behavior. He felt crazy thinking it, but it was as if the *Mike* sitting next to him wasn't the same man he'd known for the past fifteen years, and wondered if it wouldn't be best to order Wicker to take Jones's advice and head on home.

The prisoner continued, "We returned for the other bodies and heard screaming in the cellar, followed by silence. We assumed Herr Fitzgerald was dead and went downstairs to investigate what Bell had done to him. When we got to the bottom, the man was tied to a chair facing his family. His lips were sown shut with a shoelace…"

Don opened and closed a fist.

"… and Bell was bent over Herr Fitzgerald next to a table with a leather tool roll open, filled with surgical instruments. His face was splattered with blood. In a hand, he held a saw and then he began sawing. Herr Fitzgerald's eyes shot open and he muffled a scream." The prisoner paused and rubbed his lips. "Neither Deitrich nor I could speak… but rather than stop the madness and end the father's suffering, we went upstairs."

Don swallowed hard, forcing down bile. Wicker's expression remained unchanged.

"Later that day, Bell left the cellar to shower and wash his blood-soaked fatigues. While they were drying in a new contraption I had never seen before, he went to the garage for a portable stove and to the kitchen for a plate, silverware, a wine glass, two bottles of wine, and several jugs of water. It took a few trips to carry everything into the cellar, though I noticed he took nothing downstairs to eat. We thought little of it, since Bell had rations, as we did, in case we were unable to forage. I remember the madness in his eyes. Like a feral animal. And that grin…" the prisoner said as his gaze returned to Wicker.

Don's forehead furrowed as Wicker licked his lips. An image of a hungry wolf popped into Don's head.

The prisoner continued, "Bell closed the door, and we did not see him for three days. We listened to Herr Fitzgerald's muffled screams until they ceased. Only then did we see Bell again, caked in dried blood and holding his rifle. I asked if we could bury the bodies before they started to smell, but he swung his gun around and placed the muzzle on my shell's forehead and said, *'If either of you touches those bodies, I will exorcise you both.'* And then he carried more jugs of water and two more bottles of red wine into the cellar and did not come upstairs again until this morning. That was shortly before your sheriff arrived at the door, and Dietrich shot him through the peephole. That is also when I learned how the General had ordered this to end. We were to die. I could not allow Joshua's life and eternity to be squandered like that. He is a good man and good father. So, I tried to escape for his sake. Shortly before that, Bell had ordered us to bury the bodies because he could no longer stand the stench. That is when I saw what he had done to Herr Fitzgerald. We never got the chance to bury the family since that was when Bell observed DeMure pass the observation post and called the General to let him know it was time to execute Plan B."

Don's chest felt tight as he breathed through flared nostrils. Speechless at first, he finally found enough spite to speak. "And you did nothing to stop him? Nothing?! It's convenient that none of your friends are alive to corroborate your story. But I have to say I believe you. At least the part about you sick, demented fucks torturing Jeremiah for three days as you chopped and sliced off pieces and ate him while he was still alive. Not to mention, you sadistic freaks forcing his eyes open, so he had to watch it happen and stare at the dead bodies of his wife, son, and daughter until, and even after, he was dead. I don't want to hear another word of your bullshit. I'll tell you this—I will personally do everything in my power to see that you get the death penalty, even if it's much less than you deserve. Wicker, you'll need to watch this piece of shit, or I swear I'll strangle him. I have a press conference to give."

Don pressed stop, put the recorder in his pocket, and stormed out of the courthouse.

Sixteen

Franz listened to the cacophony erupt. "Give me ten minutes, and then I'll update you on what happened today," he heard Glickman say. "No comment! I said ten minutes."

Franz watched Wicker leave the jail museum. The deputy was not who he appeared to be, but whoever had possessed him, had blocked his mind to deeper probing. Of course, it did not take a V2 scientist to figure out who the demon inside might be. He examined Joshua's hands and nodded. Franz's mindheart was content. He had not allowed these hands to be bloodied.

Wicker returned a few minutes later, eyed Franz, and smiled. "Hey Franz, how are you doing?" he said with a deep, articulate southern drawl. "It is your friend Morgan Bell behind these eyes. The General wanted me to convey his deepest displeasure with the songs you been singing and to let you know that the Curator has marvelous things planned for your sweet Johanna."

Franz closed his eyes as contentment dissolved and his mindheart ached. He opened his eyes and said, "I suspected it was you."

Bell smiled and laughed. "Say it ain't so. What, might I ask, gave me away?"

"The settling at the medical center. I did not think much of it until you came on too strong when you arrived here. I probed Jones's, Guzman's, and Glickman's minds and sensed that Deputy Wicker's friends did not recognize what lay beneath his mortal shell."

Bell grinned. "Yes, I am still not very good at this. But frankly, my dear Franz, I do not give a damn, and that is why the Curator keeps using me. You, on the other hand..."

"How did you do it without a contract?" Franz asked.

"Oh, oh, *thaat* little thing? Seems Wicker wanted a little revenge after Dietrich killed the sheriff and his partner John, Jake, Joe—well, I do declare I should get my best friend's name straight. I would hate to forget it again when I am talking to his grieving widow. Anyhow, when Wicker finished off Rice with a bullet to the noggin, well, let us just say, his vengeance opened a little door, and I hopped right through. Once in control, I was about to perform a full metal exorcism on the former Colonel, but I was not able to make it outside before Wicker's friends swarmed around you. Then I lost control of the deputy until after your current performance was well underway. It was convenient how you avoided the firefight and a direct order not to be taken alive." Bell smirked. "But it is a good thing I did not execute Stone. How was I to know that the Boy Scout from Boston was a little project of the Curator? Anyhow, enough about me. The General wanted me to let you know that the Curator is willing to give you one more chance to save Johanna from what he has planned for her. All you have to do is keep your end of the bargain and harvest Stone's soul. In fact, I am even gonna make it easy for you. You simply have to kill the deputy. And believe it or not, the deputy is going to hand you his fancy pistol."

Bell removed the gun from Wicker's holster, verified that it was loaded, and made sure it had a chambered round. He grabbed the iron keys, opened the cell, and entered with the pistol pointed at the floor.

Franz stayed seated.

Bell pulled invisible strings and lifted the deputy's wounded left arm and tapped Wicker's forehead. "Just one round here," he said with a big grin, and then pressed that finger against Stone's forehead and tapped, "and another right there." Bell motioned with Wicker's head and eyes for Franz to take Wicker's gun.

Franz regarded Bell's malicious eyes with contempt. "I know the Black and White Rule and the loophole in the Curator's contract buried in the fine print which the Man in White did not allow Stone to read before he signed. So you can put the gun in Stone's hand. You can place his finger on the trigger. You can even press that finger to kill the deputy, but it will only be another life added to your soul's tally. I hope Johanna will understand, but I know that she will not after all I have taken from her. But I will not damn another soul to Hell to save hers. As for Joshua Stone, I am terminating his contract."

Bell guffawed, then stopped before attracting attention. "Heavens be, I swear, you care too much for these fleshy beings. You will have to excuse me because I do not understand. Hell, I did not care much for these mortals when I was one, except for a few, of course. I tell ya, I surely do miss my son Jefferson and my sweet Cordelia, Atticus, and Carol Ann. But unlike your Johanna, they are in a place that I can never be." He sighed, and continued as his tone became progressively demonic. "But I do digress. Anyhow, when my good son was gone, murdered by that bastard Horace Greenly's mob…"

Franz knew nothing of what Bell spoke of but listened as the demon rattled on.

"… I only cared about making Horace suffer before he died and erasing his line from this earth. And, of course, how he and his line tasted before they died. I must admit the taste of fear goes well with a fine red. Anger is even better but so much harder to produce once the carving starts. Mmmm. Mmmm. I know what you are thinking, but do not knock it until you have tried it. Well, have fun when you are dragged back into the Black Water. I have heard your playlist is quite unpleasant, but I imagine Johanna's new one will be *farrr* worse," Bell said, widening his eyes as bitter glee burned through. He pulled a phone from his pocket and walked into the hall.

Franz wept as he beat the back of Stone's fists against the wall. He had two options. Allow Stone to go to trial, be convicted, and executed, or kill him using his own hands. Either way, he would die, and his family would be disgraced. Yet, if Franz kept him pure to the end, Stone would have a chance to be reborn or enter the paradise of his choice and possibly reunite with his family one day. Killing him would only send him to the purgatory for those who murdered themselves.

Bell returned a few minutes later. "You drive a hard bargain," he said, drawling out the *hard* and the *bargain*. "The General tells me that the Curator is willing to compromise. He says he will settle on Stone's suicide. In return, Johanna will continue at his lab in this reality and will never have to return to the Black Water again.

Seriously, I would take the deal. The General told me what the Curator has in store for Johanna if you do not accept the Great One's generous offer. Viking, Spanish Inquisition, and some tasty tidbits from Ivan the Terrible's playlist. I do declare—her potential eternity even makes me feel a little green behind the gills," Bell said and raised his eyebrows, smiled, shrugged, and shivered. "So, use the bedsheet. It will make a dandy noose. And that pipe running across the ceiling looks like a great place to tie it. Oh, and by the way, thanks for being such a stubborn sonuvabitch and not killing my gracious host. It will be nice to stroll the streets of Packer City again. There are still many scores left to settle. See you in Hell, Franz."

Bell slowly raised Wicker's right arm, and flicked a Hitler salute. He kicked his feet together, snapped a finger to his upper lip to imitate Charlie Chaplin, spun, and goose-stepped into the hall.

Franz sobbed. He knew he had no choice and tried to rationalize sending Stone to the Asylum of Silence. It would cause him no physical pain, yet psychologically it might be far worse than the Black Water grave.

He pulled the sheet from the bed and trembled as he lifted one leadened leg, and then the next, onto the bed. His arms felt just as heavy as he swung the sheet over the pipe, pulled it down, and fashioned then secured a noose with shaky hands. He slipped the noose over Stone's neck, and cried for his soul. "I am sorry. I am sooo sorry," he said and stepped off the bed.

Seventeen

Joshua squinted as his eyes adjusted to the bright light. It quickly dimmed to yellowing black and white. Bars surrounded him in a room that reminded him of an old western jail cell. He saw three black doors in the center but only the middle door was open.

He sensed someone in the cell, turned, and saw a pale-skinned man dressed in black. His jaundiced complexion and silverish hair contrasted with his black Stetson, trench coat, shirt, pants, and boots. Whoever it was, they reminded him of Johnny Cash, who he'd never much cared for. Next to him, a body dangled from a bedsheet. His jaw dropped when he recognized the body. *Am I dead?* he thought.

"What happened?" he asked with an Atlanta, Georgian accent. "I mean, last I remember, I was discussing a security contract with someone named Frederick Chance. He looked like... well, he kinda looked like you, just not as old and wrinkly. No offense."

"None taken," said the man.

"He even dressed like you. Just younger and wore all white, right down to the cowboy hat. Then everything went black. So, why am I hanging there? Is this a dream?"

The Man in Black glared and his nostrils flared. He pursed his lips, shook his head, and said, "No—this is no dream." He gritted his teeth. "You committed suicide, and now I will guide you to a place called the Asylum of Silence. It's the only place in the Afterworld open to you now."

"What? That... that's bullshit. I didn't kill myself. I was murdered—I had to a been."

"Yes, it is bullshit of the highest degree. The one who killed you did so voluntarily with your hands. A technicality, but I don't make the rules. I don't even agree with most of them. My job is only to guide you to where you have to go."

"But... but what will happen to my baby girls?" he asked, his voice breaking through trembling lips. "And what about Alli? What will they do without me?"

"I don't know. That's no longer your concern. It's all in the hands of Destiny and Fate now. Now hurry and go through the open door. I'm in no mood to argue."

"Fuck that... I ain't going. This is wrong. I shouldn't be dead."

"I agree. Fine—stay. Maybe in the aging of Timethy, I'll make it around again to check on your Underspirit to see if you've had a change of mindheart."

"Timethy? Underspirit? Change of what?"

"Not important. But I have to warn you that the four barred walls around you will be your world until you choose to pass through that middle door."

"You're fuckin' kiddin' me."

"Oh, I wish that I were."

Joshua glared into the old man's eyes, sighed, and said, "Shit." He closed his eyes and shook his head as the Man in Black gently patted his shoulder.

Joshua opened his eyes, said, "Goddamnit," and stepped into the dark hallway.

Eighteen

Dr. Morgan Bell returned and found Stone dangling, eyes bulging, red, and fixed. He breathed deep as if inhaling a sweet spring breeze as his lips curled into a satisfied smile. He nodded and headed outside.

"Yes, Julie," said Glickman, pointing at WNN's Ms. Florid.

Morgan whispered in Glickman's ear, almost forgetting to turn off the southern drawl. "There's a... there's a problem with our prisoner." *Well now, if that is not the understatement of the past two centuries*, he thought and guffawed in Wicker's mind.

Morgan locked eyes with Glickman, and gave him his best *this-is-really-bad* face which he would have loved to have admired in a mirror.

"I apologize, Julie, there's a matter I have to attend to. I'll address your question when I return."

Morgan watched blood drain from Glickman's face and fought the grin that was creeping onto his lips. He followed the interim sheriff inside as shutters clicked and flashes flashed.

When Glickman stepped in the jail museum, he whispered a yell, "Goddammit! How did you let this happen? You were supposed to be watching the prisoner. Where the hell were you?!"

"I... I had to take a shit."

"Not... another... fucking... word. Hand me your badge and gun and go home, now!" said Glickman. "I don't wanna see your face. I don't wanna hear your voice."

Morgan handed him Wicker's badge, gun, and deputy starred cowboy hat. He walked down the hall wearing a subtle, uncontainable grin, but stifled it in time to pass through the media throngs without even a *"no comment"* as two police officers (whose names escaped him) arrived in a fancy smancy black vehicle that had replaced the old horse and buggy. He jogged Wicker's mind and retrieved the names, *Jake Tolliver and Lawrence Lombardi*.

"Where's Don?" asked Tolliver.

"He's inside. He's a little upset. He thought it would be better if I headed home," Morgan said without inflection.

Lawrence handed him Wicker's keys and Morgan climbed into the fancy contraption called a Jeep. He took a moment to find memories of how to drive it, and then backed up too quickly and almost hit a reporter. Morgan stopped to re-calibrate and once he got his bearings, he headed north toward the deceased former sheriff's home where Wicker's shell lived with his mother-in-law, Patsy Maxwell, and wife, Mandy Wicker.

Part II

Cannibal Surgeon of Packer City

Nineteen

11:09 a.m. EST, Wednesday, October 3, 2007. The Pentagon, Washington, D.C.

General Cornelius Adamson savored the oxygen he was allowed to continue breathing. Plan B had failed but it had been in accordance with the Great One's purpose. How foolish he felt doubting the Benefactor as War agreed inside his head.

How foolish indeed. True, it would be difficult replacing the good soldiers sacrificed for the Benefactor's greater plan, but the Great One had always provided since Cornelius had inked the Man in White's contract so many years ago.

Cornelius pressed a temple, and a Reality Window appeared on his desk. Dr. Antonia D'Amato's face appeared on the virtual screen. Her eyes were their usual spiraling green, not Delores Destiny's farseeing blue that he would have preferred.

"You look well after your meeting with the Benefactor," said Cornelius. "Is he currently driving Dr. Caine?"

"Unfortunately, no," D'Amato said in a light German accent. "But we can speak. Dr. Caine is receiving the new test subjects." She scoffed. "But I do protest—these new rats are far less desirable than those in the first group."

"Ah, yes, but they are the best I could provide due to our nuisance in Seattle."

"Yes, the detective," said D'Amato.

"And why has this *nuisance* not been dealt with?" Cornelius asked. "Or might I say, why hasn't the Farseer seen a path by which we can make this nuisance disappear."

"In time she will," said D'Amato. "For now, Destiny has a plan for the detective that she has not revealed to me."

"Then I will defer to the greater plan that is beyond our understanding or need to comprehend." Cornelius sighed and asked, "Any word on Mender and DeMure?"

"No, but I do know they have left Mears County, Colorado."

"Where are they now?"

"Destiny is currently unable to pinpoint past, present, and future blind spots but suspects our couple is in the wilderness south of Greenly Mountain. Unfortunately, they will soon be beyond her sight."

"How is that?"

"Has the Benefactor not divulged Destiny's weakness to you?" she said in a tone that made Cornelius wish he was at the lab within reach of her throat.

"No, he has not," he said, tensing his lips.

She snorted a chuckle and said, "According to Destiny, it all has to do with a squabble between the gods. The details are unimportant other than there is a large area in the southwest U.S. that her farseeing eyes are blind to. It's the area between four mountains called Diné Bikeyah."

"Does she think they are headed there?"

"It is definitely possible. Louis Suerte's passenger did send her to find a healer named Manycows. Our Mary may be attempting to take Mender there to find a cure for the Touch that she gave him when they first bonded. It would fit her personality, but it is just as possible that Mender will attempt to reach his grandmother's family in Mexico since he has little connection with his relatives in New

Mexico and Arizona. Regardless, if they continue south, they will soon pass through at least part of this shadow land."

"Why is Destiny unsure?" asked Cornelius.

"Why? Because she only saw up to Mary's accidental healing and the transfer of her curse. No doubt, Mary's power to block her farseeing eyes is related to her ancestral blood. It is why she was chosen. Like Mender's power, hers was amplified by their connection. If the symbiosis continues to grow, Destiny fears that she may be unable to see our way through to the harvest. If so, our plans will be in the hands of her sister, Gladys Fate."

Cornelius chewed his lip as Caine's face appeared on the Reality Window behind D'Amato. The doctor looked lost as if wondering who D'Amato was speaking with. Cornelius tapped his left temple twice and thought, *invite Dr. Albert Caine*. As he waited, he eyed the crimson ink pen on his desk pad and the scarcity of white that remained between the many red double-crossed ankhs that he had doodled on the large sheet.

Dr. Caine tapped his temple and said, "Good morning, General, sir."

"Surprisingly, it is. What is the word on my new meat puppets?"

"Sixty-eight are currently incubating in the Hole and the remaining thirty-two are in transit to the lab," Caine said with his shaky voice.

Cornelius had the urge to say *"BOO"* to make him jump, but decided against it, and said, "Good. And you made sure to remove their easy exit option?"

"Yes… as you ordered."

"Good boy." Cornelius's desk phone buzzed. He tapped his temple without saying goodbye. The Reality Window vanished.

"General, sir," said Sergeant Major Skip Fossum.

"Yes, what is it?" snapped Cornelius.

"President Cranston needs you to speak at noon on the situation in Packer City and your plans to deal with the growing terrorism threat in Colorado."

"Very well."

"May I ask something, General, sir?"

"By all means."

"Can I get you some coffee? I realize you had a late night and figured you could use some."

"Yes, you may. The usual."

"Which usual?"

"Red Velvet Frappuccino… extra raspberry… and add four shots."

"Yes, sir, General, sir."

Twenty

8:15 a.m. PST, Wednesday, October 3, 2007. Federal Way City Hall, Federal Way, Washington.

Junior Detective Bob Roberts regarded Senior Detective Doug Thorfinnson. His new boss was sipping coffee with his eyes glued to the crowded conference room's TV for the latest news from the once peaceful town Bob had left a month earlier.

Bob liked Thorfinnson even though he was a straight arrow with the mouth of a saint and was obsessed with a cold case that left warmer ones collecting dust. He was older middle-aged, shorter by a few inches, and wider than Bob around the middle. He had cherubic cheeks and graying auburn hair combed to the right, with a balding line separating the left quarter of a hairdo that went out of style in the 1930s.

Bob's attention returned to the news from Mender's fallen Watchtower. Over the past month, Bob's former home had been the center of attention, but the latest was too ghastly to comprehend even though much of it he was hearing for a second time.

WNN's Julie Florid patted her short-cropped blonde-do and continued, "*Packer City, Colorado's three week lockdown ended yesterday. It'd been initiated following an isolated case of Ebola-Colorado which claimed the life of Alex Mender, son of Berets star, Ryan Mender, and grandson of R&B legend, Norine Jasmine Jones. The improbable case and subsequent abuses by those enforcing the lockdown during the first few days of the quarantine appeared to be the low point of the town's troubles when no further fatalities were reported. Sadly, it was the calm before the storm.*"

The story clipped to news chopper footage of burned out ruins and associated debris atop Tower Rock at the base of Greenly Mountain. The entire rock and adjacent area was blanketed with sparkling dark blue ash. "*New accounts have been pouring in since yesterday concerning the battle at the home of Ryan Mender southwest of Packer City. As you can see, the home and local landmark, known as the Watchtower, was destroyed during the battle. According to reports, at least three- to four-dozen Black Berets were killed during the firefight. Three Black Hawk helicopters were also shot down and a fourth crash-landed nearby. So far, no survivors have been found at the site and the incident is being called the Mender Massacre. The actual number of casualties is still unknown but include Suzanne Mender. Ryan Mender still unaccounted for, but he is presumed dead."*

Photos of two of Bob's closest friends appeared on the screen. He chewed his lip as Florid continued, *"As the massacre on Tower Rock ended, a shoot-out took place between local police and Black Berets at the base of the rock. During the skirmish, Mears County Sheriff Peter Maxwell and Undersheriff Joseph Turner were killed. The short standoff occurred at the home of Mender's closest neighbor which had been commandeered by Helix Eternal Laboratories' security contractors sometime during the lockdown. According to Interim Sheriff Don Glickman, County Deputy Michael Wicker was shot but managed to kill one or two of the shooters and wound the third."*

The piece cut to the previous evening's press conference with Don Glickman in front of the Mears County Courthouse. *"Julie, uh, you have to understand, Undersheriff Turner was Deputy Wicker's best friend and Sheriff Maxwell was his father-in-law. As you can imagine, Deputy Wicker needs time to recover, grieve, and comfort his family. I've placed him on extended leave to do what he needs to do. With him out, I'm the county's only full-time peace officer. Of course, surrounding departments have been gracious enough to lend our community a helping hand during this time of crisis and have sent all available officers to assist."* The camera had panned to several nodding police officers. A few were red-eyed, possibly from crying. *"I also want to thank agents from the Colorado Bureau, FBI, Homeland Security, and ATF who will be here shortly to help with the ongoing investigation concerning today's tragic events."*

Julie Florid segued from the previously recorded news conference and continued her update with details concerning the Fitzgerald murders. She gave a content warning before sending the report spiraling into the surreal. Bob covered his quivering lips with a shaky hand as his eyes fought to stay dry. It was hard for him to see the bullet-riddled home and hear again what happened inside. He'd known the family. Been in their home many times. Played baseball, hiked, and backcountry skied with the family. He'd hunted with Jeremiah, Sarah, Zeke, and Blossom. He'd spent days alone with Jeremiah on several tricky rescue operations for which the devout Presbyterian had always been more than eager to volunteer.

Florid's report returned to the previous evening's news conference. Bob continued to fight back tears as Glickman described the grisly details. A hail of questions followed, few of which Glickman had answered. Among the evasions, he had refused to speculate why the Black Berets were still in the area, why three of them had set up a base at the Fitzgeralds', why they had killed the family, or why they had attacked Mender's home in the first place. His stock answer was, "*It is currently under investigation and further details will be released as soon as we know more.*"

Glickman had pointed to the next raised hand. Bob saw his pained expression when he had realized the overeager appendage belonged to KNW's Kristen Kettlemeyer.

"*Interim Sheriff Glickman, what more can you tell us about the suspect and sole witness to the Fitzgerald quadruple homicide who just committed suicide while in your custody?*"

Glickman had wrinkled his nose and had answered with thin lips, "*The suspect voluntarily identified himself as former U.S. Army Colonel Joshua Stone of Boston, Massachusetts. Before his apparent suicide, Stone asked for his statement to be recorded. He was very cooperative but I can't give you full details of what was said. When the interrogation can be released to the public, my office or whoever is in charge of the investigation will let you know. But I'll tell you this much—Colonel Stone confessed* without coercion to his role in the Fitzgerald murders, as those recordings will show."

"Well, can you at least explain to the public why you chose your town's archaic jail museum to hold Colonel Stone? According to my research, your jail hasn't held a prisoner in over thirty years."

"That's... that's not exactly true. It worked just fine when Helix Eternal Laboratories' security contractors locked up our entire staff."

"Yes—that's right. They did. I apologize. That was unfortunate, but... but why use the museum when there is a brand new state-of-the-art lock-up facility in Grayson, Colorado, where Colonel Stone could've safely been held and monitored?"

"Look, as interim Sheriff, I wanted to question the prisoner first, especially after everything that went down earlier in the lockdown. Also, with the enormity of what happened today, there wasn't a lot of time or manpower to transfer him."

"*Really?*" Kettlemeyer had looked around with incredulous eyes as a camera panned to several officers, some of whom Bob recognized from Grayson and Silver City. "So, what you're saying is that none of these fine officers who have been standing out here with us could've taken Colonel Stone to Grayson an hour before he hung himself?"

Glickman's nose had flared and his lips had pursed. He didn't answer the question and had pointed to the next hand. "*Yes, Julie, you have a question?*"

"I do," Florid had said. "I'm also curious to hear your answer to Kristen's question. But my question is—why was Deputy Wicker guarding the prisoner in the first place? You said yourself that he was wounded and lost his best friend and father-in-law. And then we all watched him leave the courthouse around the time of Stone's suicide. I'm sure the public would like to know why you waited until then to place him on leave?"

Glickman had closed his eyes and abruptly ended the press conference without another *"no comment."*

Florid's report continued with another twisted layer as she reminded viewers of the strange death of KNW reporter Kenneth Prattle following an altercation with Mender before the massacre. She segued to a tearful interview with Kettlemeyer concerning her deceased fiancé. Kettlemeyer had recounted Prattle complaining of a burning sensation after being manhandled by the former Army Ranger. With the express permission of KNW, WNN replayed the footage of Mender gently removing the reporter's hand from his chest. The report then clipped back to Kettlemeyer as she recounted Prattle's severe gastrointestinal discomfort before she had found him dead in the restroom of a local grocery store.

The segment clipped to an earlier Florid interview with the Grayson County Coroner, Francis T. Pickens, outside Earth First Food Market. *"Yes, Julie. There are some similarities to the Anderson murder but all I can say is that Prattle died from hyper-acute hemorrhagic enterocolitis. As with World War II Veteran, Melvin Anderson, Prattle's death was followed by accelerated necrolysis."*

Bob's head buzzed. He zoned as Florid continued. Mike Wicker was, and Pete Maxwell and Joe Turner had been, among his best friends. And it'd been on the night of Bob's going away party when everything in Packer City had gone to shit. Bob felt sick and had since Glickman had called him the last night after fumbling his news conference.

Glickman had tried to maintain composure as he described the destruction and carnage at the Watchtower and the Fitzgeralds' and then how Brigham Norsworthy's ghost had played a role in the mayhem. He didn't know if Mender had been aware of the Watchtower's defense system, but couldn't imagine how. And then there'd been a strange weapon deployed during the battle that'd left the area cobalt blue. Glickman had never seen anything like it, and no one who'd visited the scene had the foggiest what it might be. After killing and scorching everything in its blast radius, the device had left behind the snow-like ash (that Bob had just seen on TV) which had smothered the flame and smoke and left the area colder than ice. There'd been another odd detail. The two dead pilots of the crashed chopper southwest of Tower Rock and Suzanne Mender had been undergoing the same *accelerated necrolysis* that Coroner Pickens had described of Prattle and Anderson. Don had also expressed concern over Strickland's and Jones's—not to mention his own—exposure to the ash. Coroner Pickens hadn't eased his mind.

Pickens had no idea what the substance was, and had felt it best for everyone to wear hazmat suits anywhere near the dark blue snow, or *Ethereal,* as he was calling it. He also recommended masks and gloves be worn for several hundred feet outside the blast zone. Additionally, Lake Hotchkiss Road had been closed north of the Crown Lake campgrounds. Residents around the smaller lake had been evacuated and unauthorized persons barred from entering Watchtower Private Drive.

To add insult, Glickman had been demoted back to deputy and sidelined from the case by Colorado Governor Claudius Thorp. Now, multiple agencies were wrestling for jurisdiction, but it appeared that President Ethan Cranston was poised to allow Homeland Security to lead the investigation, citing national security concerns.

Glickman went on to tell Bob about Colonel Stone's tale of multiple personalities and his *so-called* confession. As crazy as it sounded, the Fitzgerald killings had reminded Bob of the town's infamous Cannibal Surgeon Greenly murders which occurred not far from the scene. What'd made it even more bizarre was that Jeremiah Fitzgerald was a direct descendant of one of Greenly's two surviving daughters. Of course, there'd been at least one additional copycat killing spree in the Midwest inspired by Packer City's infamous town doctor. Still, it was an unsettling coincidence.

Before Glickman had hung up, he told Bob about a fourth Black Beret killed at the Fitzgeralds' place. The body was still buried in their backyard when Bob and Glickman had spoken. According to Stone's other personality, Jeremiah Fitzgerald had blasted a hole in the guy with a shotgun right before a Black Beret had knocked him out and began torturing and eating him alive. Stone had identified the fellow contractor as former Navy Captain Martin Rice. As it turned out, Rice was the same man who'd shot Wicker before Wicker had killed the former SEAL.

Glickman had believed Stone had made up the whole story to cop an insanity plea, but after the Colonel used a bed sheet to escape trial, he wasn't sure what to think about anything anymore. Well, except that he should now have his head checked for leaving the suspect alone with Wicker.

Twenty-One

8:18 a.m., Wednesday, October 3, 2007. Federal Way City Hall, Federal Way, Washington.

Doug Thorfinnson stood aghast, watching the TV as he massaged his sore lower back—a consequence of an old skiing injury, a weak core, and extra pounds from endless hours of desk duty. He glanced at his new partner. Detective Bob Roberts was almost his opposite. Taller than average, he was skinny, but muscular with an oval head and ears that stuck out. The ears were a bit odd, but didn't distract from his ruggedly handsome, stubbled face. Currently, that face looked ill—a little paler than usual—but he doubted Roberts had anything contagious. Doug took a sip of his venti swill that Starbucks called coffee and continued watching Florid.

"In other news, the woman sought in connection with the murder of Packer City resident and World War II veteran Melvin Anderson was positively identified as Mary Celeste DeMure of Walnut Hill, Washington. Ms. DeMure was reported missing last October after being abducted from..."

"What the…" Doug said as Ms. DeMure's photo appeared on the screen. His jaw dropped and he squeezed the cup. The lid popped off. "Owww, dangit," he said, as scalding coffee burnt his hand and spilled onto his new tie and white dress shirt.

The name and face of the twenty-year-old woman had filled most of his waking thoughts and many of his sleeping ones for the past year. Ironically, since Roberts replaced his former partner, the two had frequently spoken about the situation in Packer City. Most often it concerned the search for a woman that famous Army Ranger Ryan Mender had rescued after she drove Anderson's Jeep into a local lake. No way could Doug have fathomed that he and Roberts had been searching for the same person.

Doug wiped his shirt with a napkin, looked at Roberts, and rhetorically asked, "Well, partner, you up for a trip to Colorado? 'Cause that's where we're headed."

"One step ahead of you, boss man. I spoke to Don Glickman last night and was already planning the trip. Now I have another reason to visit. I'll fill you in over lunch with everything I know. Much of it, the media isn't aware of yet. After a bite, I'll go online and snag us two seats for the first available to Grayson, Colorado."

Twenty-Two

1:17 a.m. MST, Thursday, October 3, 2007. Horseshoe Lab, Helix Eternal Laboratories Main Complex, Undisclosed Location.

Dr. Albert Caine heard a scream. He threw on his robe and ran down the hall. He placed his hand on the ID panel and the door opened.ABraham D'Amato was in the midst of a grand mal seizure.

Albert tapped his temple. Nothing happened. He tried again but his Ethereal driven implant wouldn't connect to his Reality Window, so he frantically punched the archaic intercom's call button. "Code Blue, Code Blue. Need orderlies at Dr. D'Amato's quarters immediately. Bring valium and restraints."

He chewed his fingernails as D'Amato's graceful form shook, her teeth chattered, and her mystical blue eyes bounced about in their sockets.

Four orderlies dressed in white with black bowties rushed into the room. They strapped D'Amato to the bed as she vibrated. One orderly placed an IV catheter as Albert drew up a dose of valium. With the catheter placed, he slowly injected the valium until the tremors lessened. He waited. The shakes continued but her teeth stopped chattering and her eyes closed. He gave a little more and the seizure ceased.

"You may leave now," said Albert.

The orderlies filed out and the door slid shut. He watched D'Amato sleep as he once had before he signed the Man in White's contract. How he missed her touch and the things she did that Cassandra never would. He wondered how his wife was doing, how the kids were, and whether he would ever see them again. But more than that he wondered if the Benefactor would ever allow him to enjoy D'Amato's body as he once had. He wanted to touch her. *She'll never know*, he thought. Why would it matter if she did? His mortal shell had been with her last night or so he suspected after he had awoken wandering the hall, naked, sweat drenched, and smelling of sex and her rose perfume.

He leaned forward and stroked her hand and let his fingers leisurely roam up her arm.

"Don't you dare," said D'Amato as her eyes opened and glared. They were green now.

Albert snatched his hand away like she was a hot stove. "I, I, I was just, uh, checking your pulse. You, uh, had a seizure."

"Yes, I did. Something has happened. I do not know what, but the Farseer is no longer with me."

"What do you mean, *she's no longer with you*?" asked Albert. He felt queasy.

"I mean exactly what I said. She is gone. Last I remember was a pain like nothing I have felt before. Like someone had replaced my eyes with flaming coals. And then… and then, all pasts, presents, and futures went black."

"Ohh. That's not good," said Albert. "That's not good at all."

Twenty-Three

1:17 a.m. MST, Thursday, October 3, 2007. The Fasthorse Ranch, West of the Rock with Wings, Navajo Nation in Arizona.

The Eye greater than Destiny's slammed shut and two very old mortal ones opened as a coyote howled outside the hogan.

Curtis Chee, grandson of Manycows, sat up and a warm hand grabbed his wrist. He turned to the beautiful silhouette as moonlight from a waxing gibbous outlined Emma Fasthorse in silver.

"Is everything okay?" she asked.

"Yes. My *sight* is gone," he said in an elated tone. "The prophecy has come to pass. My cousin and his lady friend will be here soon and then we can begin."

Emma smiled and patted Curtis's hand.

Another coyote howled.

Emma shook her head and grabbed the AR15 by the side of the bed. "I'll be back in minute. Can't let those tricksters get another of my sheep."

Twenty-Four

Before dawn, Thursday, October 4, 2007. SeaTac International Airport, SeaTac, Washington.

Doug settled into his cramped coach class seat two rows behind Detective Roberts. He had no love for flying and wasn't looking forward to the next three-and-half hours, followed by the one-hour connection in an even smaller plane. Though he despised the journey, he looked forward to being back in Colorado.

When he was a kid, and up until his fall off a cliff at Steamboat, he'd loved skiing at Breckenridge, Keystone, Vail, and Aspen. However, he never had the opportunity to visit Mears County or hit Crested Butte north of Grayson. All the same, his excitement seemed ghoulish. The situation was fiendish, to say the least. And he still couldn't wrap his head around the fact that Mary DeMure's unsolvable disappearance was now leading him into an investigation of a home-grown terrorist organization. But how was Ms. DeMure connected with Tuesday's events? And how did she end up as a suspect in the murder of a World War II veteran who had died from the same thing that had killed Kenneth Prattle, Suzanne Mender, and two Black Hawk pilots? He had his suspicions, and they were dreadful. As the 737 left the tarmac, he drifted back to how he had become involved in Mary DeMure's case on the evening of Friday, October 27, 2006.

The day had been a blur of counting hours and minutes until he could leave to see his daughter, Elli, after a week of waiting for her to come home from Pullman. As Doug was leaving, he'd spied a skinny, heavily tattooed, and multiple pierced young woman with blue hair sprinting toward the front door. She kept looking back as she ran and when she hit the door, it'd almost hit him in the face. She'd ran past, babbling about people trying to kill her. Doug had suspected she was strung out on meth or something else or a mix of things.

Doug had listened as she continued on about two casually dressed men who'd attempted to abduct her from her apartment. They'd introduced themselves and told her she'd been selected for a drug study. Then one had allegedly pulled out an air pistol, fired a dart, and missed her. His partner had tried to finish the job, but she'd kicked him in the shin and made him shoot his friend. She'd run away screaming as two similarly dressed men had picked up the chase. Fortunately for her, she hadn't been far from the station, and her disturbance had scared off her assailants.

While Doug had been interested in learning more, he was hungry and desperate to leave on time for once. So, he'd bunted the case to his partner, Keith Foley, and left. Sure, he'd felt guilty but wasn't about to cancel dinner reservations at *Stanley and Seafort's* in Tacoma with his wife, Loretta, and their future veterinarian.

Traffic through Fife had been epically terrible that evening, and when he'd finally arrived at the restaurant overlooking Tacoma Harbor, he'd apologized to Elli and Loretta for being late (as usual). He had then grabbed a handful of calamari, filled his mouth, and while speaking and chewing, he'd told them about the strange last-minute case that'd literally ran through the door.

Elli's attention had peaked when her father mentioned the drug study.

"*Hey, that sounds kind of like the drug study Bridgette told me about,*" Elli had said. Bridgette Dudley was Elli's best friend and was then attending Green River College in Auburn, Washington. "*She's super bummed she wasn't accepted. The company doing the trial promised to pay her well if she got picked, but that's not why my girl's bummed. She's struggling with a medical condition she's been dealing with for years and wanted to try something new. And this new drug—it sounded pretty amazing to her. I'm really worried about her. She's really depressed. Most of the stuff her doc's given her doesn't work, and what does help makes her feel crappy.*"

Doug had expressed empathy but had nothing else to add, so the conversation had shifted to vet school and life in Pullman.

Over the weekend, Doug had done his best to think about anything but work but couldn't get the terrified girl or Bridgette's seemingly unrelated story out of his head. He'd wondered if, by strange happenstance, the two were connected.

By Sunday afternoon, curiosity had got the best of him and he called Foley about the girl. His partner had said the woman's name was Clarice Moonflower. Like Doug, he'd suspected she was strung out and asked if she'd taken anything. Foley said she'd looked offended and welcomed him to test her. He did, and she'd tested negative for even THC and zeroed the breathalyzer. As it turned out, she was enrolled at Green River College and had applied for what sounded like the same drug trial Elli had mentioned. Like Bridgette, Ms. Moonflower had heard nothing until *company representatives* had showed up at her doorstep with air pistols.

Later that afternoon, Doug had asked Elli if Bridgette would mind speaking with him concerning Moonflower and the drug trial they'd both applied for (assuming it was the same one). After explaining why, Elli had said, *"I can't imagine why not. I'll call my bestie and have her give you a call."*

Bridgette had called that evening. Doug had thanked her for taking the time to talk and asked, *"I was wondering, do you know a Clarice Moonflower?"*

"Elli asked me about her, but the name doesn't ring any bells."

Doug had described her and bells had begun ringing.

"Oh, I know who you're talking about. I've seen her in the halls. She's not an easy person to miss, but we don't have any classes together and I've

never spoken to her. But she was definitely at the presentation you wanted to talk to me about."

"So, tell me what you remember about the presentation."

"Well, I guess I'll start from when I saw the flyer on the bulletin board in Salish Hall. The flyer's gone, but I remember what it said:

'Looking for applicants wishing to participate in a phase three drug trial for a new therapy for the treatment of CFIS (chronic fatigue immunodysfunction syndrome) and other autoimmune disorders. Selected applicants will be well compensated and have the opportunity to be the first to benefit from our life-changing therapy.'

"Yeah, it sound really good so I called the number on the flyer. A woman with this sweet German or Dutch accent, I guess… well, she answered and told me her name was Johanna Müeller and asked me for some basic information and meal preferences, and then she said she looked forward to meeting me in Salish Hall, Room #313 at 9 a.m. on Saturday, September 28. Anyway, I hung up and then I was late for class.

"Well, that Saturday, I was surprised with the turnout. I'm sure most came for the money, because I can't see why else the room would be packed for a riveting talk entitled: How DNA manipulation can cure genetic, immunodeficiency, and immunodysfunctional disorders and prevent disease and cancer."

"Well, after the presentation, several people woke up and skedaddled after learning the screening details. In fact, only eight were left sitting when Ms. Müeller finished her spiel. Like I told you, Clarice was there, and there was also this amazing girl named Mary DeMure. I just love her. She is such a sweetheart.

"Anyway, the first part of the screening was this long, very personal questionnaire that Ms. Müeller said we had to answer truthfully and completely before we could move on to the next stage. Yeah, that took a *while, but that was the easy part. I tell you, like you, I mean, no offense, Mr. Thorfinnson, but I'm not in the best shape and I swear Ms. Müeller almost killed me with her stamina test. It lasted hours. It was crazy, and I wasn't sure I was gonna make it. Well, when we stumbled back into the room, everybody was sweaty and nasty, but before we could catch our breath, Ms. Müeller and another representative collected blood, saliva, and hair samples and gave us cups to pee in. Oh, wait—I said everybody stumbled into the room. I meant to say everybody except Mary. She wasn't even breathing hard after blowing us away."* After that, Bridgette couldn't stop talking about the girl.

While Bridgette and Mary hadn't spent time together outside school, she'd made a lasting impression before the presentation. She had inspired Bridgette to study harder and not let her condition get her down. Then Bridgette told Doug about Mary's hard-luck story.

Her mother had OD'd on heroin when Mary was three, and she never forgave her for dying the way she had. It'd been Mary's widower grandfather who'd raised her at his home in Walnut Hill, Washington. Life had been almost perfect until he died of a stroke after losing everything in the stock market when she was sixteen.

Her grandfather, Thurston DeMure, was her life, and she had few, if any, close friends. They had done everything together. Mary had loved to fly, and occasionally her grandfather would let her take the wheel of his Cessna. She had loved to play baseball, and they rarely missed a Mariners home game. Her grandfather had taught her to hunt with a rifle and bow. They'd hiked together and had even climbed the tallest mountain of every continent before she was fourteen. She even had a black belt and had been trained by one of Bruce Lee's students, Taky Kimura. Her grandfather had been proud of that accomplishment since Kimura had trained him before Lee died young and had been buried at Lake View Cemetery in

Seattle's Capitol Hill district. Also, while her grandfather had been a great skier and nearly qualified for the Olympics, Mary had been a world-class snowboarder and had seemed destined to fulfill her grandfather's dreams.

Even with all of her extra-curricular activities, Mary had been an honor student and always near or at the top of her class. But what made her active lifestyle and academic achievements even more impressive was that she'd done it all while suffering from CFIS.

After her grandfather died, Mary had continued excelling in school, but everything else had faded away. She'd continued living in her grandparent's home on the shore of Lake Forest next to the park where she'd spent her childhood. She lived alone and had even fewer, if any, friends. Despite everything, she was never late for school at Walnut Hill High School and maintained a four-point-O. She'd hoped for a free ride to Harvard (her grandfather's alma mater) to honor his memory now that her Olympic dream was dead. She also had feared becoming like her mother, who she barely remembered, or her father, who was out of the picture before she was born.

Mary had graduated valedictorian of the WHHS Class of 2006. Still, the scholarship offers hadn't been enough to cover what she'd needed for nearby University of Washington, much less Harvard where she'd been *enthusiastically* accepted. There'd always been the option of selling the house, and in that seller's market, the lakeside home would've sold quickly and covered any scholarship deficit with lots of spare change. Yet, she'd refused to give up the one thing left from the only father she'd ever known or the memories of happier times contained within its walls.

Much of the money she scraped together went toward paying property taxes and utilities, leaving her just enough for tuition at

Green River College that fall. That was where Bridgette had met Mary in psychology class.

Mary only came to class a few more times after the presentation. After a week passed without seeing her, Bridgette went to admissions to find out if she was okay. The woman at the desk had said Mary withdrew that morning. Bridgette had asked for her phone number, and the lady reluctantly gave it to her. She'd called and found the number disconnected, so she looked up her address, and went to Mary's house. Bridgette had told Doug in a tearful tone, "I wanted—no, I needed to know why she gave up and dropped out. I wanted to let her know the difference she'd made in my life and encourage her to come back to school. I wanted to tell her that if she needed help, I'd always be there for her. But no one was home, and after going by her place a few times, I gave up."

When Bridgette finished her story, she remembered another student who hadn't been in class for a few weeks. Like Mary and Clarice, the guy (whose name she'd forgotten) also had completed the screening process. He was a quiet kid who'd sat on the back row of Psychology, had never spoken unless spoken to, and had kept to himself. He was practically invisible, and his absence would've been forgettable had Doug not asked Bridgette about the presentation.

Before Doug hung up, he'd asked if she still had the number that she'd used to RSVP. Bridgette had said, *"I threw it away. It doesn't matter anyway. The number was disconnected when I tried to call."*

The next Monday, Doug and Foley had visited Green River College to inquire about Mary and the boy Bridgette mentioned. They also had hoped to find information about the pharmaceutical company that rented the room in Salish Hall. The woman in admissions was very helpful and had identified Mary as Mary Celeste DeMure, age nineteen, and the young man as Leonard Royce

Grimes, age twenty. Both students had withdrawn on the same day, and neither had done so in person. Also, like Clarice Serena Moonflower, all three had lived alone, had few, if any, friends, and no one locally to report them missing.

When the police had searched Mary's home and Leonard's small apartment in Kent, it was clear that neither had been home for weeks based on spoiled food on the kitchen counters and in the refrigerator. That evening, they were declared missing, and the search had begun. Both had been presumed dead until Mary DeMure was sighted two days earlier in Packer City, Colorado.

Concerning the presentation's sponsors, the room at Salish Hall had been reserved by an unnamed subsidiary of DNAXIS Pharmaceuticals. When Doug had contacted DNAXIS, he'd run into a wall of corporate confidentiality. Finding no one helpful at corporate and lacking evidence to obtain a subpoena, he'd tried a different approach.

Since he'd been unfamiliar with therapies for CFIS, he started researching potential breakthroughs in the treatment of immune dysfunction disorders. While it'd taken some digging, he found a 2004 article from *Immunology Today*, which discussed a promising new drug called Curitall. After phase one trials, it'd appeared to be the miracle drug of the new millennium. DNAXIS stocks had soared in anticipation of phase two results and FDA approval; however, the report had been anything but encouraging.

In phase one, twenty-seven rats had been treated with Curitall. One week later, both groups had been weighed and examined. The test group had increased lean muscle mass, stamina, and speed on the wheel. Next, both groups had been infected with a variety of highly infectious agents. Every rat in the control group had died, but the treated rats had survived and appeared stronger and healthier than after their first post-Curitall examination. When researchers had necropsied the treated/infected group, no evidence of disease or immunological response to infection had been detected. Yet, when phase two results were released, DNAXIS stocks plummeted when a report surfaced that two researchers had died after contact with one of the Curitall treated/infected rats. No other information was released, nor were the researchers' autopsies made public. The phase two trial was repeated, and the moment the Food and Drug Administration had learned the results, further testing of the miracle drug was banned.

When Doug had finished the article, he'd seen a link entitled, *Shakeup at DNAXIS*. He clicked it and had pulled up a news blog concerning one of the company's founders and the creator of Curitall, Dr. Albert Caine. Following the FDA ruling, DNAXIS's board of directors had discontinued funding for Curitall research and Caine's related projects.

Caine had been furious and was quoted as saying, *"I'm disturbed with DNAXIS's lack of vision for the future after such a minor setback. As such, I am severing my relationship with the company that my blood, sweat, and tears built."* The next day, Caine and twelve of his assistants resigned.

The blog had named his assistants, and over the next few weeks, Doug and Foley had followed up on each. When former associates, friends, and family members were contacted, none knew of their whereabouts nor had they heard from them since they'd left DNAXIS. According to Caine's wife, Cassandra, a man from another pharmaceutical company had come to their home and offered Caine a grant and a contract to continue his work. Caine didn't tell his wife the company's name and had disappeared the next day.

As months passed, Doug had become obsessed with the case, yet every lead had led to more dead ends. He'd even called other community colleges across the state, and then the country. He'd asked about presentations for drug trials and antisocial students who'd withdrawn from school after applying. Since students frequently came and went from these schools, and those without connections were hard to trace or even verify if they'd been abducted, no other missing kids fitting the profile had been identified.

Doug had attempted to get a subpoena to investigate DNAXIS, but no judge would consider it without solid evidence that a yet-to-be-identified local suspect hadn't abducted the two missing students. Each judge had been unmoved by the fact that both had withdrawn and disappeared on the same day. Nor were they phased by the presumption that articles and blogs about a failed drug trial pointed to the possibility of a rogue scientist abducting kids and experimenting on them like rats. It'd sounded crazy to Doug, too, but he couldn't get the possibility out of his head. Without other colleges reporting missing students fitting the same MO, his chances of solving the case had seemed slim to none. That'd changed yesterday morning.

When Keith Foley had moved to Los Angeles in August and was replaced by Bob Roberts, Melvin Anderson's strange murder case was one of the first things he and Roberts had discussed. What was striking was Roberts's description of Mr. Anderson's body and what he called *accelerated necrolysis*. Grayson County Coroner Francis Pickens had coined the term, and they had an appointment with him at 1:00 p.m. After that, they were scheduled to meet with Grayson Undersheriff Danny Griggs and then planned to check out the

Anderson crime scene before heading to Packer City. It was going to be a long, busy day.

Twenty-Five

Near noon, Thursday, October 4, 2007. Grayson, Colorado.

Doug glanced at Roberts and shook his head. Since leaving Seatac, he'd felt like he'd flown alone since Roberts hadn't acknowledged him during the flight nor had he looked up from the book he was reading when he grabbed his carry-on with his free hand. He also didn't utter a word during their late breakfast or two-hour layover or the short flight to Grayson or after Doug picked up their red rental 4Runner.

As Doug neared the Grayson County Mortuary and Coroner's Office, Roberts lifted his nose from his book, and said, "Pickens is a bit odd but I think he can help us."

Doug smirked as he pulled into a parking space at the courthouse. He trotted across the street and tried to keep up with Roberts.

A heavy-set, balding man with thick-framed glasses stood in the mortuary's doorway. "Detective Thorfinnson, I presume," said the man in a high-pitch, cartoonish voice. "I'm Coroner Francis T. Pickens." He extended a hand.

Doug's eyebrows rose and his forehead furrowed in surprise at such a small voice coming from the big guy, not that he could talk about the big guy part. He recovered his professional face and firmly shook his hand.

Pickens turned to Roberts. "And it's so good to see you again, Bob-Bob."

Bob-Bob? thought Doug as *"Bob-Bob"* and Pickens shook hands.

"Welcome to Grayson, Detective Thorfinnson," said Pickens. "Come on in. Let's talk in my office."

Doug followed and passed through the showroom where the newest coffin models were on display and opened for prospective customers to check out creature comforts they'd never enjoy. Before leaving Seattle, Bob had informed him that Pickens was the only mortician in Grayson and Mears County and that his place was *"like a one-stop-shop from here to eternity after a short drive to the old cemetery on the eastern outskirts of town."*

"Would you like some coffee?" asked Pickens.

"That'd be nice," said Doug.

"Room for sugar and cream?" he asked as they passed through the embalming room and formaldehyde stung Doug's nostrils.

"No, I like mine black," Doug said as he entered Picken's office where the formaldehyde was cut to a tolerable level by rose scented plug-in deodorizers.

"Leave some room for me," said Roberts. "I like mine with a little half and half."

Pickens nodded and said, "You got it," as he pushed his spectacles up the bridge of his nose.

Doug sat by Roberts in a matching soft leather chair in front of a large oak desk as Pickens filled two Styrofoam cups from the Mr. Coffee coffee-maker on a sparkling white counter next to the desk. The only other item on the counter was a microscope with a view screen. He prepared both cups and added a stir straw to Roberts's.

"You are just going to love what I have for you guys. Interesting stuff," Pickens said and chuckled as he set the steaming cups in front of the detectives.

The big man walked around the desk, settled into his chair, and adjusted his glasses again. He slid a tan folder across the desk. "In that file, there are a bunch of photos of Melvin Anderson's corpse and what little I learned from his autopsy," he said with more enthusiasm than Doug thought appropriate. "I even made a video of the crime scene. I'm telling you—you will have to see it to believe it."

Doug opened the file and perused the gruesome images, studying every detail for clues. In each, Mr. Anderson appeared progressively different, as if each photo were taken days apart, but the one hundred photographs were taken over a span of fifteen minutes. When Anderson's corpse reached the morgue, the body reminded Doug of some of Ridgway's earliest victims, whose graves had been located six years earlier after the arrest of the Green River Killer.

Once he and Roberts finished perusing, Pickens pulled up a video on his desktop of the same fifteen minutes. Doug watched in stunned silence. It was like watching a time-lapse video. Only gently fluttering grass next to driftwood and the sounds of passing vehicles betrayed that he was watching a man decay in real time at breakneck speed.

"As you can see, it... it's almost as if Mr. Anderson's body was undergoing *accelerated necrolysis*. I just don't know how else to describe it. In fact, as you saw in the photos, there wasn't much left of him to autopsy by the time he reached my morgue. It seemed almost... uh, supernatural to a born skeptic. I... I'm embarrassed to admit it, but I was a little freaked out. I figured the man was exposed to some kind of biological or toxic agent or some weird form of radiation. To be honest, I didn't know what to think, so I called the CDC, who called the three I's: the CBI, the FBI, and the HSI."

"Have you come across any similar cases of what you're calling *accelerated necrolysis*?" asked Doug. "I mean, other than the ones you documented in this area over the past month."

"Never. No. Nothing remotely like this."

"Well, have you heard of a pharmaceutical company named DNAXIS and its failed Curitall trials a few years back?"

"Curitall? That's a silly name for a drug—never heard of it. Then again, many drugs never make it out of trials and are forgotten. Now, DNAXIS—I've heard of them. It's a huge company at the forefront of gene therapeutics. Why do you ask?"

"I'm sure Roberts told you why we're here."

"Yes—he said something about a missing person case you've been working on for some time, but not how it relates to Melvin Anderson's death."

Doug summarized his involvement in Mary DeMure's abduction case, and then delved into his suspicions about a DNAXIS connection. "… and that's why we're here. We need help getting a subpoena for DNAXIS's records concerning the autopsy of those two dead researchers and the second phase-two Curitall trial. We also need to prove that DNAXIS is still connected and funding Helix Eternal Laboratories. Additionally, we need to know where every presentation for that phase-three drug trial was held. I suspect Green River College wasn't the only location, and I don't believe that DeMure and Grimes were the only students abducted. Mr. Pickens…"

"Oh, please, call me Francis. No need for formalities. We're out in the boondocks—I prefer first names."

"And you can call me Doug. Anyway, Francis, as I was saying, I was one of several detectives who worked with Dave Reichert to bring the Green River Killer to justice. Gary Ridgway specifically chose victims who could disappear without anyone noticing—society's so-called *forgettables*. While it remains to be proven, I suspect that's how H.E.L. chose human subjects for Dr. Albert Caine's illegal Curitall research."

"Sounds fascinating," said Pickens. "I would love to read that article. I have to say, it sounds like, I don't know, like someone's trying to create the perfect biological weapon. With the security detail involved in the lockdown and the massacre on Tuesday, I wouldn't be surprised if this goes much higher than a pharma firm. And with the death of that reporter after Mender's touch—well, that's… that's, uh, too much of a coincidence. I suspect your missing woman infected Mender with whatever she was carrying. Somehow, it didn't kill him and made him a carrier while killing Melvin Anderson in a way too terrible to imagine if I hadn't seen it with my own eyes. Kill with a touch… and then let the evidence destroy itself." Pickens rubbed his chin. "Hmmm. I don't think there'll be any problem convincing a judge to grant a subpoena now. However, you should contact Ryan Mender's father as well. His name is James Mender. He's a lawyer in Grand Junction and has been on a legal rampage since his grandson's death. He has, uh, all the connections you'll need to cut through the ol' red tape. Just convince him that DNAXIS is somehow connected to the Ebola quarantine and… well, let's just say, it won't be pretty."

"What? You think the Ebola quarantine and the death of Melvin Anderson are connected?" asked Doug.

"I have my suspicions… like a lot of people. The fact that the lab which the CDC contracted to manage things never allowed an independent evaluation of Alex Mender's body seems very strange to me. Especially when you consider the draconian measures they employed during the first few days of the lockdown. And doesn't it seem odd that an isolated case of Ebola would show up in an area where there's never been a case before? Also, the victim had never traveled to endemic areas or been exposed to anyone who had. And no one exposed to the Mender boy, including his parents, became ill during the lockdown. When I heard about the case, I offered my services. You know, years ago, I was volunteering with the Peace Corps in Uganda when we were hit with an outbreak. In fact, Dr. Raymond Boyd, who was the Mender boy's doctor, was in my group. The outbreak killed a few of our fellow members, but Raymond and I were lucky enough not to get sick and gained first-hand knowledge of what the disease can do in a short time. After the death of Melvin Anderson, followed shortly thereafter by the Mender boy, I was curious if there was a connection and believed the doctor who'd confirmed Alex Mender's cause of death had made a mistake. So, I reached out to the CDC in Fort Collins. They gave me a number to call, but no one from Helix Eternal Laboratories ever called me back."

"Really?" Doug said, rubbing his lips. "Thanks, Francis. You've been a big help, and we'll take your advice and contact Mr. Mender. But first, we have a few stops before we head south to Packer City to chat with Sheriff Glickman and ask around about Mary DeMure. She's probably through to the next town, but someone must've seen her and helped her after Ryan Mender rescued her from drowning."

"Bob—Don didn't tell you, did he?" asked Pickens. "He must've forgotten in all the craziness."

"Tell us what?" asked Bob.

"The whole reason why the Mears County Sheriff's Office was at the Watchtower minutes after the attack. Sheriff Pete had a hunch that this Mary DeMure was going there to see Ryan. That, um, maybe they knew each other. That maybe they were tied up in this whole mess together."

"That's impossible," said Doug. "I feel like I know everything about DeMure. I've read her journals. I've spoken with her teachers. I feel like I know her as well as my own daughter. She's as spotless as they come. Just a bookworm loner whose life ended when her grandfather passed."

"Hmmm. What did Ms. DeMure like to read?"

"Nathan Miller, Tony Hillerman. She was fascinated with the southwest. A lot of Stephen King, Dean Koontz, Ernest Hemingway, J. K. Rowling, J. R. R. Tolkien, books on Eastern philosophy, to name an armful. Why?"

"No reason. Just curious. What did she like to do?"

"Not much besides reading and writing in her journal after her grandfather, Thurston DeMure, died. Before that, she was a competitive snowboarder. Almost went to the Olympics. Hiked a lot. Climbed the highest mountains. Loved baseball and Seattle Mariners. Even after her grandfather was gone, she still inspired others, even if she didn't open up to friendship. I imagine she was afraid of losing someone else." Doug sighed as he tried to tame a trembling lip. "Francis… I have to find this woman… and have to find her alive. I just have to," he said, choking on his words as he held back a tear.

Pickens sighed even deeper than Doug and somberly said, "Don told me Tuesday evening that the Black Beret who killed himself said your girl was at the Watchtower at the time of the massacre.

Don't get your hopes up. Even though her body hasn't been found, it's unlikely anyone survived what happened up there."

Doug closed his eyes, exhaled, and opened them. "Well, I have to see the site. I have to know for sure. Bob, you think you can twist Glickman's arm into taking us up there?"

"Oh, about that," Pickens said out of turn. "I have to warn you—the Feds are not very sympathetic about your missing girl. And they aren't happy at all with Don and what's left of the Mears County Sheriff's Office after the only suspect and witness to the Fitzgerald murders and Mender Massacre committed suicide on their watch. So, I doubt Don will be able to help you guys get anywhere near the crime scene since Homeland Security restricted his access. Not to worry, though. I know one of the HSI guys in charge. His name is Matt Matthews. He's a sweetheart, but I don't care too much for his partner, Jeff Fuller. I can… I can give Mattie a call and warm things up if you'd like."

"Thanks, I'd, I mean… we'd appreciate that," said Doug. "Before we go, may I ask a favor?"

"Sure."

Doug handed Pickens his business card. "Would you mind scanning everything in Melvin Anderson's file and sending it as a PDF along with a copy of that crime scene video to the email on my card? There's no rush."

"Of course. Will do as soon as I can. But before you leave, there is one more thing I'd like to show you."

"Alright, what do you got?" asked Doug.

"It's some of that strange blue powder I collected from the massacre site," Pickens said as he opened a desk drawer. He retrieved a silver thermos and removed the lid, exposing the glistening substance inside.

Doug leaned back and covered his mouth and nose. Roberts did the same.

"Oh, don't worry. Stuff's completely harmless. I was worried at first. Now, I feel bad making the starred PC boys in blue or brown think they'd be looking like Chernobyl first responders in a flash. My bad. But it wasn't too smart trudging through the stuff after that *Blue Bomb* exploded. Don did tell you about that, didn't he?"

"Yeah, he mentioned it," Roberts said, lowering his hand as he examined the container's frosty contents.

"I didn't know what the stuff was," said Pickens, "kind of like I didn't know what to think when I watched my first corpse melt before my eyes. I still don't know what it is, but I call the stuff *Ethereal*. So far, the substance appears to be harmless but maintains a temperature of almost exactly thirteen degrees Fahrenheit. I've never seen anything like it. I wonder if it's an undiscovered element. A lot more testing is needed, but if it is, I could be famous someday. All I know is that it instantly smothers flames and even smoke. I mean, that's pretty useful. Here, look at some under the microscope. It's *ether-unreal*," he said raising his eyebrows as he chuckled. His chair creaked as he stood.

Doug missed the humor and Roberts smirked as they followed Pickens to the microscope.

Pickens set the container on the counter and grabbed three pairs of gloves from a box on the wide, long windowsill above the scope. He handed a pair to each detective and pulled on the third. He opened a drawer below the coffee maker and rummaged through straws, packaged chopsticks, ketchup and mustard packets, plastic forks and spoons, until he found a pair of fairly clean surgical forceps and a box of slides and coverslips. He set them on the counter and picked up an orange Starburst that had been hiding under the slide box, unwrapped it, and popped it in his mouth. He grabbed the forceps, wiped them on his shirt, and nabbed a glistening pinch from the container. He placed the crystalline substance on the slide and gently pressed it into a dark transparent layer under a coverslip.

Doug was mesmerized as it twinkled like a starry mountain night.

Pickens sealed the container and sat on the stool. He placed the slide on the stage, adjusted the light, and focused on the high dry.

"Here, check this out, Doug," said Pickens.

He got up, and Doug sat down.

"Wait," said Pickens. "Let me turn on the screen so Bob can see what you're looking at."

Doug peered through the objective. Hundreds of beautiful, shimmering cobalt crystals phased in and out. They seemed ghostly as they took on familiar and impossible forms, and then transitioned into new, equally fantastical ones. *Ethereal? Hmmm, not a bad description,* he thought as he adjusted his seat. He pulled closer and slammed his shin into a cabinet corner. "Owww, dangit." He shook off the pain and looked through the objective. "Francis, you need to see this," he said, pushing away from the counter.

"We're seeing it," said Roberts.

The crystals were vibrating under the coverslip and pulsating flame-like radiation. The slide cracked, and the coverslip melted. The crystals rapidly returned to their former surreal state.

Pickens grabbed the frosted pieces.

"What the hell happened?" asked Roberts.

"I hit my shin," said Doug.

"Not you. Francis—what was that?"

"Iiii don't know," he said with a nervous chuckle and a shaky smile as he scratched his shoulder, "but I think it would be a good idea to keep the biohazard signs up at Tower Rock until more testing can be done. I guess Ethereal is not as harmless as it seems. My bad."

Twenty-Six

Early afternoon, Thursday, October 2, 2007. Grayson, Colorado.

Doug shook Pickens's hand after Roberts thanked him for his time. They left the coroner's office through the back, and crossed the street to the courthouse that housed the police department.

Grayson Undersheriff Danny Griggs was on the phone when they stepped into his office. Griggs held up a *hold-on* finger and used the same digit to point to a pair of seats in front of his desk.

They waited as Griggs spoke little except for, "Yes, I understand," and, "Okay, I will," until he finally said, "It was nice speaking with you, too, Governor Thorp. Thanks for letting me know. And thanks for your confidence in me." He hung up.

"I can't talk long. This Mears County situation has me running in every direction. That was Governor Thorp. He just appointed me interim Mears County Sheriff by executive order, which wouldn't have been a tall order, but under the circumstances... well. So, Bob-Bob, what can I do for you and your partner... Dean, is it?"

"Doug, Doug Thorfinnson, of the Federal Way Washington Police Department," Roberts corrected.

"Uh, where exactly is that?"

"Between Seattle and Tacoma."

"Oh, that's right. Well, you two are way out of your jurisdiction. I apologize upfront that I can't give you much time today."

"That's okay. I'll keep it short," Doug said and proceeded to summarize a year's worth of collected information and suspicions in five minutes.

"Hmmm," Griggs uttered as he tapped steepled fingers together. "That's interesting, but a bit far-fetched, if you ask me. Like Francis told you, there's not a lot of sympathy for your girl around here after what she did to Melvin Anderson, who pretty much everybody knew and loved in Grayson, PC, and Silver City. The President is even interested in the situation, and the Governor has agreed to turn jurisdiction in Mears County over to Homeland Security."

"Yeah, we heard," said Roberts.

"Well, then I guess you also heard they're convinced your missing person is a terrorist and needs to be captured or killed if she's not already dead. Someone likewise convinced them that Ryan Mender was turned after he left the Army, killed his wife, and is currently working with Ms. DeMure—that is, if Mender's still alive. The President and the Governor are under the impression that they're both involved with the radical militia group, BNM, or Brigham Norsworthy's Minutemen, in case you didn't know, Dean, I mean Don. Doug?"

Doug nodded.

"Sorry. Anyway, they, uh, believe this group is intent on bringing down the U.S. government and have something called Blue Bombs they plan to deploy in multiple federal buildings across the country. Well, it was nice to meet you, Detective Thorfishing. And Bob-Bob, always a pleasure, present circumstances… well, you know. But hey, that's all the time I have for you guys. Good luck with your search for the other kids, but I'm afraid your Mary is, uh, excuse the French, fucked," he said, wide-eyed for emphasis.

Doug's eyes shot needles, but Griggs smiled as if overjoyed with the unhealthy pile of crap he'd shoveled. Doug pursed his lips and exhaled through his nose. He returned a similar grin, still glaring, and said, "Thanks for your time, but I need to ask you one more question. It concerns the Land Rover they found at the site of Melvin Anderson's suspected murder. According to Bob, it's registered to a Louis Suerte. Have you been able to locate him, and if not, do you have any information concerning who he is?"

"Not a clue. The guy's a ghost. Turns out, the registration was a forgery, and the Land Rover was stolen. Hey, I hate to cut you off again, but I really gotta run."

"Alright. Again, thank you for your time," said Doug.

"No problemo," said Griggs.

Twenty-Seven

Still early afternoon, Thursday, October 4, 2007. Grayson, Colorado.

"Is Undersheriff Griggs always such a dick, and I don't mean detective?" asked Doug as they headed west.

"Yeah, pretty much. He's a grade-A jackass. Always has been. He deserves a *Kissed-Ass-to-the-Top* plaque for his wall. Damn… Danny Boy in charge…" Bob sighed. "Talk about pouring salt in PC's wounds. Hey, pull over here—this is where Suerte's Land Rover was parked," he said, pointing to a wide shoulder within a micro-canyon.

They got out, stopped to let a truck zip by going twenty over, and jogged across the two-lane highway.

"The Grayson Reservoir Bridge and road to Packer City is an eighth of a mile up from here. This is the lowest I've seen the river in the ten years I lived here," Bob said, pointing at the Grayson River that was nearly a dry bed.

Doug nodded, then looked left and right down the highway and around at the cozy little canyon's walls. His gaze returned to the brushy grass and driftwood-lined bank next to the trickle masquerading as a river. The road was visible for about a hundred feet in either direction but not the crime scene. He glanced at Bob.

Bob nodded and led him to the weathered yellow tape nestled in driftwood.

Doug looked back at the 4Runner and said, "That's a long way to drag a body."

"Yes, it is."

Doug shook his head and frowned. It disturbed him that DeMure had tried to hide what she'd done. *Could I have been wrong about her?* he thought.

He took out his camera, snapped some photos, and continued snapping on their way back to the rental, retracing DeMure's likely path to the veteran's Jeep. *Why would she murder someone who stopped to help her?* It made no sense like everything else in this twisted case. Unless, of course, his theory that Pickens had expanded was correct. But of the people he'd confided in, only his wife, his new partner, and Coroner Pickens didn't believe he was two skis short of a set.

Twenty-Eight

Early Afternoon, Thursday, October 4, 2007. Grayson Highway South.

Doug stretched his eyelids. He glanced and saw that Roberts was lost in another novel entitled *Cell* by Stephen King. Doug released an exasperated sigh, and couldn't restrain himself any longer. "I have to tell you, Bob. You are the worst traveling companion I've ever had the displeasure of traveling with."

"Hey, sorry, it's a good book about cellphones turning people into zombies. Did you know King doesn't have a cell phone?"

"No, um… I didn't," he said, feigning the interest of a non-reader as they passed a sign that advertised *Dr. Morgan Bell's Curiosity and Souvenir Shop 40 Miles This-a-way*, with an arrow dripping crimson above the *This-a-way*.

Doug had heard Bell's name mentioned on the news in conjunction with the Fitzgerald slayings, but didn't know much about the century-old case and hadn't had time to learn more before the flight. Of course, Bell sounded like another Jack the Ripper, and he'd never understood the fascination with psychopathic degenerates like Ridgway, Dahmer, Gacy, Bundy, Ackerman… Doug could think of a slew more. It was bad enough seeing their faces on t-shirts and in the cameo appearances in horror flicks and television series that he sought to avoid that his daughter Elli and her bestie Bridgette enjoyed. And that billboard—Doug couldn't fathom how any town or city would celebrate another of their homicidal alumni in such a way. He wondered if someday there might be Green River Killer tours in Seattle or a big plaque on the house where Bundy lived or a U-Dubb Bundy Walk of Infamy.

Roberts sighed. "Yeah... hey... but seriously—I'm sorry I'm not better company. I'm just trying to keep my mind off what we're driving into. If I don't, I'm gonna lose it. I'm sure Joe Turner's wife and the Maxwell family are inconsolable. Glickman was a basket case Tuesday night when we spoke, and things haven't improved since. I can't imagine Wicker's doing any better after seeing his father-in-law and best friend murdered, and then getting shot and then letting a key suspect kill himself. And there's no telling how the other guys are doing, not to mention the town in general. Things like this don't happen in Mears County, or at least they haven't for a long time."

"It's okay. I'm... I'm just giving you a hard time..." *No you're not,* thought Doug. "... I can only imagine what it's taking for you to keep focus. We'll solve this case, and when we do, some heads are gonna roll."

"Yeah. If it wouldn't be too much trouble, can we stop by Patsy Maxwell's place before we meet with Glickman?"

"Of course. So... so, who's this Morgan Bell guy I keep hearing about on the news?" asked Doug.

Roberts shot him a skeptical glance. "Seriously? You don't know who Morgan Bell is? And to think you helped bring down the Green River Killer, but you don't know the story of Dr. Morgan Bell, the infamous Cannibal Surgeon of Packer City, Colorado."

"It might surprise you, but I hate my job because it has to exist. When I'm off, I don't spend my time reading about every psychopath who has ever walked the earth. I'm from the Pacific Northwest. We're known for salmon, clam chowder, Mount Rainier, and... ah yeah, serial killers. Oh, and we also have some good microbreweries. So, indulge me. Close that damn book and tell me a story, or I swear I'm going to nod off and drive off the edge of that canyon there."

Roberts looked left at the gulf beyond. He chuckled, closed the book, and set it aside. "Hmmm. So, you want to hear Morgan Bell's story. PG or R-rated?"

"Like you said—I helped Dave Reichert take down Gary Ridgway. How much worse can it be than what I saw on that case?"

"Good point. Okay—R it is." Roberts rubbed his chin, took a deep breath, and exhaled. "Where do I start? I guess I'll start from the beginning, long before Bell was known as the Cannibal Surgeon of Packer City."

Roberts cleared his throat and continued with the best southern drawl someone who obviously wasn't from the south could pull off—slow, thick, and a bit over the top with added high-pitch vocal squeaks to get the nineteenth-century stereotype right. "Morgan Jefferson Bell was born on April Fool's Day, 1841, in Montgomery, Alabama. He was the son of a cotton plantation owner. As such, he grew up like any other plantation owner's son with all the creature comforts a staff of negro slaves could provide. But when that wily varmint Lincoln was elected President, Morgan answered the call and volunteered to fight for the Confederacy to preserve state's rights and keep his daddy's plantation full of free labor.

"Now, Morgan was a scrawny specimen—not much good on a battlefield except for catching lead. So, he was put to work as a field surgeon's assistant, where he gained plenty of cutting-edge experience." Roberts paused.

Doug glanced over, caught his grin, and returned a smirk.

"Sorry. Bad pun. Couldn't help myself."

Roberts returned to character. "Anywho—Morgan survived the war—obviously—and returned home. But after the Emancipation Proclamation, the property became unmanageable and fell into disrepair. During those lean years, he met and married the love of his life—a woman named Cordelia. They had three children who lived, named Atticus, Carol Ann, and Jefferson. The other three died at childbirth or when they were very young, which weren't that unusual back in them days.

"As the plantation's fortunes declined, Morgan learned of the Colorado gold and silver rush, and specifically about a mountain of gold around the newly established town of Packer City. However, he chose to stay and tried to build a new life in Montgomery. He became a barber and continued doing work as a surgeon. Soon after, he was inspired to become a doctor after learning about the novel techniques of Joseph Lister. He had watched scores of young men die from minor wounds and even greater numbers after successful amputations. He was intrigued that Lister had found a way to reduce the post-surgical death rate by using carbolic acid to keep instruments and wounds clean. He began to employ those methods in Montgomery and was making a name for himself when another doctor in town, critical of Lister's techniques, began to slander him. Scrawny Morgan—as he was called behind his back—challenged the doctor to a duel and won but was run out of town after the man died two weeks later from an infected gunshot wound."

Doug smirked and sniffed a laugh.

"With no real options in Alabama, Morgan decided to take a chance and headed west with his family to that mountain of gold in Colorado. They traveled by train, and along the way, Comanches attacked. The Indians killed the conductor and his crew, and then ordered the passengers off. That day, Morgan was forced to watch his sweet Cordelia scalped and then raped. Atticus and Carol Ann were pulled from the train by their hair and looked like porcupines when the Indians got done filling them with arrows. But not Morgan's baby boy, Jefferson. The Comanches left him for dead with just a few quills. He survived, but his mother died a few days later. Inexplicably, Morgan was left unmolested and allowed to live while the Indians raped and/or massacred the rest of the passengers."

Doug lost his smirk.

"A month before the incident, the Indians in question were out hunting when the U.S. Army surrounded and slaughtered everyone in their camp. Only women, children, and tribal elders were there at the time. You know, in better times, only Morgan and Cordelia would have been mercilessly butchered and the children mighta been taken as slaves and incorporated into the tribe. But these warriors were on the warpath, and Morgan's family was collateral damage. Every one of them Comanches responsible—and several who were not—were either killed outright by Texas Rangers or rounded up and hung without trial. But I do digress."

Doug's lips were a line—his eyes fixed on the road as an old sepia western rolled on the big screen in his mind.

"Morgan buried his wife and two children in what would become Abilene, Texas. There, he worked as a doctor until Jefferson—who was nine at the time—was healthy enough to travel. That is when they hooked up with a prospector on his way to the San Marcos Mountains. Like Morgan, he had lost his family and wanted to start over and find his fortune in those mountains of gold and silver.

"They arrived in Sur Del Rio in mid-summer 1881. The town was the closest railroad stop and supply junction to Packer City, which was still ninety miles away. From there, the three planned to travel by wagon and mule the rest of the way. Yet, as fate would have it, about the time they were to leave, Jefferson broke with Scarlet Fever and was sick for weeks, during which time the prospector died. When Jefferson recovered, Morgan was more determined than ever to continue on to Gold Mountain, even though several people in town warned him about chancing Bullion Pass that late in the season. It was mid-October when Morgan and Jefferson finally arrived at the foot of the San Marcos Mountains near the headwaters of the Rio Grande and what is now the Mears/Silver County line.

"As they ascended the trail to the pass, a family of four unmounted Utes heading south stopped to warn Morgan about a coming storm. After the Meeker Massacre up north from there, wild Utes were rare. Since then, the whole state was on high alert for an Indian invasion that never happened. It was not safe for Utes to wander off the reservation and it is possible the family got separated from a larger illegal hunting party and was headed back to Southern Ute Reservation when they happened upon Morgan and Jefferson Bell.

"Anyhow, the Ute man spoke his native tongue, which Morgan did not understand. And when he turned his head to point in the direction they came, Morgan pulled an ax from his belt and hit the man in the head with the backside. Knocked him clean out. Morgan quickly grabbed his rifle from the wagon, pulled the lever on what was probably a Winchester 1873 or 1880, and aimed the gun at the Ute woman and her two children. He instructed Jefferson to tie their hands behind their backs and then together into a rope chain gang. When the father came to, Morgan had Jefferson direct the Ute man and his family at gunpoint up the trail while he contemplated what to do with them to exact revenge for the death of his sweet Cordelia, Atticus, and Carol Ann. He did not care in the least that they were not Comanches since he was of the same opinion as the current Colorado Governor, Frederick Walker Pitkin. The governor believed the only good Indian was a dead Indian. On that, the southern Democrat and western Republican could agree," Roberts added with a sarcastic bite.

"Anywho, continuing on. Only after the snow began to fall did Morgan understand what the Ute man was trying to tell him. By then, it was too late. They had only enough rations for a few weeks, but Jefferson had shared most of his with the family. Oh, that Jefferson. Bless his heart. He was a soft-hearted fella, much to his father's disgust. And this softness gave Morgan an idea what to do with the family. First, he walked the mule off the edge of a canyon near the camp. Then, until they exhausted their rations, he and Jefferson shared their remaining food. But when the food was gone, Morgan decided to teach his son a life lesson about feeding savages and other animals of their sort. He shot the father in both legs to shatter his femurs and then tied a rope tightly around each leg to keep him from bleeding out. The cold helped, too. He then forced the man to watch as he scalped his wife and two children while scolding Jefferson whenever his soft eyes looked away. Then using his surgical instruments, Morgan sliced off pieces of the man while he was still alive and ate them raw since there was no means of cooking without dry wood. And, of course, he made Jefferson partake in his madness. The man did not live long, and after he died, they continued eating him and his family until there was nothing left but bones and inedible parts. When they could travel again, Morgan and Jefferson dumped the remains to hide what they had done in the same canyon near the pass where Morgan had killed the mule."

Robert's voice returned to normal. "While we're in town, I can take you up to Cannibal Canyon where it all happened, if you'd like."

"If we have time, that might be interesting," Doug said to be polite since he doubted extra time would be a luxury they'd get to enjoy. He glanced at the rolling landscape of stubby grass, short pine-covered hills, buttes, and small mesas.

Roberts returned to character. "Now, killing Indians in that day and age was not frowned upon, but eating them was a bit over the top. So, Morgan and Jefferson never spoke of it. Oh, and it was said that those who witnessed their arrival at the Gold Mountain mining camp thought it odd that the two looked as healthy as they did—well-fleshed and rosy-cheeked after such a harrowing ordeal.

"Well, soon after staking his claim, Morgan became the town doctor and found a decent silver vein with a respectable amount of gold mixed in. He made a small fortune, especially after selling it to the next prospector, who was not quite so lucky. The vein was located under what is now Greenly Mountain, which was named after the not-so-lucky prospector, Horace Greenly. Now, Horace, he was a very religious man and the town's school teacher. And, he always believed Morgan had swindled him.

"Anywho, concerning Jefferson Bell—he never got over the death of his mother and siblings or what his father made him do to that Ute family. They say—whoever *they* are—that he was a peculiar teen and fell in with the wrong crowd. The worst among them was a dance hall and brothel owner named Buford Redman. He was part Comanche, whose mother had been taken as a slave several years back. Their mutual hate for the tribe was their bond. To make matters worse, Horace Greenly was cruel and abusive to Jefferson in class until the day he graduated. Horace swore many times in front of the other students that Jefferson was the spawn of Satan himself. More than once, Morgan confronted him, but to no avail. He even contemplated a duel but never followed through after his last successful contest.

"One night, Jefferson went out drinking with Buford at his dance hall brothel in Hell's Acre on the southside of Packer City near the mining camps. The brothel was located where a restaurant called the Old Prospector would be built many years later and long before Ryan Mender and his wife...." Roberts paused, exhaled, and swallowed hard enough for Doug to hear. Doug glanced over as Roberts rubbed his mouth.

"Sorry. Well, anyway..." he said, missing a few beats before regaining his narrator voice. "Anyhow, there was... there was a disturbance later that night at a house on the north side of Packer City—or the church side, or Acres of Heaven, as they called it back then. Sheriff Bo Bridger went to check on it. It turned out to be the home of former Union General Rutherford Hotchkiss, the richest man in town. As a matter of fact, the big lake south of town is named after him, and there's even a monument near the courthouse dedicated to his prowess for ordering blue-coats into slaughter at Gettysburg. Anywho, when Sheriff Bridger came knock, knock, knocking on Rutherford's door, there was no answer, but the door was slightly ajar. So, Bridger entered with a hand on his grip and immediately heard a clicking hammer. Before he could draw, the room lit up with a single shot from Redman's Colt 45 Peacemaker, which hit Bridger in the chest. Both Buford and Jefferson ran from the scene and might-a got away with the crime had Deputy Ulysses Carlton not shown up in time to hear Bridger's last word, *Redman.*'

"When Deputy Carlton confronted Buford at the brothel, the half-breed still had the revolver in his holster and a single spent casing in the cylinder. Since Jefferson had been seen with him earlier, Deputy Carlton went to Morgan Bell's home and arrested his very drunk son. When Jefferson woke up in a jail cell the next morning, Carlton questioned him. Morgan's boy could not remember much of anything after arriving at the dance hall, but he did remember a flash from Buford's gun and a face that looked like it was on fire across a room, wherever it was that he might have been. He actually thought it was a dream. It was obvious Buford had killed the sheriff and that Jefferson was only guilty of being at the Hotchkiss house. But that did not matter to Jefferson's former schoolteacher, Horace Greenly. He raised a lynch mob to break into the jail and hang the mix-blood savage and the demon spawn. The Deputy tried to stop them, but the mob pushed him aside and tied up Buford and Jefferson and carried them to the Howard Creek Bridge. Under a blood moon, they hung them from beams and left their lifeless bodies dangling there for a week.

"Horace Greenly could not help but treat the event as an object lesson. The next morning, he paraded his class by the bodies and told those poor kids, *'These are the wages of sin in this town.'* As you can imagine, many of the children had nightmares for years to come. And many of those who participated in the lynch mob swore they saw the ghosts of Buford and Jefferson walking around the bridge and riverbank with nooses tied around their necks, red-faced with eyes bulging out and bloodshot. When the two bodies were finally cut down, the severed ends of the ropes were left hanging on the beams for years. The ropes were eventually removed, as were the beams, to erase any memory of an event that has not been forgotten.

"Well now, Morgan was inconsolable, and at first, he threatened revenge on the town. Then he seemed to calm down. He started going to church. Even said he found God. He apologized for his unkind words and publicly prayed for his son's soul. He even reconciled with Horace and apologized for selling him that worthless mine. He claimed he had seen the light and that Jefferson was justly punished for associating with a degenerate half-breed like Buford. Morgan continued as the town doctor, and for a spell, everything seemed right as rain.

"One night, not long after, Horace and his family boarded up their home near Crown Lake and abruptly left town. No one questioned their absence since a letter was sent that morning by Pony Express to a friend in Grayson who was also a teacher. In the letter, Horace said he was leaving to care for a sick aunt in the new town of Durango and that—God willing—he and his sweet wife, Loulou Belle, son, Elijah, and daughter, Ester, would be back by next spring. The friend became the town's substitute teacher, and life went on.

"Several weeks later, a prospector found Horace's wagon and decaying horses at the bottom of what is now Greenly Gulch, located between McMann and Crown Lake. All the supplies needed for the journey south were mixed amongst the wreckage, but there were no human remains. That is when Sheriff Carlton checked the boarded-up Greenly home."

Roberts's voice returned to normal. "The home was located northwest of where Brigham Norsworthy built his Watchtower on Tower Rock. It's ironic that Jeremiah Fitzgerald built his home near the Greenly place after inheriting the land from an uncle who was Horace's great-grandson." Roberts shook his head and choked a little as he continued. "They were such a nice family. Tragic and senseless what happened to them, but then you're probably used to this sort of thing."

"I never get used to it. And if I ever do, I'll retire before the end of the day," Doug said as he weaved the winding roads of a canyon with a rock wall to the right and yellow, orange, and red-leafed aspens and the river to the left. He passed the *Welcome to Mears County* sign.

"We're almost to my old home," said Roberts. "I'll finish up the story before we get to Patsy's. It's about ten miles up ahead. Really nice place. Well… Let's continue. Where was I?"

"Uhh, Sheriff Carlton was investigating the Greenly home."

"Yeah. The Greenly home." Roberts resumed the drawl. "Anywho, inside the home, Carlton found dried blood all over the front room. And on the kitchen table, there was an empty bottle of wine, an empty glass, and a plate with some dried trim fat. There was also an overwhelming stench of death permeating everything. After searching and finding no cause for the smell above, he checked under the house and found four corpses. Loulou Belle, Elijah, and Ester were dressed in their Sunday best with a bullet hole in each of their heads, but otherwise, they were unmolested. That could not be said for Horace's body. He was naked and ravaged by hate, mutilated and half-eaten, with the pieces sliced off like one would carve a roast or Thanksgiving turkey. And all the mutilations and amputations were done with surgical precision."

"Wait—isn't that the same way the Fitzgeralds were killed?"

Roberts's voice returned to normal. "Almost exactly, even down to the wine. But Martin Rice isn't Morgan Bell's first copycat killer. There was another named Gregory Foreman back in the seventies and eighties who slaughtered nine families in the Midwest before he was brought to justice." He scoffed. "He was a Sunday school teacher of all things. Foreman ended up getting the electric chair in

Nebraska back in '95. He was the last one before the Nebraska Supreme Court outlawed the chair as *cruel and unusual punishment*," he said with finger quotations. "Yeah, like there was nothing cruel and unusual about what Foreman did to those families. Bastard deserved to fry. Still, it was too nice for that psycho. But off my soapbox and back to the story."

The southern drawl returned. "Sheriff Carlton could think of only one person who could have done this deed and had the motive, and that was the good doctor, Morgan Bell. When questioned about where he was on the night of the family's disappearance and for several days after, Morgan did not have a good alibi, so Ulysses arrested him. When word got out that Sheriff Carlton suspected Morgan killed the Greenly family and ate Horace, the town surrounded the jail and demanded justice. This time, Ulysses was able to talk some sense into the townsfolk and convinced them to let the justice system do its job. In the famous court trial that followed in the Packer City Courthouse, Morgan broke down on cross-examination over the town murdering his boy. After that, he admitted to his crimes in gruesome detail, including the Ute family he and his boy had eaten in the winter of 1881.

"When asked why he only ate Horace, Morgan admitted, '*I didn't have anything against Loulou Belle and the kids.*'

"'*So, why did you kill them,*' asked the prosecuting attorney.

"Well, now, Morgan replied, '*It made Horace taste better when I ate him alive. There's nothing like a little anger, sorrow, and fear to season up the meat.*'

"There was a collective gasp in the courtroom, and several looked like they might be sick, and a few were and ran outside to do their business. They say Morgan just grinned and that his eyes turned devilish before he added, "*Do not knock it until you have tried it.*'

"Once Judge Ripkin had restored order, he sentenced the not-so-good doctor to hang and said, '*You do not deserve mercy on your soul. May you burn in hell, Morgan Bell,*' and then demanded, '*Sheriff Carlton, remove this demon from my courtroom immediately.*'

"Morgan's hanging would be the first official execution in Packer City. Sheriff Carlton wanted to do it right and festive, so he sent out some *real* nice invitations to everyone in the surrounding mining towns, Grayson, Silver City, Bakersville, and Quenche. And woo-doggy was it a party, and the finale… watching Morgan Bell swing like his son near the ravine we just passed named in Bo Bridger's honor."

Roberts's voice returned to normal. "Turn left there," he said, pointing to a road that led to a small bridge over the Grayson River and continued around a rock wall at the edge of another small canyon.

Doug turned onto gravel.

"It's about a mile down this road. Anyway, the story doesn't end there." The drawl returned. "Many claimed for years of seeing Morgan Bell standing in the middle of the Howard Creek Bridge every time there was a blood moon. That is, until the ropes were taken down that reminded everyone of the evil they had done. Several townspeople went insane and were committed, including Sheriff Carlton. And Judge Ripkin… well, he had unrelenting nightmares and died of shotgun indigestion. Eventually, everything went back to normal, and Dr. Bell, the Cannibal Surgeon, became a macabre legend. Even the makers of that popular trashy adult cartoon *South Park* made a musical about the whole chain of events.

Didn't do nearly as well as the cartoon or the play on Broadway about the Mormons."

Roberts's voice returned to normal. "Yeah, it's crazy. As you saw, if you noticed that billboard, Packer City has this hate-to-love relationship with the old surgeon. On one hand, they don't like being known as the site of Bell's heinous crimes, and on the other... well, you'll see." He laughed. "We'll have to drop by and eat at Dr. Bell's Cannibal Saloon. Their specialty is called the *Cannibal Burger with Finger Fries*. As disgusting as it sounds, it's actually really good—a big hit with seasonal tourists. We also could've stayed at Doc's Cannibal Cabins, built where his home and office used to be. But I think you'll like the place I picked. It has a nice view overlooking the town. Well, here we are. Pull up behind Mike's Rubicon."

Doug rubbed his forehead as he parked in the driveway crowded with five other vehicles. "That...that was a messed up story, and you told it so well. Thanks for keeping me awake. Now I might not sleep tonight," he said with a wink.

Roberts chuckled and drawled out, "My pleasure, pawdner."

Twenty-Nine

Mid-afternoon, Thursday, October 4, 2007. The Maxwell House.
Doug tried to count the bullet holes in the passenger side of the black Jeep, and then stepped out and followed Roberts to the front door.

Roberts knocked, and Mrs. Maxwell answered. Her eyes were red and puffy. Roberts hugged her and lost it. They sobbed together as he stroked her back. He let go and wiped his eyes.

Mrs. Maxwell wiped hers, sniffed hard, and asked, "Who's your friend?"

"This is my new partner, Senior Detective Doug Thorfinnson of the Federal Way Police Department."

Her lips curled into a tragic grin. "Nice to meet you, Doug. Sorry, I'm just a mess. I'm still in shock. I can't believe my Pete's gone."

"No need to apologize. From everything Bob told me about your husband, he sounds like he was a great man, and his death, a senseless tragedy."

"He was. And thank you… thank you, Doug. Let's go inside. I'll introduce everybody."

Three men and a young, middle-aged woman sat in the front room around a large coffee table.

Starting from her right, moving counterclockwise, Mrs. Maxwell pointed and said, "This is my youngest, Matt, and that's Luke, and this is my oldest, Mandy. And over on the couch is my son-in-law, Mike."

Deputy Wicker was reading a newspaper. He was wearing a blue and orange Broncos *Elway #7* jersey and his left shoulder was bulked up with a bandage. The others were likewise dressed in *knocking-around* chic. Mrs. Maxwell's children acknowledged him and Roberts with a nod, but Wicker didn't glance up.

Roberts hugged each of the grown children and said what he could to console them. Doug noticed that Wicker still hadn't looked up and was grinning as if something was funny. He didn't look sad, and his behavior contrasted with the scene like a clown juggling at a funeral. Doug thought it strange and very unlike the *Mike* his new partner had described more than once over the past month.

When Roberts finished speaking with Mrs. Wicker, he went to the couch and said, "Mike, I'm sorry I wasn't here. I can't help feeling like... like maybe I could've done something."

Wicker set the newspaper on the table as his grin melted into a somber line verging on a mournful frown. For some reason, it seemed contrived to Doug.

Wicker replied calmly, measured, with a dash of sorrow buried deep in his words, "There's nothing you could have done. Pete was dead at the Fitzgeralds' doorstep before they—I mean *we* got out of our vehicles. So, who's your friend? And how you been doing?" he asked mechanically as if rattling off a formality-to-do list.

"This is my new partner, Senior Detective Doug Thorfinnson. And how am I doing? I was adjusting fine to Seattle until I heard about Pete and Joe and Suzanne and the Fitzgeralds, and before that, the Mender kid. I just feel sick. How you hanging in here?"

"It was hard losing Pete and Joe, that's for sure," he said. "And I feel like a Goddamn idiot leaving Colonel Stone alone long enough for him to kill himself. Now, we have nothing on those Black Beret bastards except that insane pile of garbage Stone gave us when he confessed to his part in the Fitzgerald murders. Seriously, not worth watching or listening to. Rantings of a *seriously* deranged mind if you ask me. Yeah, I'm sure you heard by now that Glickman suspended me. Rightfully so, of course. I would've done the same thing had I been in his shoes. But it's for the best. I needed some time to clear my head anyway. As a matter of fact, I'm taking a little vacation up at the cabin to do just that."

Doug stepped closer to the coffee table and glanced at the newspaper to see what'd been so funny. He figured Deputy Wicker had been reading the comics, but instead, he saw an article about the Fitzgerald murders. Wicker noticed him looking at the paper and Doug sensed unease as he read the first few lines of the article. He pursed his lips to one side and thought, *Everyone deals with grief differently, and this man's experienced something that can change anyone, but...*

"Anyone for coffee?" asked Mrs. Maxwell.

"Coffee? Seriously?" said Wicker. "I'm sure Bob and Doug would rather have a beer or something stronger."

"Coffee's fine," said Doug. "It's going to be a long night, and I don't drink while I'm working."

"Suit yourself," said Roberts, "but I'm having a beer with my old buddy. A few shots would be nice, too. You're driving anyway. Got any Coors?"

"Of course. I always stock the fridge with your favorite," said Wicker.

The Maxwell boys grabbed two chairs from the dining room and set them by the coffee table. As Doug sat, Mrs. Maxwell handed him a steaming cup and set the creamer on the table. He skipped the creamer and took several sips as Wicker and Roberts slammed shots of Jameson and cracked open two Silver Bullets.

Doug interrupted the reunion and said, "Deputy Wicker…"

"Call me Mike."

"Okay, Mike—I know you've been through a lot, but would you be willing to answer a few questions about the local search for Mary DeMure? She's the reason Bob and I are here."

"No, not at all. Not much to say, though. Ms. Demure only appeared out of nowhere two days ago. Before that, we'd given her up for dead after we were unable to find her."

"Well, can you tell me anything about what happened at the Mender place? Was she there when it was attacked?" asked Doug.

"Can't help you there either," said Wicker. "I took a round at the Fitzgeralds' after taking out one of the two shooters and wounding a third. But why they were there? And why they killed Pete and Joe and did those gruesome things to that family? I don't have a clue. I'm sorry I can't be of more help." He looked at Roberts. "After that asshole shot me, your replacement rushed me to the clinic to get patched up. I was already gone by the time the other guys investigated Captain Rice's basement of horrors and the aftermath of the Mender Massacre."

"Okay, then, can you tell me what you know about former Army Colonel Joshua Stone?"

Wicker glared as his lips rose to a sneer. His tone became less than cordial. "I've told Glickman and Homeland Security all I know, and I'm on suspension because of it. I already told you that. I don't want to talk about the Colonel anymore." His face softened, his lips quivered, and his eyes welled but didn't overflow.

"Hey, Doug, lay off the man," said Roberts. "We'll see Glickman soon enough. We can ask him these questions then."

Doug exhaled. "I'm sorry, Mike. I really am. I've been searching for Mary DeMure for almost a year, and her case has been making me crazy ever since. Ms. DeMure was just an innocent kid trying to stay out of trouble and make a better life for herself when she was abducted with another kid, who went to the same college south of

Seattle. And it could've been three. If not for the one that got away, no one would've known they were missing."

"Hey, I'm sorry," said Wicker. "I didn't know the whole story about DeMure. I just thought she was some cold-blooded terrorist who killed an old man and stole his car." He sniffed and wiped his eyes.

"There's a lot more to it, but I can't prove it yet. I'm hoping to find clues that will get us closer to a subpoena for records..." Doug looked around the room. Everyone was listening. "But... I can't go into the details right now since much of it is speculation. Look, I know this is difficult for you, but would you mind joining Bob and me at the station for our meeting with Deputy Glickman?"

"You mean Sheriff slash Undersheriff?"

"No," said Roberts. "He was demoted back to Deputy by an executive order from the Governor. We were in Grigg's office when the Governor named him interim sheriff."

"Damn. I really feel bad now. No—I especially don't want to face him now. And hey, my Rubicon is already packed and ready for some alone time in the mountains. I figure a week away from this place will do me some good."

"I agree, but don't forget the Jameson," Roberts said with a grin. "Hey, how about one more shot for Pete and Joe? Come on, Doug—one won't kill you. Anyone else want to join?"

Doug didn't argue and joined the others in the dining room as Wicker filled seven shot glasses. Doug grabbed one, raised the glass with everyone else. He sang with the choir, "To Pete and Joe," swallowed the firewater, and coughed.

Thirty

Late Afternoon, Thursday, October 4, 2007. Mears County Sheriff's Office, Packer City, Colorado.

Deputy Don Glickman looked up as a familiar, smiling face entered the office. He hopped from Sheriff Maxwell's chair to greet former Deputy Bob Roberts as an unfamiliar chubby face joined them. "Good to see you, Bob," he said and gave him a man hug.

"Good to see you, too," said Roberts. "This is my new partner, Doug Thorfinnson. New partner—this is Don Glickman."

"Nice to meet you," said Thorfinnson as he shook Don's hand.

"Here, let me get you a chair," said Don. He pulled up two, set them on the side of the desk in the small office, and returned to the old chair with Pete's imprint in the worn leather.

"How you holding up?" Roberts asked as he sat.

"About the same as when we spoke the other night. The Homeland Security guys the President put in charge are all over us after Mike's fuck up. Now, they've locked us out of the investigation, except for the honor of crime scene guard duty. Don't know if you heard, but the Governor made Danny Griggs our Interim Sheriff, but he hasn't assigned an Undersheriff yet. Danny's Goddamn useless here with his hands full in Grayson."

"Danny's pretty useless with his hands empty," Roberts said with a droll grin.

Don cracked a smile and released a chuckle.

"Yeah… we heard," said Roberts. "We were in Griggs's office when Governor Thorp promoted him."

Don shook his head and scoffed. "Yeah, Griggs left us here with our dicks swinging in the wind. I want to blame Wicker for this, but it's my fault. I should've never left him alone with the prisoner after what happened. But those damn reporters—always needing their headlines and sound bites. I should've waited until Tolliver and Lombardi got back. I could tell Wicker wasn't himself, but I thought he was okay enough to watch Colonel Stone for a few minutes while I fed the vultures. Instead, I ended up being their meal. Wicker's a good cop, but he hasn't been the same since Joe and Pete were gunned down. It was hard for me to suspend him. And at that moment, it was even harder not to strangle him when he told me Stone killed himself while he was on the crapper. I tell you, Bob, I wish you were still here. I really need your help and guidance."

"Don't beat yourself up too much more. I'm not sure I would've handled the situation any different or better. Now, let's get down to business. Doug here has been searching for Ms. DeMure long before Melvin Anderson's death…"

Bob gave him a quick rundown of the investigation, suspicions, and theories thus far.

"Curitall, huh?" said Don. "I lost a shit-ton of money on DNX because of that drug."

"It gets weirder," said Thorfinnson. "Seems the creator of the drug disappeared along with twelve of his assistants shortly after the FDA banned further testing…"

"… and my investment went to pennies on the dollar," Don scoffed. "Sorry—go on." He sucked air through his nose, shook his head, scrunched his lips, and exhaled.

"Well, apparently, the drug's designer, Albert Caine, signed a contract with an unnamed laboratory and left his wife and kids the next day. He wasn't heard from again until…"

"What? You're kidding. Dr. Albert Caine? That bastard and his bitch, Antonia D'Amato, lured us into the courthouse at the start of the lockdown, then had their Black Beret goons lock us up in the jail museum for two days without food, water, or access to facilities. It was disgusting in there by the time the National Guard released us." He looked at Roberts. "Yeah, lucky you. You were already gone when your replacement's shit hit the old wooden floor."

"Yeah, I heard what happened to you guys," said Roberts. "I've also heard Caine's story several times on the news, but we didn't connect Melvin Anderson's death to Albert Caine's new job. We also spoke with Francis Pickens this afternoon and told him the same thing we told you. He suspects the Mender boy and Melvin Anderson's deaths are connected. The theory only sounds crazy until you start connecting dots."

When Thorfinnson was sure Roberts was finished, he asked, "Deputy Glickman…"

"Seriously, call me Don."

"Okay, Don, um, can you tell me about Kenneth Prattle's death and the state of Suzanne Mender's body when you found it?"

Don sighed and felt sick as he rubbed his clean-shaven chin. "Yeah, sure. I didn't see the reporter's body, but I got a good description from our town's doctor when I spoke to him Tuesday night. He arrived on the scene shortly before being called into the medical center to treat Wicker's and Stone's gunshot wounds. He found Prattle in the bathroom of the Earth First Food Market a few blocks from here. The condition of Prattle's body was similar to

Francis's description of Melvin Anderson when he got to the scene outside Grayson on September second. I suppose it's possible that Prattle was exposed to Ms. DeMure somewhere in town, especially since we still don't know who was helping her or where she was hiding. But there's no shadow of a doubt that Prattle came into contact with Mender less than an hour before he died. His fiancé—you know that annoying fame monster, Kristen Kettlemeyer?"

Roberts nodded.

"Well, she said Prattle complained of a burning sensation where Mender touched him shortly before complaining of stomach cramps. Ahh, but I'm sure you heard about it on the news. Anyway, when I told Dr. Boyd that Suzanne Mender's corpse was undergoing *accelerated necrolysis*, he said he suspected Alex's death was related to Prattle's and that Ryan was the source of infection of all three, as well as the chopper pilots who crash-landed near the massacre site. Like Pickens, Dr. Boyd doesn't believe Alex Mender died of so-called Ebola-Colorado, but he can't understand why Prattle's symptoms were so different from the boy's. It would've been nice if Dr. Boyd could've examined Alex's body again, but Helix Eternal Laboratories moved his corpse to an undisclosed location the same day he died."

"Hmmm," murmured Thorfinnson, rubbing a finger over his lip. "If... if Dr. Boyd and Coroner Pickens are right about Mender having the same abilities as Ms. DeMure, how did he survive direct contact on September first? I mean, if she had this deadly touch like Mender demonstrated with Prattle, he would've been dead in less than an hour."

"Well, you have your theories, and I have mine. You read much?" asked Don.

"Yes. Well, no. Sometimes. Depends what it is. Why?" asked Thorfinnson.

"Well, if you haven't already done so, you need to read Nathan Miller's novel, *The Menders: A First American Story*. It's about Ryan Mender's family tree and not just Norine Jasmine Jones's, which everybody and their dog and/or cat—or if they have a guinea pig—knows."

"I've heard of it. I know several people who've read it—my wife is one of them. She's probably the biggest Norine Jones fan there is… or at least that I've known for over thirty years. She said it's a great read, but I haven't had a chance to check it out."

"Well, you should. One of the best books I've ever read. But then Miller is a master. That's just my opinion, but that's not important. What is important is that the book contains the history of the blended Mender family. A lot of good stories, but one in particular, I didn't believe until last January. It was about a nineteenth-century Ute medicine man/healer named Healing Hands. To this day, he's still a legend among the Utes and other southwestern tribes. Even enemies and victims of the Utes still speak of him with reverence. Healing Hands was Ryan Mender's great-great-great-grandfather. According to the legend, the healer could absorb and consume illnesses, including cancers, and even resurrect the dead. In doing so, he made his patients healthy and whole again and became stronger every time he cured or resurrected someone. After Healing Hands died, no one in Mender's line had shown any healing potential until Ryan resurrected his son and cured his leukemia."

Thorfinnson's head cocked back and his eyes narrowed.

"I know. I know. It sounds far-fetched. But the boy was dead—clinically dead. And there were a bunch of witnesses who saw Alex die in his father's arms and then come back to life and walk on his own. And nothing, I mean nothing, was helping that boy's cancer before the end came. Even his oncologist was so surprised by the boy's recovery and complete remission that he believed Ryan was one of the healers described in Miller's book."

"Healers?" Thorfinnson scoffed. "That's hard to swallow. Then again, what I saw in Grayson, I wouldn't have believed had Coroner Pickens not shown me the photos and the video of Anderson's corpse. The possibility that a human could be weaponized to kill with a simple touch is a bit of a mind-bender as well. So, hypothetically speaking, if by chance Mender is a so-called *healer*," he said with finger quotations, "then theoretically he may have cured Ms. DeMure. If so, why couldn't he save or resurrect his son and wife? Also, if Mender is infected, he must've consumed whatever Ms. Demure was afflicted with and is now the carrier. All I can think is somehow, the process initiated by Curitall, which Mender corrected within DeMure, must've corrupted his ability to save lives. And if she learned she'd infected the man who'd rescued her and that Mender had cured her, she might've gone to his house to warn him and his wife if he was still unaware."

Don's brows furrowed.

"Hey, look, I feel like I know this woman. It sounds like something she would do. Then again, I could be wrong about everything. It's all speculation, and it's all nuts."

"Maybe not. When I spoke to Bob, I forgot to mention that Colonel Stone confessed that she was at the Watchtower at the time of the attack."

"Yeah, Pickens told us," said Roberts.

"Well, did he also tell you she was the whole reason the observation post was set up at the Fitzgeralds' in the first place?"

"Uhhh, no… Francis didn't mention that," said Thorfinnson.

"Well, Colonel Stone said that Martin Rice killed the family to get rid of witnesses and was following orders from some unnamed General. But Rice did a lot more to Jeremiah Fitzgerald than just kill him. It was almost like he was re-enacting what Morgan Bell did to Horace Greenly. But I figure you already know the story of Dr. Morgan Bell."

"Actually, not until Bob told me on the drive down."

Don raised a brow and looked at Roberts.

Roberts shrugged and said, "Yeah, he'd never heard of Morgan Bell."

"That's not exactly true," said Thorfinnson. "I heard about on him on the news before we flew to Colorado."

"But you didn't know the story of Morgan Bell? Huh. Wow." Don scratched under his nose and asked, "Did Bob tell you that Jeremiah was related to Horace and that the Greenly family murders occurred near the Fitzgerald home?"

"Yeah, he mentioned it."

"Now, if that isn't a totally messed up coincidence, I don't know what is. Anyway, Stone, Rice, and another operative named Jim Stevens waited there until Ms. DeMure made contact with Mender after the lockdown. There was a fourth named Hunter Harrison, but Jeremiah killed him when he found the Black Berets in his home. Stone and Stevens buried Hunter in the backyard. Okay…" Don took a deep breath, exhaled, and continued. "So, let's just say Mender has some kind of deadly touch, and Ms. DeMure lost hers.

It still doesn't explain the blue powder explosive device that was deployed during the assault. DeMure or Mender must've deployed it since it would've made no sense for the contractors to bring such a dangerous weapon for a snatch-and-grab op.

"But even before the bomb went off, booby traps inside the house—heavy machine guns mounted behind paintings, poison-laced nail bombs—crazy, crazy shit, just happened to come alive and explode, taking out a couple dozen contractors. Not to mention three pop-up pill towers outside with more concealed machine guns and RPGs that killed several more outside and downed three Black Hawks. I assume that the hi-tech Blue Bomb finished off any reinforcements. But not all the dead were killed by the home defense system or the bomb. Some were shot at close range, and one was decapitated. You gotta understand—according to Stone, these were highly skilled contractors, and the ones Stone ID'd were decorated and respected ex-Rangers, SEALs, and Marines. How could two people hope to have a chance against these guys unless they were prepared and working with Brigham Norsworthy's Minutemen as the Governor and the President have been led to believe?"

"You got me," said Thorfinnson as Roberts rubbed his chin and held a pensive expression.

"Well, so far, Mender and Demure's remains haven't been found or identified. And until they are, we have to assume they're on the run together. That makes Mender look even worse since his wife Suzanne was found dead in their bedroom from the same thing that killed Anderson and apparently Prattle, and probably their son. If they're on the run, they would most likely have gone west or south. Currently, all roads in those directions are closed for the season, and exits and trailheads are being closely monitored. Still, they have a two day start."

Thorfinnson nodded and said, "Yeah…" He rubbed his lips. "There are a lot of unanswered questions… that's for sure. Would you mind if Bob and I looked through the crime scene photos, including those from the Fitzgerald's? Also, I'd like to watch Stone's confession."

Don scoffed. "Homeland Security took everything. They didn't want to take any chances of us losing evidence after we lost their only witness. Assholes. But…" He swiveled to face the desktop and clicked the file icon at the bottom toolbar. "… I made digital copies of everything, including the audio-only second half of the interrogation."

Roberts shot Thorfinnson a curious glance.

Don shrugged. "Hey, I had to improvise after Wicker dropped Jones's camcorder. I used Pete's old micro-cassette recorder and dubbed it onto his computer with a desktop mic. A bit archaic, but it worked. The audio isn't great, but you can understand everything that nut job said." He sighed. "I'm with you guys—there's more to this than some trumped-up conspiracy about a dead man's militia group trying to overthrow the government. Oh, and welcome to my nightmare. Well, I'll let you boys enjoy the photos and Stone's show while I go get a cup of coffee. I don't want to see those pictures again. Oh, and I almost forgot—I made a bunch of notes and a timeline of the day and left them in a Word doc in the interrogation file. Anyway, call me when you're done, or come over to the courthouse. I'll be in the breakroom. Oh, and Bob, I got something for you," he said and shuffled through a drawer. He removed a crucifix attached to a silver necklace, rosary beads, and paperbacks of Stephen King's *Carrie* and *The Dark Tower*. "You left these when you moved."

"Thanks. Figured they got lost," said Roberts as Thorfinnson eyed his partner.

"Hey, I'm a backslidden Catholic," Roberts said with a shrug.

Don chuckled and stood. "Well, you boys have fun," he said and stepped out.

Thirty-One

Late afternoon, Thursday, October 4, 2007. Mears County Courthouse.

Don moved down the hall with a grimacing glance at the locked door to the jail museum. On it was a sign that read CLOSED UNTIL FURTHER NOTICE attached to a cross of yellow police tape. Below it was a second notice—AUTHORIZED PERSONNEL ONLY—with a Homeland Security symbol.

Don entered the breakroom and filled a Broncos mug half full with the house blend. He reached under the sink for a half-filled black labeled bottle. Before Tuesday, he hadn't touched a drop in years. Since then, he'd done his best to act sober.

He unscrewed the cap and took a decent pull. He savored the burn and filled the cup to the rim.

"Hey, I thought you didn't drink," came Guzman's voice.

Don turned to see the new guy. He was wearing his deputy-starred cowboy hat. Like Tolliver and Lombardi, he was now full-time.

"Sorry. It's been a rough couple of days. Just needed something to cut the edge."

"No worries. Don't let those assholes get to you. I know you were trying to do a good job in an impossible situation."

"Thanks, Guzman. Do me a favor—keep this between us."

"Of course. Hey, it'll get better in time, you know. We're all hurting, so never feel like you're alone."

They locked eyes. Guzman patted Don's shoulder. Don nodded and Guzman filled his coffee cup and left.

Don sat at the table, sipped his first spiked java in a few hours, and stared at a blank wall for thirty minutes.

"You wouldn't by chance have James Mender's phone number?" asked Thorfinnson, startling Don. He looked down at the empty cup.

"Of course. Leth me get it for you," Don said with a lubricated lisp.

Thorfinnson and Roberts followed him to the sheriff's office where Don flipped through Pete's Rolodex to *M* and read the number as Doug wrote on a sticky note.

"So, wad… so, wad did you think of Stone's confession?" asked Don.

"We haven't had a chance to watch the video or listen to the recording yet."

Don concentrated on clear speech and said, "I warn you, that guy is batshit crazy, but he's good. I found myself slipping into his dilutions—I mean, delusions—a few times. I thought he was working on an insanity plea, but then he… he hung himself. Yeah, I told you that… on the phone last night. Now, I'm not so sure what's real. I feel like I'm slipping myself."

Roberts nodded, and said, "It's okay. I understand."

Thorfinnson added, "Yeah, I feel the same way after what I've seen and the conversations today. Bob and I will let you know what we think. Maybe we'll find some truth in between the delusions. By the way, anything good to eat in town? My stomach's grumbling. I just remembered Bob and I haven't eaten since our layover in Denver."

"Mama Maria's Sou…" Don stopped at the sight of Robert's somber face.

"Damn shame," said Roberts. "Mender's restaurant was the best in town. I guess we can go to Dr. Bell's and get you one of those *Cannibal Burgers* I was telling you about," he added, his aspect recovering quickly and brightening as he smiled and made *woo-haha* hands.

"Is there any place else?" asked Thorfinnson. "After that story on the way down and looking at those photos… nothing remotely related to Bell sounds appealing."

"Suit yourself, but *do not knock it until you have tried it,*" Roberts said with the accent, a wink, and a wicked grin. "There's another good place up the street I think you'll like. Don, you wanna join us? You could probably use something to eat after all that coffee you been drinking. We'll come back in an hour or so. Then we can watch and listen to that madman's confession together and eat some popcorn."

"I'd love to, but I have some things… some things I'm working on. I'll see you guys later."

Thirty-Two

After dark, Thursday, October 4, 2007. The Maxwell House.

Deputy Michael Wicker's mortal shell hugged Wicker's mother-in-law, Patsy, and kissed his wife, Mandy, at the door, and then went to his black Jeep. Morgan threw a black duffle in the back, climbed in the new age box seat, and waved. The fair ladies smiled and waved back and then Morgan drove off like he knew what he was doing. Once out of sight, he made a call.

The blood-spattered phone connected, and in his thick Alabaman accent, Morgan asked, "General sir, what would you have for me to do right now?"

"Something you will enjoy. We are sending you on another chaos mission," said the General. "The Curator has instructed you to do what you do best and have fun doing it. Also, when or if you are caught, dispatch the deputy's shell immediately."

Morgan guffawed and said, "Trust me, before I am through with Michael Dwayne Wicker, I will have done for the police what my friend and fellow demon, John Wayne Gacy, did for clowns."

Morgan continued north and slowed just south of the *Welcome to Mears County* sign. He flipped off the headlights and pulled into the driveway to the right belonging to Eugene and Charlotte Lee. Everyone in town knew that Eugene was the nephew of Brigham Norsworthy, but more importantly, his wife, Charlotte, was the great-great-granddaughter of none other than Horace Greenly, another descendant Morgan wished to cross off his list. But this would be a special flavor of revenge. It was a half-mile east, across the Bridger Ravine, that he had hung and swung until he was dead. It was also there that the town desecrated his mortal shell. Morgan still smarted over that.

The dining room light was on. Morgan could see two people through the front window sitting at the opposite ends of the table enjoying their dinner, though their unpleasant faces might lead one to believe otherwise. The one on the right was a rotund woman, overdressed and wearing too much makeup for the hour. The one on the left was a scrawny shriveled-up specimen in a red mackinaw long-sleeve picking his teeth with his finger.

Morgan stepped from the Jeep, opened the back door, unzipped the duffle bag, and retrieved a black hoodie and black sweatpants. He removed the Broncos jersey, and put on the hoodie and sweats. He shoved the jersey into the bag, closed it, and retrieved a Ginsu knife from a side pocket. He regarded the blade in the light from the front window. He turned it slowly as if twisting it in a liver, and grinned at the glints off the fine steel.

He put the knife back in the duffle, moved the bag to the front seat, and retrieved the tranquilizer pistol from the glove box which he'd swiped from Rice's mortal shell. He chambered the first dart and slipped the pistol into the hoodie's front pouch. Morgan unlatched the backseat and pulled the backrests forward for his oversized load. He closed the door ever so gently and opened the back end. He unfolded a large blue tarp and spread it over the bed. He left the back open, went to the front door, and rang the bell.

After ding-donging several times, Mr. Lee yelled something about a "Goddamn asshole" at the front door. Morgan heard angry huffing and more expletives before the scrawny-specimen of the house opened up and looked like he meant harmful business.

"What the hell do you wa…" Mr. Lee stopped in mid-syllable as his scowl softened to a look of confusion. His jaw dropped enough to see his tongue and a piece of meat stuck between his teeth. His eyes widened as he saw the gun. Morgan fired into his chest and followed the dart with a fist hammer between the eyes just for fun. Mr. Lee hit the foyer floor with a *THUD*.

"Eugene, what in damnation is going on in there?" snarled Charlotte as Wicker's mortal shell entered the dining room.

"Michael Wicker, what in tarnation do you think you're doin'? You put that gun down right now!" she scolded like Wicker was some young whippersnapper whose hide she was about to tan.

Morgan cocked the deputy's head sideways and said in an over the top, demonic drawl, "Mrs. Lee, Mikey's not here right now." He fired a dart into a buxom bosom.

Mrs. Lee fainted and her face slammed into a heaping helping of pork chops, mashed potatoes, and gravy.

Thirty-Three

Eugene opened his eyes. His head hurt *really* bad. He tried to move and realized he was taped to a wooden chair. Flickering lantern light across the room barely brightened in a what appeared to be a small cabin. He blinked several times to clear his vision. It didn't help much. Still, he could tell he was in a small living area and could make out an open door to a bedroom. He was cooking hot—sweating like a pig. To his right, a wood-burning stove crackled, and flame figures jigged and jagged beyond the tempered glass. A large blurry silhouette sat facing him in a chair a few feet away. Orange and yellow light pranced and skipped with shadows over the body, surrounding floor, and the ceiling. The large form was slouched forward with head down and chin resting on a wide chest. As Eugene's head cleared, his eyes went wide with horror. The silhouette was Charlotte. He tried to scream, but his mouth was taped shut.

As he tried to wriggle free, his gaze was drawn to a kitchenette table where Deputy Michael Wicker sat with perfect posture with his face lit up with lantern light. He was dressed in a Broncos jersey and was delicately chewing something. He had a fork in one hand and a wine glass in the other. A dark bottle, a large kitchen knife, and a revolver sat by the plate in front of him. Wicker swirled the glass, sniffed, drank, and swallowed. The deputy closed his eyes. He seemed to really be enjoying whatever he was eating and that made Eugene's stomach growl. He remembered that the sonuvabitch had interrupted his dinner when he shot and punched him. Eugene's nose throbbed. He had no doubt it was broken. He looked at Charlotte again, forgot about his stomach, and realized he was too damn scared to think about eating.

Wicker set the glass down, picked up a large knife, sliced another piece of meat, and raised the fork to his mouth. He laid the morsel on his tongue and closed his lips. Eugene's stomach growled again as Wicker chewed slowly and made exaggerated sounds of delight. Wicker set the knife down and took another sip of wine without swirling or sniffing this time.

Eugene glanced again at Charlotte and saw dark liquid dripping from her left arm. He squinted and saw that a large slice of upper muscle had been removed. His gaze shot back to Wicker as the deputy began cutting another bite, and began frantically murmuring in an effort to say "Oh, my God, oh, my God, oh, my God. I don't want to be eaten. I don't want to be eaten." His chest tightened and sharp pains shot down his left arm.

Deputy Wicker looked Eugene's way. He smiled as he chewed. He swallowed and said in a southern drawl that matched Charlotte's, "Ahh, now if it is not Prince Charmin' awake from his slumba. Did you sleep well?"

Eugene mumbled a continuation of his previous ramblings and wondered why Wicker was talking that way since he was from Colorado where folks had no accent.

"I am sorry," said Wicker, "but I cannot understand what it is that you are sayin', so why don't you just sit back and relax for now. There will be plenty of time for screamin' or cryin' or whatever you would like to do before I kill ya. After all, we cannot begin this ritual until your sweetheart awakes. I do apologize, though. I was so famished I could not wait. She is quite delectable with a dash of salt and pepper." Wicker cut another piece and raised the fork for Eugene to see. "You are welcome to try some of her if you would like."

Eugene tried to scream again, but only a muffled symphony of dread and anguish escaped. Sweat cascaded from his forehead and mixed with fresh tears. He struggled to break free as his efforts were greeted with rolling laughter.

"Now, this is goin' to be fun," Wicker said as his smile turned sinister in the lantern light.

Thirty-Four

Late night, Thursday, October 4, 2007. Deputy Wicker's cabin.

Morgan watched as Mrs. Lee lifted her head and acknowledged her sweety across from her. Her head went to flopping and she started wiggling and jiggling beneath her adhesive bindings as she mur-mur-murmured under the tape covering her mouth.

"Wait, wait. Keep up that anger. It makes the meat taste so much better," he said as he grabbed a knife and moved like a tom cat pouncing on a mouse. He leaned in to slice her.

Mrs. Lee swung forward and hit him like a cinder block. A Fourth of July spectacular went off in Wicker's head. Mrs. Lee's noggin rebounded and the chair tipped backward, slammed to the floor, and shattered under her substantial girth.

Morgan shook off the blow and said, "Alrighty, all mighty, I am excited now," he exclaimed as Mrs. Lee thrashed to free herself. "You are one ornery cuss. Not a frightened little philly like Horace was. Oh, and if you are wondering why you will be dying after I eat you alive—well, you can thank your great-great-granddaddy for that. I know it is not your fault that you have some of Horace's blood coursing through your veins. But it is my solemn duty to eradicate his line from this reality. And it has been good having friends in low places to help me in my quest from beyond the grave."

Morgan grabbed her permed blonde hair, and it came off in his hand, exposing baldness. He looked at the wig, smirked, and dropped it in the blood puddle. He left her there, grabbed a new chair, and set it next to the broken one. He licked his lips, and approached her with the knife. She gasped and closed her eyes as he punched her in the face.

Thirty-Five

Charlotte smiled wide as visions of long lines of eager customers danced like sugar plums through her head. It was hard to believe that her little coffee shop had gone so far so quickly as she picked up a fancy pen to ink that fat contract at the Starbucks' corporate table for her hostile takeover. Soon the whole world would be clawing down the doors of her humble establishments all over God's creation for a taste of gustatory perfection and a dash of heaven.

"Wakey, wakey, darlin'," came a pleasant southern voice from above.

She looked around at the corporate types and said, "No. No. I have to sign the contract."

SMACK.

The dream bubble popped and her eyes shot open as her cheek caught fire. With a flick of a wrist, tape was torn from her mouth. She saw Michael Wayne Wicker standing in front of her.

"Oww, you sonuvagun. To Hell with you, Michael Wicker. I have had all the guff I'm gonna take from you," she hollered as she worked herself into a frenzy to free a leg or an arm or whatever to give that whippersnapper what he deserved and a little more.

Wicker guffawed and lost his breath. He tried to speak, but couldn't on account of continued chuckles that made Charlotte madder than a wet hen.

Wicker bent down for something and Charlotte's leg came loose and her foot connected with his face. "Oww," she and he both said as lightning pain shot from her toe to the top of her skull, and Wicker stumbled back as twin fountains erupted from his nose.

Wicker snarled and yelled, "You harlot!" He stood straight and proper as the jersey soaked up scarlet. He huffed and puffed, shook his head, and backhanded her.

Thirty-Six

Eugene's eyes went wide as Charlotte's head hit the floor hard enough to split a coconut but not quite hard enough to split her head. His eyes watered but he wasn't sure if it was tears or sweat rolling down his cheeks.

Wicker's face shot his way. "Are you crying?" he asked with a mocking grin. He guffawed and spat blood as more leaked from his nose and dribbled and dripped from his chin. He licked his lips. Wicker returned his attention to Charlotte and finished taping her legs to the new chair, and then set her upright.

Charlotte came to, shook her head, and roared, "Michael Dwayne Wicker, you crazy son of a bitch!"

"Ahh, do not be so hard on Michael's mother. I am sure she had some delightful qualities. I am sorry I did not formally introduce myself. Believe it or not, I am not usually this rude. But you have already heard of me. I am a legend in this town, thanks to your great-great-grandfather. My name is Dr. Morgan Bell. And don't be too hard on poor Michael. He is unaware of what I am doing with his mortal shell, but he will get the blame, and his family will get the shame. I can tell by the look on your face that you are a might bit puzzled."

"You… You are insane!" Charlotte said as Eugene observed Wicker's back.

"Yes, and no, and most people would say *yesss*. But frankly, Mrs. Lee, I do not believe you give a damn and just want to live more than a few more days. Unfortunately, that is not going to happen. But as for your sweet Mr. Lee, I only eat Greenlys, so he is going to have to die now."

Wicker went to the table, grabbed the pistol, and strolled to Eugene.

Eugene shook his head back and forth as if it would stop a bullet. The twinges in his chest intensified. It felt like someone had reached inside him and was squeezing his heart like a stress ball.

Wicker placed the gun barrel to his temple, and cocked the hammer.

Eugene regarded Charlotte with a look he hadn't shared since their wedding day.

Charlotte's demeanor changed. The anger was gone. "No, please. You don't have to do this," she said with quivering lips.

"NO, NO, NO, NO. None of this fear and sorrow. I want anger. I never get an angry meal, dagnabbit!"

Thirty-Seven

Wicker continued ranting, but Charlotte wasn't listening. She was thinking how uncomfortably warm she was—like she was being roasted alive. She hoped she'd been good enough in this life to avoid a place that was a lot warmer. She thought about her Starbucks dreams and realized there would be no hostile takeover. She also wondered what her nephew, Francis Pickens, would do with all the money she'd left him as a surprise. She hoped that God had windows in heaven so she could watch Francis's pudgy little face when he learned he wouldn't have to sell coffins for a living anymore. She smiled. Surely that good deed would guarantee her a golden mansion on a hill in the hereafter. She sighed, eyed the floor, and spied the stove's iron kindling shelf. It was slightly to the left, a few feet away. Her gaze fell on Eugene and she mouthed, *I love you.*

His sad peepers seemed to reply, "*I know.*"

She glared back at Wicker and tore into him, "Michael Dwayne Wicker, you can go to Hell, you people-eating son of a bitch. You like this? Well, you ain't eatin' Charlotte Lee alive."

She violently rocked forward to the left. As she fell, she jerked her head back, and then forcefully forward.

Thirty-Eight

Morgan's mouth fell open as Mrs. Lee's head hit the shelf. It didn't bend as her skull gave way, bounced up, and slammed cheek down on the floor. A red pool quickly followed. He ran to her, but she was already dead. "Well, dammit. Now the meat is just ruined." He glared at Mr. Lee with the blackest hate, pointed the Colt 45 Peacemaker, and then uncocked the hammer. He lowered the piece. "I suppose you will have to do."

Mr. Lee gasped for breath and turned deadly blue.

Morgan rushed to him and ripped the tape from his mouth, but it was too late. Wicker's nostrils flared as Morgan glowered at the dead man. His jaw clenched and he ground his teeth as he rumbled like a baby volcano about to be born. His hands trembled and words erupted, "ARE Y'ALL KIDDIN' ME?"

He roared and kicked the dead man's chest. The chair fell like a sprung mouse trap and rattled the window sills. Morgan stomped to the 45, turned to the warm corpse, and emptied the cylinder. He dropped the gun, picked up the knife, and returned to Mr. Lee. He frowned down as pressure built for a second eruption. He huffed and puffed like a bull who'd seen red. And there was a lot of it, all around. It covered him and dripped from his chin onto Mr. Lee. He snarled. "HOW DARE YOU DIE ON ME!" he hollered.

He fell to his knees, and went berserk, plunging the knife in and out of Mr. Lee's chest. Again and again—shredding flesh and cartilage and breaking ribs with such ferocity that the thick knife stuck in the floor several times and bent.

Morgan stopped after stabbing Mr. Lee's spent shell more times than anyone would ever be able to count. He panted hard, sweating blood, as he gritted and ground his teeth behind trembling lips. He writhed with uncapped fury. His head ticked as one eye twitched. He wiped below that eye and felt something wet other than splatter. His gaze bore down on the finger. "What is this? I am no crier. I am far beyond grieving for you, Jefferson." Morgan's demon spirit was the embodiment of hate and had no time for sorrow. He wiped his eyes and examined another borrowed tear, savoring it with bitter ecstasy as he rubbed it between his fingers. He dipped his pointer into Mr. Lee's ground-up heart, removed it, and watched blood dribble down Wicker's palm and forearm. He sat back on his knees, beheld his handiwork, and smiled at the grimacing death mask before him. He looked again at the finger and dipped it once more in the chest's gaping maw.

He stood and went to Mrs Lee's corpse. It was still secured to the chair. He kicked her over onto her back, knelt, and examined the bruise around her forehead's split-skin-indentation. He cocked his head to the side as he drew a heart around the bruise with Mr. Lee's blood. He tilted his neck the other way and saw Mrs. Lee's wig sopping up red sauce. He snagged it and replaced it on her bald head, and let her rest not so peacefully, looking like a plus-size southern belle.

He regarded Mr. Lee's mortal husk. "Now, isn't that sweet?" He chuckled lightly, then not so lightly, until it became rolling, hardy belly laughter that made him fight to catch Wicker's breath. When the wind of borrowed lungs returned, he wiped the bent blade on a clean part of Mrs. Lee's blouse and surveyed the meaty shoulder that was no longer oozing. "What a shame. Will not be nearly as tasty, but…" He sighed. "… a Greenlys, a Greenly."

Thirty-Nine

Eugene was stuck in a terrible dream. Try as he might, he couldn't wake up. It seemed so real as he watched a man that he'd seen in photos at the Mears County Historical Society repeatedly stab a body that looked like his own. If fact, Eugene felt like he, himself, was in one of those yellowish black and white photos. Weird. And then there was everything that happened since he opened the door to that Goddamn nightmare, Michael Wicker. It gave him chills, though he felt neither warm nor cold within the terror. At least it would be morning soon, and then he could drink to numb it all away.

He started to weep as he watched the same man, who, just moments before, had Michael Wicker's face, draw a bloody heart around the bruise on Charlotte's forehead. The man mouthed something at his corpse, laughed without sound, and started carving slices off her shoulder with the ruined kitchen knife.

Eugene scanned the room. He glanced down, and his and Charlotte's corpses were gone, along with the face-changing psychopath who murdered them in this God-awful dream. All the blood was gone, too. It seemed so real... and familiar. Strangely familiar but different. He wasn't making any sense, but how often did dreams make sense... or good ones come true?

"I'm sorry I'm late," came a deeply apologetic, grandfatherly voice.

Eugene spun and saw a pale man that made him look young. His white hair was tucked uncomfortably under a black Stetson. He wore a matching open trench coat over a black shirt unbuttoned at the collar. His pants and fancy boots were black as well.

"Neither of your Underspirits needed to see that," said the Man in Black. "I tell you—these work-ins are killing me and my sister keeps adding more." He sighed. "I've tried to correct the problem, but Fate blames it on unreliable forecasts from our sister Destiny's department."

Eugene scratched his head and said, "This is hands down the worst nightmare I've ever had. When I wake up, I swear on my mother's grave I'll never drink again. Okay, maybe a shot or two to calm my nerves, but nothing after that. And I'll be nice to everyone, and go to church more."

"Eugene Jonah Lee, first off, this is not a dream, and second, I regret to inform you that you're dead."

"Whaaa..."

The Man in Black held up a finger.

Eugene's mouth slammed shut. He tried to open it but couldn't.

"Please don't interrupt. That's rude. Now, I understand that dying can be disorienting, especially in the horrible manner in which you and your wife passed. So, introductions are in order. My name is Morton Death, but you probably know me better as the Grim Reaper. And grim doesn't begin to describe my job."

Eugene felt his lips loosen up. "Well, Goddammit, this is bullshit. If I hadn't been tied up, I would've kicked Michael Wicker's ass," said Eugene. He punched his palm. "Oh, well... What's done is done. I guess I'll have to make the best of it. So, how do I get to Heaven from here?"

Three black doors appeared, but only the middle door was open.

"Regretfully, that door is locked."

Eugene's bravado evaporated and he whimpered, "No. No, I don't wanna go to the bad place."

"Not to worry, you're not going there either. Lucky for you, your war stories were made up. And lying's not a prosecutable offense, nor is making the lives of mortal shells, unfortunate enough to be around you, miserable. That just makes you an insufferable bastard. No, you get another chance to be a better man or woman or..."

"What the H-E-double-hockey-sticks are you talking about?" Eugene said as he glared at Death, "I... I was a war hero!"

"Hmm. No, you weren't."

"The hell I wasn't!"

"Umm, no—no, you weren't. You have to understand—in the Afterworld, things are not exactly like you've been led to believe. Not all heroes go to heaven, and not all villains go to Hell. Needless to say, you are neither. I reviewed your file before entering your White Room. I know everything about you. It's part of the reason I was late. So, calm down. You're getting another chance to not be such a self-serving curmudgeon on your next turn of the Wheel. Look, I'm not gonna argue with you. You need to go through the middle door now. Like always, I have a lot of work to do, and thanks to you and your wife, I'm behind schedule. So, if you wouldn't mind..." Death gave Eugene an impatient smile and extended a hand toward the open door. "Once you pass through, walk straight until you to *get to Samsara Station. And remember, like I've warned your Underspirits umpteen Timethies before..."*

"Huh?"

"Of course, you don't remember, so I'll tell you again. Karma will not put up with your Underspirit's crap. If you want a chance to improve your lot on your next turn, you best keep on her good side. Know this and remember it well—if you cross that little Eternal, she can be very vindictive. You know what vindictive means, right?"

"Yeah—I'm not stupid. Karma's a bitch," said Eugene.

"You got that right."

Eugene looked at his sepia yellow tennis shoes, and then at Death. He started to speak, but stopped. What was the point? He looked away, dropped his chin, and stepped through the middle door. It slammed shut.

Inside was a strangely familiar, extremely long hall that seemed to go on forever. Heeding Death's warning, Eugene kept quiet and tried not to think how pissed he was with his current situation. He had no way of knowing if Karma could read minds like the Grim Reaper could review his life.

Eugene walked for what seemed like days... or had it been months or years? He lost track but eventually he entered a massive waiting room that reminded him of New York's Grand Central Station. He remembered visiting there once when he was young; yet, this station was many times larger.

Beyond the entrance was a large wooden, ornately carved archway. Beneath the archway was a small kiosk and a sign that read, *Take a Number*. From the archway he could see the snaking lines waiting for their turn with Karma. He nodded and scrunched his lips. He tried not to think of the daunting wait ahead of him and escaped to his less unhappy place, like he would when he was a little guy and the bullies would use him as a punching bag or a door mat.

He looked around. The station was one of the finest places he… he could vaguely remember seeing at least once or more. Its walls were carved and sculpted and lined with statues that he suspected were famous people from around the world. He didn't recognize most of them and many of the statues he suspected were of heathen gods, goddesses, and other pagan monstrosities. Above the statues were massive jumbotrons all tuned to a small, brown-skinned woman sitting at a desk reviewing a large stack of files. She was dressed colorfully like one might see in India. Not that Eugene knew more than what he'd seen on television or in photos at that Indian restaurant Charlotte had dragged him to once for her birthday. That was about all the culture he could stand, and after that, he'd insisted on good ol' 'Merican food.

He studied the number dispenser and noticed there wasn't a number on the tongue of paper sticking out. "Hmmm" he murmured, careful to heed Death's warning and watched his mouth and brain as he pondered, *Does a ghost have a brain?*

He shrugged and tore off a ticket. He looked at both sides, but it was blank. He flipped it again and numbers began to appear, faint at first, and then bold and screaming *1,234,567,890*. He smacked his forehead and said, "Ahhh, noo. No. This is bullshit!"

He slapped a hand over his mouth and looked up at the screens. The small woman was peering down on all of them, her brown eyes piercing through Eugene like the knife his murderer used to send him to the station. She rolled her eyes, frowned, and shuffled through several files. When she found the one she was looking for, she opened it, and made some notes. He smiled slyly and laughed softly. She closed the file and returned to the one she was reviewing before the disturbance.

Eugene glared at the big number as if staring hard enough would knock the last nine numbers off the ticket. As he continued looking at the number, memories began seeping into whatever passed for his ghost brain. Odd memories that didn't make any sense. Memories of other people's lives... *Or were they?* There were even animal recollections which made him feel sorry for all the dogs and cats and other critters he'd kicked or done much worse to. More and more memories seeped into Eugene until his ghost felt like a faltering dam about to bust. As memories mounted, puzzle pieces of the lives began to fit together until he came upon a certain memory. It was a memory of a recurrent dream or a feeling that had stuck in the craw of his consciousness whenever he'd been near the Howard Creek Bridge or sat inside Mama Maria's Southwestern Bar & Grill... or the Old Prospector before the Menders bought the place. Eugene's ghost eyes went wide and he gasped as he was sucked into the déjà vu.

Eugene's hands were tied behind his back. He felt a rope around his neck and tried to focus on the mountains around the creek... anything other than the town that he despised. As a breeze cooled the warm wetness of his tears, his focus faltered as his gaze strayed to the crowds on either side of a creek dressed in their Sunday best. He glanced at the wooden rail under his boots, and the rocks and water far below. He regarded the grinning faces and frowning ones with nodding heads and eyes that glared approval. Only one set of eyes was shedding tears. It was his father with his stylish curl and chin beard, wearing his favorite bowtie, his polka-dot vest, and his patched and slightly tattered black dress coat with large metal buttons. He was glowering fathomless hate at everyone around him. Eugene felt a push and fell for a long second. He felt sharp pain as his neck broke the fall but didn't snap. He struggled to breathe and flailed and spun. Eugene felt like his head might explode if his eyeballs didn't pop out first. He bounced against the bridge and saw another man hanging, motionless, beside him. The man was a half-breed Indian and Eugene's only friend. Light narrowed and spots appeared. As light winked out, Eugene remembered the name of the man hanging beside him; Buford Redman, and his own, Jefferson Bell.

Forty

Friday morning, October 5, 2007. Northside Lodge, Packer City, Colorado.

Doug sat at the motel room's desk. He felt drained. He hadn't slept well and had tossed and turned after staying up late watching and re-watching Stone's interrogation. Doug had dealt with his share of deranged suspects over the years, but there was something different and unsettling about the former Colonel gone insane. Luckily, Roberts used to work for the Boston PD and had been able to make some calls and pull some strings to obtain Stone's military and medical records (and more) on extreme short notice. Doug had just finished reading the last of the records and none of the emailed files contradicted what Stone's alter ego confided. Before joining the Black Berets in late July, Stone had been a decorated soldier with no history of mental instability. Something obviously must've been missed. He knew war could change a man, and there was no way of knowing everything he'd experienced. And if he was crazy, what made him choose a distant cousin of Adolf Hitler as his alternate personality?

Based on his experience and Stone's mannerisms, Doug suspected he would've flatlined a polygraph when asked questions about his imaginary, murdered Jewish wife, his job at Auschwitz/Birkenau, and his time working for Dr. Josef Mengele. The same would be true concerning Stone's visions of the Grim Reaper, of Hell, and of striking a deal with a demon named the Curator. Though it was far outside his jurisdiction, he believed understanding the Colonel was crucial to understanding the people who took Mary DeMure and Leonard Grimes. Doug knew he would just have to dig deeper and find Stone's dark side, if one existed; yet, based on his record, he'd been, both figuratively and literally, a Boy Scout. No, there had to be something else going on. But demon possession? Doug shook his head and scoffed. *I can't believe that. I won't believe that. But if not, what happened to you, Joshua?*

Doug threw on his coat, left Roberts snoring, and stepped outside with his camera. He sucked in mountain air, looked over the town, and clicked some photos. He lowered the camera to drink in his surroundings. He looked west and east at the lower snowcapped mountains, which were taller than Mount St. Helens used to be. He looked south to a pair rising above the others that were nearly as high as Mount Rainier. He loved the Pacific Northwest, but at that moment, Packer City was heavenly with its multicolored aspen-lined streets and Grayson River rolling south under the Northside Bridge. The place was an island among forgotten settlements that died when the gold and silver dried up. The fact that the town survived was a testament to those who stayed and kept it alive against all odds during the lean years. While it never returned to its glory days, Packer City had a rich history Doug planned to delve into when he had time. For now, he had to focus on the case and hope for a happy ending which seemed less likely again and something he didn't want to think about, not at *that* moment.

He slid the camera in his pocket and peered down the steep, shale-covered hill that separated Northside Lodge from Mount Capitol Suites. A dark brown man was pushing a laundry cart along the milky motel's single row of the sky-blue doors. The man looked up, smiled, and waved.

Doug waved back and asked, "Excuse me, where's a good place to get a cup of coffee?"

"Oh, I recommend Charlotte's Espresso. No one makes coffee better than Mrs. Lee. Her café is located five blocks south of here. From the bags under your eyes, I suggest her signature Frespresso. It will carry those bags away."

"Thanks—I'll take your advice. I'm pretty beat," Doug said with a croak as he scratched his morning shadow.

He stepped down a steep path, approached the man, and handed him a card. "My name is Detective Doug Thorfinnson of the Federal Way, Washington, Police Department."

"Nice to meet you. I am Rajesh Batra, the owner of Mount Capitol Suites. I used to live in Gresham, Oregon, before moving here. You are very far from home. What brought you to Packer City at this time of year? You do not look like a hunter."

"Well, I am, in a sense. I'm on the clock and looking for a woman who came up missing from my area about a year ago. I thought she was dead until she showed up in your town three days ago. I can't say anything else since her case is part of an ongoing Homeland Security investigation. But you probably know who I'm talking about. Her name is Mary DeMure."

Batra hesitated and then said, "Yes, I have seen her... on the news," he added with a slight stutter that tickled Doug's detective senses. "She looks like a very nice girl. I hope she is okay. I cannot believe she is responsible for killing Mr. Anderson."

"Yes—she is a nice young woman, or at least she was. Right now, some bad people are trying to find her. I heard on the news that she hid somewhere in town during the lockdown. I'd love to talk to whoever helped her. It would definitely help my search. Ms. DeMure is a friend of a friend of my daughter's. Anything they said would be off the record, of course."

"Hmmm. I wish I could help, but I do not speak to many people in town. If I hear something, I will call you." Mr. Batra glanced at the card. "Goodbye, Detective Thorfinnson. I have much work to do. Enjoy your coffee, and I hope you find your girl."

"Goodbye, Mr. Batra. Hopefully, I'll see you around."

Batra nodded and pushed his cart to the next room.

Doug turned and headed down another steep path. He couldn't shake the feeling that the motel owner knew more than he was saying. He made a mental note not to forget Rajesh Batra.

Charlotte's Espresso was closed when Doug arrived. He checked the sign for the posted hours. It read: *Charlotte's Espresso / Home of the World Famous Frespresso / Open Weekdays and Saturdays, 7 a.m. to 5 p.m. / Rain, Shine, or Snow / Closed on Sundays for our Lord and Savior.*

Doug waited fifteen minutes, gave up, and headed back to the motel. Roberts was dressed and brushing his teeth when he walked through the door.

Roberts spat and asked, "Where'd you go?"

"I tried to get some coffee, but the café by the school was closed."

"Charlotte's? No way. It's 8:06 a.m. and it's not Sunday. That's not like her. As long as I lived here, she always opened on time. She only closes on Sundays and during the dead months from November to February. But then everything except the country store and the gas station shutters for winter. Seriously, that woman rarely takes vacations or sick days when she needs them. Well, until recently. Not many people know this, and I only learned it second hand from someone who does, but she has cancer—lymphoma. Should already be pushing up daisies, but she's a fighter. As I understand it, she's still undergoing chemo in Denver but refuses to move closer since her family has deep roots here. They've lived in Mears County off and on since Packer City's founding. She's even related to Horace Greenly, and her husband is related to Brigham Norsworthy. Of course, she has a southern belle's accent because her parents left for a while. Wanted to see new horizons. So, she was raised in Alabama and only moved back here shortly before I moved here from Boston in '97, or maybe a little longer—I don't know. Besides her coffee and what I told you, I don't know her that well."

Doug furrowed his forehead after hearing what he considered an adequate biography.

"Well, as far as your dream cup of java goes, you're shit-outta-luck today," said Roberts. "She's probably headed to Denver for a doctor's appointment. Hopefully, you'll get to try one of her Crackspressos tomorrow. That drink is amazing," he said, nodding with raised eyebrows.

"Look, I don't care. I just need some caffeine."

"Alright, we can get some at *The Greasy Spoon*. I just got a text from Pickens. He set up a meeting at nine with that HSI agent he knows and the partner he warned us about."

Forty-One

8:56 a.m. Friday, October 5, 2007. The Greasy Spoon.

Doug parked by a blue Jeep Wrangler, the only other vehicle in front of the corner café with a Victorian facade. Across the street was the Earth First Food Market's empty parking lot. A cross of yellow police tape covered the market's front door.

Roberts opened the corner doors and let Doug enter, then asked the man behind the counter for a booth for four.

"Seat yourself," said the early middle-age man with dark brown hair and a short beard. He wore a red-checkered long-sleeve flannel. Behind him was a National Rifle Association logo next to a red, white, and blue BNM sticker boasting membership to the late Brigham Norsworthy's militia.

Roberts chose a booth by the window.

The bearded man set two glasses on napkins, filled each with ice water, and asked, "Coffee while you wait for your friends?"

"Yes, and leave the pot," Doug said. He noticed the man's dirty finger nails and a bit of scrambled egg in his beard.

The man nodded and filled two cups as Doug watched four deer stroll by. The deer stopped and grazed on sparse grass along the sidewalk in front of the vehicles. He glanced at the closed market again and thought about the reporter's death after breakfast at the *Spoon*.

The waiter set the pot on a coaster as a black Hummer pulled up next to the rental, blocking Doug's view of the market. Across its side in large white letters was HOMELAND SECURITY INVESTIGATIONS. Two men wearing matching black slacks, warm field jackets, and brown leather work boots stepped from the vehicle. Each wore a white shirt with attached ID badges and a red power tie. Golden HSI shields hung from their necks. The light tan HSI agent with brown hair and a handlebar mustache was smiling. The clean-shaven blond one with the perfectly sculpted do was not. The one with the handlebar said something to the bearded man at the counter. He pointed as if Doug and Roberts could be missed.

"Agent Matthews, I presume," Roberts said as he slid out of the booth. He extended a hand as Doug followed.

"Yes, but please just call me Matt," said the one with the handlebar. He firmly shook each hand. "This is my partner, Jeff Fuller."

Fuller looked annoyed, avoided eye contact, and shook each extended hand with a soft grip. He said nothing as they sat.

"I'm Detective Bob Roberts, and this is my partner, Detective Doug Thorfinnson. As Francis probably told you, we're here from Federal Way, Washington."

Matthews glanced at Fuller, then said, "Yes, Coroner Pickens called me last night and filled me in on who you are and why you're here. Detective Thorfinnson, may I call you Doug?" asked Matthews.

"Yes, of course."

"Doug, I understand Mary DeMure was abducted from Walnut Hill, Washington, last year and that you've been searching for her ever since. Is that correct?"

"Yes, but she's not the only one. There was another kid from the same school named Leonard Royce Grimes. We only learned about the abductions after a woman from the same school came into our station. She reported that four men from a lab attempted to abduct her for a phase three drug trial that a friend of my daughter also applied for."

"Yeah, Francis told me everything about your investigation and the subpoena you're seeking for DNAXIS records concerning a banned drug called Curitall. Have to say it sounds far-fetched, but you must've done a good job convincing my old friend. I can report that we haven't found any evidence that Ms. Demure is dead, but we believe she was at Mender's residence; otherwise, none of this makes sense. But we also can't find evidence that Ryan Mender died, even though some of the bodies are still being identified based on dental records. So far, we can say with a high degree of certainty that forty Black Berets on the ground, eight helicopter pilots, and Suzanne Mender are among the dead. Of course, there was also the Fitzgerald family, and the town's Sheriff and Undersheriff, but that was an unrelated incident. Unfortunately, we don't have any suspects to verify what happened at the residence."

Doug raised a finger.

Matthews ignored him and continued. "And yes, we watched and listened to Colonel Stone's interrogation. We didn't find it very helpful."

"We watched and listened to it last night, and I have to disagree," said Doug.

Fuller's eyes narrowed. "Wait, how could you have watched it? That buffoon, Glickman, was supposed to turn over everything."

Roberts broke in, "Deputy Glickman made a copy. I guess he forgot it was still on Sheriff Maxwell's computer and didn't see any harm in getting an outside opinion. I'm sure it was just an oversight by someone who isn't used to handling cases like this, you know, like you guys. Look, you have to admit, it's a little strange for two decorated veterans to go batshit crazy in a matter of two months, and at least one of them go off and murder a whole family, copycat style, near the site of the famous Greenly Murders."

"Matt, this is a waste of time," said Fuller, shaking his head as he glowered at Roberts. His tone grew increasingly sarcastic as he continued. "Next thing you guys will start talking about is demon possession and that the devil made Mary DeMure kill that World War II veteran and steal his Jeep. This is a simple case of some loser kids who were recruited by a homegrown terrorist organization. Everything that's happened since Ms. DeMure entered this town is our government's attempt to stop them and keep you, your families, and everyone else safe. Ms. Demure killed Melvin Anderson and stole his Jeep after her last ride belonging to Louis Suerte, or whatever his real name is, broke down outside Grayson. Suerte's body still hasn't been found, but I'm sure he was a co-conspirator who had a falling out with Ms. DeMure. There is little doubt that she was trying to escape the dark ops on her tail who were attempting to capture her before she could set off one of those Blue Bombs. It's very likely the group she's working with designed them and used her as a mule. We also suspect that the Blue Bomb detonated at Norsworthy's Watchtower was not the only one she was carrying."

Doug scoffed softly and asked, "So, how do you explain Ms. DeMure's accident at Lake Hotchkiss? Nothing incriminating was found in Mr. Anderson's Jeep… at least to my knowledge."

"Accident? Seriously?" Fuller looked at Matthews, and then back at Doug. "Is there really any evidence of an *accident*? Any witnesses other than Mender? No—there's not. I believe they met at the lake where she passed Mender the bombs or bomb-making material and the tactile toxin she used to kill Melvin Anderson. Then they drove Anderson's Jeep into the lake and parted ways until they met again on October second. The only reason Mender contacted Sheriff Maxwell on September first was to make up a story to throw him and everyone else off the scent of what was really going on here. Also, it's very likely that Mender and Demure were having an affair based on Sheriff Maxwell's conversations with the former Army Ranger. After they parted ways that night, we also suspect DeMure contacted another local BNM member..."

Doug saw the bearded man behind the counter glower at Fuller and suspected the militia sticker belonged to him.

Fuller didn't notice (or was purposely poking the bears) and continued, "... who provided her safe haven throughout the lockdown—a lockdown meant to contain both suspects while obtaining enough evidence to bring them in together or take them down. It seems clear that Alex Mender came in contact with the tactile toxin inside the Mender home. It is also likely that Mr. Mender used that toxin to kill reporter Kenneth Prattle out of malice and that he or Ms. DeMure killed Mrs. Mender after she discovered what her husband was involved in. Or, maybe, it was because she learned her husband was responsible for their son's death. Or, maybe because Mrs. Mender learned her husband was having an affair with Ms. DeMure."

Doug tried not to glower as he breathed deep and heavy through his nose as Fuller's face turned redder and his tone became almost a growl. "Makes my blood boil. That, and the fact that he could be so cruel and calculating as to associate with DeMure after she murdered the man his entire family had to thank for their prosperity. And that was long before his father married Norine Jones, or Nathan Miller made him the subject of a best-selling novel. If they are still alive—which seems *very* likely—they'll soon be in custody or, more likely, dead because we're not taking chances after what happened Tuesday."

Doug glanced at Roberts. He looked ready to explode as Doug asked, "Okay, then how do you explain what happened at the Fitzgeralds'?"

"That's easy. Martin Rice snapped due to some PTSD he was dealing with and killed the whole family. Probably thought he was back in Iraq or Afghanistan. Maybe he read the story of Morgan Bell the night before. Hell, I don't know, and I don't really care. Some people snap. I figure the same thing happened to former Colonel Stone. Lost his grip on reality after seeing what Rice did to that family, then slipped into some Nazi fantasy world. It's funny, but not really. He even used the name of one of the doctors who worked for the lab to play the part of his murdered Jewish wife. What a nut job. But both Rice and Stone are dead, the latter thanks to Deputy Glickman's abject ineptness. But they're not the issue here. Mender and DeMure are."

"And what of Leonard Grimes and Clarice Moonflower?" Doug asked.

"Grimes? He's probably another sleeper cell. Who knows where he'll pop up. And Clarice Moonflower—seriously? With a name like that, double nut job. Question—did they ever find any evidence confirming that four men attempted to abduct Ms. Moonflower? Were there any witnesses other than those who heard her screaming as she ran into your police station? I'll answer that for you. No. And no. I've read everything in your case files. You want me to believe that a major pharmaceutical company was in some way responsible for abducting two college students, attempting to abduct a third, and abducting many others yet to be identified? And for what purpose—to experiment on them? To create assassins with a deadly touch?" Fuller furrowed his brows, rolled his eyes, and glanced at Matthews. He shook his head and asked with palms up, "Come on—you don't actually believe that?" He peered into Doug's eyes, and his face fell. "You do? You really do? Damn."

"At least I haven't closed my mind to the possibility that more might be going on than meets the eye. The truth is not always the easiest explanation. Look, the reason we wanted to meet with you and Matthews was that we'd like to do our own walkthrough of the crime scenes. You seem intent on taking DeMure and Mender dead or… dead. My goal is to try to bring Ms. DeMure in alive and find out what happened to her and why."

"Whatever. If it wasn't for Matt, I'd say you have no business being here, because you don't. Your girl is a terrorist, and this isn't remotely your jurisdiction. However, I'll respect my partner's wishes and allow it, but he'll be shadowing you to make sure you don't fuck things up any worse than Glickman already has."

"Thanks, Bob and I *appreciate* your graciousness," said Doug.

Fuller smirked. "No problem. And make it quick. Who knows? I might change my mind. Well, you boys enjoy your breakfast." He slid out of the seat and started for the door.

"Will you be eating?" asked the bearded man.

"Seriously? At *The Greasy Spoon*?" He rolled his eyes. "Matt, I'll be in the Hummer."

"Okay. Be there in a minute."

Fuller straight-armed the door open and exited.

"Look, he's not always this bad. He lost his brother at the Pentagon on 9/11. He's not about to let another terrorist attack happen if he can help it. Well, I have to go. I'll meet you guys at the Crown Lake at eleven."

"Thanks, Matt. We really appreciate your help," said Doug. "I know your partner has already convicted DeMure, but I believe she's an innocent victim in all this, like Mender."

"Prove it, and I think Jeff will come around."

Forty-Two

Late morning, Friday, October 5, 2007. Lake Hotchkiss.

Doug thought about the night before as he and Roberts neared the big lake. After watching and listening to Stone's interrogation several times, Roberts had suggested they review Sheriff Maxwell's notes before calling it a night. Of course, while Roberts had called it a night thereafter, Doug had continued working. Upon reading the slain sheriff's impressions of Mender's words and mannerisms after DeMure's rescue, he understood why Fuller was convinced Mender was involved. What would any rational person think about someone who would defend a suspect after learning that they'd voluntarily, or involuntarily, killed his family's closest friend?

But Melvin Anderson was much more than Mender's grandfather's war buddy. When Edwin Mender left his Utah reservation following the war, Melvin repaid his brother-in-arms by giving him a job to help feed his family, and later, paid for Edwin's only son's college and law tuition. Of course, a semi-rational person might consider that Mender believed DeMure was innocent or that extenuating circumstances led to Anderson's death. Nothing about Mender's character led Doug to believe he was a terrorist, had an affair, or for any cause, would sacrifice his wife and son, whom some say he resurrected from the dead (that last part required one to let go of the rational altogether). With everything that had occurred in the past month, this was a case Fuller would be incapable of grasping. Whatever Doug learned about DeMure and Mender, he planned to be keep between Roberts and himself.

On the way to Watchtower Private Drive, Doug stopped at the site where DeMure drove Anderson's Jeep into Lake Hotchkiss. He stepped from the vehicle and looked around. Roberts stayed in the rental.

The skies were cloudy, and the weather was frigid. He blew into his hands as he walked a short distance to where the grade was less extreme. He descended to the shoreline, knelt, and dipped his fingers in the water. *Ice cold,* he thought as his gaze rose forty-five-degrees to the road. He took a deep breath and struggled up the steep slope. Regardless of Doug's weight issue, the climb would've been difficult for most, and the shale slid easily under his feet, causing him to slip several times before he reached the road.

He panted hard and wheezed. He looked at the lake, then up Gold Mountain's daunting slope. According to Maxwell, Mender had said, *"When the woman came to, she was scared. Real scared. She kicked me in the nuts… and threw me off like a rag doll. Then she scurried up the mountain like a packrat being chased by a bobcat. I tell you, she wasn't fazed at all by that head wound or thin air."*

Doug chalked it up to adrenaline, maybe shock, and based on what Bridgette had said about Mary, she'd been in great shape when she was abducted. Even so, the slope to the road was hard to climb dry, and it was wet at the time of the accident. He surveyed skid marks, then his gaze drifted to the ditch across the road. Hair and bones of a dead buck rested there, twisted and broken above the pelvis. He went to the carcass and saw two one-centimeter holes in its skull.

Forty-Three

10:50 a.m., Friday, October 5, 2007. Ten miles southwest of Packer City.

Doug passed several parked vehicles north of Crown Lake and arrived at the first roadblock a thousand feet from Watchtower Private Drive. Fog hung over the lake and beyond, but he could still see news vans, SUVs, Jeeps, and trucks about a hundred feet from the second roadblock. Journalists with proper credentials lined the roadside, waving arms for sound bites as Doug gazed at Greenly Mountain and the burned-out husk of the fallen Watchtower poised on Tower Rock. He lowered his window as two officers approached.

"Hey, that's Jake Tolliver and Lawrence Lombardi," said Roberts as one of them came around to Doug's side.

The officer ignored Doug, peered across the seat, and asked, "Is that you, Bob?"

Roberts leaned and said, "In the flesh. Good to see you, Jake. Just got into town yesterday. Turns out my new partner, Doug Thorfinnson here, was searching for the same Mary as we were. What're the odds?"

"No shit. That's crazy. It's nice to meet you, Doug. I'm Jake Tolliver, and this is Lawrence Lombardi."

Tolliver extended a hand and Doug shook it.

Lombardi stepped up, did the same, and asked, "So, Bob, what're you two doing here?"

"Waiting for Agent Matthews. He's babysitting us on a walkthrough of the Fitzgerald and Mender crime scenes. Doug's been trying to crack DeMure's abduction case for a year now. He suspects whoever took her did something to her, but we can talk about that later. Anyway, Doug believes whatever happened here might help our investigation."

"Well, let me give you a heads up," said Tolliver. "Agent Matthews is okay, but his partner is a triple-A asshole."

Roberts chuckled. "Yeah, we met him earlier. Real charmer."

"Yeah," Lombardi said, shaking his head. "Also gotta warn you—the smell inside both places is diabolical. The bodies are gone, but that odor's never coming out of those walls. Of course, that doesn't matter for the Watchtower—that place is toasted. The respirators in the hazmat suits will cut the smell up top, but you'll want to pack your snoz with Mentholatum at the Fitzgeralds'."

"Thanks," said Roberts as Fuller and Matthews arrived at the campground.

Fuller stepped out and was thronged by the media. Matthews ran down the road and across to the rental.

"It's okay. Let 'em pass. They're with me," said Matthews as he climbed into the back seat.

"Matt, I know these guys," said Roberts. "Jake, maybe you and Lawrence can get everybody together tonight at Dr. Bell's for some drinks. First round's on Doug. It's my mission to get him to try a *Cannibal Burger* before he leaves town," he finished with a grin.

"It's a date, brother," said Tolliver, trying not to laugh. "Doug, it's nice to meet you. Welcome to our *peaceful* mountain town."

Matthews directed Doug to park in the Fitzgeralds' driveway behind the gray, bullet-riddled 4Runner. To his left, Doug saw the Watchtower's carbon-scored chimney jutting above the trees.

Roberts' face fell when he looked toward the front door. His lips quivered as he got out and went to the Sheriff Maxwell and Undersheriff Turner's initial resting place. He covered his mouth, closed his eyes, and wept.

Doug stood by Roberts' side and gave his partner time to collect himself. Roberts nodded with thready breaths when he was ready.

"Here, you're going to want some of this," said Matthews as he removed a jar of Mentholatum from his coat pocket, opened it, and offered it to Roberts.

Roberts wiped his eyes, grabbed a dab, and stuck the finger up each nostril. Doug got some and did the same before Matthews applied some himself. Matthews replaced the lid, put the bottle in his coat, and pulled out three pairs of gloves and handed a pair each to Doug and Roberts.

Doug opened the door and smelled menthol and a tolerable trace of rancid. Roberts hyperventilated behind him, and calmed himself as Doug stepped inside.

"You okay?" Doug asked, seeing that he wasn't as Roberts stared at a dining room table and four empty chairs.

Roberts rubbed away tears and said, "No. No—not in the slightest," he said, sighing, "but I need to do this." He nodded.

Doug patted his shoulder and they moved on.

Two more outlines greeted Doug in the front room and kitchen. From the audio only portion of Stone's interrogation, he deduced that the first belonged to ex-Marine Lieutenant Jim Stevens and the second, ex-Navy SEAL Captain Martin Rice. The black blood spray in the kitchen marked where Wicker had taken out Rice. The three walked the hall and up the stairs to the second floor. There was a large black stain on the carpet at the top and blood splattered in the direction of a couch in the open family area where Mr. Fitzgerald had killed ex-Army Ranger Specialist Hunter Harrison. It appeared that Stone or Stevens had tried to clean the carpet unsuccessfully.

Doug returned to the first floor, continued to the basement, and descended into Rice's kill room.

Outlines of Mrs. Fitzgerald and the children were jumbled in the corner to the left. The chair where Mr. Fitzgerald was tortured, mutilated, and eaten alive faced the outlines and was stained with old blood. The freezer where Mr. Fitzgerald's limbs had been found was open and empty. There were more outlines on a picnic table of a tool roll, a Coleman stove, and a plate.

Doug returned to the dining room and went to the back door. He glanced at the kitchen, paused, and gently pushed the door open. The frame was broken and the strike was ripped away but the hinges were intact. There were bullet holes in the frame and a dark burgundy splash.

Doug re-created Wicker's movements starting from outside. Extending a two-hand finger pistol, he slow-motion kicked open the door, stepped inside, and imagined a 5.56mm round slamming into his left shoulder. He dropped his left arm and continued gripping the imaginary gun as the force knocked him back. He looked at the wall, the door frame, and the door. He examined the pair of bullet holes in the wall. *A three-round burst*, he thought and returned to the re-creation and directed his finger gun to where the shots were fired and to the outline of a spent Carbine magazine on the linoleum. *Rice's magazine was empty*, he thought.

Doug fired his finger once, twice, thrice, imagining each shot hitting Rice. He went to the outline and examined the splatter. A bullet hole was at the predictive angle in the right cabinet above the sink. Rice was shot once in the chest and shoulder. The third matched the one in the cabinet... And then there was a fourth—a headshot. The blood splatter and brain matter on the broken doors below the sink didn't make sense. It was directed downward as if Wicker was standing over Rice... *who held an empty rifle. He executed him,* thought Doug. *Yeah, the guy was probably gonna die, but he was a witness—a valuable one—just like Stone... and he put him down.*

"So, what do you think, Doug?" asked Roberts, as he stood by Matthews.

"Nothing. Just trying to get a feel for what happened here. Let's go out back. I wanna see where Specialist Harrison was buried."

"What in the world does that have to do with DeMure?" asked Roberts.

"Look, partner, I've been doing this for decades. You never know what you'll find until you've retraced every step."

Forty-Four

Early afternoon, Friday, October 5, 2007. Tower Rock.

The three headed up the drive to a white van parked at the perimeter of the blackened and blue-dusted switchbacked drive. The crystalline ash sparkled and seemed to dance in the sunlight. Doug saw a burned-out chopper to his left. Matthews opened the back of the van and they put on a hazmat suit, turned on the respirators, and began hiking up the driveway to the massacre site.

On the way, Doug passed several yellow flags scattered in a thin layer of ash, marking the site of body parts, most of which had already been delivered to the Grayson morgue or elsewhere. He stopped several times to catch his breath. At the third switchback, he looked down at the second fuselage at the misty bottom. Late morning fog still obscured another fuselage in the field to the southwest.

Beyond the switchback, the ash deepened and the air became brisk even through the respirators. Soon, Doug rounded the final bend to the wide main driveway. A chopper's melted husk sat at the epicenter of an explosion with a blast radius extending a good hundred feet above and several hundred feet around and below the twisted mass of metal. More flags dotted the driveway and hillside.

The garage door was open, but Doug decided to enter through the front door where three outlines greeted him on the porchway. To the right, he saw a smashed, flat-screen TV surrounded by more flags in a terraced garden. He stepped into the foyer and saw more complete outlines, but beyond, they became amorphous or were shaped like arms and legs (or parts of arms and legs) and intermingled with a variety of ash-covered debris.

Doug peered into the office to the left. Plate-sized high-caliber holes dotted the lower half of the wall into the adjacent utility room. Smaller plate-sized craters peppered the office floor, washer, and dryer, but not the outside wall. The utility room's garage-side was cracked and pushed in.

He entered the living room. A collapsed second-floor balcony obscured his view of the dining room and kitchen. A narrow pathway was cut through the mass of debris and led to the precipice that was the tower's face. The room was blackened and sprinkled with cobalt and dried gore. Numerous nails were stuck in the hardwood and a mass of outlines congregated near where a sliding glass door had been.

He stepped around the outlines and went out on the deck. Roberts and Matthews followed. To the right, the deck was missing. Doug paused for a glance, and then moved up the cut-rock steps to the remnant tower top. More outlines and flags. He passed the chimney, the fire pit, solar panels, and stopped at the sunken pill tower's dome. He knelt for a closer look.

"Find something interesting?" asked Matthews as he stood by Roberts.

"No. Nothing." Doug sighed. "I'm beginning to think I wasted your time."

Matthews nodded with an unreadable face, and then directed Doug and Roberts down the way they came up.

They exited the front door and headed up the cedar steps to the main bedroom. Each step had an alternating blood-black footprint in the blue ash. The footprints continued along the deck to the doorless bedroom.

On the right side of a king-size bed was a body outline and one of a revolver to the outline's left. In Glickman's photos, Doug had noted a Smith & Wesson Model 27 sitting there. A half-folded white sheet covered the bed's other half. On the floor on that side, there were clothing shards stuck to burned skin. He knelt and carefully peeled apart what looked like jeans and saw a melted but identifiable elastic band for a pair of thermal underwear with a fragment of a *FRUIT OF THE LOOM* size S tag. There were also remnants of a winter jacket and Seattle Mariners beanie attached to charred skin. He regarded the folded sheets. He lifted them and noted a black-blood impression of a second body, approximately the same height as the outline on the right. He gazed through the doorless threshold, and then to the open door and short hall that led to the angled floor that had collapsed into the first. He saw more outlines. Doug returned to the deck, passed Roberts and Matthews, and continued to the garage.

Mender's truck was embedded in the utility room wall and numerous bullet holes polka-dotted the tailgate. The windows were shot out and the driver's door was open. Inside, Doug saw no sprays, drops, or dried blood puddles. He glanced back and up and saw hundreds of bullet holes concentrated on the left side of the garage door. The wall to his right was dotted with matching holes around a water heater that looked like Swiss cheese. Along the mountainside wall, a partially shredded sixty-liter backpack and an equally ruined child's pack hung between a breaker box and an empty hook for a third. Doug looked in the truck again and thought about the photos he'd seen in Glickman's office. There were no backpacks in the truck, and none were found elsewhere on the property. That wasn't to say they hadn't burnt up in the inferno, but it gave Doug hope that there was at least one survivor.

Doug headed toward the door to the dining room and kitchen.

"You'll need a flashlight in there," said Matthews and handed Doug his.

Doug took it and led the way into the house. He headed down the hall and stopped when the ceiling creaked. He peered up at what might crumble onto their heads at any second. More blue powder. More black spatterings. More outlines. He saw a metal door on the wall to the left that he knew from Glickman's photos hid a heavy machine gun on a swiveling apparatus.

Doug eyed Roberts, then turned to Matthews and said, "Matt, thanks for everything. I think we're done here. Thought I might find something. Again, sorry for wasting your time. If you don't mind, I'd like to check out the fourth chopper's crash site—you know—to be complete."

"Sure, why not? And if you're right about DeMure and Grimes, whoever abducted them needs to be brought to justice. I wish you luck getting that subpoena," he said, sounding sincere.

"I appreciate that," said Doug.

Doug reentered the garage, looked to the two shredded backpacks, and went to examine them as Roberts and Matthews stood by the destroyed water heater. Doug leaned his head sideways and peered inside the open breaker box. He'd almost forgotten the curious red switch and the strange message from the crime scene photos.

"Hmm. Hey, Matt, what does the red switch do?" he asked.

"Oh, that..." Matthews almost stifled a laugh. "That's a dumb joke from the previous resident."

"Has... has anyone flipped it? You know, for poops and giggles, at least."

"Uh, no. But, you're welcome to be the first."

Doug nodded and tried to flip the switch. It wouldn't budge. He added a little more force and it popped. He looked at Roberts and Matthews as the wall next to them silently slid open and a room beyond bathed them in ghostly blue.

"Oh, shit," said Roberts.

Doug's jaw fell open and he was sure his face matched Matthews's skinnier one.

Matthews grabbed his handheld and pressed the talk button. "Jeff, you need to get up here now."

"What is it?" asked Agent Fuller as his voice crackled over the speaker.

"You just need to get up here. Detective Thorfinnson found the Watchtower's safe room."

Forty-Five

Very early afternoon, Friday, October 5, 2007. At the fallen Watchtower.

Doug entered the hall beyond the hidden entryway. He stepped forward, rapt by a knee-level conduit lining the left wall that shimmered with waves of blue. The three men followed the conduit as it descended two long flights of stairs. At the bottom, it turned left and continued into a tunnel with an end beyond sight. To the right, the ghostly luminance was smothered by incandescent wall fixtures in a short passage to a half-open gray metal door. Past the door, black and white light flickered from dozens of monitors on the left. Most were tuned to static and white noise, but a few showed aspects within and around the fallen Watchtower.

Beyond the control room, another door opened to a hall that turned left. Along the right side was a large weapons cache displayed like a military Toys-R-Us. Someone had removed weapons from the display, and a few drawers below were left open. Several ammo boxes were disturbed, with spaces for others now missing. Halfway down on the left, steps descended into an underground firing range that dead-ended into a colorful patriotic display of the second amendment in original script large enough to read from that distance.

Doug knew what this meant. Whatever he believed about Mary DeMure and Ryan Mender no longer mattered. Homeland Security had all it needed to crucify them. In the current political climate, they would get their mandate to hunt and capture or kill DeMure, Mender, and anyone else they believed was a member of Brigham Norsworthy's Minutemen.

Forty-Six

Dejected Doug and frowning Roberts passed Agent Fuller in the driveway next to the chopper fuselage. Fuller was dressed in matching Hazmat.

"So, you still believe Ms. DeMure is the little angel you thought she was?" asked Fuller. "Why don't you head back to Seattle and let the big boys handle this? I'm sure there are plenty of cases that you two can work on in your area. As for this one, it's no longer your concern."

Neither Doug nor Roberts replied. Doug walked past without eye contact as Fuller turned to continue his jibing.

"Yeah. That's what I thought."

Doug and Roberts started the descent. Blue ash swirled behind Roberts as he blazed a furious trail and Doug struggled to keep up all the way to the white van. They removed their hazmat suits, tossed them in the back, and continued in silence to the rental. Doug got in and slammed the door. He was livid and felt like he'd just betrayed a friend or a daughter and knew he'd done both. He reversed much faster than he'd pulled into the Fitzgeralds' driveway, shifted into drive, and spun his wheels more than once until they reached the roadblock where Tolliver and Lombardi sat in lawn chairs by the barrier.

Roberts rolled down his window and put on his good old boy mask, though his tone barely concealed his vexation as he said, "Hey, Jake, Lawrence, see you at Dr. Bell's around six. Hey, Doug, you up for a few drinks with some good friends of mine?"

"Definitely," Doug said with no effort to hide his bitterness.

Tolliver nodded with an implacable smile. "We're looking forward to it. We already radioed everyone. Don's the only holdout. Said he wasn't sure if he'd be able to make it. Other than that, it'll almost be like old times."

Roberts smiled softly, laughed under his breath, and murmured loud enough for Doug to hear, "Like old times? If only."

Tolliver added, "Oh, and Agent Fuller said you two are to leave this crime scene immediately and ordered us not to let you back on the premises."

Doug smiled spitefully as Roberts rolled up his window. Doug turned southwest onto Lake Hotchkiss Road instead of northeast. He watched Tolliver and Lombardi grin in the rearview as he and Roberts entered the restricted area. Doug glanced back once more when Tolliver and Lombardi were ant-sized in the rearview.

"Bob, I'm gonna check out that other Black Hawk. I don't care if it upsets Fuller's apple cart. I'm not leaving Mears County until we've finished what we came here to do. The chopper's in an open field a short hike to the southwest."

"Yeah, this'll piss off Fuller if he finds out," said Roberts. "But I don't see how it'll help our investigation, which just turned to shit. I mean, we already have this information, and it'll probably further incriminate Demure and Mender. I'm sure Fuller believes they killed the pilots while fleeing the scene."

"I need to be complete. I won't sleep otherwise, and I'm already not sleeping as it is," Doug said as he glanced over to see Roberts nod.

Doug continued further down the dirt road and stopped at yellow tape that blocked the trailhead to the crash site. They got out and Doug stopped at a historical marker next to the tape. On it were faded yellowing photos of Horace Greenly and his family, including the two surviving daughters. Further down the panel was a photo of the monster himself, Dr. Morgan Bell. He was odd-looking, skinny, and unattractive with dark hair combed into a Bob's-Big-Boy curl. He had a chin beard and wore a bowtie, white shirt, polka-dotted dark vest, and dark dress coat with large metal buttons. Doug skipped the text since he already knew the tale better than he would've liked.

Roberts lifted the tape, and they started down the trail. "According to Don, the chopper's about a half-mile from here."

Doug nodded, tripped on a rock, and nearly tumbled into Roberts but recovered.

The narrow trail leveled at a rotten fence that peeked above the overgrowth and continued along a wagon road filled with aspens and other plant life. A short distance further, they came to a large white marble pyramid covered with algae. The inscription was written in fancy Blackadder script, still clear except for a few missing letters. Doug stopped and read:

On this site / Horace Greenly and his loving wife Loulou Belle, / son Elijah, and daughter Ester / were Brutal*y murdered / by that Scoundrel

Morgan Bell / May th* Greenlys rest peacefully in Heaven / and / May Morgan Bell and his kind rest uncomfortably in Hell.

Roberts walked ahead as Doug studied the memorial. Doug looked up and lumbered to catch up. When he did, Roberts picked up his pace. Doug struggled again and was soon huffing and puffing and rubbing his back. He stopped, caught his breath, and stretched.

"You good?" asked Roberts.

"Yeah. Stupid back. Hey, I have to level with you. This walk isn't to check out the fourth chopper or get under Fuller's skin. Though I have to admit, I don't mind screwing with that jerk."

Roberts chuckled.

"Maybe I'm paranoid," said Doug, "but I think Fuller bugged our vehicle. I purposely left it unlocked when I realized he wasn't joining us. Matthews and Fuller were obviously playing *good-cop-bad-cop* at the restaurant. When we get back to the rental, I'll check all the places I'd hide a listening device. If I'm right, we best check our room, too. I'd also mind what you say on any phone."

"Yeah, you sound paranoid, but Fuller's a snake."

Doug nodded and they continued to the bank of the Grayson River and forded a shallow, rocky part. "I can't believe nobody checked that switch. And what was I thinking flipping it? It could've deployed those heavy machine guns again, or who knows what else. Worse, I seriously messed up our chances of getting any judge to grant us anything concerning Demure's case. We need Mender Sr. more than ever. This is life or death for his son. We need to wind this up here and head to Grand Junction A-SAP."

"Hey, don't beat yourself up. You didn't know," said Roberts. "Even the smartest people do dumb things some…" He paused to get his toes out of his mouth. "Umm, every other person that walked by or saw that breaker box thought it was a joke by the crazy old coot who built and owned the Watchtower before the Menders. And before the Menders bought the home and opened their restaurant, it'd been vacant for a dozen years. After a falling out with his children and almost everyone else outside his militia, Brigham Norsworthy amended his living will. In it, he restricted access to the Watchtower to everyone except his nephew, Eugene Lee, you know, in the event he was incapacitated or had to be maintained on artificial life support for an extended period of time. Of course, this all happened before I moved to town. Glickman told me it was weird, like Norsworthy knew something was gonna happen to him. He had a stroke a week after making the changes. Glickman told me he even added a clause that under no circumstances was he to be removed from life support. It's like he was terrified of death and wanted to extend his life by any means necessary. And he had the money to do it, too, but his body eventually couldn't sustain the vegetative state.

"Anyway, Eugene must've known what was under the house. I mean, I've always wondered how Charlotte could afford her chemotherapy selling coffee in a small, seasonal town like Packer City. Their benefactor must've been Norsworthy. I know Eugene was family, but from what I heard, Norsworthy wasn't known for his generosity. And if you ever meet the Lees, I doubt you'll believe he helped them out of the goodness of his heart. He must've worked out something with Eugene before his stroke in '93. Most in town knew that Eugene maintained the grounds to keep the pack rats from destroying the place. They're a real problem around here. You know, there was once a mansion on the island in the middle of Lake Hotchkiss, but the owners had to raze the place after the rats came down the chimney one winter."

"You know where Mr. Lee lives?" asked Doug.

"Sure."

"Great. Maybe we can drop by on our way out of town and ask him a few questions."

Roberts chuckled and shook his head. "Eugene Lee. Ohh, man. We can do that, but I have to warn you—the guy's a real piece of work. Real charmer, even sweeter than Agent Fuller. Just make sure to ask Charlotte about her *World Famous Frespressos* and make sure you say the full name. Tell her you were unable to try one since she was closed today. I'm sure she'll whip one up just for you. You'll love it, trust me. Then give her a compliment or two, and she'll keep Eugene in line for your questions."

"What makes these Frespressos so special? Sounds like something you can get at any Starbucks or any corner coffee stand."

"I have no idea, but it's…. it's good, and probably illegal," Roberts said and snickered.

Doug paused, caught his breath, and wiped sweat from his brow. He removed his jacket and wrapped it around his waist, though the sleeves were barely long enough to tie. "Bob, I want to get your take on a couple of things I noticed at both scenes. You know, the burned clothing next to the bed… it likely belonged to DeMure. If she survived—which there's no indication that she didn't—she would've had horrible burns from the explosion. Mender must've also been injured but strong enough to carry her out of the inferno up to the bedroom. Somehow, even after sustaining these injuries, they escaped the Watchtower. It was definitely through that tunnel that we didn't have time to explore. But what I can't understand is how Mender didn't know what was beneath his home. I mean, he lived there for almost a year and a half. Unless, of course, he also got a good laugh out of the red switch and message like everyone else, then randomly let his curiosity get the best of him, like me…" Doug rolled his eyes "… and flipped the switch when Norsworthy's worst nightmare came true."

"Or maybe," said Roberts, "he just never had a reason to check the breaker box until that morning. Glickman did mention a strange darkness that lingered until the Fitzgerald shoot out. He thought it was weird enough to mention and couldn't explain it. I didn't think much about it until now. Mender probably flipped the breaker for battle advantage."

Doug nodded as Roberts continued, "But concerning the message, Sheriff Maxwell told me old Brigham was always going on about government conspiracies. He really believed that black helicopters would one day come for his guns. Even that painting on the wall in that photo Reserve Deputy Jones took immediately after the massacre spoke volumes to his paranoia. That was obviously the Watchtower, and I suspect the ravens were the Black Hawks. But the black wizard and the Joan of Arc defending the tower… Mender and our Mary… Now that…" He paused wagged a finger in the air, adding, "… that's just freaky. And why the raven warning in his home? And how did he know that October 2, 2007, would be D-day and that Ryan Mender would be the one living there to flip the switch and defend the tower? Man, it makes my head hurt. I mean, Mender was fourteen when Norsworthy had his stroke. Even the theory that he was recruited after Almawt Lilkifaar makes no sense. Norsworthy's Minutemen aren't known for being inclusive. That group has always been as white as mayonnaise."

Doug stretched and wiggled his back. Something popped. "Ooh… that's much better," he said, nodding. He cracked his neck and grinned with relieved glee as they hiked on.

"To para-quote Churchill," said Doug, "it's definitely a riddle, wrapped in a mystery, inside an enigma. But it's our job to figure out this riddled, mysterious enigma. Everything has a logical explanation. The challenge sometimes is figuring out the logic. Hopefully, we can learn more from Mr. Lee tomorrow. Alright, there were a few things I noticed on our walk-through that I also need to get your take on. First, DeMure was wearing men's thermal underwear."

"Yeah, so what? Probably whoever hid her during the lockdown supplied her with fresh clothes. They might've had limited shopping options during the high-level lockdown."

"Exactly, but it would've had to have been a man about her same height. How tall would you say the owner of the Mount Capitol Suites is?"

"Raj Batra?"

"Yeah. I spoke to him this morning."

"Well, I'd say he's… around DeMure's height. A little wider around the middle, though."

"Okay, so he's not a perfect fit. Like I said, I spoke to him before my failed caffeine quest and told him why we were here. When I mentioned DeMure's name, he seemed nervous."

"You know, I can definitely see him hiding her. He's a quiet guy unless spoken to, but he's very kind. He's the town's only Hindu, and it's like he's greedy for karma points to trade in for the next life. I heard his wife left him, won custody of his kids, and moved to Florida. At the time, he lived in Portland, Oregon, and only stumbled onto Packer City while driving home after visiting his kids several years ago. When he got back to Portland, he sold his house and bought the motel and a cabin outside town. He's been living in

Packer City year-round ever since. The only other thing I know about him is he hikes a lot and loves snowboarding. Of course..." Bob paused and tapped a finger on his lips. "Now you got me thinking. He does sort of fit the MO of a sleeper cell... or a serial killer. Seriously, an Indian-Indian guy from Portland moving to the most remote and very white county in the lower forty-eight. Huh. Maybe Agent Fuller isn't that far off track, and maybe Mr. Batra is tied to some terrorist group. I mean, who would expect a terrorist safe house in Mears County, Colorado?" Roberts gave Doug a wry grin. "But I think that's as much bullshit as Mender being part of BNM. Batra is a good guy. A little strange, but we've never had reason to suspect him of anything other than being a clean freak and being willing to give someone the coat off his back in the middle of a blizzard."

Doug pondered for a few seconds. "Still, it would be nice to have a private, off-the-record chat with him to see what he knows. If he's the one who hid DeMure, he might know where she and Mender are headed, granted, if they're still alive after those injuries."

"I agree," said Roberts. "You said you noticed *a few things* you needed my take on. That was one. What else is bothering you?"

"At the Fitzgeralds', did you see what I saw in the kitchen?" asked Doug while locking eyes with his partner.

Roberts bit and chewed his lip for a second. "Yeah, I did. Mike executed Captain Rice. And what's more, I knew something was wrong with him yesterday, even if I didn't let on. He didn't seem like himself, and his emotions were, uh, I don't know, insincere. Contrived. Even his tears were unconvincing, like he had to push them out. I mean, he just lost his best friend and father-in-law. It was strange. I heard Mike's voice and saw his body, but someone else seemed to be pulling his strings. Crazy, huh?"

"Not really. I'd never met him, but he seemed very different from the person you'd described last month. Granted, a lot has happened since you moved to Seattle."

"Still, the man walking around in Mike's body isn't the Mike I know. The *Mike* I know would've never left Mandy alone at a time like this to *clear his head*. He always thought of everybody else in times of crisis, and no one more than Mandy. Alone time wasn't his thing. Drinking too much with his buddies and watching the Broncos or the Rockies play—that was the Mike I knew for the past ten years. I've watched him struggle through hard times. The worst was when his father and mother passed close together a few years back. He's always been a good cop, but I guess he snapped when he killed Rice. As painful as it is to think it, I question what happened to Stone as well.

"Yet, Glickman and Pickens didn't mention anything to suggest a struggle before the Colonel's suicide. But, under the circumstances, they didn't consider Mike a homicide suspect. Hell, until an hour ago, I would've never believed my buddy could be so stupid as to let his emotions drag him over the thin blue line. Yeah—I'm not mentioning this to Glickman. As shaky as he is, I don't think he can handle it quite yet. I wanna be sure. I'll call Pickens on Monday and ask him if he noticed anything unusual on his examination of Stone's body Tuesday or during his autopsy. I mean, I assume one was done."

"Bob, I'm sorry we have to do this. I know what Mike means to you. This isn't what we came here for, but my gut tells me this is an important piece of a larger puzzle."

"Don't be sorry. If Mike did this, he has to answer for it, but I want to talk to him face to face before acting on what we learned. You think Matthews suspects anything?"

"If he does, he has a winning poker face," said Doug. "I have no idea about Fuller, but he wears his heart on his sleeve, so I suspect he would've mentioned any such suspicion."

"I'd like to hear what the other guys think who were there when it happened," said Bob. "Maybe they can shed some light on Mike's behavior after he executed Rice. I mean, we'll be casual about it. Let the drinks oil the conversation."

"Of course. Casual," said Doug.

The earlier mist had cleared in the meadow beneath Tower Rock. Doug saw yellow flags and two twisted, but complete body outlines about fifty feet from the Black Hawk downed. Pines and aspens surrounded the dark, blue-dusted meadow. He looked up to where they'd been standing earlier below the Watchtower. The front of the tower would've been visible on Tower Rock early Tuesday morning.

Doug shivered as goose bumps covered his arms. He put on his jacket and pulled on exam gloves from the Fitzgerald crime scene. They continued to the chopper. Doug wiped blue dust from the cockpit and peered inside. It was empty, and there was no visible dried blood. He inspected the fuselage. It was untouched except for the ruined tail rotor. The landing had been rough but controlled. He scratched his head. It was hard to tell if this *raven* had been knocked from the sky before or after the Blue Bomb was deployed. Maybe one or both the pilots were injured and it might have taken some time to exit the chopper. For that reason, he believed it'd probably crashed before the Blue Bomb exploded. He pictured the pilots running or limping as fast as they could before they were caught by blast radiation that acted similar to Fuller's described *tactile toxin*. Accelerated necrolysis would have followed. *So why didn't the body parts and the rest of the corpses undergo the same?* he thought. *Did Mary or Mender do this?*

He rubbed his forehead, trying to erase the thought, but failed. Then his mind unwound. *Mary and Leonard's abduction. Mad scientists. Human experimentation. Ryan Mender's resurrections and pestilent touch. The bogus quarantine. The Black Berets. Joshua Stone's suicide. Contracts with the devil. Stories of demon possession. Morgan Bell copycat killers and cannibals. Joshua Stone's suicide. The massacre at the Watchtower. A dead man's secrets. BNM...* How were they all connected in this metastasizing enigma? And now this so-called *Blue Bomb*... It was just another piece of a seemingly impossible puzzle.

"You okay?" asked Roberts.

"Yeah. Yeah, just peachy," Doug said, rubbing his temples.

They left the site and headed toward the 4Runner. Fuller and Matthews greeted them at the river ford.

"Are you boys lost, or did you forget that Homeland Security took over this investigation?" Fuller said from the opposite bank.

"My apologies," Doug said unapologetically. "I didn't think it would be a big deal if we took a look at the fourth chopper before we left town. It's the least you could let us do after we located an underground armory and terrorist training facility for you pros."

"I appreciate your help. I really do," said Fuller with an exaggerated wink. "But concerning you or your ex-Hazzard County deputy and partner, I care a great deal about you trespassing here. And I'm pretty sure Deputies Lombardi and Tolliver told you that you were no longer welcome at this crime scene. As I said, you two need to head home. And if I catch either one of you on the wrong side of my tape again, I'll have you arrested."

"Duly noted, Agent Fuller," said Roberts as he and Doug crossed the river. "Question—how did you know we were down here?" asked Roberts.

"Reception out here is terrible, and we needed to head back into town to make some calls," said Fuller. "As we were leaving, I asked Deputy Lombardi which way you two headed. You know, just to make sure you hadn't wandered off somewhere you didn't belong. He pointed this way, and it wasn't too hard to figure out where you went."

Roberts smiled. "Oh yeah, I could've told you the reception out here is shitty. You gotta have a Sat phone. Surprised you hadn't figured that out 'cause you guys are *tho* smart. Well, good luck with your investigation. Hope you find your terrorists," he finished with sarcastic flare.

Fuller didn't reply. His face was red and his eyes and mouth were three lines.

Doug brushed past Fuller and Matthews without making eye contact and headed up the trail. Doug felt Fuller's glare bore into his skull as the HSI agents followed. He clambered up the trail, bent under the yellow tape, got into the 4Runner, glanced once at Roberts, then u-turned, and headed toward town. He watched Fuller and Matthews in the rearview. Fuller's stare never left them as he and Matthews climbed into the Hummer and followed far behind. Neither Doug nor Roberts spoke until they reached the Sheriff's Office.

Forty-Seven

Mid-Afternoon, Friday, October 5, 2007. Mears County Sheriff's Office.

Bob faced Glickman in the file room outside the shared office. "Seriously, Don, the guys would really like to see you at Bell's tonight. You don't have to stay long, but it'd mean the world to them... and me. After all, Doug and I are leaving for Grand Junction tomorrow to meet with James Mender. I mean, we'll be back in town Monday for Pete and Joe's funeral, but after that, we have to head back to Seattle. There won't be another chance to get everybody together again."

"Alright, alright. I'll be there," said Glickman. "Might be a little late, but I'll be there."

"You better, or I'll drag your fat-ass there."

Glickman cracked a smile. "Yeah, it'd be fun to see you try. And hey, my ass isn't that fat. I've been working out. Wanna see?"

"No, I'll pass. Plus, I don't need to. There's supposed to be a full moon tonight anyway."

Don chuckled. "Oh, by the way, Pete and Joe's funeral is tomorrow," he said as his smile faded. "And then we'll keep spreading the joy next week with the Fitzgerald family parade to the same cemetery." He sighed as some color left his cheeks.

"You're kidding me. For some reason, I thought it was Monday."

"No. That's the Fitzgeralds'."

"I hope I'm not interrupting anything," Thorfinnson said as he approached.

"No, not at all," said Bob. "But we need to reschedule or push back our meeting with James Mender. I had the day wrong for Pete and Joe's funeral. It's tomorrow. I'm really sorry."

"No problem. I'm sure Mr. Mender will understand. If he can meet with us tomorrow evening, we might be able to catch a flight home from Grand Junction early Sunday. I'd love to spend the afternoon with Loretta and Elli before my little girl heads back to Pullman."

"Sounds good," said Bob. "By the way, I twisted Don's arm into coming to Dr. Bell's Saloon. Oh, and Don, Dougie here is gonna try the *Cannibal Burger* tonight."

Glickman forced a smile and chuckled. "Don't worry," he said as he patted Thorfinnson's shoulder. "That burger's tasty. Before the Mender's opened their restaurant, it was as popular as Charlotte Lee's Frespressos. Everyone new here has to try one unless they're vegetarian or vegan. And you don't strike me as a veggie killer."

"Okay, okay, I'll try one," Thorfinnson said with a hint of a grin. "Deputy Glickman, you think you could show me the courthouse? I hear that's where Dr. Morgan Bell's trial took place."

"Again, just call me, Don. And that's correct. Not a great chapter in our town's history, but as you can see, the town has turned tragedy into profit. The tourist dollars really help. If it weren't for the lake, hunting, and the Cannibal Surgeon, we'd probably have gone the way of McMann, Howard's Mill, and the other ten ghost towns in the county. So, by all means, I'd be happy to give you a guided tour."

Glickman put on his hat, and Bob and Thorfinnson followed and stopped between the Sheriff's Office and the courthouse.

"What's wrong?" asked Glickman.

Thorfinnson whispered, "Homeland Security is bugging us."

"Yeah. So what? They're bugging me too. Fuller's a real asshole."

Thorfinnson shook his head and motioned with his eyes for Glickman to come over to the rental.

Bob opened the driver's side door, casually pointed under the steering column, and lipped, *Bugging us.*

Glickman made *Oh* lips.

Bob closed the door and moved away from the 4Runner.

Once out of listening range, Thorfinnson told Glickman about their meeting with Fuller and Matthews, what they discovered in Norsworthy's garage, and their suspicions concerning Eugene Lee. He also recommended that Glickman sweep his office. Thorfinnson skipped the part about his suspicions concerning Raj Batra. Bob thought that was nice of him since he knew the man would have to live here after he and Thorfinnson were gone.

"Thanks for the heads up," said Glickman. "I'll search my office and vehicle. Damn, I can't believe they're doing this. I've worked with the Colorado Bureau on several cases. They were always easy to work with and even appreciated what we had to contribute. But Fuller? He's a cliché made-for-Hollywood asshole. Regardless, still looks bad for Mender and that woman. Even I hate to admit it, but after what you found, Fuller's theory is solid. In fact, without some supernatural explanation, his is the only one that makes sense."

"Yeah. You don't have to remind me," said Thorfinnson. "Once this hits the news and Homeland Security starts rounding up BNM members, it'll be nearly impossible to get any judge to listen to us, even with James Mender's help. Then DNAXIS will get away with what they've done or at least had a hand in covering up…" he said, then sighed, adding, "… and all those kids like DeMure and

Grimes..." He bit his lip and couldn't finish. Thorfinnson pursed his lips, narrowed his eyes, and breathed heavily through his nose. Bob glanced at Glickman and wondered if he should worry about his partner.

"Look, I hope you clear Mender because I like the guy," said Glickman. "Everyone in town does, except maybe Eugene Lee. But nobody cares much for Eugene, except maybe his wife, Charlotte, but even that's debatable. Yeah, everyone who mattered loved Mender's wife and son, too. I swear Ryan is one of the most honorable men I've ever known, just like his grandfather and Melvin Anderson. He's a no-bullshit American patriot and a war hero. I'll believe that 'til the day I die, no matter how much assholes like Fuller and the news media try to drag his name through the mud... Changing the subject. Did you really wanna see the courthouse?"

"Actually, yes," replied Thorfinnson. "I'm trying to learn everything I can about your town's famous psychopath."

Forty-Eight

Doug and Roberts headed back to Northside Lodge. In the minutes it took to reach the room, they made small talk and added tidbits of misleading information. Roberts also suggested it might interest Doug to check out some graves at the town cemetery across from the motel. Doug parked outside the room, and then they walked across the road.

"Why didn't you remove the listening device?" Roberts asked as they passed through a rod-iron gate with *Packer City Cemetery / 1876* written above in rusted letters.

"I didn't want Fuller and Matthews to know we found it. We can use it to funnel misinformation. For now, let's assume they've bugged our room and are monitoring our calls. Don't say anything you think might remotely help their investigation. I've already helped them enough."

"I won't. I noticed you didn't mention Batra to Glickman. I understand. Don's a great guy, but I've always had the impression he doesn't like Batra, and I don't know why. It's just the guy is a little different than the average Packer City resident."

"Yeah, I noticed," said Doug. "That's why I felt better not taking the chance. Of course, with Fuller's tunnel vision, he'll probably be directing HSI to be on the lookout for redneck white guys with guns, Confederate flags, and NRA and BNM stickers. For now, Batra is probably above suspicion. We still need to talk to him, though. If he's not the one who hid DeMure, we need to find whoever did before Fuller or Matthews does." Doug looked around at the old tombstones and changed the subject. "So, where's Sheriff Bridger's grave?"

"Right over there," Roberts said, pointing.

They headed to a black rod-iron fence that surrounded the grave near the cemetery center. Its monument was ornate, weather-beaten white marble. Engraved upon it was *Bocephus Andrew Bridger / born July 3, 1852 / died May 31, 1892 / May he live on forever / in our hearts and minds.*

After a few seconds of respectful silence, Roberts went on to show Doug the grave of Judge Ripkin, who committed suicide a few months after the trial. He then showed him the Greenly family plot with its two rows of four graves. In the first were Horace, Loulou Belle, Elijah, and Ester. In the next were the other two daughters,

Mable Ferguson and Clara Belle Stewart, who weren't living at home when the murders had taken place. Beside each were their husbands, Scott and Patrick.

Roberts said, "Mable and Clara Belle survived to have large families and their descendants number in the hundreds. Several are even buried here."

Doug lingered, examining the headstones.

"Hey, Doug, I have a few more graves to show you."

Doug nodded, and the two detectives moved to the cemetery's less-visited, poorly maintained section. Roberts pointed to the graves of Buford Redman and Jefferson Bell. The names on the old stones were barely legible.

"After what you told me, I'm surprised they're buried here," said Doug.

"Well, they weren't initially. They were dumped in an unmarked grave, and only a few people knew the location. But after the town had a chance to reflect on the whole chain of events that ended so terribly... I think it was after the trial judge killed himself... Well, the townsfolk thought it would be a good idea to reinter them here to quiet some angry spirits. It was a way for the town to heal and at least get a little justice for Jefferson."

"So, where was Morgan Bell buried?"

"Uh, yeah," Roberts said with a humorless chuckle. "That was the part of the story I didn't tell you. No one in town would allow the *good* doctor to be buried in the cemetery, so, it was decided that the disposition of his body should fit his crimes. So, they tied his body to an aspen tree out in the woods on the other side of Bridger Ravine. They wrapped him in a fresh deerskin and hung a necklace of venison around his neck. The next spring, it was obvious that he'd provided a nice meal for a hungry creature or two since his bones were gnawed on, pulled apart, and scattered around the tree."

"Dang... And it all started over Greenly feeling cheated after buying Bell's tapped out mine?"

"Yup. Pretty much," Roberts said, nodding. They turned to the cemetery entrance. "Never ceases to amaze me what people will do for the love of money or the loss of it."

Forty-Nine

Late afternoon, Friday, October 5, 2007. Mount Capitol Suites.

Doug headed next door while Roberts cleaned up for dinner with Packer City's finest. On the way, he sniff-checked his pits to confirm his suspicion that he probably should've followed Roberts's lead.

Doug peered through the front office window and saw Batra sitting behind the check-in desk, holding an open book. He opened the door and a pleasant tingle-linging followed.

Batra hopped to his feet, closed the book, and set it on the counter. He stood tall for his short, round stature in front of two Hindu icons hanging on the wall. Doug read the cover of the book. *Nathan Miller. Among the Dead.*

"What can I do for you, Detective Therfishen?"

"Detective Doug Thorfinnson," he corrected as politely as possible.

"Oh, very sorry. Again, what can I do for you?"

"Mr. Batra, if it wouldn't be too much trouble, would you be willing to answer a few questions concerning the town?" Doug asked, admiring the icons as he tried to identify them. The one on the left with the elephant head was Ganesha. He recognized the other, but couldn't remember the god's name.

"Sure. What would you like to know?"

"Any chance we could speak somewhere private?"

"Yes, indeed, but what if someone walks in and needs a room?"

Doug glanced outside. There were three vehicles parked in the dirt lot. He assumed the place was packed three days earlier, but the media's fast trickle from town began yesterday. And between the lockdown and the massacre, seasonal hunters were likely going elsewhere to kill hooved, hairy things. Now, only media skeleton crews remained, and they were camped at Crown Lake. "Just put a sign up," said Doug. "Say you're out for coffee and will be back in fifteen minutes. I promise I won't take much of your time."

"Okay, I think I can spare fifteen minutes."

Batra locked the door and put up a clock sign showing the office closed for a quarter-hour. He paused, adjusted the minute hand to twenty, and said, "Follow me upstairs."

Doug followed Batra to a small room over the office with a twin bed, refrigerator, a standard water cooler with a hot and cold dispenser, microwave, sink, and a small bathroom with a stand-up shower. There was a strong smell of curry in the air. In one corner was a shrine with another icon of Ganesha, one of Shiva, the same one downstairs whose name Doug couldn't remember, and another he didn't recognize. Out of place in the room was a poster of Shaun White and a *Never Summer* snowboard leaning against a wall with a gorgeous snow-capped mountain design.

"Come—sit. Would you like some tea?" Batra asked as he directed Doug with an open palm to a pillow and low table next to the shrine.

"Yes, thanks," Doug said as he sat.

Batra filled a tea kettle with hot water from the dispenser and set two cups with saucers on the table. He placed a bag of Earl Grey Black in each cup, filled each with hot water, and set the kettle in the middle.

As they dunked their bags, Batra asked, "So, Detective Thorfishnet, what is it that you would like to know?"

Doug didn't bother to correct him, took a sip, and said, "What I'd like to do first is tell you a story about a little girl."

Batra listened as Doug told him what he knew of Mary DeMure's tragic tale up to when he became involved. When he finished relaying his suspicions about what he believed had been done to her, he said, "But I think you already know this story, and that's why you protected her."

Batra swallowed hard, his eyes barely restraining tears. Then one escaped. "She did not mean to kill Mr. Anderson. She told me everything about her life, about the abduction, about the horrible things Dr. Caine and Dr. D'Amato did to her, what the mad General, whose name she never said, did to her, and what they made her become, and the things they made her do." His voice became shaky, higher pitched, as words fought to break through sorrow. "They were trying to kill her when she escaped. It was a man named Louis, a Black Beret himself, who helped her. She loved him, and I know in my heart that he loved her, too. He was killed during the escape, but he provided her with the means to be free and supplies to get to where he told her to go. But Louis's vehicle broke down, and it was

Mr. Anderson who stopped to help Mary. He was... he was just like me. He was only trying to help her, and he... and he accidentally touched her." Batra paused and wiped his eyes and runny nose. He sniffed hard, looked to the ceiling as if to Heaven, and then out the window overlooking the town.

He collected himself, and his soulful gaze returned to Doug. "After Mr. Anderson was dead, she took his Jeep and continued to Packer City, following the directions Louis had given her. She planned to hike through the mountains to get to Arizona and the Navajo Nation. There, she planned to search for a great shaman who had the power to reverse what Dr. Caine did to her. And that was how she ended up here. Ryan Mender saved her life, but he did not die like Mr. Anderson. Instead, he cured Mary and became a carrier of the deadly touch you speak of. She was headed to see him Tuesday morning. Mary knew what she had done to him and that she was responsible for the death of his child. She... she wanted to... she wanted to save Suzanne Mender's life. Now... now they are all dead." He wiped his eyes again. His hands trembled as he sipped his tea.

Doug did what he could to not match Batra's aspect. He breathed deep, albeit shakily, and asked, "What if I told you there's a good chance that Mary and Ryan are still alive?"

Batra's lips trembled. "What? But what about... what about the explosions? The news lady said no one could have survived what happened there."

"I agree. I don't know how anything could've survived, but Mary and Ryan did. But I believe both are badly injured."

Batra smiled slightly, his lips quivering as he sniffed. He stood, went to Doug, beckoned for him to stand, and hugged him. "Thank

Brahma, Vishnu, Shiva, Ganesha, and all the other gods and their avatars," he said and gripped Doug tightly, then released. He stood with an ear-to-ear smile, sniffing, and wiping his eyes. They sat again.

Doug asked, "Do you know where she was told to look for this medicine man? I need to find them before Homeland Security does. The agent in charge has already convicted them. And until I can prove that Albert Caine and those financing him are the real terrorists, there's no way Mary or Ryan will get a fair hearing, especially in this political climate."

"No, as I said, she only told me she was going there to convince Ryan Mender to go with her to the Navajo Nation to find the shaman. She never said his name or where she might find him. It was Louis who told her about him, but I think he was killed before he could tell her everything she needed to know. They had planned to escape together and find the healer. As I said, she loved Louis, and once she was cured, she planned to run away with him to someplace where the lab could not find them."

Doug nodded. "Thanks for your help, Mr. Batra. Like I said, this is all off the record for now. But when the time comes, would you be willing to testify in court to what you just told me?"

"If it will save Mary, I would give my very life."

"May I ask you one more thing?"

"Yes, of course."

"Did she ever say what happened to the others like her?"

"Yes… She told me they are all dead. She said some took their own lives. Many died from the experiments or during the training process to turn them into the General's assassins. The mad General killed the rest after he decided the survivors did not suit his purpose.

Louis helped Mary escape after he learned that the General planned to kill her."

Doug felt acid bubble up as his hands trembled. He set the tea cup on the saucer. "How... how many were there?" he asked, his voice cracking with each word.

"Mary said, including her... one hundred."

Doug rubbed his forehead and put a hand over his mouth. He breathed faster and gulped down the acid.

"Thank you. Thank you, Mr. Batra." Doug's lips quivered as his hands continued to shake.

"I am sorry you did not find them in time, but Mary is still alive," Batra said with a hopeful sparkle in his bloodshot eyes.

Doug finished his tea. It was cold. He looked at his watch. They'd been sitting there far longer than twenty minutes. Doug said nothing as he rose from the pillow. He only nodded, turned, and left.

Fifty

Early evening, Friday, October 5, 2007. Northside Lodge.

Doug returned to the motel room. He was sure he was a few shades paler. Bob was dressed in blue jeans, boots, and a Patriots sweatshirt. He was sitting on his bed watching a horror flick. A blood-drenched prom queen was on a stage glaring as psychokinetic powers set everyone's world on fire.

Roberts turned and asked, "What's wrong?"

"Oh, nothing. Everything's great. Just peachy," said Doug.

"You don't look so good. You coming down with something?"

"Just missing Loretta and Elli. I hate being away from home."

"I'd say I understand, but I've been a bachelor for over ten years." Roberts sighed. "Yup, I've gotten used to a quiet apartment. Well, you ready?" he asked, and then furrowed his forehead and held a hand to his nose. "On second thought, you might wanna take a shower."

Doug smirked and headed that way to a chorus of screaming teens and teachers. The movie credits were rolling when he stepped out, dressed, and readied himself to do some drinking.

"You want to walk or drive to Bell's?" asked Roberts.

Doug heard Roberts but didn't respond as he leaned on the sink and examined dark puddles under his eyes in the mirror. He felt stiff, fatter, and his back hurt. He wasn't hungry. Honestly, he didn't want to go and wanted to be alone to bawl his eyes out and collect his thoughts for the next century.

"Hello. Seriously—are you okay, partner?"

"Huh? Yeah, yeah," Doug said and turned to face Roberts. "Hey, it's not that far. Let's walk. And besides, neither of us will be legal by the time the nights over."

"I thought you weren't much of a drinker."

"I'm not."

Fifty-One

It was cold and the skies were clear, and stars were already appearing along the Milky Way's catwalk as the scheduled blood moon peeked above the horizon. On a twenty-minute walk, Bob listened as Thorfinnson conveyed the ghastly details of his conversation with Batra and informed him that they were no longer working on just a kidnapping case. It was now a quest to find Ms. Demure and deliver justice for the victims of three mass murderers: Albert Caine, Antonia D'Amato, and an unnamed General.

They arrived at Dr. Bell's Cannibal Saloon a little before six. To Bob's surprise, Glickman was already there with a half-finished mug of beer.

"So glad you came, Don," said Bob.

Glickman smiled like it wasn't his first drink. "Well, I... I didn't feel like being dragged up here."

Bob lifted a finger to get the attention of the attractive blonde, blue-eyed waitress he knew well from his decade in PC. She was wearing a gray Coors sweatshirt, tight blue jeans, and white high-tops with dark blue Nike symbols. "Ethyl, can you get me two Silver Bullets?"

"Sure, sweetie. Who's your friend?" she asked, strolling to the table like she was at a fashion show.

"Ethyl, meet Doug Thorfinnson. Doug meet Ethyl McMann. She's the best thing that ever happened to Bell's."

She laughed, gave Bob that look, and slinked a hand over his shoulder. "Always the flirt, huh? And a heartbreaker, but we won't get into that, *sweetie*. Well, it's nice to meet you, Doug. So, Bob, how you been?"

"Still settling into my new life in Seattle. Crazy month you've had here."

She scoffed. "You noticed, huh?"

"Yeah, it's the reason I'm back so soon. The suspect in Melvin Anderson's murder case was from the Seattle area," he said as he pointed at the month-old wanted poster on the bulletin board by the door. "Turns out Doug here was searching for the same woman for the past year."

"Really? Do you think she's a big, bad terrorist like the media and the Feds want us to believe she is?"

Bob glanced at Thorfinnson who held a *can-we-change-the-subject* expression. "I wish I could say. There's still a lot we don't know. But keep an eye on the news, they might get it right yet."

Ethyl walked away and returned with two silver-wrapped aluminum bottles and set them in front of Bob and Thorfinnson as Tolliver and Lombardi stepped through the door.

"I see you three started without us," Tolliver said with a wide grin. "There's some old friends outside as well as the new guy."

Fred Strickland, Ronnie Jones, and someone Bob didn't recognize entered. Bob hopped up and gave each a man-hug until he reached the Chicano.

"Oh, this is Juan Guzman from San Pedro, California. He arrived just in time for the lockdown. Fun times," said Tolliver as he patted Guzman's back.

Bob shook the new guy's hand and introduced everyone to Thorfinnson by job title. When he was done, Bob said, "And everyone, this is Detective Doug Thorfinnson of the Federal Way Police Department. He's one of the best detectives I've had the pleasure to work with."

"Hey, Bob, let me get this round," said Thorfinnson.

Bob scoffed. "Nobody's stopping you."

Thorfinnson raised a finger to get Ethyl's attention. She came over, and he ordered six more Silver Bullets.

Tolliver placed his hand on Glickman's shoulder. "So, you decided to come."

"Yeah, I wasn't feeling good when you called, but I feel much better now. It's been a rough couple of days." Glickman sighed. "And hey, it's good that we can get together while Bob-Bob's in town."

Tolliver found his seat and took a drink.

Strickland asked, "So, Bob, you coming to Pete and Joe's funeral tomorrow?"

"Definitely. No way I wouldn't be there." He glanced at Thorfinnson.

Thorfinnson's gaze shifted, suggesting that he hadn't called James Mender with the change of plans.

Thorfinnson pulled hard on his bottle, gulped three times, and set it down. He unsuccessfully suppressed a hardy belch, and then asked, "What time is the service?"

"Eleven a.m.," said Strickland.

"We'll be there. I know how close Bob was with Pete and Joe."

Jones regarded Bob, and said, "Patsy and Mandy and definitely Jos will be happy to see you there—that's for sure," he said with a subtle raised eyebrow that made Bob uncomfortable.

Bob chewed his lip, nodded, and looked away but kept it together in front of the guys. He took a large pull from the bottle. He remembered the many dinners over at Turner's home. Jos (as most people called Jocelyn Turner) was always overly friendly, and Bob would be lying if he said she wasn't smoking hot. That was the reason he always avoided being alone with her since people in small towns talked. Joe Turner was a good friend, and Bob never once contemplated betraying him for a little carnal pleasure, though the sandman allowed a fantasy or two to slip through, making him wake up with guilty morning wood. But that was it, not a thought outside dreams. *Bullshit. That's a lie. Oh, it would've been amazing.* It was a bitter thought he'd rather not have had right then or any time after Joe's death, and was why he'd left the mountain town he'd grown to love. The Turners' marital trouble had been their business, but Joe was gone now, and Jos would be delivering Joe's child soon. No one but Jos knew that she was the reason he'd left for Seattle. It was also the reason Bob hadn't visited her since returning to PC.

Fifty-Two

Early Evening, Friday October 5, 2007. Dr. Bell's Cannibal Saloon.

"You'll have to excuse me," said Doug as he stood. "I need to make a call."

Everyone nodded and went back to their conversations.

Doug stepped outside and punched in James Mender's number but got his after-hours answering service. He left a message telling him about the funeral and that he and Roberts would be unable to be there until tomorrow evening. He gave him the option of rescheduling for another day but reiterated that he and Roberts needed to speak with him face-to-face as soon as possible. He left his number, hung up, and went back inside as McMann was taking food orders.

Doug sat and perused the menu. He reluctantly eyed the *Cannibal Burger and Finger Fries* that he would undoubtedly be strong-armed into trying. There was no description, only Dr. Morgan Bell's infamous quote from the trial, "*Do not knock it until you have tried it.*"

Before Doug could object, Roberts said, "Cannibal Burger and Finger Fries for my partner here."

Doug rolled his eyes and shook his head. He wasn't in the mood but had no *argue* left in him. *When in Rome…* he thought and sighed in his head.

Everyone except Jones ordered the same. He ordered the southwestern grilled chicken sandwich and a salad instead of Finger Fries.

"Ethyl, what exactly is a *Cannibal Burger*?" asked Doug.

"It's a three-quarter pound venison and buffalo double patty mixed with some red wine, our secret spices, and a lot of cannibal love. The fries are cylindrical cut and sprinkled with our secret seasoning. Don't ask me what the spices are, or I'll have to eat you and then kill you in that order," she said with a disarming grin.

"You people are sick—you know that, right?"

"Hey, don't knock it until you try it," said McMann. Everyone at the table chuckled.

Doug nursed his beer as conversations ran out of steam and the bar got quiet.

"It's sure quiet in here tonight," said Strickland. "Hey, wait a second. Where's Eugene?"

"Who cares?" said Lombardi. "Ever since Mender kicked him out of his bar, he's been coming to Bell's to annoy everyone here. I swear if he disappeared, the only person who'd care would be Charlotte, but that's even questionable."

Doug rolled his eyes and thought, *This town really hates this guy.*

"I heard Charlotte's café was closed this morning," said Roberts. "Is she okay?"

"No idea," said Lombardi. "Why you so worried about her? Miss your *Frespresso* fix?"

"Yeah—kind of. If her café isn't open tomorrow and Charlotte skips the funeral, I'm gonna swing by the Lees' on our way out."

Doug noticed Roberts skipped the part about speaking with Eugene.

Fifty-Three

After another round of Silver Bullets, Bob began probing for information concerning Mike's strange behavior as Thorfinnson shamelessly devoured his burger and fries as if it was the first and best of both he'd ever had. Bob's brows raised as teetotaling Thorfinnson slammed his beer and ordered another.

Everyone had noticed Wicker's behavior, but like Bob, they chalked it up to losing his best friend and father-in-law.

Guzman chimed in last. "I've only known Wicker for a month, but I have to agree, something's not right with him. I'm the one who drove him to the medical center, and he didn't say a word the whole way or when he was at the clinic. I figured he was in shock. I mean, I would've been. But then he walks into the jail museum where Stone's being held and acts like nothing's wrong and interrupts everything, pulls rank, and tells Jones and me to get a drink. Next thing we hear, Wicker leaves the suspect long enough for him to hang himself and then breaks the news in the middle of a news conference. Top that, he broke Jones's camcorder, but I guess that doesn't matter now."

Glickman raised a palm to interrupt. "Excuse me, Guzman, and everyone else. I've heard enough and I really don't feel comfortable talking anymore about Mike when he's not here to defend himself. He made a mistake—simple as that. I've known him for years, and when he returns from his suspension, he'll be good to go. I don't want to hear anything more about this. Understood?"

"Yes, sir," said Guzman. "You're right. I'm… I'm sorry."

Everyone but Bob and Thorfinnson nodded.

Bob looked at Tolliver and the other guys. The look on their faces said they agreed with the new guy. Glickman had done a good job on the worst day in the town's history. Everyone around the table respected him as if he were still the Undersheriff, regardless of the demotion that came on the heels of his promotion. Tuesday had been like the town's personal 9/11. Glickman had stood at ground zero like President Cranston and taken control of the situation. They all knew Wicker was the reason Homeland Security was able to shut them out of the investigation in their own county. Now, HSI was taking advantage of Sheriff Maxwell's death, so some Fed with a chip on his shoulder could trophy hunt while Cranston got a much-needed bump in his sagging approval ratings. Bob still worried how Glickman would handle it when he learned Mike had executed Rice. When HSI figured it out—if they hadn't already—the suicide would look as suspicious as Guzman had described.

Ethyl started clearing plates. She smiled and set her twinkling blues on Thorfinnson. "So, how'd you like the burger and fries?"

Thorfinnson snickered. "Have to admit. It was… it was pretty amazing," he said, sounding like the Silver Bullets were doing their thing.

Ethyl smiled wider showing teeth that were far past braces. "Another satisfied Cannibal."

"Could you get us a round of some fine Irish whiskey?" Glickman asked as he spun his finger in the air.

"Tullamore Dew okay?" asked Ethyl.

"Yeah, that'd be great."

"I'll pass. I'm on duty tonight," said Strickland.

Like Jones, Strickland drank little. Both had stopped at two beers.

"One shot won't hurt," said Tolliver.

"Okay, fine. Just one," said Strickland, like a little boy who'd been told to do chores before he could go out and play.

"Ronnie, you down for a shot?" asked Tolliver.

Jones nodded.

Ethyl brought eight singles and set them on the table.

Glickman grabbed one, stood, and held the glass at arm's length. "To Pete and Joe."

Everyone at the table stood, as did everyone in the bar eavesdropping Glickman's cheer. They repeated in a loud chorus, "TO PETE AND JOE," and emptied their glasses or mugs of whatever they were drinking.

Part III

The Exorcism

Fifty-Four

Saturday morning, October 6, 2007. Northside Lodge, Packer City, Colorado.

Doug's head pounded as his eyes opened. He felt nauseous, but his back felt great, or he failed to notice the usual ache. He remembered little after the second whiskey shot. Blurry snapshots. Muffled voices. Laughter. And the blood moon overhead as he staggered back to the motel while his best friend, Bobby Bob-Bob, old buddy, old pal, that wasn't his old buddy, old pal, but his new buddy, new pal, helped him every step of the way as he trudged forward on wobbly legs. Yeah, the moon. It looked like twins or triplets, but mostly twins set in a bed of fuzzy stars. So many stars. When Doug had narrowed his eyes, he'd drawn the crimson spheres into one, morphing the moon into a malevolent blood-drenched face that looked strikingly like Dr. Morgan Bell. At least his sleep had been dreamless, or if he had dreamt, his subconscious lips were sealed.

Doug rarely drank, and never as much as he did the night before. There were few things he hated more than a bad hangover, the stale taste of vomit, and residual throat burn. As horrible as he felt, he had no regrets. He'd needed a break from the roller coaster, or he would've snapped. He'd felt it coming, building inside. If the dam broke, he would be worthless to Mary. She was all that mattered now—she and anyone else Caine's laboratory had abducted since killing all but Ms. DeMure in her group of human lab rats.

He went to the bathroom and peered in the mirror. He looked terrible. He grabbed a glass from the sink, filled and emptied it in one gulp, then repeated the action three times. He set the cup on the counter and cringed into the mirror again. It suddenly dawned on him that he hadn't called Loretta since arriving in Colorado. She hadn't either because she knew how he was when he was consumed by a case.

It hadn't been that long since he'd helped convict the Green River Killer, but he wasn't the lead detective—"Davey" Reichert was. And it was Davey's twenty-one-year obsession and a remorseless serial killer's fumble that had helped capture Ridgway. It haunted Doug that justice had taken so long to find its way to that maniac. Before it was over, the deranged degenerate had murdered a confirmed forty-nine of society's forgettables and, after his capture, Ridgway took credit for at least twenty-two more. It'd only been a year since DeMure's abduction and a little over twelve hours since he'd learned he was right all along—one hundred times over. And, like Reichert, he'd solved the case too late. Now, he had to find a mass murderer named Albert Caine and those who'd financed him before he killed again.

Doug drank a few more glasses, popped two antacids, and splashed his face. He sat at the end of his bed and called Loretta while *sleep-of-the-dead* Roberts slept in the next one.

"About time you called. I was beginning to get worried," Loretta said with her delightful voice.

"I am so sorry. You won't believe the situation here, but it's no excuse."

"I understand. You need to find that girl and bring her home. I only hope you can find a lead on that other missing kid."

Her words were like pins in a voodoo doll, but the truth was something he couldn't divulge over the phone.

"I love you, Douglas. I know this is something you have to do. If I didn't, I would've divorced you several big cases ago. Just stay safe and come home as soon as you can. So, where you off to today?"

"I'm attending the funeral for the County Sheriff and Undersheriff, who were gunned down during the Mender Massacre."

"I'm sorry," said Loretta.

"Yeah—and after that, Bob has to check on a sick friend before we head to Grand Junction to meet with James Mender. I got a text from him this morning. Says it's okay for us to come by his place this evening. He said Norine would feed us, and Bob and I could crash in the guest quarters by the horse barn. It's close to an airport, and I hope to catch the first flight out tomorrow."

"Oh, that'd be wonderful. You might catch Elli before she heads to Pullman."

"That's the plan."

"Hmmm. Norine, huh? So, you're on a first-name basis with the Queen of R&B?"

"I was just repeating the text."

"And I was just giving you a hard time. If it were a better situation, I'd be envious. You know how much I love Norine Jones and every song she's ever written."

"Of course, you've only told me a million times. And I know the story by heart about you going to the third from her last show on her *Farewell My Love Tour* in Seattle."

"You want to hear it again?" she asked.

Doug laughed as his head pounded out tears. He tightened his face and gritted his teeth. "If it's not too awkward, I'll let her know you're her numero uno fan," he said, squinting.

"Don't you dare. Leave that poor woman alone."

"I'm just kidding. It's another bad situation Bob and I are stepping into. In the past month, that family has lost a best friend, their grandson, and now their daughter-in-law."

"I heard rumors their son, Ryan, might be among the dead but that his body hasn't been identified," said Loretta. "I also heard he was radicalized after Almawt Lilkifaar and is now part of a domestic terror group called Brigham Norsworthy's Minutemen. They say he detonated some kind of mini-nuke and killed a bunch of ex-specialists like himself who were sent to capture him. They say Mary might be involved."

"Yeah, don't believe everything you hear on the news or anything you hear from Jeff Fuller's lips. He's already pegged Mary and Mender as a modern-day Bonnie and Clyde crossed with Osama Bin Laden. The man's blind to extenuating circumstances related to her abduction or any other explanation for what's going on. He also believes the Black Berets are the good guys, even after what happened to the Fitzgerald family. He thinks it's all a government-sanctioned dark-op organized to keep us safe."

"Is there any word on where Mary might have gone after she left Packer City?"

"Loretta, I love you, but I can't discuss anything more about the case with anyone outside Homeland Security or the local police at this time. When I can, I'll tell you everything."

"Is she still alive? Can you at least tell me that?"

"Seriously, I can't say anything."

Loretta sighed. "I understand. I can't wait to see you. We'll go out someplace nice and then talk."

"Sounds great. I can't wait."

"Oh, and in case you don't get back in time to see Elli, she wanted me to tell you that Bridgette says hi. She really misses Mary. It's been tough for her. She was on cloud nine when she heard Mary was still alive and then crashed when the news broke that she might be dead again. She wants you to know she doesn't believe anything the media says about her."

"Tell her I'm doing my best to bring her friend home safely, but I need to go now. I have a double funeral to attend."

"Then you think she's still alive?"

"Seriously, I can't discuss the case."

"Okay, I'm sorry. Geez. And, yes, I'll let Bridgette know. Drive safe this afternoon, and don't forget to call me after you settle in at *Norine's*," Loretta said with extra sugar. "Bye, now. I love you."

"I love you, too," said Doug.

He hung up and sat for a few minutes with head in hands, rubbing his temples. He finally shook Roberts until he reluctantly lifted his eyelids.

Once ready, he drove Roberts to the still-closed Charlotte's café and then to the Greasy Spoon and ordered breakfast and more humdrum coffee. Neither felt much like eating, but the coffee and water helped with the hangovers.

Fifty-Five

10:30 a.m. Saturday, October 6, 2007. Packer City Baptist Church.

Bob rubbed a temple as he stood next to Thorfinnson and scanned the church parking lot and surrounding area. It was filled with cars, trucks, Jeeps, and SUVs. There were police vehicles representing departments from all over Colorado and even a few from surrounding states. Near the front steps, a crowd mournfully mingled under clear, blue skies. Most who journeyed for the double funeral would watch the service on large screens set up outside by WNN and KNW. Everyone in town was there... well, almost. Bob didn't see Mike or the Lees.

Bob weaved around mourners on his way up the steps, through front doors, and into the foyer. He paused before entering the packed sanctuary. Every pew was filled with police officers in full attire and several men and women dressed in military uniforms. Patsy Maxwell, her three grown children, and a very pregnant Jocelyn Turner sat on the front pew dressed in funeral black. Two places were reserved for Bob and Thorfinnson, but the place next to Mike's wife, Mandy, was empty.

Bob took a deep breath and entered the sanctuary and walked with leadened feet to the front where two closed caskets, on either side of the pulpit, were draped in U.S. flags for military veterans. Behind the casket on the left was a photo of Peter Allen Maxwell, and, on the right, Joseph Yukon Turner. Bob's lips trembled as Thorfinnson placed a comforting hand on his shoulder. Bob was used to open casket funerals but these metal boxes would remain sealed due to the disfiguring head wounds that no amount of Pickens's mortuary magic could make presentable.

Bob saw no dry eyes during the service, and after the pastor said his piece, everyone sang *Amazing Grace*. When the sanctuary was empty, Bob rose and joined Glickman, Tolliver, and Lombardi to carry Maxwell's coffin while Strickland, Jones, Guzman, and Interim Sheriff Griggs carried Turner's to the hearses waiting outside. From there, the procession led to the historic city cemetery where Bob had taken Thorfinnson the day before.

At the cemetery, the pastor said a few last words, which were followed by a traditional three-volley salute. The U.S. flags were then folded. Out of respect, Griggs allowed Glickman to hand Pete's flag to Patsy and Joe's to Jos.

Everyone filed out of the cemetery and headed back to the community school auditorium, where a reception and luncheon were being held. Patsy Maxwell, her grown children, and Jos Turner stood at the front of the hall.

Bob watched from a distance as everyone came and offered Jos condolences and words of support. After well-wishers had wished her as well as could be wished under the circumstances, he walked up and hugged her.

Jos released him and asked with her subtle hill country drawl, "Bob, you stayin' in town long?"

"I wish I could, but my partner Doug and I have to head to Grand Junction to meet with James Mender. He's expecting us for dinner. I also wanna stop by Mike's cabin to see how he's doing."

Jos moved away from the Maxwell family, motioned with her head for Bob to follow, and whispered, "I can't believe Mike didn't come to the funeral. I understand him upset over everything that's happened, but he needs to put on his big-boy pants. This is so unlike him."

"I know. That's why I need to drop by and see how he's doing. He wasn't himself when I spoke to him Thursday at Patsy's. But enough about Mike, how're you doing?"

Jos pursed her lips, sighed with tragic eyes, and said, "It's tough being alone in that big house. I can't stand it. Next week, I'm moving back to Austin. I'm stayin' with my brother Ricky for now, at least 'til Joseph's born. After that, I'm not sure what I'll do. You know as well as anybody, Joe and I had our differences, but damnit, he was my life."

"I know. Hey, if you ever need to talk, you can call me anytime. You know that, right?"

"I know. God, I miss you so much."

Bob hugged her again, and Jos started sobbing on his shoulder. He broke down before breaking the embrace.

As they separated, Jos held one hand as Bob wiped his eyes with the other. "Jos, I'll call you soon—I promise. And if you stay in Austin, I'll come visit you and Little Joe. But hey, I gotta go."

"Okay. I can't wait to chat when you have more time."

Jos halfheartedly let go of his hand as her gaze held on longer.

Bob nodded. His gaze remained locked to her puffy red eyes for a few precious seconds longer, and then he turned and hastily moved to the 4Runner.

Fifty-Six

Doug glanced at Roberts as they pulled away. His eyes were red and angry as he rubbed a fist over his mouth. They passed Tolliver and

Lombardi, who were headed toward the auditorium. The two deputies waved. Doug waved back, but Roberts didn't seem to notice as Doug turned onto Grayson Highway.

"I cannot believe that sonuvabitch," spat Roberts. "We need to make a detour to Mike's cabin before we head to Grand Junction. I need to talk to that asshole. I know he wanted some alone time at the cabin, but there's no excuse for not being at the funeral. I know Patsy and Mandy are putting on a strong face, but I guarantee they won't forget this. Hell, never mind—I don't want to see him."

"Look, you two have been friends for a long time. You need to talk. He's been through heck, and when this blows over, he's going to have to deal with how he handled the situation. Maybe you can say something that might make a difference. I mean, how far out of the way are we talking?"

"About a two-hour round trip on bumpy dirt roads. And we still need to drop by and see how Charlotte's doing," said Roberts, careful not to mention Mr. Lee to listening ears.

Doug sighed. "Look, I'll just call Mender and tell him the funeral ran over. I'll see if he can meet with us tomorrow or Monday. That way, you'll have plenty of time to talk to Wicker or beat the crap out of him. Whatever you need to do," he said with a grin.

Roberts laughed and snorted. "Thanks. I won't be worth a damn until I get this off my chest. He's being a selfish prick, and I need to call him on it and tell him to get his ass back home where it belongs while he still has a home to get back to," he said as they passed the city limit sign.

"Where do the Lees live?" asked Doug.

"Right before the *Welcome to Mears County* sign."

Bridger Ravine came into view soon after.

"Turn there," Roberts said, directing Doug to turn into the driveway on the right.

They passed under an open ranch gate with a metalwork sign that read, *The Lees*. The dirt and gravel drive led to a house surrounded by aspens nestled a stone's throw from the ravine. Beyond the house, Doug saw the crumbling tan mesa on the opposite side. A red Ford truck that'd seen better days was parked next to a sparkling black Lexus sedan. Roberts got out, and Doug called James Mender.

He watched Roberts approach the porch as the phone rang on the other end. The front door was open.

"Eugene, Charlotte, you home?" Roberts asked loud enough for Doug to hear.

Doug watched Roberts wait for a few seconds and then step inside the home as the call connected.

"James Mender?"

"Speaking."

"This is Doug Thorfinnson. I hate to keep doing this to you, but the funeral ran over, and I have some more business to deal with in town…" He paused as Roberts ran back to the SUV with a troubled look.

"Doug, you gotta see this," he said.

"Bob, hold on. Sorry about that, Mr. Mender. I need to see if we can reschedule our meeting for tomorrow or Monday."

"Tomorrow will be fine," he said. "Monday, I hope to act on whatever I learn from our meeting. What time should I expect you?"

"Let's shoot for lunch around one—I mean, if that's okay."

"Sounds good to me. Looking forward to meeting you and seeing Bob again."

"Likewise, and thank you for your patience."

"De Nada."

Doug disconnected and asked, "What the heck?"

"You gotta see this. On second thought, hand me some gloves. You should put on a pair, too."

Doug peered into the front hallway. There was dry blood on the floor. He stepped around the smear and walked down the hall to the dining room, where the lights were on. On a dining room wall scrawled in dripped blood was *Killer Pig*. Doug swallowed hard.

He moved slowly through the one-story rambler, and then went outside to check the home's crawl space. There were no dead bodies or abnormal smells. Roberts checked the backyard for turned dirt, but there were no signs of fresh graves. With both vehicles in the driveway, Doug had no doubt it was the Lee's blood that the psychopath had used to sign his or her work.

Doug closed his eyes, shook his head, and sighed. He would be calling Mr. Mender to cancel tomorrow's plans and knew he wouldn't be leaving Mears County anytime soon. Also, for the time being, he'd be unable to continue his search for DeMure. He only hoped she was safe and well and that she and Mender could evade capture until then. At this point, he could care less if Fuller or Matthews eavesdropped his calls since James Mender and Norine Jones deserved to know that their son was alive. Still, he would make sure whoever listened in was detoured to *nowhere-close* to Mender and DeMure's destination. He had an idea. It wasn't a great one and he hoped the Menders would forgive him.

Fifty-Seven

Early afternoon, Saturday, October 6, 2007. Doc's Cannibal Cabins, Packer City, Colorado.

HSI Agent Matt Matthews sat with headphones plugged into a laptop. Across the room, Agent Jeff Fuller's eyes were closed as he reclined against the pillows propped against the headboard. It was Matt's turn to listen into the conversations of Detective Doug Thorfinnson and his partner, Bob Roberts. Clearly, the detectives were oblivious to the listening devices Jeff had placed in their 4Runner and motel room.

Matt thought about the previous day and tried not to laugh at the games Thorfinnson had played at the Fitzgeralds'. Matt knew Deputy Michael Dwayne Wicker had executed a key witness and suspected he'd staged the suicide of retired Army Colonel Joshua Stone to cover his tracks.

He chuckled at the gift the bungling Keystoners had given him and Jeff at the Watchtower. *Ahh, the look on Thorfinnson's face when he flipped that switch. Priceless. Just priceless,* thought Matt, and then grinned, thinking about Jeff's reaction when he'd learned what lay beneath Brigham Norsworthy's old mansion. He glanced back and licked his lips, remembering the *thank you* he'd received when they returned to the cabin.

Matt scanned his partner's body, starting with his bare feet and manicured toenails. He stopped at the soft bulge in his black sweats, then continued up his shirtless body, pausing to admire his ripped six-pack and sculpted pecs. He swallowed and adjusted himself below the desk. He turned to the computer, breathed heavier, and watched audio waves.

The waves had been flat during Sheriff Maxwell's and Undersheriff Turner's funeral but had come alive since. It was more bad news for the small town. Apparently, the Keystone detectives had learned that a local elderly couple was missing. Matt had heard of Charlotte Lee and her famous Frespressos and had hoped to try one before leaving town. From the sound of the chatter, her café would be permanently closed.

Suddenly, the feed got interesting.

"Mr. Mender, I hate to do this, but I have to cancel our meeting tomorrow," said Thorfinnson. "There's been a... another incident in Packer City, and Roberts and I will be tied up for the next few days."

"What happened?" asked James Mender.

"Missing persons case. A couple named the Lees, and from the looks of their house, it doesn't look good."

"I know them. Unfortunate. Charlotte Lee made a good cup of coffee. If something bad happened, her Frespressos will be missed."

"Yeah... Yeah, I'm sure they will... um, I need to let you know there's strong evidence that your son is still alive and on the run with Mary DeMure. I can't reveal my source, but they said Ryan and Mary—I mean Ms. DeMure—plan to cross the border at El Paso or somewhere around there. From there... well, my source didn't know anything else. You have any idea where they might be headed?"

"Ryan's probably headed to San Luis Potosí. We have a lot of relatives there on my mother's side. Haven't seen them in quite a while, but I'm sure they'll keep him and DeMure safe until we can sort this out. And... thank you... thank you for this. I can't tell you how much this means to us... to me. Norine has been a wreck, and happy doesn't cut it for how she'll be when she learns our boy's alive. I don't hug, but if I were there right now, I'd make an exception."

"Yeah. I'll...I'll get those files over to you tonight. Talk to you again soon."

"Most definitely."

Matt ripped off the headphones, tossed them on the desk, and said, "I got you... I got you, you sonuvabitch. Jeff, wake up and get dressed. I know where Mender and DeMure are headed."

Jeff's eyes snapped open. He shook off sleep and asked, "What? Where?"

"We're going to El Paso, and if we miss them crossing, we'll be having margaritas in Mexico."

"Seriously?"

"Yes. Mender and Demure are headed south to his grandmother's side in San Luis Potosí."

"Well, that sucks. Why couldn't Mender have family in Cozumel?"

"When we're done with this case, we'll be able to go anywhere you want," Matt said with a wide smile.

Jeff scoffed. "This confirms it. They knew each other before their so-called *accidental meeting*. We're going to nail these assholes to the fucking wall along with the rest of Norsworthy's Minutemen and then retire in style as the pair who stopped the next 9/11. Then Lindon can look down and smile on his little brother." Jeff chuckled as his eyes glistened.

Before Matt could put his headphones back on, Jeff went to him, leaned over, wrapped his arms around his chest, and kissed his neck, taking Matt's breath away. He set the headphones on the desk, turned his head, and met Jeff's lips, and then pulled away. Matt peered into Jeff's misty eyes and wiped a tear running down his cheek.

Jeff smiled. "I need to take a shower. You wanna join me?"

Matt shifted his legs. "Oh, I'd love to, but I need to keep listening in case our friend gives us more gifts."

"Okay, suit yourself."

Matt put on the headphones and watched Jeff drop his sweat bottoms and underwear, and then thought of last night as he sauntered to the bathroom. Once Jeff closed the door and the water was running, Matt removed the headphones, stepped outside, and made a call.

"General, sir. This is Agent Matt Matthews. I know where they're headed."

"Are you sure?" asked the General.

"I am…"

"Because you well know the consequences for failure."

Matt swallowed hard. "I… Yes, sir, I am fully aware. And I would not be wasting your time if I wasn't sure. Detective Thorfinnson's source told him Mender and DeMure were heading south to meet up with Mender's relatives in San Luis Potosí."

"Makes sense. Did Thorfinnson name his source?"

"No, sir, he didn't. But I didn't expect him to over the phone."

"How do you know he's not playing you?" asked the General.

"Sir, uh, Thorfinnson and Roberts haven't given any indications that they're onto us."

"Good. Have you told Agent Fuller about your contract?"

"No, sir. Absolutely, not. Agent Fuller doesn't suspect a thing. I plan to keep it that way, too. But you can count on him to pull in everything at his disposal to capture Mender and Demure."

"Excellent, then proceed with all available forces while I tend to contingency plans."

"Yes, sir, and what does the Benefactor want us to do when we capture them?"

"He wants you to liquidate them by any means necessary. But, remember, they must be harvested together."

Harvested? Huh? Matt thought and said, "You can count on me. The Contract Maker came through. And believe me, I read the fine print before I signed. I fully understand the consequences if I don't deliver."

The cabin door opened.

Matt turned.

Jeff was in the doorway, his waist wrapped in a white towel. "Who you talking to?"

"Uh, I decided to take a break after all. I needed to call my mom. Mom, um, I'll call you back," he said to a dial tone with barely a stammer. He paused to make it look good, and then closed the flip phone. "I remembered I hadn't called her since we arrived in Packer City. You know how she worries about me."

Jeff laughed. "Such a mama's boy. It's one of the reasons I love you." Jeff grabbed his hand, pulled him inside, and slammed the door.

Fifty-Eight

Early afternoon, Saturday, October 6, 2007. The Lees Residence, Packer City, Colorado.

Bob was sitting in the rental when Glickman, Tolliver, Lombardi, Strickland, Guzman, and interim Sheriff Griggs arrived on the scene ten minutes later. Glickman gave Bob a quick nod and headed inside with Griggs, followed by Tolliver and Lombardi. Strickland and Guzman moved to the perimeter and started searching the yard and trees for clues. Glickman was inside no more than a minute, and then exited with shaky hands. Bob exited the 4Runner, followed by Thorfinnson, and went to him.

"I can't take much more of this," Glickman said out of ear shot of the other guys. "I moved to Packer City for the quiet. I thought I'd be rescuing stranded hikers, or dealing with the occasional town drunk or thief, or calls asking when to expect an obnoxious bear to start hibernating. Now, someone's abducted the Lees. Goddamnit, Bob—what the hell happened to this town?"

"I honestly don't know."

Agent Fuller and Matthews arrived in their Hummer as Griggs, Tolliver, and Lombardi stepped from the house. Fuller rolled down the driver's side window and shouted, "Hey, Sheriff Griggs, it looks like Agent Matthews and I are done here."

Griggs approached the gas-guzzling monster as Fuller continued in his normal volume. "We found evidence that Mender and DeMure are alive and currently on the run together. We aren't sure where they're headed, but we do know they headed south after exiting a few-mile-long tunnel under the BNM Watchtower. We suspect they're headed to the border, but they have a four-day head start. Hey, Thorfinnson, since you seem to know so much about this Ms. DeMure, you have any idea where she might be headed? It would definitely help us. And who knows, maybe you're right. Maybe she is innocent—pure as the driven snow."

"I wish I knew something that could help. You know how much I want to see Ms. Demure safely brought into custody so I can prove she's not the monster you think she is."

"Well, it was worth a shot. Matt, let's go. And Undersheriff Griggs—I mean, Interim Mears County Sheriff Griggs—it has been a real pleasure working with you."

"And you, as well, I hope you find your terrorists. Let me know if there is anything else I can do to help."

Bob added to the glare from the rest of the guys that would've burnt through Griggs had they all been Supermen. Bob knew Grayson's Undersheriff didn't have a clue what was happening in PC and only came down that morning for the double funeral.

Fuller laughed as he rolled up the window. He backed up and spun around, leaving a rut in the lawn before speeding down the driveway. He turned north.

Griggs turned to Glickman, and said, "I need to head back to Grayson. Why don't you handle this missing persons case? I have faith you can do a good job. After all, you haven't screwed up anything in the last three days." He grinned and released an obnoxious chuckle. "Tell you what I'm gonna do. I'm promoting you to Undersheriff, effective immediately. Congratulations, Don."

"Thanks, Danny," said Glickman with the look of someone contemplating serious harm to another human being.

"Don't mention it. I think you got a raw deal. I also think you should run for Sheriff in the special election. I just don't have the time for this job, especially after a week like this. Whew."

"Thanks for your, uh, vote of confidence," said Glickman, chewing his words as he gave Griggs an irreverent grin.

Griggs smiled and got into his white Jeep Cherokee.

Glickman was red-faced and seething as he drove away. "Tolliver, go out back and get Strickland and Guzman. I need to speak to everyone. Now!"

The group huddled by Thorfinnson's rental as Glickman spoke through intermittently gritted teeth adding spittle for emphasis. "We need to find the piece of shit who did this. Someone call Jones. And since reception is shit at Wicker's cabin, can someone please drive out there and let him know his suspension's over—and so is his vacation. I'd say call his sat-phone, but I know Wicker never takes his when he heads to the cabin. We need everyone out looking for the Lees, whether they're dead or alive, and regardless of how you might feel about them."

Tolliver and Lombardi glanced at each other.

Bob raised a hand and said, "Hey, we were heading to Mike's before we stopped to check on Charlotte. We'll tell him to head back into town. And if there's anything else Doug and I can do to help, please let us know."

"Weren't you and Thorfinnson headed to Grand Junction to meet with James Mender?" asked Glickman.

"Doug already canceled the meeting. We figured you could use the extra bodies."

Glickman sighed. "Thanks as always. Don't know what I'm going to do when you head back to Seattle."

Fifty-Nine

Early afternoon, Saturday, October 6, 2007. Terrarium Central Dome, Helix Eternal Laboratories Main Complex, Undisclosed Location.

"Mexico? Thorfinnson must be mistaken," the Benefactor said through Albert Caine's lips as he regarded General Cornelius Adamson's image through an primitive video chat window. Curiously, all Reality Windows in the Afterworld and the Realities had gone on the fritz when Delores's farseeing eye went blind. A coincidence? The Benefactor doubted it, but neck-wringing in Hell or elsewhere had thus far failed to stimulate a plausible theory for the cause or a solution for the existence-wide blackout.

"Great One, I only humbly report what my informant has told me," Adamson replied in his deep, precise, and gravelly voice. "According to Matthews, DeMure and Mender are headed to San Luis Potosí and will likely cross the border around El Paso, if they have not already."

"Tell me, who is Thorfinnson's source, and is there any chance the detective is feeding us lies?"

"My contact does not know Thorfinnson's source, but I suspect he or she is the same person who harbored DeMure during the lockdown. I cannot rule out that the detectives might know about the listening devices, but I asked Matthews if there was any indication that Thorfinnson or Roberts were holding back information. He said they did not appear to suspect a thing. Great One, I humbly apologize that I cannot give you better assurance than that. May I ask, why you have not asked Destiny? And why has she suddenly become so useless to this operation?"

The Benefactor fumed and opened Caine's lips to answer but Adamson boldly continued, his voice becoming less reverent.

"Everything rested on her guidance, and now we are operating blind. It cost me forty-eight excellent shells. With all due respect, those are not easy to replace in this reality. And besides that, the more that pass through Death's realm, the greater the chance that your Council will learn what we are doing and of the greater plan which you have not fully confided to me."

The Benefactor gritted Caine's teeth and seethed at his minion's tone, but now wasn't the Timethy to scold the mortal pissant. "I will speak with Destiny and see if her vision has improved. For now, the good doctor's escapades with Michael Dwayne Wicker's shell will create the chaos and misdirection we need and make it harder for anyone to interfere."

Adamson continued with his insolence. "I know you have faith in Morgan Bell. And I cannot deny that he has an excellent work record, but he is impulsive and takes his job too personally. He is also in this reality illegally. If Death learns of his presence now that Captain Rice's contract has expired, it could greatly complicate things."

The Benefactor put his thoughts of Adamson's torments on the shelf. "Ahhh, Cornelius—you worry too much for such a young soul. As you know, I've been around for a long, long… well, longer than that," said the Benefactor, drawing Caine's lips over his teeth. He chuckled and continued, "Know this, Cornelius—by the time Death figures out what's happening, DeMure and Mender will be out of his reach and that of Gaia and the rest of the Council. Have

Matthews direct all available forces to intercept our sweet couple before they cross the border. And if by chance they do, make sure your agent pays the Federales and Policia in every town and city from Ciudad Juarez to San Luis Potosí. We need to make sure they receive the proper welcome."

"With the abilities Mender demonstrated at the Watchtower, how should they be approached?" asked Adamson.

"It doesn't matter now—it's time for the harvest. But as I've said before, make sure they're harvested together. I'll know if I have what I need when they arrive in my corner of the Afterworld."

"So be it, Great One," said Adamson. The video screen turned black.

The Benefactor left the lab and returned to the Terrarium, where D'Amato's shell sat in its usual place.

"Delores, has your sight improved?" he asked. "I need to know if Thorfinnson and Roberts are deceiving us."

Dr. D'Amato's eyes opened slowly. They were cobalt rather than this mortal shell's unnatural swirling green. "I've been trying for the past few days," said Destiny, "but I still can't see them. I don't understand the disturbance which tore me from D'Amato's shell, but my third eye has been blind ever since. All pasts, presents, and futures are black to me. It's as if the Eye has been gouged out."

The Benefactor gritted Caine's teeth, scowled, and spoke to her like a mortal. "Then you should take a break from D'Amato and get the Eye checked, because you are *worthless* to me as you are. And while you're at the Prison, send my best Dark Inquisitors to the Diné Nation and have them possess the Skinwalkers. They'll be our eyes while your Eye is blind in case Adamson's source misled us."

Sixty

Mid-afternoon, Saturday, October 6, 2007. Deputy Michael Wicker's Cabin.

Doug's back had the right to remain screaming but his mouth was silent. Mercy only came when he turned off the ignition following many miles of ups and downs on a mountainous dirt and snow-covered road to arrive an hour away from anywhere. On the drive, Doug spoke to keep his mind off his spine, but, like Roberts, avoided any mention of DeMure or Mender. Both knew that one slip of the lip might sink the ship carrying Fuller and Matthews on a misdirected cruise to Mexico. Of course, it was unlikely the receiver was still in range, but why take chances?

There was no vehicle out front, but Doug saw tire tracks in muddy snow, u-turning away.

Roberts rubbed his chin and said, "Well, damn—wonder where the hell he went." He sighed. "I guess we can head on to Grand Junction. No telling how long he'll be gone. When we get back to civilization, I'll call Glickman to tell him Wicker wasn't here. And, if we're lucky, we might catch him on the road back."

Doug rubbed his back. He twinged his lips as his eyes closed.

"You okay?" asked Roberts.

"Yeah. I'm fine. It's just my back."

"You know, I don't mind driving. You could kick back in the seat."

"No, I'm good. Plus, that's not gonna help on that road. Look, I deal with this all the time. I just need to rest my back and maybe do some stretches, you know, before we hit that roller coaster again."

"Alright—suit yourself," said Roberts as he leaned back and turned his head to the window and the sparsely snow-covered aspens and pines that shrouded the hills and mountains as far as Doug's eyes could see.

"Umm, you think Deputy Wicker would mind if we waited inside?" asked Doug.

"Nah—not at all. In fact, he'll wonder why we're sitting out here."

Doug struggled from the SUV and stood slightly hunched, feeling like someone thirty years older. He winced as he tried to straighten and followed Roberts in short, careful strides.

Roberts turned the knob on the front door. It was locked. "That's weird. I've been out here more times than I can count—Mike never locks the door. I mean, no one does out here, or in town. It's one of the things I loved about living here. Shoot—let's check the side door."

Doug followed with slightly longer strides as the stiffness eased.

Roberts checked. It was also locked, and every shade was pulled down. He scratched his head and said, "No worries. Mike leaves a key around back in a hidey-rock."

Roberts retrieved the key, opened the side door, and light poured over a table, slicing through dust eddies. He stepped inside.

A familiar metallic rot slammed into Doug like an angry mountain goat. His gag followed Roberts's. Doug covered his mouth and nose as his eyes watered.

"For God's sakes, Mike—take out the trash," Roberts said to the darkness.

Doug saw a dirty plate on the table next to an empty wine glass and glanced at Roberts as he tilted his head with a puzzled looked on his face.

"Hmm. That's odd," said Roberts.

"What's odd… other than that smell?" asked Doug.

"Oh, nothing. I've just never known Mike to be a wine drinker. But he's one helluva a slob when Mandy's not around," Roberts said with a chuckle. "I'll lift the shades and let in some light. There's no electricity out here, but Mike's got a gas generator we can fire up. Leave that door open and let this place air out. I'll open the front."

"No offense, I'll…" Doug retched. "I'll… I'll wait outside."

Doug turned and stopped as he eyed something unexpected below the windowsill where Roberts was headed.

Roberts trudged forward as Doug's eyes adjusted and began to register what that *something* was.

"I tell you, Mike and I had some good times out here. I gotta tell you about the time when…" His next step made a sticky pop when he lifted his boot. He tripped over the *something* and barely kept his balance.

"Ohhh, my," Doug said as he reached into his coat pocket for his camera.

Roberts looked down, and Doug watched his face fall. At Roberts's feet was a badly mutilated corpse. Its chest was a dark, jagged cavity. The camera flash removed the shadow obscuring the head for a split second. As the initial shock eased, Roberts stepped backward and turned to the door.

Doug handed him a pair of gloves.

Roberts put them on and went into auto-mode as Doug's flash and Roberts's Maglite lit up the scene.

The man was tied to a downed chair. His neck was bent at an odd angle against the wall under the window. A wide, black puddle surrounded the body.

"That's... that's Eugene Lee," Roberts said into his sleeve. He coughed.

Doug nodded as he studied the corpse and his camera clicked away. Mr. Lee had been dead for at least one or two days. The chest was gouged out, filled with bloody gelatin, bone chunks, and a chopped-up devilish chili of heart and lungs. Two small-caliber wounds were visible on the neck and right cheek below the eye. If there were more, it was hard to tell from where Doug stood. And stab wounds... forget about counting stab wounds.

Roberts's light shone over blood splatters on the blinds, walls, and wood around the body, testifying to the crime's viciousness.

Doug's attention returned to the shredded chest cavity as Roberts moaned and said, "Mike? No. No, please. No." He retched, but nothing came up.

Roberts shakily panned the beam left. Beyond the black pool was a wood-burning stove. Below it was another dried puddle that led to the head of a corpse of a rotund, late middle-aged to early senior female. Her face was bruised, mottled gray, and black.

"Oh, God... it's Charlotte," said Roberts.

His beam moved to the wood-burning stove's iron shelf.

Doug saw a bent kitchen knife and boot prints.

Roberts panned the beam in a rough triangle between Mrs. Lee's corpse, the square dining table, and the kitchenette. The beam returned to Mrs. Lee's battered face. A blonde, blood-soaked wig rested askew above the forehead that was caved-in on the right side. A heart had been finger-painted with blood around the crater. The trembling light drifted to Mrs. Lee's arms. The upper parts were filleted with some muscle removed to the bone.

"Fuck. Fuck. Fuck-fuck-fuck," Roberts said as he sucked in and out and staggered to the door. "We gotta get back to town. This… this is unfuckin' real. There's gotta be some explanation. Mike would never do anything like this. Someone must've forced him out here after abducting the Lees. Mike's dead. Mike's fuckin' dead—he has to be. The killer must've taken his Jeep."

Doug followed him outside.

Roberts shook as tears formed. He bent over, breathed heavily, and then paced and muttered as Doug continued watching his partner come apart. He'd known Roberts for less than a month, but it was long enough to know he buried his emotions. Now, Roberts looked lost, floundering, grasping for a life preserver to buoy him in the confusion and denial pulling him under into realms he wished not to visit. Doug knew that only Wicker could've done this. For what reason, he couldn't imagine. It was doubtful Wicker had gotten so annoyed with the town's unpopular couple that he decided to abduct them, sign his work at their home, and then, ritualistically and brutally, kill and eat one of them. Doug closed his eyes, took a deep breath of fresher air, and then re-entered the hellscape and studied every inch of the cabin again, starting with the square table and ending with Mrs. Lee's corpse, taking care not to add anymore boot prints.

Doug stepped back outside and pondered as Roberts stared off somewhere in the distance as tears bathed his cheeks. *The plate. The wine glass. Charlotte's arms trimmed of marbled meat. Nauseating.* It reminded Doug of the Fitzgerald murders, but without the dismemberment that Mr. Fitzgerald had suffered. He wondered if the loss of Wicker's father-in-law and best friend and execution of Rice before seeing the Fitzgeralds had… *Wait,* thought Doug. *Wicker never saw the bodies or the photos. He was on his way to the medical center when Tolliver made the grisly discovery. He only witnessed Stone's audio statement.*

Doug recalled meeting Wicker Thursday. The Deputy had been reading about the Fitzgerald murders and seemed amused rather than dumbstruck or appalled. And according to everyone Doug had spoken with on the Mears County force, Wicker's strange behavior began immediately after he killed Rice. Had Wicker lost his mind, or was Stone's story about hell and demon possession something more than a psycho's fairy tale? Obviously, Wicker wasn't in his right mind, but if not his mind, then whose? Questions like that made it clear to Doug that he was overdue for a psych-eval, especially after learning the fate of others taken with DeMure. *Yeah, Dr. Ungol's couch will do me some good,* he thought as he nodded and continued to watch Roberts. *And maybe Bob and I can get a two-for-one special.* Doug sniffed out a snicker though nothing seemed funny.

Doug pondered deeper as he ran his fingers through his hair and massaged his forehead. Lines and dots began to come together. *Martin Rice, now Michael Wicker—each a copycat of the not-so-good Dr. Morgan Bell. Each gone acutely insane with no prior criminal record or evidence of mental illness or instability. Jeremiah Fitzgerald, Charlotte Lee—both eaten, and both descendants of Morgan's arch-enemy and last human meal, Horace Greenly. Family members sadistically murdered but not eaten. And what about Greg Foreman, the Midwest Family Killer? Easy to check… Noo. No way.*

Doug banished the thought that Packer City's legendary cannibal had returned from the dead—maybe more than once—to wreak vengeance on the descendants of the man responsible for his son's death. Doug sniffed out another snicker. *How can I even consider such a thing? There's no such thing as souls, ghosts, evil spirits, or any other mumbo-jumbo attached to the insanity of immortality. But if not Bell, then what… or who?* he thought as he rubbed a temple.

Doug laid a hand on Roberts's shoulder. "Look, I got an idea—maybe whoever did this still has Mike's cellphone. I mean, he does carry his cellphone, doesn't he?"

"Yeah. Probably," Roberts said with croaky voice. "But like Glickman said, when Mike heads out here, he puts the *do-not-disturb* sign on his door to the rest of the world."

"Well, it's still worth checking," said Doug. "If he has his phone on him or the… the killer has it…"

Roberts closed his eyes and sighed.

"… there's a… there's a good chance we can trace it, but we have to… we have to make this place look like no one's been here. Nothing we can do about your boot prints or the tire tracks, though. Bob, you have to consider your friend may have snapped."

Roberts faced Doug and said, "I know. I know. But Mike? No. No, I just can't believe it," he said, and then shook his head and pursed his lips.

"I know—it's hard to imagine, but… but everyone has a dark side, and anyone can be pushed over the edge given the right circumstances."

Roberts wiped his eyes, nodded, then sucked up his emotions like a sponge. He took a few deep breaths. "Yeah, but this is way over that edge. Okay… I can do this. Yeah…" He rubbed his mouth.

"Yeah, we need to keep this between us… and a deputy or two we can trust. Glickman can't know—not yet. This shit'll push him over the edge." He released a sour chuckle. "I need to know Mike wasn't involved. And I know if he wasn't, my friend is dead." He swallowed hard, teared up again, and glared at the sky.

"Well, at least we have one of the murder weapons," said Doug. "The first place to look would be Mrs. Maxwell's to see if she's missing any expensive kitchen knives."

Bob nodded. He closed and locked the door.

The 4Runner bounced back toward Grayson Highway. On the way, Roberts stared out an open window at passing pines and aspens that progressively lost their snow. Doug gripped the steering wheel with arthritic knuckles that ached and tingled as his back shrieked for relief.

While the mind-numbing discomfort helped, Doug could think of nothing other than everything consuming him. He needed to think of something else. Something light and happy. He needed a mental break other than a binge that cured what illed his brain until the next morning.

A sharp pang and a pop almost sent a yelp to his mouth. A delightful sigh followed and his back felt better. Unfortunately, this only allowed his focus to gravitate to memories of the Green River Killer. Ridgway was the worst he'd personally witnessed of humanity's inhumanity to humanity, but the psychopath barely scratched the surface of what was happening here. Additionally, Doug was wrestling with disbelief in forces outside his narrow, rationally-minded reality that made Ridgway look like an altar boy. And how was Wicker connected to the investigation that led him to

Colorado? Or was he connected? Doug wasn't sure, but his gut told him otherwise, and his gut rarely failed him. Well, at least he had a theory, but that theory was sure to earn him a stay at Bellevue's Psychiatric Specialty Hospital.

Suddenly, Doug's wish was granted. He found something to occupy his mind—another *gut* feeling. But this one was more of a rumbling and a cramping. He moaned as he realized he was in for a longer, more miserable drive to the Maxwell House. It wasn't the diversion he'd hoped for, but it did the job.

Sixty-One

Time/Date, Not applicable. Prison of Homicide (AKA Hell), Afterworld.

Delores Destiny fumed. Marduk had never been so cruel... well, at least not to her. They'd been together through untold mortal millennia since he and Gaia had separated following the creation of those despicable two-legged beasts. And now that her powers were on the fritz—her ability to see all pasts, presents, and futures in the Reality 313 removed—Marduk (or the Warden, the Curator, the Benefactor, or whatever he was calling himself this mortal week) had cast her aside like a piece of garbage, or a mortal. *He treats his pets and bastards better than he does me*, she thought.

Marduk would be nowhere without her. It had been her visions from the first murder to the previous mortal day that had made everything possible. Every twist. Every turn. It was her doing. *Beware an Eternal scorned—I won't forget this*, thought Delores.

She angrily strolled down the obsidian hall with its pearl-white floors as grotesque demon guards parted for the storm. Delores slapped a hand on each gray door she passed and each creaked open. Inside, black tendrils ripped naked souls from the viscous darkness covering the floor.

"Up and at 'em, maggots. Your master has a job for you. Do it right, and he may slash your torment time."

A mix of slim to corpulent spirits wafted from the cells dripping Black Ethereal in the hallway. They formed a line and stood erect like soldiers before a drill sergeant.

Delores soured further, disgusted by the eye poison. *In our image? I think not, Gaia.* "Get dressed, you rancid rejects," she commanded.

Memories of clothing spread over them, covering their nakedness with vestments of priests and friars from the Spanish Inquisition. One stepped forward. His head was bald except for a crown of shit-colored hair.

"Did I say you could step forward, Tomas?"

"No, Great Destiny. I apologize for my… for my insolence, oh Great One," said the Spanish Inquisition's first Grand Inquisitor, groveling in the Afterworld's universal language. "I, I am quite eager to know what job your grace has for us. We are but the Curator's faithful servants," he said, chuckling nervously with reverent prayer hands. "We will do anything not to face the torments of the black water grave. Tell us—what is the bidding of our one true Lord and Savior?"

"I'll get back to you soon and let you know. For now, enjoy the indulgences in the Rec Room," she said, directing Tomas de Torquemada and the eyes of the other Dark Inquisitors to the soft, inviting light at the end of the hall.

De Torquemada nodded at the others. Several licked their lips.

"Thank you. Thank you. Thank you. May the Curator bless you," said De Torquemada with the silky voice of a creeper.

Delores shook her head with revulsion, turned, and stormed off the way she came.

Sixty-Two

Early Evening, Saturday, October 6, 2007. The Maxwell House, Packer City, Colorado, Reality 313.

Bob exited the rental with a faux-face as Thorfinnson stiff-legged to the door, knocked, and then knocked again.

Patsy Maxwell answered.

"Where's your restroom?" Thorfinnson asked in a husky, urgent tone, as he shifted from foot to foot while holding a hand to his stomach.

"Second door, down the hall on the left," said Patsy, pointing in the general direction.

Thorfinnson moved down the hall, into the bathroom, and slammed the door.

"Is he okay?" Patsy asked Bob.

"Yeah. Probably. You here alone?"

"Yeah—kids went out to eat. Matt and Luke are heading out Monday for opposite sides of the country. Then it'll just be me and Mandy. Not looking forward to it. God, I miss Pete so much." She sighed and pursed her lips. "Oh, and Jos Turner's hitching a ride with the boys to Denver for her flight to Austin."

"Yup, she told me she's staying with Ricky until Little Joe arrives."

"Yeah. She's leaving everything behind now that…" Patsy sighed deeper, "… now that Joe's gone."

"Hey," Bob said with open arms.

She accepted and wept on his shoulder. Bob wanted to cry, too, but he'd used up his tears at the cabin.

After the Maxwell boys left Monday, only Mandy would be there to help Patsy through the difficult days ahead. It'd been a horrible day and week for her, and for everybody's sake, Bob hoped she wasn't missing any knives. He sat in the recliner and lent his ear to Patsy for the next fifteen minutes.

When Thorfinnson joined them in the living room, he looked peaked. He sat on the couch across from Bob.

"Can I get you guys something to eat or drink?" Patsy asked from the dining room/kitchen entryway.

"Patsy, come on—sit. Let me take care of you," Bob said as he stood. "By the way, you heard from Mike?"

"Thanks, Bob. Always the sweetheart," she said as she sat in the recliner. "And yes, Mike called this morning."

Bob glanced at Thorfinnson.

"He said the quiet time's doing him wonders. He feels just terrible leaving Mandy alone, and even worse missing Peter and Joseph's funeral this morning. He really appreciates everybody's patience and understanding and plans to make it up to us when he gets back."

Bob paused, and asked, "Did he say where he called from?"

"No, he didn't."

Bob nodded. He realized his façade had slipped.

Patsy looked at Thorfinnson, and then back at Bob. "Why? Is something wrong?"

"Uhh, no—it's nothing. Hey, you got any cheese and crackers?"

"Um, yeah. Crackers are in the pantry, and the cheese is where you'd expect it to be," she said with a soft smile.

Bob chuckled lightly and asked, "Either of you want any, or something to drink?"

"No, I'm good," said Thorfinnson, not looking so good. He swallowed like he might not be done in the restroom.

"A glass of water would be nice," Patsy said with a raised eyebrow and a look of concern. "You sure you're okay?"

"Oh, yes. I'm… I'm fine," said Thorfinnson.

Bob entered the kitchen and scanned the counter next to the refrigerator where Patsy kept her fancy knife holder. *Oh shit,* he thought. The largest Ginsu was missing, and the rest of the set matched the knife at the cabin.

"Nice knife set," Bob said as his stomach rumbled while grabbing two glasses from the cabinet.

"Yeah, it was a birthday gift from Pete. I'm so pissed off. One of my knives is missing. I've looked everywhere, but I haven't seen it since yesterday… or maybe it was the day before."

Bob set the glasses on the counter, brought a hand to his lips, and ran toward the restroom. He vomited in his mouth before he got there. He stepped inside, closed the door, and fell to his knees. Retching and splashing followed.

"Bob, you okay?" Patsy asked through the door.

"Yeah, just fine," he said, not feeling fine. More retching, gagging, and panting followed. "Must've been something I ate." He retched and purged again.

"You guys didn't eat at the Greasy Spoon, did you?"

Silence.

"You did, didn't you? After what happened to Kenneth Prattle… Well, I hope you both feel better soon."

After retching a few more times, Bob stood on shaky legs, gargled with Listerine, and returned to the living room feeling ghostly.

"Are you sure you're okay?" she asked again.

"Yeah—much better now," Bob lied. "Could you do me a favor? Could you call Mike and have him call me? There's something, um, important I need to ask him. I've tried to reach him, but he's not answering."

"That's because he accidentally took Mandy's phone. His phone is in the guest bedroom. I guess the ringer's off 'cause I never heard it ring."

"You mind if I look for something on his phone?"

"Why would I? You guys are like brothers."

Bob went to the guest room, found Mike's NOKIA on the nightstand, and flipped it open. The screen was locked, but Bob knew the code was nothing more secure than *1234*. Once unlocked, he scrolled recent calls. There'd been none since Tuesday morning, shortly before the shoot-out at the Fitzgeralds'. He set the phone back on the nightstand and noticed an empty velvet-lined display case on the wall that usually housed a restored vintage Colt 45 Peacemaker. *Well, I know where Eugene's bullet holes came from,* he thought. Bob hoped that was all he was armed with but asking Patsy for the firearm safe code would raise suspicion. He returned to the living room.

"Did you find Mike's phone?" asked Patsy.

"I did. Was looking for a number, but Mike didn't have it."

"No worries. I called Mike. He should be calling you soon. He said he's finishing up something and couldn't talk."

"Thanks, Patsy. In case he gets tied up, can I get Mandy's number?"

"Sure, no problem," she said. She wrote the number on a sticky note and handed it to him.

"Thanks, Patsy. I hate to leave so soon, but I need to speak to Jake Tolliver concerning another missing persons case."

"Oh, my. Who… who's missing now?"

"It's early in the case, so I probably shouldn't say."

"Seriously?"

"Alright—its Eugene and Charlotte Lee."

"Really? Do you think its foul play?" she asked, leaning forward.

"Patsy, I can't say. You know how it goes."

"Sadly, I do. Well, if it is foul play, I'm just surprised it hasn't happened sooner. Those two are the worst, but Charlotte does make a good cup of joe…"

Bob's face flinched at the mention of his fallen friend's name.

"… um, I mean, coffee. You know, it may be her only redeeming quality."

Bob turned serious but stayed gracious for what she didn't know. "I know they weren't nice people, but they don't deserve this," he said, taking care not to speak in the past tense.

"No. No, of course not. I was just saying that... that if the Lees were, I doubt they'd be missed. I mean... uhh... I'm gonna stop talking."

"Patsy, uh, we need to head out," said Bob. "I'll drop by again before we leave town."

"Okay, sweetie. Thanks for coming by. I'm dreading Monday and the lonely days after."

"I know... I know you are," Bob said.

Sixty-Three

Time/Date (Not applicable), Warden's Throne Room. Prison of Homicide, Afterworld.

Marduk—also known as the Warden, the Curator, the Benefactor, God of Gods, Mightiest of the Fallen, and countless other names—sat on his massive throne centered against a wall overlooking two titanic white marble courtyards. A long, wide, obsidian walkway bordered by Afterworld-high ivory columns led to two enormous black iron double doors that opened into the Prison of Homicide and its thirteen levels of Hell. Unlike the earlier whenever, the room was now quiet except for soothing moans and cries of the damned staked in the war pit to the left or the messes in the courtyard to the right.

His gaze drifted to the right where Sirrush—or Rushie as he liked to call the beast—loved to play with Lucifer's three-headed dog, Cerberus. The play area was empty now and stained with writhing soul-shits that Marduk hadn't felt like rising to clean up. Cerberus was gone. Lucifer had taken his faithful companion to another level to spread terror. Oh, how Marduk hated when Cerberus was off chomping the damned elsewhere. Though Sirrush couldn't speak, he worried that his great beast got lonely. *Rushie, if only you could get along with the other beasts. You're just as wrathful as your master, I guess,* he thought as his doting gaze fell on the sleeping dragon balled and snoring at his feet.

Marduk stared forward and regarded the massive white columns. Each column was decorated with gods and demons from the Mesopotamian and Sumerian pantheons. Several columns illustrated the epic of Gilgamesh and other lost stories from Marduk's favorite epoch. This made his mindheart drift back to the good old days when he'd ruled as himself in the cradle of civilization, before mortals gave him countless other names, and pretenders created pantheons mimicking the one he created for Babylon. He'd ruled those lands until Xerxes's armies had lost to the Greeks. After that, Marduk had become bored with his narrow role, and had retired to the Afterworld. But that was only a blink of Timothy's eyes ago—no more than two and a half mortal millennia.

Marduk stroked his chin as the iron doors swung open and a speck of white, contrasting with the obsidian, approached. Initially, the speck was dwarfed between the columns and seemingly no larger than an ant. As the speck grew, pale skin, deep blue-eyes, and blond hair under the white Stetson hat became distinct as did his matching trench coat, shirt, pants, and cowboy boots. The Man in White continued to grow until his size matched Marduk's titanic form lounging on the throne. The young Eternal did not look happy.

"Ahh, Frederick, if it isn't my favorite Eternal. Thank you so much for agreeing to see me."

"Fuck off. What do you want?" asked the God of Mischief, Chaos, and Luck.

"I need my Contract Maker back in the fold. We've come too far to end things like this."

"You and Delores used me."

"Of course we did. If you knew what was going to happen, the whole plan would've never worked."

"Whatever. Say what you will, but I'm not helping you hurt Mary any more than I already have."

Marduk laughed.

Frederick's pale skin turned a delightful shade of furious red.

"You do realize she's a siren?" asked Marduk. "A Merelder, like Helen? Back when we could weave magic in the mortal worlds without the fear of disapproval of the Council, sirens were common. Their voices beautiful. Their songs irresistible. Mortals desired them, and their tribes went to war over them. You, yourself, know that Troy was destroyed because of one, and from the ashes, Rome was born. Many mariners have dashed their ships on the rocks trying to get close to them. Are you going to let this siren lead your ship onto the rocks and ruin the good thing we have going?"

"You don't understand," the Man in White said through clenched teeth. "I couldn't help you if I wanted to."

"Of course, you can," said Marduk. "Tell me how you know this Manycows that your previous shell sent Mary Demure to find, and where I can find him. You know your sister has no powers within the sacred mountains where he resides. As it stands now, she has no power at all. And anyway, you owe me."

"I don't owe you shit. Look, I'd never understood how your ex could love those two-legged creatures until I met Mary. Yeah, descended from Merelders—so what? She means more to me than the magic inside her. I can't and won't do anything *else* to harm her."

"Hmmm." Marduk pursed and rubbed his lips with a prayer hands steeple. "Alrighty then. Let me put it this way. You do realize that under the Black-and-White Rule, she's already mine?"

Frederick glared.

Marduk grinned and continued, "And you also know the eternal punishment prescribed for any immortal-to-be whose shell has broken the Black-and-White Rule? Need I quote it to you?"

Frederick's hateful glower didn't waver.

"No? I didn't think so. And I guess, most importantly, you know what happens when I don't get my way. So, let me put it this way. I can make her stay in the Prison a delightful dream, or subject her soul to every… imaginable… horror," he said, turning on his most demonic voice for *every*, *imaginable*, and *horror*.

"You're a real bastard, you know."

Marduk scoffed, smiled wide, and said in a mocking tone, "Bastard? Not that I know of. I was just sort of created, like you, only bigger and far more terrible and awesome. Honestly, I'm not sure how the whole Eternal baby thing works. My creator never gave me that *talk*. You have to understand—it doesn't serve my purposes to make your mortal sweetheart suffer during her stay here." He paused and stroked his chin. "You do realize she will hate you for eternity once she learns what you did to her life and the lives of almost everyone she ever loved?"

Frederick worked his jaw, but didn't blink.

Marduk sighed, and looked at sleeping Sirrush. "He doesn't seem to care, Rushie." He regarded Frederick, and lowered his tone reticently. "I see that now. You really do love her. Listen, I'll make you a deal. I won't make you give up the location of the healer. Believe it or not, I'm a romantic at heart. Well, at least I once was, but that was before your creation. I have to say—it is kind of sweet. A lovesick Eternal using a mortal shell with the crazy notion that he could enjoy the rest of a life revolution with the mortal he loves, away from Delores's prying eyes. It's kind of funny… but I'm not laughing," said Marduk, his tone darkening. He paused as he leaned forward and narrowed his eyes. "Your advice to Mary put her exactly where Delores had foreseen she would go, and where your sister had made sure Ryan Mender would be. Then at the moment of transfer, your sister went blind to Mary's destiny as if a bubble formed around her that also protected Mender when she was near. And then, a few mortal days ago, Delores's powers vanished altogether as if her far-seeing eyes had been plucked out of her Eternal head. Now she's utterly useless… and that bothers me. What also bothers me is that I don't know who this Manycows is or why you believed he could reverse Albert Caine's formula. With or without your sister's special gift, this Manycows would've been able to hide from your sister inside the land of the Four Sacred Mountains. And now, even if your sister could see, it's too late to screen your last shell for answers. That shell has been shed, and its Overspirit refuses to reveal anything about Manycows, no matter how many torments I put it through." Marduk glanced to Sirrush's play yard and a screaming pile of soul-shit and then back at Frederick. "Rushie here has already eaten and shat it out more than a hundred times. Few Overspirits make it through my dragon more than once or twice before cracking. Yes, this Overspirit will crack… eventually. They all do. But I'm starting to get… very, very impatient. If I discover you are in league with my ex, Mary will suffer, and I will make you watch."

"Look, you fucking asshole, I hate you from the bottom of my heart, but I would never help that bitch other than what is required of me as the Contract Maker. I mean, especially after she ganged up on me with the other gods and cheated me out of my kingdom—and you helped."

"Ah, yes, true—I did. But what was I to do as a Councilone? And besides, Gaia's payback was *hell*, wouldn't you say?"

"Yeah." Frederick grinned and chuckled lightly. "I guess it was. A bit of overkill, don't you think?"

"Nope. Gaia had it coming for what she did. You got your revenge, and I took the fall. And what thanks did I get? You and your brother tried to have me extinguished. But I forgive you. Plus, I knew Gaia was too weak to do what needed to be done. So here I am, banished to the Prison of Homicide. You know, we've had some good times. You remember when I had you mess with the master weather control for the realities?"

"Yeah—that was classic." The Man in White snickered. "Nearly drowned all those five-fingered buggers."

"Whew—was Gaia pissed. I swear that woman can't take a joke," Marduk said and laughed through a wide smile before it faltered. "Though it did kill a lot of creatures my son, Timothy, loved."

"And you tried to blame the whole thing on me—dick. But hey, you did give mortals a prophecy about the flood and plans for the arks."

"That's right, I did. I was merciful, and Timothy was happy that a few mortals listened and didn't kill all the prophets, or else our favorite creations, the horse and the dog, wouldn't have survived. It does feel good being merciful sometimes. Also, if all the mortals had drowned, the rest of eternity would've been very boring. I mean, what other creature would I use to make Gaia's eternity miserable?"

Frederick smiled. "Look, I didn't warn Gaia about your plans. And whether I hate you or not, I'm on your side as always."

Marduk raised a brow.

"Okay… almost always."

"Splendid, because I need mortal shells to locate and capture Mary and her new boyfriend. As you know, they have to be harvested together; otherwise, I won't be able to control the White Horseman, Pestilence. That's why I need you to travel to the land inside those cursed mountains and speak with my Diné witches. I need my Skinwalkers to find Ryan Mender, Mary DeMure, and this *Manycows*. General Adamson believes they're headed to Mexico, but I suspect deception. Of course, the Council and your brother, Morton—the eternal pain in my ass—have bound me to follow the Rules of Immortal and Eternal Conduct. As you know, your contracts are the only way my Dark Inquisitors can pass into the Reality 313 without needless trouble from the Council that will only slow the inevitable. So, if you would be so unkind to convince the witches to allow my Dark Inquisitors to use their shells to locate your precious Mary and my lead horseman, I will guarantee her a delightful afterlife in Hell."

Frederick paused, and then said, "And you promise she won't suffer after her wind is taken?"

"I promise. Would I lie to you?" Marduk said, palms up.

"When have you not?"

"True, but then, what choice do you have but to trust me now?"

THRIPPssss.

Frederick glanced at the sleeping dragon and wrinkled his nose and forehead. "What are you feeding Sirrush?"

"Oh, nothing unusual, just souls I've had trouble converting. My apologies. Some Overspirits don't agree with his delicate digestive system. You know, I hardly notice the smell anymore. I guess Rushie needs to dump some Overspirits back into their Black Water cells. How I hate when Rushie drops them in the play courtyard. Leaves a stain that's hard to clean up, and sometimes… well, the beast sends them right back through the ol' grinder. Disgusting when he licks me."

Sirrush opened its eyes, lifted his long neck, and turned its head toward Marduk. The beast leaned forward, and Marduk scratched the dragon between its horns. Sirrush let out a mix of a purr and a low growl that was as pleasant as a chainsaw. "I just love this beast. Now leave us. You have work to do. Do it quickly, or I might change my mind about Mary's afterlife." His gaze returned to Sirrush.

Sixty-Four

Dusk, Saturday, October 6, 2007. Packer City, Colorado, Reality 313.

Bob tried to call Wicker twice on the way to Tolliver's place, but each time the call went to voice mail, and each time he left an urgent *call-me-immediately* message. On the east side of the Northside Bridge, cattycorner southeast from their motel, Bob asked Thorfinnson to pull over so he could get some air. Thorfinnson did and Bob got out and motioned for him to follow down the bank to the river's edge. There, they discussed what Bob had learned at the Maxwell house and from Wicker's phone and what he hadn't. He confirmed that the knife at the cabin was Mrs. Maxwell's and that Wicker hadn't used his phone since Tuesday morning.

"… But he had to have used someone's," said Bob. "I didn't think about this until now, but according to Glickman's notes, Mike called Mandy right after breaking Jones's camcorder and before the audiotaped portion of Stone's interrogation. The question is, whose phone was Mike using? It wasn't Mandy's 'cause he didn't grab hers until he left for the cabin Thursday evening and there were no calls on his phone after Tuesday morning. I need to find out where Mike's call originated from this morning. I also need to know if Mandy received a call from Mike on Tuesday around four p.m. Look, I'm gonna call the phone company to see what I can find out before we bring Tolliver into this."

Thorfinnson paced as Bob found a helpful operator and learned that a call originated from Wicker's phone in Grayson at 9:03 a.m. that morning. But on Tuesday, there were no calls between 11 a.m. and 6 p.m. After that, there were several long ones from Albany, New York, and Carlsbad, California, and various places in between. The ones to New York and California would've been from the Maxwell boys.

Bob got in the mud-coated 4Runner and brought Thorfinnson up to speed as they continued to Tolliver's place. "Mike was definitely in Grayson this morning, but there's no telling where he is now. Hopefully, he'll call soon. I wish there was some way to check if anything was missing from the dead operatives at the Fitzgeralds', but everything's locked up in Grayson."

"Why?"

"Well, I would guess they had phones, and I'll go out on a limb and guess that Rice's was missing along with an air pistol that every other Black Beret was carrying. It's likely he used Rice's phone to make the missing call to whoever—we'll probably never know—but I doubt it was Mandy like he told Glickman. And the air pistol—I figure Mike had to use something to incapacitate the Lees to transport them to the cabin."

"I understand the first part. And the second. But how does that information help us find Wicker?"

"Look, there's still a lot you don't know about me. Believe it or not, I was once a *hail-Mary-full-of-grace*, rosary-bead-carrying Catholic."

"Yeah, I kind of figured that out when Glickman handed you your cross and beads. So, you're a Catholic. So what? Bob, you're losing me now."

"Just… just bear with me. When I was a kid in *Bawstun*, I was an altar boy and was faithful to the church up until a nasty divorce. Then my faith was rocked by that sex scandal in the archdiocese a few years back. I left the church and haven't been to mass since."

Thorfinnson's eyes narrowed.

"And no, I wasn't diddled by my priest. What I'm trying to say, and not so well, is that… I… I still believe in the power of God to do good in the world and in the power of Satan to tear everything down. I tell you, something bad's going on here."

"Really? You think?" Thorfinnson said sarcastically.

"No, it's something more. Something demonic. *Really demonic*. Don't take this the wrong way, but I have to ask, do you believe in God?"

"Uh, no, I'm an atheist… or at least I was. I don't know what I am anymore. You know, over the past few days, I've been struggling with my beliefs, too. There's just no... no rational explanation for what's going on here."

"I know. Let me ask you another question. Do you believe in demon possession?"

"Umm, no. No, I don't."

"I understand. It's not something that's easy to wrap your head around unless... unless of course, you've seen proof. But whether you believe in demons or not, they believe in you. They're real, and so is the power of the exorcists who cast them out."

Thorfinnson rolled his eyes.

"You can believe it or not—doesn't matter. But the process is different than what you see in the movies. My old priest back in Boston is still an exorcist. His name is Reginald O'Malley. Anyway, it was after I saw *The Exorcist* that I became curious. So, I asked my padre what it was like to go toe-to-toe with a demon. That afternoon, he showed me some videos of a few he'd performed. Stone's interrogation reminded me of one of them. The possessed was a middle-aged Chinese homeless woman. She'd been committed after running naked through Chinatown stabbing people with dirty needles before she was tazed on the Common. Anyway, before Father O'Malley sent her demon back to Hell, it spoke French and referred to the woman as its *mortal shell*. O'Malley translated—he speaks like six languages. Well, there was no green vomit, and her head didn't spin around, but the demon did claim to be a dead serial killer named Dr. Marcel Petiot. Not that that matters, but Petiot said he was from the same place—if you can suspend your disbelief long enough—that Franz Schicklgruber described. He even called the Devil in his hell the Curator."

"What? Why didn't you say something sooner?" asked Doug as he pulled into Tolliver's driveway behind a black Toyota Tacoma.

Bob paused to take in the magnificent early evening view of the Mount Capitol beyond the high ridge in the near distance. "Sorry. Beautiful view."

Doug looked.

"But really—you just said yourself that you don't believe in this shit. Plus, we've only known each other for a month. I figured you'd think I was crazy if I told you what I thought after I listened to Stone's statement. Not a very good way to further a working relationship. Am I wrong?"

"No, you're right. I thought I was going crazy myself. I'm just glad I'm not the only one."

"Well, my theory is that the spirit of Morgan Bell possessed Martin Rice, forced his mortal shell to kill the Fitzgeralds, then jumped into Mike after my buddy finished off Rice. Bell has been controlling his actions ever since."

"Okay, granted you're right—no matter how ridiculous that sounds—what do we do about *your* buddy?"

"Well, each of the demons O'Malley exorcised attempted to harm or kill the host before being sent back to the abyss. If Mike is possessed, Bell will try to destroy him if cornered. It would be nice to have one of those tranquilizer pistols that are locked up in the Grayson evidence room. But there's no way Griggs will let us in there, even if we bring Glickman into the loop, which we'll have to do sooner than later. And there's another problem—Mike's armed with at least a vintage Colt 45 Peacemaker. I believe that's what he used to unload a cylinder into Eugene Lee. I noticed it missing from its display case after I checked his phone. You know, I've only seen it out of the case a few times when Mike and I took it out to fire it. It works just fine, and he has plenty of ammo for the relic. If he starts shooting or if Bell decides to use it on Mike, there won't be any way to bring in his *mortal shell* alive. When we find him, we have to move fast. We'll need backup and an ambulance close by in case something goes wrong. And we'll need to do it without alerting the Cannibal Surgeon."

Tolliver stepped onto his porch. "Hey, you guys coming in, or are you just going to sit out there all night?"

"Yeah, yeah. Be right in," Bob said as he stepped from the vehicle.

Sixty-Five

Dusk, Saturday, October 6, 2007. Near Kayenta, Navajo Nation in Arizona.

The Man in White stood on a straight stretch of desert Highway 160, staring at a clear orange and yellow horizon and the darkening blue sky. He inhaled the cold, clean air. It was refreshing after leaving the Warden's Throne Room. It was real, unlike the air of the Afterworld, where breathing was optional, and something Immortals did to remind themselves of what it was like to be alive. Sure, there was the sensation of breathing when he was in control of a mortal shell, but it was nothing like this.

Frederick Chance never had a body per se. He only had the ones he conjured when he played the role of the Contract Maker. Or when he'd played the part of Gavrilo Haus when he'd hung out with his good friend Nathan Miller… who he'd been leading down a spiral staircase to Hell for a while now—but they'd had so much fun. It'd all been part of the greater plan which had become complicated as his feelings grew for the famous writer, though they'd never be as intense as they were for the siren named Mary. And like with Mary, he knew that the fun with Nathan would eventually end. He sighed and enjoyed the natural sky.

How Frederick wished he could be a real mortal just once. He missed Louis's shell and wished he could touch Mary, make love to her, and make her happy for one life revolution. But alas, he was an Eternal. He'd once not existed, and then he did. Where he came from, or where any Eternal came from, he didn't know. Marduk once spoke of an Upper Realm and a Master Creator, but Frederick wondered if it was just more of his lies. Like most Eternals and Immortals, he believed there was nothing beyond the Afterworld and the mortal realities that Marduk and Gaia created for their son, Timothy. It was a depressing prospect that had made him more than once consider taking the plunge into the Abyss.

He watched a rapidly approaching truck. It was rusted and moving backward due to a lack of forward drive. As it passed, the driver located the lone mud puddle remaining after the short-lived snowfall of a few days earlier, splashed him, and colored his suit brown.

Frederick gritted his perfect teeth and lifted a hand toward the truck already some distance away. He made a fist, and then opened the palm. The driver's luck ran out as a well-worn tire exploded.

The truck veered to the right and flipped over and over as screeching, crunching metal sounds tore through the desert air. The soon-to-be lifeless mortal was ejected on the third roll.

Frederick grinned and slowed time to watch the rocket-man soar, guiding his flight upward with a flat hand. The hand arced, and then shot straight down.

The man lifted his arms as if they'd soften the impact. They snapped, and his head exploded like a melon, painting the pavement brainy red. *Better than frying ants with a magnifying glass*, he thought.

The Man in Brown waved a hand from his hat to his boots and sparkled again like the glistening teeth of his winning smile.

Across the road, a dirt driveway led to an old hogan. In front was a rusted-out old Ford truck on blocks and another beside it that looked barely drivable. He headed toward the hogan as an emaciated mutt hobbled his way. The dog peered up and waited for a pat on the head.

The Man in White melted. *What a pitiful beast*, he thought as he knelt and stroked the remaining fur on the gray, scabbed, thickened odiferous skin.

The dog licked Frederick's hand and sauntered away as best he could, satisfied.

Frederick smiled and strolled to the dwelling with his mindheart warm and full. He knocked on the east-facing door and waited. He knocked again—harder and louder this time—and heard the occupant yell something in Diné, which Frederick understood with the All-Speak ability of Eternals and Immortals.

"I'm coming. I'm coming. No need to be so rude," a man bellowed in a raspy, cantankerous voice.

The door opened.

Before Frederick stood a crouched, late-middle-age, skinny Navajo man wearing a flannel shirt and long johns. The man scratched his ass and straightened his junk.

"Oh, it's you. Come on in. Come on in," said the man. "I will make you somethin' to eat and pour ya some coffee."

"Billy Darkstorm, you know I don't eat," said the Man in White.

"Ahh, that's... that's right, I forget. So, Contract Maker, what brings you to my humble hogan?"

"The Curator has a job for you and your Skinwalkers."

"Really? What is it? What is it? You know, I, uh... I'm always happy to serve the Master."

"He wants you to be on the lookout for Ryan Mender and Mary DeMure, and we need your special skills to find them. He also wants you to find an Hataalii named Manycows."

"Hmmm, well, there's not a lot of Manycows around. And no singers that I know of. There was one who had a grandson who became a singer, though. Still around, too. His name is Curtis Chee. All Diné know him, and he's an easy man to find if he wants to be found, an' nearly impossible if he don't."

"Well, then I'd start by finding him to see if we can solve this mystery. I know that's what the Curator would want you to do. He'll also need a blood mark to allow his Dark Inquisitors to ride along with your witches. You never know when you might run into one of Gaia's angels who might need to take a dip in the Abyss."

"Of course, whatever our Lord wants, his faithful servants will happily comply. I will send word to the others to meet in the caves tonight," said Darkstorm.

"No need—I'm meeting with them as we speak."

"Pardon me. I forget sometimes that your kind can be in all places when you want to be," he said.

Frederick opened his white jacket and removed a dagger from a sheath on his belt and an ink well from a coat pocket. He laid both on a small kitchen table beside a plate with a half-eaten, fried bologna sandwich. From another pocket, he retrieved a black leather roll tied with a brown leather cord. He undid the cord, unrolled the leather, exposing yellowing parchment, and set it next to the dagger and the ink well. Paragraphs of calligraphy covered the document, specifying the contract's legalese in the Diné language. Frederick pulled an ivory quill from his shirt pocket—its silver nib engraved with a double-crossed ankh. He placed it by the contract opposite the dagger and ink well.

The witch regarded the Contract Maker, nodded, and sat. He took a bite of his sandwich and grabbed the dagger.

"Aren't you going to read the fine print?" asked Frederick.

"Should I? The Master already owns my soul, an' I am hoping for special treatment when my unholy wind leaves this body. So, what do you want us to do when we find the famous Ryan Mender, the girl, and Curtis Chee, if he turns out to be the Hataalii you're looking for?"

"They are to be harvested, but don't bother using your corpse poison on Mender. He'll only absorb it and use it against you. And concerning the *girl*..." Frederick said, glaring into the witch's eyes, "... she is not to suffer when you or your Skinwalkers put her down, or else I'll peel off the skin of the one responsible and wear it."

Darkstorm's hand holding the dagger trembled. He stammered, "W-w-what if our passengers use our shells against our will?"

"I have no power over the actions of Dark Inquisitors, but rest assured, for the mortal shells that I do, I will have my vengeance and see to it that their stay in the Prison is even more unpleasant than usual."

Darkstorm glanced at the contract, and then into the Contract Maker's lethal blue eyes. He swallowed hard, sliced his left palm in one fluid motion, made a fist, and squeezed until the inkwell was full.

Frederick handed him a white handkerchief.

Darkstorm wrapped it around his bleeding hand and picked up the quill with the other. He dipped the nib in the well and signed on the line in mortal red with the Diné words for *Darkstorm*.

The Man in White turned his left palm up and a doeskin pouch appeared.

The Witch Chief smiled and drooled over and around rotten teeth and through toothless gaps. He swiped the ice cold pouch from the Contract Maker's hand and undid the tie string as he danced in his seat. He stuck a thumb and index finger inside and removed a glittering pinch of cobalt paradise. He brought the fingers to his nose and bumped hard. His face contorted in sweet agony and tensed as his eyes closed to contain the maddening brain freeze. He opened them slowly. His brown eyes were now dark blue and glistening.

"Is this what I think it is?" asked Darkstorm.

"Yes. Only the best Dead Blow for the Curator's witches."

Sixty-Six

Twilight, Saturday, October 6, 2007. Deputy Tolliver's Place, Packer City, Colorado.

Bob sat in his small living room across from Thorfinnson.

"Can I get you a beer?" Tolliver asked Thorfinnson.

"Got any coffee?"

"Yeah, I'll put on a pot. How about you, Bob?"

"Beer, please."

"So, did you talk to Mike?" asked Tolliver as he opened the refrigerator.

"Not exactly," said Bob. "Maybe you should grab that beer and sit down before I tell you what I have to tell you."

"On second thought, forget the coffee," said Thorfinnson. "I could use a beer, too."

Tolliver returned with three open bottles of Shiner Bock and set two on the coffee table. He plopped in the recliner, took a big guzzle, and asked, "So, what's on your mind other than the obvious?"

Bob rubbed his mouth and began with what they found at Wicker's cabin, and then continued with everything he and Thorfinnson had observed and learned about Wicker before and after the grisly discovery. Bob expressed fear that Wicker might try to harm himself if confronted but didn't say why.

Tolliver looked sick. "We have to tell Glickman."

"Are you sure he can handle it?" asked Bob.

"Are you fucking kidding me? What choice does he have? Hell, you should have gone to him first. He's the head lawman in this county now. I mean, what choice do any of us have now? Wicker is one of us."

"Yeah. You're right. But I'd keep this between the four of us for now… that is, until we have a good plan to bring Mike in alive," said Bob.

"Agreed. Let me call Glickman and tell him to get his ass over here as soon as possible."

Sixty-Seven

Glickman arrived ten minutes later and sat in a rocking chair between the recliner and the couch. Tolliver handed him an open Shiner. Glickman took a big gulp as Bob skipped formalities and got straight to it as Thorfinnson handed him his camera. Glickman set the bottle on the coffee table and listened with a stony face as he perused the macabre photos. When Bob finished, Glickman stared at the floor.

After a thirty-second silence, Bob asked, "Are you okay?"

"Be quiet, Bob. I'm thinking," Glickman said in a calm and deadly collected voice. Another minute passed, and then another. Finally, he spoke. "I didn't turn over everything Pete and Joe had on DeMure. It wasn't on purpose, though. Our office manager found DeMure's backpack yesterday—you know, the one Pete pulled from Melvin's Jeep. It was sitting in the corner of a storage closet at the office. I guess Fuller and Matthews missed it when they came by the office on Wednesday, demanding everything on the Demure case. I mean, Pete should've turned it over to Griggs that first week after Melvin Anderson's death. I guess with all the craziness, he got distracted and forgot it was there. I started looking through the backpack yesterday before the get-together at Bell's Saloon. In it, I found a map of the Four Corners states with a path drawn to Arizona with *find manycows* written on it. Before he died, I think Pete was following up on something. On his desk pad, he wrote, "*find Manycows?*" I don't know what it means unless it's the name of the Navajo medicine man Mary Demure was trying to find. But if Pete was on to something, I couldn't tell you. He didn't mention it anywhere in the copy of his notes I turned over to Homeland Security. That doesn't matter right now, but it might be helpful when you talk to James Mender. To get to my point, I was planning to give the evidence to Griggs after the funeral so he could take it up to Grayson. After all, Anderson's murder case was in his jurisdiction before he became Interim Sheriff. After your call from the Lees, it completely slipped my mind. So, I feel it would only be right and proper to drive this stuff up to Grayson tonight and put it in the evidence locker myself. Maybe I can borrow a pair of those tranquilizer pistols from the Mender Massacre."

"Uhh, that... that would be great," Bob said as he glanced at Thorfinnson.

Glickman held up a *shut-the-fuck-up* finger and continued, "Anyway, Dr. Boyd told me whatever was used on Mender after he beat the shit out of two of those beret-wearing cocksuckers works faster than anything he's seen. Well, at least according to his office manager. She watched those contractors take down Mender with two darts in less than ten seconds. Obviously, it didn't kill him."

"Thanks, that might just work," said Bob. "Once we know where Mike is, I think it would be best if only Doug and I went in. If he sees us going in heavy, this won't end well. Mike has his wife's cellphone, and the last call this morning was from Grayson. Patsy and I called Mike and I'm still waiting on a call back, but as soon as he does, we'll know exactly where he is."

"Maybe I'll catch him heading back this way," said Glickman. "But we can't go near that cabin until we know."

Bob nodded, and then asked, "Don, how long have you known me?"

"Ten years. Why?"

"And have you ever considered me an irrational guy?"

"Never. Get to your damn point," said Glickman.

"Well, before I do, I need you to assume that everything Stone told you was true. It's the only way this'll make sense."

"Okay, whatever."

"What did the Fitzgeralds and the Lees have in common?"

"I don't know—Jeremiah and Charlotte were cousins."

"Yes, and who in this town's history are they both related to?"

"Horace… Horace Greenly, of course," said Glickman.

"Okay. I need to tell you another thing about Mike. He executed Rice, and right after, he started acting strange."

"Yeah. Yeah, I know. I know he did. I didn't want to think about it. I mean that asshole and his friend… they killed Pete… and Joe. I'm not sure if I could've restrained myself any better had it been me standing over Rice. Definitely not after I saw what he did to the Fitzgeralds." He clenched his lips and breathed hard through his nose.

"But Mike didn't know about that, or shouldn't have. So, what else did Rice and now Mike have in common, other than performing killings and a cannibalistic ritual reminiscent of Dr. Morgan Bell?"

"Nothing, except they had no prior criminal records and were apparently decent people before the murders."

"Exactly. I have a theory I haven't had time to check out yet. It concerns a serial killer named Greg Foreman."

"The Midwest Family Killer?" asked Tolliver.

"Yup. The former Sunday school teacher murdered each family and ritualistically ate the father or mother, but not both, and not the children if they had any. It was exactly what Bell did with the Greenly family, right down to the red wine. I suspect we'll discover, like Jeremiah and Charlotte, every one of the fathers or mothers was a direct descendant of Horace Greenly."

"But... but how? That makes no sense."

"Yes, it does. But only if Joshua Stone—or, more correctly, Franz Schicklgruber—told the truth. Martin Rice, Mike, and, I suspect Greg Foreman didn't voluntarily kill anyone. And now the spirit of Morgan Bell is pulling Mike's strings. And we need Mike captured alive to prove it."

Glickman sighed, looked at Tolliver, and asked, "What do you think?"

"I'm trying not to. Just tell me what you need, Bob," he said as he shook his head.

"Tolliver, head up to Grayson with me in case we run into Wicker, and I need backup. And Bob, call me immediately after Wicker calls. If you're correct, we need to know if Horace Greenly has any descendants in Grayson."

Sixty-Eight

8:27 p.m., Saturday, October 7, 2007. Northside Lodge, Packer City, Colorado.

No sooner had Bob faded into sleep's soft darkness did a chiming ringtone tear him from impending slumber. He sat up, fumbled for his phone on the nightstand, and found it. He rubbed his eyes, and flipped it open. The caller ID read *Mandy*—it was Wicker, or least his shell.

Thorfinnson glanced away from the WNN newscast.

Bob waved for him to lower the volume. He did and Bob pressed the green *L*.

"Hey, Bob, Patsy told me you've been trying to reach me. What do you need?" Wicker asked, sounding put out.

"Did you listen to my messages?"

"No, I saw you called, after I told Patsy that I'd call you back when I had time. So, here I am calling you back. What do you want?"

"Yeah, uh, sorry to bug you, but it was Glickman who asked me to give you a ring. He wants you back in town. The Lees are missing, and he needs everybody out there searching for them. Where are you now?"

"In... Grayson... getting supplies. Shit, why didn't he call me himself? And why can't he handle this? I'm trying to get my head straight and I still have a few more days of vacation."

"One—you have Mandy's phone. Two—I don't know, Mike—maybe his hands are full with all the shit that's gone down lately. Look, Glickman said vacation's over, and so is your suspension. He needs you."

"Goddammit. Whatever. I'll be back in town tomorrow afternoon."

"Hey, look, I'm sorry I got testy," Bob said, lowering the tension. "Everybody's under a lot of stress."

"It's okay. Look, I'm gonna let you go now. I'll talk to you tomorrow if you're around."

"Wait," said Bob, looking at Thorfinnson. "Can I ask you one more thing?"

"Yeah, what?" said Wicker.

"Would you mind if I took Thorfinnson out to the cabin? I want to show my new partner where we used to hang out. Maybe barbeque something. Have a few cold ones."

"I'm… I'm sorry, but I'm doing some repairs right now. Maybe some other time?"

"Sure, Mike. Looking forward to it. Maybe on another trip. Probably for the best anyway. Me and my partner have an appointment with James Mender tomorrow evening. Norine's making dinner. Can you believe it? You want to know something?"

"Bob, I really don't have time for this."

Bob kept talking. "Thorfinnson's wife is a big Norine Jones fan. I'm talking a fanatic. I mean, rough situation we're walking into. Still, hella-cool for him to meet the living legend. Besides being talented, she's an amazing per…"

"I am sorry to cut you off, Bob," said Wicker, faltering into a southern drawl, "but I am quite busy right now. Can I call you later?" he asked, recovering his no-accent accent.

"Oh, yeah, sure. Why not? Sorry," Bob said, and chuckled, "you know me, always mister talkative. You remember the time…"

"Goddammit, Bob. Shut the fuck up! I gotta go. Bye!" Dial tone.

"You think that was long enough?" asked Bob.

"Absolutely. But you realize you don't have to keep someone on the line for a trace on them anymore?"

"Yeah, I know. But after watching so many cop shows growing up, it's a quirk I have. Plus, the *good* surgeon slipped and lost Mike's voice for a second."

"Really?" Doug asked as a hand came to his mouth.

"Really."

Sixty-Nine

Morgan hung up with a huff. "I do declare that Detective Roberts is an annoying cuss," he said to the middle-aged, graying man duct-taped to a chair. The man's blood was drip, drip, dripping on the fine ceramic floor. "I cannot for the life of me understand how Michael Wicker can suffer him. Do you not agree?" he asked as he picked at a stubborn piece of meat between his teeth with a toothpick.

The unlucky man did not reply. He only looked through Morgan as if he were not there. Like Jeremiah Fitzgerald and Charlotte Lee, his only crime was being born to Horace's bloodline that led to his two oldest daughters. At the time of his infamous crime, they were married and no longer lived in Packer City. While they were the only surviving members of Horace's family, his progeny had multiplied and spread like a plague.

Morgan peered into the vermin's sad eyes, and his lips drew into a toothy smile as he followed the man's gaze into the front room.

There, the man's lovely wife reclined in a rocking chair with her head askew while their daughter and twin teenage sons sat nice and proper on a fine leather couch. They were spectators for the macabre spectacle and were watching with unblinking interest. Well, not really. The black hole in their foreheads and the maroon trickle that had stopped dribbling past their chins made it clear that they were no longer interested in anything in this reality. Unlike the father, Morgan did not know their names, nor did he care to know. They were Greenlys, and that was good enough for the old Surgeon.

He smiled at his handiwork as the bleeding man passed out again. He checked the man's pulse. It was still strong. He sighed and lamented what could have been earlier that week. Mr. Lee dying from a heart attack Thursday had left him feeling hollow and unfulfilled. And while he tried to enjoy his previous Greenly feast, Mrs. Lee had not satisfied his fussy palate after she'd done killed herself to prevent an even gruesomer end. He'd tried to make the best of it but had felt queasy early that morning and decided to pick up some supplies from a hardware store in Grayson. He'd got some odd looks since Wicker's face was quite bruised and swollen from that insufferable fat Greenly bitch. After leaving Wicker's Jeep in the parking lot, he'd found another ride, disposed of its driver by the river, and decided to pay a visit to the next Greenly on the list—a list the Curator had so kindly provided.

Morgan felt much better now. While anger was finer, the stir fried Greenly he was picking from his teeth had hit a spot which Mrs. Lee had missed. He only had a few more days at best before the authorities caught up to the dear deputy, but he was quite satisfied with this run. Two more souls for the Curator would definitely win him some brownie points. *I guess Rice and Wicker were already his, but all the shattered lives in their wake will surely count for something,* he thought. *Of course, the dividends of evil accrue with time. And ten, and soon to be eleven more Greenlys removed from this reality... well, that is nothing to him-haw about.*

If he had time, there was another family of eight in Sur Del Rio when he finished up here. Regardless, there would be infinite opportunities to eat and kill more Greenlys in the future. And by Satan, he would not rest in Hell until every last one of them was dead.

Seventy

9:03 p.m., Saturday, October 6, 2007. Northside Lodge, Packer City, Colorado.

Bob hung up with the phone company and called Glickman. "Where are you guys?"

"Just passed the Mears County sign."

"I know where Mike is."

"Where?"

"Silver City."

"Silver City? Are you sure?" asked Glickman, his voice rising to near panic.

"Positive."

"Ahh shit," said Glickman. "Councilman Duggan. If you're right about what's going on, Mike... Goddammit, I mean Morgan Bell is there to kill the Councilman and his family. Has to be. I need to call Sheriff Packwood to let him know what's going on. Where are you now?"

"Northside Lodge, room Eleven. So, why Duggan?"

"Duggan's the great-great-grandson of Mable Greenly Ferguson, Horace's oldest daughter."

"Damn."

"Yeah. Look, Tolliver and I will be at your motel in about ten minutes. We snagged a few items that might help the Mike situation. I'll ask Packwood to have his people stand by and out of sight and let you and Thorfinnson go in first. I know Packwood and he'll wanna go in guns blazing, but I'll warn him of the delicate nature of the situation and the high probability that no one will walk out alive if Wicker, or Bell, or whoever, catches wind that he's been caught. I'll send Guzman and Strickland for additional backup while Tolliver, Lombardi, and I head up to Wicker's cabin to gather more evidence. And thank Thorfinnson again for taking those photos. Look, once you have Wicker in handcuffs, I'll contact Griggs to let him know our suspect is in custody. Hopefully, you get there in time, or we'll be bagging more than the Lees."

Seventy-One

Bob was waiting outside the motel with Thorfinnson when Glickman and Tolliver pulled up with bullet-resistant vests, handheld radios (set to Silver City's frequency), and two tranquilizer pistols. There was minimal chit-chat as Tolliver handed Bob the items. Glickman nodded, reversed, and peeled off north with red and blue lights flashing.

Bob followed Thorfinnson inside. They slid on the vests and belt and side holsters. They checked the magazines of the air pistols and their SIG Sauer P226s which had been packed away since they'd left Seattle. They slid them into holsters and left. Bob drove to give Thorfinnson a break.

Strickland and Guzman fell in behind at the Howard Creek Bridge but kept a healthy distance. Once past Lake Hotchkiss Road, Bob blazed up the steep, winding asphalt to Bullion Pass, past Cannibal Canyon, and down snaking miles to the valley below. Soon he passed the *Welcome to Silver City* sign.

The Duggans lived south of town and the area to the north looked like a Texas speed trap. Closer to Duggan's neighborhood, roadblocks barred all exits. Local police waved Bob through. As he turned onto the Duggans' street, he slowed to the residential limit.

The porch lamp and a weak kitchen light were on at the one-story home. A silver Lexus SUV and a beat-up white Toyota Land Cruiser were parked in front, but Wicker's Rubicon was nowhere to be seen. Bob passed the house and continued to a side street where trees concealed the muddy red rental.

Bob followed Thorfinnson as they worked their way back to the Duggans, moving swiftly and silently with air pistols pointed down in a two-hand grip. When they came to the front steps, Thorfinnson held up ten fingers and flashed them three times, mouthing *thirty seconds*, and then continued to the back door.

Bob waited and counted at the front. At twenty, he gently opened the screen. At twenty-five, he took a deep breath. And at thirty, he kicked with all his might. The door didn't budge. He heard the back door crack open followed by the sound of an air pistol discharging more than once. "Oh, God," squeaked from the lips of a wavering atheist.

Bob panicked and kicked again and again, but the door wouldn't give. He ran to the back, entered, and found Thorfinnson bleeding on the living room floor. Wicker was standing over him with a bloody knife. Wicker's face looked like it'd been peeled off of a domestic abuse hotline poster. It was puffy and bruised, shocked and angry, and beginning to sag. Wicker staggered toward the kitchen with three darts stuck in his chest. He dropped the knife and reached for the Peacemaker on the table. Bob dropped the air pistol, whipped out the SIG Sauer, and shot Wicker in his right forearm. His eyes glared ferociously at Bob, and then a hideous smile crept onto his face. It smothered the maliciousness as his eyes rolled back and he crumpled backward to the hardwood floor.

Bob saw what was left of Clint Duggan's shadowy figure under the meager light from a bulb over the kitchen sink. Duggan was duct-taped to a dinette chair, his mouth taped shut, and his limbs were severed at the elbows and knees with stubs closed with heavy fishing line. Blood dripped from the nubs, adding to the congealing pool around the chair. Like Charlotte and Jeremiah, Duggan was missing slices. Unlike his cousins, he was still breathing. A glass of red wine sat on the table next to a fine China plate with several slices of cooked meat. Bob scanned the living room and saw three teen-to-young adults sitting motionless on the couch and an older woman in a rocking chair.

Bob felt dizzy as he moved toward Thorfinnson who was holding his side. He looked up with pleading, fearful eyes. Thorfinnson's lips trembled to speak and he spat up blood. Bob grabbed his handheld and pressed talk: "Officer down, officer down!"

Seventy-Two

Doug opened his eyes. He wasn't dead. Strangely, all his pain was gone and the living room was a strange yellowing black and white. He stood and checked his side. He wasn't bleeding. He glanced around. The dead bodies in the living room were gone and so was Roberts. An empty chair sat in the kitchen where the mutilated but living councilman had been secured and bleeding seconds before.

Three black doors had appeared out of nowhere and were now propped in the middle of the living room. The door on the left was opened a crack.

Am I dead? he thought. I'm not ready. I have too many things left to do. I, I have to find Mary. I need to see Elli walk across the stage when she becomes a doctor. I need to be there to give her away when she finds Mr. Right. I, I want more sunsets with Loretta at Cannon Beach. What I wouldn't do for just one more sunset.

He suddenly realized he wasn't alone. He looked over and saw another man in the room. It was Morgan Bell wearing a white dress shirt with a turned-up collar, dark vest, and gray-yellow slacks. He looked like he'd stepped out of the vintage photo on the Greenly Family roadside memorial placard.

Bell ran for the open door.

Doug moved faster than he'd known possible even when he was young and alive. He dived and tackled Bell. Bell's face bounced off the knob, slammed the door shut, and smashed into the hardwood floor. Doug straddled his back, grabbed Bell's head, and hammered his face again and again into the floor with all the malice he could muster.

Bell's spirit flipped face up and laughed.

Doug switched to furious fists and pulverized the not-so-good doctor's face with twin jackhammers as black spewed from Bell's mouth and nose.

Bell kicked Doug in his ghostly balls, lifting him into the air, and swatted him away like a fly. He shot to standing and staggered toward the kitchen as black streamed from his face. He grabbed the chair Duggan had been sitting in, and smashed it over Doug's head and Doug hit the floor.

Bell followed with a dropped elbow to the spine and Doug screamed as his skiing accident came back to life.

Bell guffawed as the chair reformed and returned to where it'd been.

Doug's agony faded as he refocused his enmity. He rolled over and glared at Bell's face. Like Doug's ruptured disks, Bell's mocking aspect had healed from its pummeling.

Bell smirked and dashed for the left door and yanked it open.

A third man appeared wearing a black trench coat, a matching Stetson, and shoulder-length frazzled white hair. He lifted his left hand and made a fist.

Doug froze along with Bell.

The Man in Black backhanded his right arm through the air and the door slammed shut. "Morgan Bell, I don't think you belong here. Show me your contract now," he demanded and snapped his fingers to allow Bell to answer.

"Morton, I do declare. It is always a pleasure to see you. Well, now, you will just have to unfreeze me so I can grab both contracts from ma spiritual pants pockets."

The Man in Black lowered the fist.

Doug could move again. He would've liked to resume his title bout with the psycho who'd killed him, but all he could do was lay there, awestruck, and think, Contract? Huh?

Bell reached into the front pockets. "Hold on, there. I do believe they are right here." He whipped out empty palms. "I guess I was wrong. I seem to have misplaced my papers." The demon laughed and darted to where Wicker's body had fallen and dissolved into mist.

"This has to stop," said the Man in Black. "Marduk's not getting away with this—not this time."

Who? thought Doug.

The Man in Black regarded Doug's puzzlement, smiled, and said, "I'm sorry—you're probably a little disoriented? Let me introduce myself. My name is Morton Death, and you are Detective Douglas Dean Thorfinnson, husband of Loretta Lynnette Lowery and father of a soon-to-be Dr. Elizabeth Jean Thorfinnson. I know you're a good man. And I also know you weren't supposed to die, at least not today."

Doug's mouth opened to speak, but Death interrupted. "I know you're wondering what's going on." Death scratched his chin and looked at the ceiling. "Hmmm... where do I start? So much to tell, but I don't have an eternity right now to tell you everything. And how do I not bore you with the legalese and minutia of the world beyond your last breath? I guess I shouldn't worry too much—you're a law man. Regardless, I'll stick to what you need to know. I am an Eternal, and I control the realm you currently find yourself in. It's called the White Room. I know, I know—it's more of a yellow or sepia. But like the White Room, what comes next isn't what most mortals expect. I don't have time to get into that, though.

"But concerning the White Room, most everyone has one when they die. The room separates Underspirits from their used up shells before I guide them to their destination, which isn't always the final one. Beyond this room is a place called the Afterworld, where there are other Eternals like me, Half-Eternals, Imaginaries, and Immortals like you will become. An Eternal named Marduk is responsible for what's happening here. He is the ruler of what many mortals call Hell, but in the Afterworld, we call the place the Prison of Homicide. There, Marduk is known as the Curator. He is its warden and his job is to oversee the punishment of the Immortal Damned for committing the unforgivable sin of taking the life of another shell before their appointment with me as scheduled by my sister, Gladys Fate. But Marduk doesn't play by the rules and uses his collection of killers to manipulate the many realities."

Doug's eyes narrowed as his mind swam.

"Yes, there are more than one—many more. But let's not get into that right now. I fear it might overload your circuits if they aren't already sparking. So you ask, why is Marduk doing this? I don't really know, but what he's doing is nothing new, and all Eternals and half-Eternals are guilty of interfering with mortal affairs at one point or another. But, Marduk's sins against mortal kind have been so consistently egregious that the Council of Thirteen altered the rules by which Eternals may enter the many realities. Now, the rules allow only me and my brother to enter your reality in our natural form, but we are governed by strict rules of conduct. For all others and their Immortal minions—a voluntary agreement, signed with crimson ink, is required before possession of said shell. Well, except Marduk and other Princes of Hell—they are far too dangerous to be allowed to wander out of the Afterworld and are no longer allowed to leave the Prison of Homicide.

"But as I was saying, when the agreed-upon task is complete, the Underspirit and its shell enjoys the contract's rewards until the wind of life leaves said mortal shell. Clearly, Bell flagrantly disregarded the stipulations in his original contract with Martin Rice and illegally entered Michael Dwayne Wicker. That Bell was able to enter Wicker was no one's fault but his own. When he executed Rice, his act of vengeance opened a door that allowed Bell to hide inside and take over. Since that moment, Wicker has been unaware of the crimes that Bell has committed with his hands.

Undoubtedly, Marduk sanctioned Bell's previous and current actions. I plan to prove it in the Court of the Council and expose what he's been doing with his damned collection. Douglas Thorfinnson, I sense you still have a role to play, and if I can help it, you will not die today. Mortals speak of cheating me." Death scoffed. *"Now it's my turn. Take my hand and let's return to your reality."*

Seventy-Three

Late night, Saturday, October 7, 2007. Duggan Residence, Silver City, Colorado.

Doug's Underspirit returned to the dark living room. He stood over his unconscious shell and the crimson pool beneath. The bleeding had paused. Roberts held a panicked, frozen expression with his bloody left hand firmly pressed against what had been a leaking side. The handheld was in his right. His mouth was paused in mid-sentence. In the kitchen, the mutilated and dismembered Duggan sat suspended in agony. To the left, Wicker's body lay on its back with a red puddle under his right forearm. There was a red spot on his left shoulder from Tuesday's gunshot wound. Doug glanced back. The Man in Black was there, in as much color as his old wrinkled, pale skin, and black attire, would allow.

Death knelt at Doug's body and phased a wrinkled hand through Roberts's hand and into Doug's abdomen.

"There. That'll have to do," said Death. "We need to get you to the hospital. Get ready—we're going alive." He snapped his fingers. The world went black.

Seventy-Four

Late night, Saturday, October 6, 2007. Duggan Residence, Silver City, Colorado.

Bob sensed someone behind him other than the dying Duggan and the dead as Thorfinnson's side seeped slowly through his scarlet-bathed fingers. Then the bleeding stopped. He checked Thorfinnson's pulse. It was strong. He looked to the kitchen and saw an old man in black standing over Duggan's mutilated body. Bob's phone garbled out unintelligible noises as his rapt attention was on the man in the Stetson.

The man glanced at the rest of the Duggans, sighed, turned back to the councilman, and placed a hand on his shoulder. "Don't be afraid," the man tenderly said. "You will be together soon in a much better place than this Hell you call Earth."

Duggan's face relaxed, became serene, and his head slumped forward.

Bob slowly lifted his phone to his ear.

"Damnit, Bob. Are you still there?" said Sheriff Packwood.

"Uh, yeah. Yes, my, my partner was stabbed. Councilman Duggan and his family are dead. Wicker's unconscious. We need help now!"

Bob disconnected as his gaze met the old man's dark blue pearls.

"Detective Bob Roberts, I'm…"

"I know who you are."

"Good. I slowed Douglas's bleeding, but once I return to my duties, he will have only minutes before he bleeds out. I'll stay in your reality until help arrives. I should know this, but where's the nearest hospital?" asked Death.

"At least an hour away."

"That won't do. Your partner will be dead before he passes this town's city limit sign." Death knelt and picked up the much larger man as if he were a feather. "Place your hand on my shoulder."

Bob did as the Reaper commanded.

Seventy-Five

The three appeared at the emergency room entrance for the Sur Del Rio Regional Hospital. In the blink of an eye, Bob was now forty miles away from the Silver City charnel house. He left Death holding Thorfinnson and ran through the sliding doors. "I need help now! There's a wounded officer outside!"

A doctor and three nurses responded with a gurney. When Bob got back outside, Thorfinnson lay on the ground. The Reaper was gone, and his partner's bleeding had renewed in earnest. The orderlies placed him on the gurney and rolled through the doors. Bob read the doctor's coat, *Dora Gunderson, M.D.*, and followed her inside.

"Where did this happen?" asked Dr. Gunderson.

"Silver City."

"How did you get here?"

"You wouldn't believe me if I told you."

"Okay, we'll talk later," she said and followed the gurney into the ICU.

As the team of doctors and nurses did what they could to save Thorfinnson's life, Bob called Sheriff Packwood.

"Where the hell are you two?" asked Packwood. "We stormed in a minute after you called. It's a massacre here, but we got Wicker handcuffed and he's still out cold."

"We're at Sur Del Rio Regional Hospital. My partner is in ICU."

"Huh? What? Sur Del Rio? How? But, but you just called. STAY THE FUCK DOWN! Sorry, gonna have to call you back once this piece of shit is secure." Packwood disconnected.

Seventy-Six

Ten minutes later, Saturday, October 6, 2007. Sur Del Rio Regional Hospital, Colorado.

Packwood called back. "EMS just got here. Deputy Wicker bit that new deputy. Guzman was trying to stop Wicker's arm from bleeding and that crazy bastard sank his teeth into his arm and tore off a chunk. Strickland had to knock his ass out with a frying pan. We have Wicker's mouth taped shut now. What the hell happened here, and how the hell did you get to Sur Del Rio?"

"The hand of Death."

"Ha, ha—you're a funny guy—real funny. But this ain't a laughing matter, Roberts."

Yeah, truth's not gonna cut it, thought Bob. "Hey, Wicker's a close friend of mine. He's not in his right mind. Be careful. Don't trust anything he says, but don't hurt him."

"Not in his right mind? No shit, Sherlock. That crazy sonuvabitch just slaughtered one of our council members and his family. If there is justice in this world, he'll get the death penalty or worse—a short stay in prison and a shiv in the shower."

"You don't have to tell me, but I have to know why he killed the Duggans and the Lees." Of course, Bob knew why, but like everything else, there would be no believing until they saw the truth. "Whatever you do, don't take your eyes off him. He'll kill himself given half a chance."

"Ohh, don't you worry. That piece of shit isn't escaping justice that easy."

"Thanks. I'll be back in town as soon as my partner's stabilized. I need to pick up our rental. It's the muddy red 4Runner parked a few blocks from there."

"What? A few blocks away? How'd you get to Sur Del Rio?"

Bob closed his eyes and lowered his head. "A Care Flight."

"Wow, how'd you manage that? I was right around the corner. I didn't hear or see a chopper."

"Well then, how do you explain us getting to Sur Del Rio so fast?"

"I... I can't, but... I guess it doesn't matter. I just hope your partner pulls through," said Packwood.

"Thanks. Me, too."

Seventy-Seven

Doug closed his eyes, savoring the warm sun as seagulls squawked and packs of labradors roamed the beach. Just past the changing water's edge, children leapt waves that wrapped around them and morphed into the bubbly white surf. Other little ones built sandcastles as parents watched from fire pits surrounded by driftwood benches that dotted the dry sand and gentle dunes.

Loretta sat on a towel near the fire wearing a solid yellow one-piece and mirrored sunglasses. Her feet at the ends of long silky legs were buried in the sand as her brunette hair flowed with the gentle breeze. She was beautiful and Doug's heart smiled for its fortune.

He turned to a dream house on a hill that peered down on the massive Haystack Rock sitting in low-tide's shallow surf. He remembered the far-fetched promise he'd made to buy her that house one day. He knew it was a pipe dream on a detective's salary. Even Elli's vet school stretched their finances and loans to cover the rest would strap them for years.

Doug watched Elli in the distance strolling through the sand carrying a bag of taffy. His lips curled. He looked at Loretta, closed his eyes, and drank the salty air.

Doug's eyes opened and heaven was gone. His senses returned and he realized he was in a hospital bed peering up, bleary eyed, at someone far less beautiful smiling down.

"Oh, buddy. Good to see those eyes open," said Roberts. "You had a close one. I've already called Loretta and Elli. They'll be on the next flight to Denver."

"Bob, aww. Ow," Doug said in grimacy eye-popping agony.

"Take it easy. I'll let the nurse know you need some drugs."

"No, we... have ta... talk. Everything... everything Stone said was true. I... I saw the White Room... The doors... Morgan Bell. Everything. Oww. I stopped him from... stopped him from escaping... The Man in Black helped me... helped me stop him... He's the Reaper... He said his name was Morton... Morton Death. He spoke about..." Doug took a few pained, abbreviated breaths "...

a Council of Thirteen... Eternals and Immortals... something like that. Said there was... said there was an Eternal named Marduk who uses killers... killers from Hell that possess peop... people on earth." More breaths.

"Marduk? Like the ancient Sumerian, Mesopotamian, Babylonian, slayer of Tiamat, Marduk?"

"Huh? Yeah... I... I guess.... I don't know. I... You know I don't read much... and I'm... I'm not really into mythology."

"Well, he's sort of a forgotten god. Hasn't really been a big thing since the days of Hammurabi."

"Uhh, okay..." Doug gritted his teeth and exhaled. "I... I know Hammurabi. He's the eye for an eye guy. But, whatever. Well, the Reaper said... said Marduk is also known as the Curator... And he might be forgotten here... but the Reaper said he's a big deal where he comes from..."

Roberts peered off pensively.

"But like I was... like I was saying... the Council allows it...." Another wince. "... but only if... only if they... you know, people willingly sign a contract. Oof... He... he said Bell cheated... jumped into Wicker without a contract. Said... said I wasn't supposed to die." He grabbed Roberts's hand as his lips trembled and his gaze bored into his partner's soul. "He saved me... He saved my life. I'm... I'm not crazy. It really happened... and, and Wicker's innocent... except for what he did to Rice."

"No. You're not crazy, or else we both are," said Roberts. "I saw him too, a man in black, but he was in our world. He used his hand to slow the bleeding from that gash in your side. He picked you up and told me to place my hand on his shoulder. Next thing I know, we're forty miles from Silver City, looking at the large butte behind the emergency entrance of this hospital. If it weren't for Death, you'd be dead. Now *that* sounds crazy. Our rental's still in Silver City. God, I had a hell of a time explaining to Packwood how we got here. We have to keep this between us. No one's ever gonna believe any of this unless they see what we saw or something similar. It's the only way Mike has any hope of escaping the needle. I'll call Father O'Malley and tell him we need an exorcist in Silver City A-SAP. And don't worry about Mary DeMure. I'll get in touch with James Mender and let him know what's going on. Then I'll head to Grand Junction to meet with him once you're out of the woods. I'm not letting any of this rest. These bastards are on my eternal shit list now, but I'm gonna have to do this without you because you're not leaving here anytime soon. For now, concentrate on staying alive. Okay?"

"Yeah, okay. I'll… I'll try… and… and thanks, Bob. You're not just a good partner, you're… you're a good friend."

Roberts gripped Doug's hand. "Yeah." He swallowed hard and patted the hand. "Okay. See you later today," he said, biting his lip as a nurse entered.

The nurse injected something into the line. As happiness flowed through Doug's veins, his lips curled. He closed his eyes and returned to the beach.

Seventy-Eight

Sunday morning, October 7, 2007. Sur Del Rio Regional Hospital.
While Doug slept, Bob called Father Reginald O'Malley's office in Boston before first mass.

"Saint Pahtrick's Hahly Cahthedral, Fatha Ah'Malley's ahffice. Nahncy speaking. Hah may I help yah?" said Nancy Morell in thick Bostonian. At times like these, it was nice to hear a voice he'd known most of his life.

"Is Father O'Malley available?"

"Yes, he is. May I ax who's speakin'?"

"Bob Roberts."

"Bahby Rahberts? Get ahtta haere. Hah long it's been? Ten yahrs? An' hah yah been doin'?"

"Yeah, something like that. And things have been better, but I can't talk about it right now."

"I undastand. If yah can hahld, I'll let Fatha Ah'Malley knah yahn the line. He'll be so happy to haear frahm yah."

"Thanks, Nancy."

Bob listened to *Ave Maria* and thought back to life in Boston. Father O'Malley was once a constant part of his life until shortly after he moved to Packer City following the nasty divorce from Bethany. It was fortunate that he and Beth never made kids. Then everything changed after the archdiocese's sex scandal, but O'Malley wasn't involved in the cover-up. He claimed to have no knowledge of the sexual abuse of former altar boys and appeared as appalled as anyone with an ounce of moral fiber when the allegations came to light. O'Malley had always been a good priest and devout Catholic, yet there were too many cases over several decades for Bob to believe that O'Malley was completely in the dark. Still, while he might've lost faith in the church, he never lost his belief that there was more to life and death than human consciousness could comprehend. Now faith and belief were no longer necessary. He'd seen and experienced it.

"Fadder O'Malley speakin', is dis Bobby Roberts?" said his former priest. Even after all these years, O'Malley had lost little of his North Dublin since joining the parish.

"Yes, Father."

"Ahhh, little Bobby. Well, you're na'so little no'more. It's so good to hear from you. Where are you livin' now, and how've you been?"

"Seattle. I'm a detective in Federal Way. And how am I doing? I've been better. That's why I'm calling. You're the only person I can turn to that won't think I'm losing it. I was hoping you could help me with an exorcism."

"Anythin' fo' you, Bobby."

"Well, you remember that video you showed years ago of that Chinese lady who was possessed by that demon who answered to a higher one named the Curator?"

"Tha' I do, Bobby," said Father O'Malley, his voice as grave as Bob had ever heard.

"Well, it seems this Curator is at it again, and one of his demons, named Morgan Bell, is in possession of a good friend of mine. He nearly killed my new partner and has already murdered seven people, not including the four he killed using another mortal shell named Martin Rice. And that's just in the past month. This isn't Bell's first rodeo. Back when he was alive, he murdered at least eight people, and after he was hung in 1892, he's killed at least forty-nine others, not including his current trip to our reality. He appears hellbent on wiping out the entire line of a man named Horace Greenly, who was responsible for hanging his son, Jefferson, for a crime he didn't commit."

"Are you talkin' abow'da Cannibal Surgeon of Packer City?"

"One and the same. His MO is to kill the family of a direct descendent and then dismember and eat the descendent while they're still alive. It's how he killed Horace, his wife, and two of their four children. The two surviving daughters were married and not living at home at the time of the murders. Bell's not gonna stop until every descendant of those two are dead. My partner is in the ICU in Sur Del Rio, Colorado. The doctors think he's gonna be okay, but that's only because of a man in black who appeared out of nowhere and saved Doug's life. According to Doug, who saw him too, his name is Morton Death and he's the Grim Reaper. Look—I'm not kidding."

"I know yo' not. I believe you, Bobby."

"You do? Thanks. Like I said, he just appeared out of nowhere and teleported us to the hospital. Again, I need your help or anyone you can send on a red eye… or maybe there's someone close by. And… and this exorcism has to be seen by as many people as possible; otherwise, my friend is guaranteed the death penalty even if he gets life. Jail is a sure death sentence for child killers, and even more so because he's a cop."

"I am so sorry to hear'da, Bobby. Der is no one available in your area a'dis time, so I will come. I be seein' ya soon. God bless you."

Seventy-Nine

Mid Afternoon, Sunday, October 7, 2007. Silver City Courthouse, Silver City, Colorado.

When Don hung up with Roberts concerning his plan to save Wicker, he sprung into action to lay the groundwork for the exorcist's arrival. His first stop was the office of Silver City Sheriff Dustin Packwood.

"Dustin, I have a favor to ask."

"What might that be?" he responded in a tone that sounded anything but accommodating. "This Duggan shit has me running. And don't even get me started on your Deputy Crazy Town in our lock up. We need to get his ass transferred yesterday to someplace more secure."

"I know, but this is important. I have to know why Wicker did what he did. I'd like to bring in a special counselor who might be able to help get through to him. He specializes in the criminally insane. But, bear with me because what I'm about to ask will sound bonkers."

"Look, I don't give a shit about Wicker. I just wanna see him fry. But whatever. Go ahead, ask away."

"Well, I need the special counselor to meet with Wicker in his cell..."

"Are you out of your fucking mind?"

"Probably, but that's what I need."

Packwood leaned back, shook his head, and said, "Hell, no. Wicker's already taken a chunk out of one of your deputies and that sonuvabitch bit off one of my guy's noses. We now have Wicker as secured as we can and muzzled like he's Hannibal Lector, but I don't doubt he can still do some damage. Bullshit. If you want your *special* counselor to meet with Wicker, you can work it out when he's in a deep max."

"Wow. You didn't even let me get to the crazy part of my request."

Packwood raised his eyebrows. "Well, shit—lay it on me."

"In addition to my counselor meeting with Wicker in his cell, I need their session broadcast live…"

Packwood's eyes narrowed and his lower lip drooped.

Don kept talking to keep him from interrupting. "… and it needs to be witnessed by prominent media members, maybe WNN's Julie Florid and KNW's Kristen Kettlemeyer. I need representatives from Grayson, Mears, and Silver County law enforcement to be there as well."

Packwood shook his head and said, "You *are* out of your ever-loving mind. I mean, what—you didn't get enough of a shellacking after Deputy Crazy Town killed all the witnesses in the Fitzgerald case?"

"He didn't kill all the witnesses. He… um, never mind. Look, it's a fucked up situation all around. I really need you to trust me on this."

"And make my department a laughing stock like yours? No fucking way am I letting you turn my town into a clown show. That is, unless you have one phenomenal reason that will convince me that you shouldn't get a room next to Wicker's future padded cell. If not, I'll have to ask you to get the fuck out my office."

Don bit his lip as Packwood's eyes glared and his nose flared. "Look, I can't elaborate. You have to trust me, which I know is a tall order after what happened. But this was Bob Roberts's idea. I trust him with my life and anyone's reputation. Look, I don't completely understand what he has planned… but he knows what he's doing. I'm sure of it."

"No. No fuckin' way. Not in my town. We'll handle this my way. Wicker has already maimed two officers. I'm not letting anyone else get near that sonuvabitch until he's in a straitjacket. Then, if something happens, it won't be my problem."

Don nodded. He was done being nice.

"What?" asked Packwood.

"You seem to have forgotten—you have skeletons in your closet. And what about that favor you owe me to keep my memory foggy?"

"You… you wouldn't."

"Oh, but I would. Or you can help me save Wicker and maybe get some answers about why he did what he did."

"Goddamnit. You sonuvabitch. You snake. Motherfucker. Okay, your counselor can meet with Wicker and you can have your media circus. But if this turns into a shitshow like October second, you're getting all the credit. And after this, we're *far* beyond even."

"Deal. Thanks, Dustin. I really appreciate it."

"Yeah, fuck off and get out of my office so I can get some work done."

Don left Packwood's office and called interim Sheriff Griggs on his way to his 4Runner. "Danny, think you and a couple of Grayson deputies can come down to Silver City?"

"Is this about Wicker?"

"Yes."

"Why would I wanna do that? Wicker's your problem now."

"Yeah, tell me about it. Just wanted to give you an invite. There's gonna be a bunch of media here soon and I wanted them to have the opportunity to meet the man who solved the Lees and the Duggan murder cases in record time."

"Wait, you… ahhh," Griggs said with a little pep. "Well, now. I don't wanna disappoint the media now, do I? So, when's all this supposed to take place."

"Around midnight. There's gonna be a big press conference. If you're interested, I'll warm things up for you."

"Well, that's nice of you, Glickman. I see I was right to place my trust in you and give you another chance not to fuck shit up. I'll be down there shortly with two of my finest."

Eighty

Late evening, Sunday, October 7, 2007. Sur Del Rio Regional Hospital.

Bob's mood lightened at the sight of his old priest walking into the waiting area. Father Reginald O'Malley didn't appear to have aged a day since their last meeting a decade earlier. He was still skinny, not frail, yet definitely not formidable, but held himself with a grace that spoke of immeasurable inner strength. His hair was gray, his head balding, and his face and neck had wrinkles and a few liver spots to complete the image. He wore the same round-rimmed glasses he'd worn since Bob was *Little Bobby*.

As they embraced and exchanged sincere formalities, Loretta Thorfinnson and her daughter, Elli, stepped through the ICU's sliding glass doors. Both were tall, brunette, brown-eyed, and beautiful, not skinny, but not overly plus-sized. Bob hugged each Thorfinnson. Though he'd never met Loretta or Elli, no one would've suspected had anyone else been in the waiting room after visiting hours. Considering the circumstances, the hospital had made a special exception. The four walked together to Doug's room.

Loretta stood by Doug, her eyes tear-swollen, but currently dry. Bob observed thirty-plus years of loving concern shine down on Doug as he slept.

"Thanks for staying with him, Bob," said Loretta.

Doug stirred. His eyes opened and as he floated on a morphine cloud, he croaked, "Hey, darling, so nice of you to join me on my Colorado vacation."

"You are so not funny," said Loretta.

"Dad, how you feeling?" asked Elli.

"Like I've been... you know... split in two and sewn back together. Yeah, I've been... I've been better... but having you and Mom here... sure is an improvement. You're so pretty. Isn't she pretty, Loretta?"

Elli smiled softly, bent down, and kissed her father's forehead. He lazily patted her hand, and then refocused his purple-hazy stare on Loretta.

"What happened?" asked Loretta. "Bob didn't give me a lot of details."

"Can we... can we talk about this later? My head is kind of loopy. Bob... Bob!"

"Yes, Doug?"

"Bob... Good, you're here. You are sooo awesome... Such a good friend." Doug's sluggish attention returned to Loretta. "Yeah, my friend Bob... yeah, Bob has to go to Silver City with his old priesty O'Malley... I guess that would be you." Doug waved.

O'Malley nodded.

Doug slow-glanced back to Loretta. "Yeah, Bob, Bobby, Bob-bob." He chuckled. "Yeah, he and his old Padre here have to go visit the man who did this to me. You know... I'm so glad you're here... I really need you two more than ever right now. Hey, I gotta go poop, but I can't seem to poop." He chuckled again.

Loretta sniffed out a snicker but her lips barely curled. She held and caressed Doug's hand as he smiled unevenly. "Okay, then. We'll talk later," she said. "Elli plans to stay until you're out of here. Her instructors were very understanding and are okay with her making up whatever she misses. My boss said to come back as soon as I can, but she has me covered until then."

"I see you're in good hands," said Bob. "Me and my Padre have to go see my friend, Mike, and hopefully save his soul."

Elli's eyes narrowed. "What are you gonna do, perform an exorcism?" she asked.

Bob glanced at O'Malley, and then Doug. "Like your dad said—can we talk about this later?"

Eighty-One

Midnight, Sunday, October 7, 2007. Silver City Court House.
Bob parked at the main entrance as the city hall clock struck twelve. He wouldn't have been able to park close had the spot not been reserved. Of course, there was police-only reserved parking in the back but Bob knew O'Malley needed a grand entrance that would play well on interrupted late-night TV.

Bob was thunderstruck with what Glickman had pulled off on such short notice. So many familiar faces. He wondered if everyone from Grayson, Packer City, Sur Del Rio, and towns beyond had come up and down and sideways to join the populace for a surprise engagement for someone like Norine Jasmine Jones. Had there been more time, Bob had little doubt that the crowd would've been much larger. But no one out in the cold would miss a thing since large screens had been set up by WNN and KNW.

Bob waited with O'Malley in the rental as his padre prayed the rosary for every day of the week. Bob kept a hand in a coat pocket gripping his own beads as he listened to O'Malley whisper words that were familiar which hadn't left Bob's lips in years. He thought about Mike and Doug and Pete and Joe and Jocelyn and Little Joe, who'd be coming soon. He tried not to think of everything else that was weighing him down which had brought him to this moment. It was too much. Just too much. He rubbed his mouth as he turned to one of the view screens and watched and listened to a WNN reporter ask locals why they'd come to the courthouse for the morbid midnight extravaganza. Those who were asked didn't know and were unsure what they were about to see. They were just there, curious or furious, to see the Mears County police deputy who ate Councilman Duggan and Charlotte Lee, the beloved Barista of Packer City, who invented the Frespresso.

Father O'Malley made the sign of the cross, kissed the rosary's crucifix, and nodded at Bob. He stepped from the 4Runner and walked with purpose with his hands in coat pockets that concealed the tools of his trade.

Bob got out, caught up with O'Malley, and the media descended. Cameras flashed as a din of questions was hurled. Bob answered with *"No comment"* and a *back-the-fuck-off* hand as he and his padre squeezed through the crowd to the front door.

Inside, Bob saw WNN's Julie Florid and KNW's Kristen Kettlemeyer speaking to cameras. He heard Kettlemeyer say something about the "... *special interrogation of the Killer Pig.*"

Eighty-Two

12:06 a.m., Monday, October 8, 2007. Silver City Lockup.

Father O'Malley nodded at Bob and said, "Time to do our Lord's work," and stepped into Wicker's holding room. The cameras turned to O'Malley as he entered.

The smell in the room was hellish, but unlike Bob and everyone present, he did not cover his mouth and nose. O'Malley knew that he had to appear unphased by the fiendish scent of evil. After all, this wasn't his first demon round up.

O'Malley stopped at the bars and sized up the mortal vessel he would be facing and the space in which he would have to work. Wicker was facing away in an orange jumpsuit. It was soiled brown in the back, and soaked with urine along his inner thighs to his ankles. His hands and feet were shackled and he wore a helmet that he was bonking against a wall which mostly drowned out the quieter buzz of rolling cameras and an occasional hack and gag. The cell itself was large enough to hold twenty prisoners on a good Saturday night but all that was in the cell, besides Wicker, was a mattress without sheets.

Wicker's shell perked up as if sensing a familiar presence in the room. He slowly twisted around like a reptile, revealing the protective face grate covering his mouth. He slithered with chain-shackled ankles over to O'Malley. O'Malley stared through Wicker's eyes and felt the heavy presence of unbridled evil within the damaged shell. He had never seen Wicker before but imagined that not even his mother would've recognized his purple and black, swollen, deformed face. It would eventually heal, but if successful—and O'Malley had every confidence in his faith and training that he would be—Bobby's friend would be feeling everything *very* soon.

Wicker gruesomely grinned and made hissing sounds while clicking his teeth. Then he started flicking his tongue in, out, and around as he tilted his head slowly to the left and then to the right. His head shot upright. He drew his puffy lips into a joker's smile, and, in the accent of a nineteenth century southern gentleman, said, "Hey, y'all. I'm just funnin' ya. I saw this dandy flick on my last run about what a friend o' mine gone and done to a little girl. Done made that girl's head spin clean around. Loved that pea soup bath she gave the priest. I can do that for you if you would like."

Father O'Malley heard gasps followed by gagging.

Wicker belly laughed and looked around as he played for his audience. When he could breathe again, Wicker whipped his face back to O'Malley, and in a deeper, hoarser, more hellish-sounding drawl, said, "I recognize you, but you do not appear to be dressed for the occasion. Are you here to save my soul, priest?"

"No, you ol' devil. I am here to sen' you back to Hell where you belong, Dr. Morgan Bell. Open da cell."

O'Malley's eyes fixed on the demon as he approached the cell door opposite from where Bell stood like a statue.

Bell nodded, as purplish, deformed lips rolled forward, and his grotesque face became a mask of amused shock.

An officer looked to the town sheriff for guidance. The sheriff nodded and the officer unlocked and opened the cell. O'Malley stepped inside.

Bell eyed O'Malley with a wide, hungry grin.

O'Malley nodded for the officer to lock him inside. The officer hesitated until the sheriff nodded again.

O'Malley removed a crucifix from his right coat pocket and rosary beads from his left. He wrapped the beads around his wrist and firmly held its cross.

Bell laughed. He abruptly stopped and rocked forward and back, and then roared as he moved in short, fast strides. He dived, and slammed O'Malley against the wall.

The officer fumbled for his keys.

"STAY OU'!" yelled O'Malley as he countered with a surprising grappling move. He slammed Wicker's helmeted head to the concrete and pinned his neck with a forearm. Wicker's skin sizzled as the rosary grazed it. He lifted the crucifix over the deputy's face.

Wicker thrashed, kicked, and spat as O'Malley rode the bucking shell and spoke the proper rite in perfect Latin over a litany of demon curses. "Exorcizamus te, omnis immunde spiritus, omni satanica potestas, omnis incursio infernalis adversarii, omnis legio, omnis congregatio et secta diabolica, in nomini et virtute Domini nostril Jesu Christi, eradicare et effugare a Dei Ecclesia, ab animabus ad imaginem Dei conditis ac pretioso divini Agni sanguini redemptis."

O'Malley pressed the crucifix to the deputy's forehead. The skin crackled like water in hot oil. Wicker screamed and his jaws opened impossibly wide, seeming to unhinge. White smoke poured from the eyes and nostrils, and the mouth through the grate. Wicker's shell went limp as smoke swirled around and past O'Malley. He whipped around as the smoke coalesced across the cell. He stood quickly with raised crucifix and beads.

The smoke thickened. Amorphous at first, it took the form of a body with growing, writhing appendages. The appendages became a head, arms, and legs. Hands and feet formed next. The form briefly had the appearance of an androgenous porcelain doll. The developing surface took on the textured facade of pale white skin, brown hair with a big curl, and a chin beard. Clothing followed: a black bowtie, white shirt, and a black and white polka-dot vest, black dress pants, a coat with large silver buttons, and a pair of fine brown leather boots. When the demon was fully dressed, its smooth, featureless face began to rise and sink in the appropriate places. Malevolent eyes, flaring nostrils, and a mouth filled with gritted, perfect teeth followed.

O'Malley had never seen anything like this in his many years as an exorcist—a demon spirit taking solid form. His hands trembled, and his faith faltered as fear took hold.

The unbound apparition moved like lightning, grabbed O'Malley's neck, lifted him, and squeezed hard with unyielding fingertips.

O'Malley saw Bob gripping the bars as the wraith strangled him.

The officer fumbled for his keys again.

O'Malley waved him away as he struggled to breathe. He flailed and swung his hands, directing the blessed articles at the ghost. They passed through, leaving misty swirls that quickly reclaimed their part in the solid imitation of something alive. His swings became weaker… and weaker… and weak… Stars and black spots filled his vision, dancing with each heartbeat, pulsing, swirling, merging into permanent night. Right before all went black, the demon Bell threw O'Malley across the cell like a ragdoll.

O'Malley landed with a snap. "HOLY MOTHER, FATHER, SON, AND HOLY GHOS', AMEN!" he screamed as his eyes shot open on a rocket ride back to consciousness.

He staggered to his feet, his left arm dangling with the rosary still wrapped. Sweat poured from his brow. He found his faith again and raised the crucifix shakily in his right hand, determined, fearless in the face of certain death—his faith rock-solid as a martyr in a Roman coliseum.

Bell laughed and spat. The blue sputum hit the floor and turned to mist. "I do declare—for such a young old fart, you surely do have some gumption. So, I will take my time and kill you slowly…" Bell turned his head to the audience and glared at the officers, the observers pressed against the wall, and into the cameras, and said, "… as I will anyone who interferes." The spirit let out a second battle cry and lurched forward.

O'Malley's faith did not waver as Bell hit an invisible brick wall. The wraith hung in the air inches from O'Malley, frozen as if a pause button had been pressed. Only his eyes moved and they looked scared.

O'Malley recited the exorcism rite once more, his knees buckling several times. But his good arm had lost the shakes, and the crucifix was as motionless as if it had been mounted in Golgothian stone. He stood taller as he channeled faith through the holy symbol for the coup de grace. His voice broadcasted like a loudspeaker as he repeated an impassioned plea four times, three for his faith in the holy trinity, and one for the Holy Mother.

"The power of Christ compels you."

"The power of Christ compels you."

"The power of Christ compels you."

"The power of Christ compels you."

He dropped his right arm and aimed the crucifix at Bell's feet. The ground dissolved and swirled into a dark hole beneath. A howling-sucking silence rose from the deep, indescribable in words that made comprehensible sense. Distant at first, it grew in hypersonic, nerve-rattling intensity.

Bell no longer looked scared—he looked mortified as if the cumulative terror of all his victims had filled his eyes with acid. The massive vacuum focused on Bell and took hold of him like an airlock opening into deep space.

O'Malley dropped the crucifix. It clattered on the floor, and the evil spirit was freed from its paralyzing bonds, but Bell could not break free from the vacuum.

The Cannibal Surgeon gripped the edges of the hole, but his apparitional form stretched and began to tear. The wraith cursed and thrashed and twisted as pieces fell away. When only his head, shoulders, and arms remained, his mist-like fingers slipped, and the rest of the hate that was Morgan Bell descended into the abyss. The black hole slammed shut.

O'Malley swayed and his eyes rolled back.

Eighty-Three

Mike Wicker's eyes adjusted to light pouring in and around a shadow. He found himself in a sepia-shaded room surrounded by bars with someone or something standing in front of him.

At first a silhouette, the form became a pale-skinned, silver-haired man dressed in black holding a black Stetson. The man fiddled with the hat's rim as he gathered himself to speak and said with deepest regret, "I am... I am very sorry, but you are a victim of illegal possession. Thanks to your friend, Bob Roberts, and Father Reginald O'Malley, Morgan Bell will never have the power to do this again. His Overspirit is no more, extinguished in the Abyss of Non."

"What are you talking about? Dr. Morgan Bell? And Bob Roberts? He's in Seattle. And who is Father O'Malley? And who are you?"

"Don't worry about that now. We'll meet again. For now, you'll have to deal with the damage the demon Bell has done to your life and what you have done to your own. It's time for you to wake up, Michael Dwayne Wicker."

Eighty-Four

Mike opened his eyes. He saw bars around him but realized they weren't the bars he knew for those two miserable days during the September lockdown. Every inch of his body ached or burned or itched. He could smell himself. He reeked of death and everything foul. And *that* taste in his mouth. He gagged.

He sat up, dazed and confused, and looked around. Across the cell, an unconscious man in a jacket lay on his right side. A crucifix and what he recognized as rosary beads were on the floor next to him. The man's left arm was folded over his body at an unnatural angle.

Outside the cell, numerous police officers and people with microphones and cameras stood staring at him. They looked as if they'd seen a ghost. Their faces were so pale that they could've been confused with shades themselves. That is, everyone except Bob Roberts, who was smiling through tears.

Mike's old friend asked for the keys to the cell and his shackles. Bob unlocked the door, entered the cell, and checked on the broken, older man. Relief washed over his face as he held the man's wrist.

"Hey," Bob yelled to anyone listening, "can we get some medical attention over here?"

The broken, elderly man awoke, screamed, and passed out again.

Bob went to Mike, unchained him, and helped his friend to his feet.

Mike exhaled pain and expletives, then huskily asked, "What're you doing here... and... and what happened? Last thing I remember..."

Bob interrupted, "It's a long story, but I'm here from Seattle with my partner, who the-one-using-your-body nearly killed."

"What?"

"Just let me finish. My partner is recovering in Sur Del Rio. I know what you did to that Black Beret at the Fitzgeralds'. Not that I blame you. I mean, I'm not sure I would've done anything different. But that's not the worst of it, but I know you weren't responsible for the rest of the charges you'll be facing. I think the news coverage and the witnesses around you and outside will testify to that fact. It might even save your life."

Mike's lips trembled and through thready sorrow he said, "Bob, I, I lost it... They killed Pete and Joe. I couldn't... I couldn't stop myself. After I pulled the trigger, everything went black... and all I could hear were muffled noises. And then there was light, and, and I found myself in a room like this cell with a man in black who sent me back to myself. It sounds so fucked up and insane, but that's what happened. What did I do, Bob? Tell me, what did I do?" he pleaded as tears wet his battered cheeks.

Bob bit his lip. "Before you or I say anything else, one of the locals needs to read you your rights now that you're in your right mind. We'll have plenty of time to talk later."

Mike nodded and the officer said his piece. "You have the right to remain silent..."

Mike's gaze didn't leave Bob's as he listened to Miranda's warnings.

When the officer finished, he asked, "Do you understand each of these rights I have explained to you?"

"Yeah, I do."

"Having these rights in mind, do you wish to talk now?"

"I probably shouldn't, but Bob—whatever I did—thanks for not giving up on me."

"Don't thank me, thank Father O'Malley, and the powers invested in him by the Father, the Son, the Holy Ghost, and Mother Mary." Bob's phone rang as two paramedics rushed into the cell. "Bob Roberts speaking."

He listened.

"What happened?"

His face paled.

"I'll be there as soon as I can. Bye." Bob closed his phone. "Mike, I gotta go. We'll talk soon. That was my partner's wife, Loretta. There's been a complication, and he's back in surgery. I have to get back to Sur Del Rio."

"Tell her I'm sorry. And if he makes it, please tell your partner as well." Mike sniffed hard as another tear rolled down his cheek.

"Mike, you didn't do this, and I'll do everything I can to prove it."

"I know you will."

Eighty-Five

Small Hours, Monday, October 8, 2007. Horseshoe Lab, Helix Eternal Laboratories Main Complex, Undisclosed Location.

Dr. Antonia D'Amato tapped her temple out of habit, forgetting that her RW implant, set to the same ringtone as her office computer, was still not working. She clicked the mouse the answer the video call and a face she despised appeared on the screen.

"Is Dr. Caine or the Benefactor around?" asked General Adamson in his grating voice.

"Unfortunately, Dr. Caine's passenger is presently out of *his* mind and did not tell me when he plans to return—not that the Benefactor ever does. And as for our *darling* Dr. Caine, he is working on the new formula."

"Why? The original worked just fine."

"You know Albert. He still believes that he can change the world for the better when it would be best to see it burn."

"Yes. Well, enough about the dreamer. Are you watching the news?" asked Adamson.

"I was. It is not like we did not see this coming when the Benefactor decided to use Dr. Morgan Bell."

"So, your sight is back, Great Destiny."

"No. She has not returned… yet."

"Then you are using. Why else would your green eyes be blue?"

"It is none of your concern what I do," said Antonia.

"No, it is not. But you should know that the Blue Dragon Road never ends well for mortal shells."

"I know what I am doing."

"Ah, yes—famous last words of junkies everywhere."

"Did you just call to annoy me?" asked Antonia.

"No. But it is always a bonus. The purpose of my call is to report a silver lining. If my source is correct, that annoying detective will soon no longer be a problem. At least, the demon Bell accomplished that, but War fears his recklessness will lead to repercussions that our Benefactor has not foreseen. Well, at least the wheels are in motion to bring this project to a successful conclusion with or without Destiny's eyes. But it would be nice to have those eyes."

"Yes, it would, but soon I may not need her. If only I could learn the secret of the Allseer who is greater than Destiny could ever hope to be. I just have to find the right path. I am… I am so close. Soo very close."

Adamson grinned and said, "Well, I hope you find it... or die trying."

End
of
Book 3

Continue
Mary and Mender's journey and learn what Fate has in store for our detectives

in

Hataalii
Tales for the Afterworld Book 4
Coming February 13, 2025

If you liked this title, please leave a review on Amazon or Goodreads
https://www.amazon.com/gp/product/B0CWB8WYQB

For upcoming books:
Amazon.com: V. K. Pasanen: books, biography, latest update

For updates and more:
Facebook page V.K. Pasanen

Also check out Spotify playlist:
Tales from the Afterworld
https://open.spotify.com/playlist/0zqW1pSnwzjzzuhtCw0QCC?si=cf13b4a2ad6e4fdf

Milton Keynes UK
Ingram Content Group UK Ltd.
UKHW042054080924
448054UK00002BA/9